NABARUN BHATTACHARYA (1948–2014)
was born into a family of writers, filmmakers, artists and academics.
His father was playwright Bijan Bhattacharya; his mother, writer and
activist Mahasweta Devi; his maternal grandfather, well-known *Kallol-
era* writer, Manish Ghatak. Educated at Ballygunge Government
School, Bhattacharya went on to study geology at Asutosh College
and then English literature at City College.

A journalist from 1973 to 1991 at a foreign news agency, he gave
up that career in order to become a full-time writer. *Herbert* was
published in 1992 and won the Bankim and Sahitya Akademi awards.
Some of his best-known works are *Kangal Malshat* (2003),
*Ei Mrityu Upotyoka Aamaar Desh Na* (2004) and *Phyataroor
Bombachak* (2004). Novelist, short-story writer and prolific poet,
he was also, from 2003 until his death, editor of the
*Bhashabandhan* journal.

Bhattacharya believed that every species has a right to exist
without being at the mercy of humans, and one of his landmark novels,
*Lubdhak* (2006), stems from this conviction. A devoted feeder of every
stray dog and cat in the neighbourhood, he was also a keen watcher
of insects, reptiles and other forms of life in his garden which he
tended to for at least an hour every day. He also spent a lot of his time
walking through the city, exploring its streets and lanes and bylanes,
soaking in the conversations and experiences of his subjects.

His funeral procession in Calcutta was a strange one indeed—
ministers and prominent cultural personalities marched alongside
activists, former political prisoners and a sea of have-nots, a sea of his
people. An offer of a state funeral was rejected by the family—it would
have gone against the very grain of what he'd stood for,
and written about, all his life.

# NABARUN
# BHATTACHARYA

# *Beggars' Bedlam*

TRANSLATED BY
RIJULA DAS

LONDON NEW YORK CALCUTTA

**Seagull Books, 2024**

Originally published in Bengali as *Kangal Malsat*
by Saptarshi Prakashani in 2003

Original text © Tathagatha Bhattacharya, 2024

First published in English translation by Seagull Books, 2024

English translation © Rijula Das, 2024

ISBN   978 1 8030 9 378 9

**British Library Cataloguing-in-Publication Data**
A catalogue record for this book is available from the British Library

Typeset by Seagull Books, Calcutta, India
Printed and bound in the USA by Integrated Books International

# CONTENTS

*1*

Rows of severed heads are rolling about on the banks of the Old Ganga. Ergo, something terrible happened last night. Shoved a sack full of the heads and split? So where are the bodies, then? Hacked to pieces, or sliced and diced? Are the heads all male, or female? Thus ran one narrative. The other: human skulls were canter-cavorting under a cyclone-struck grey sky. At first, there were a lot of skulls, dancing. But when the police arrived, all of them had (?) vanished but three. And while the police wondered whether to proceed or not, debated the pros and cons and sixes and sevens of getting mixed up in yet another scandal, even those three skulls vanished into the tide with a smirk. The public squatted firmly in place, clutching this particular thread, but in the evening news on a private Bengali TV channel, a long-faced police officer was heard to say that the skulls had come from the crematorium at Shiriti. They came in on one tide, and on the next tide went back to pavilion. Another faction of the police believed that the 'dancing skulls' were not the citizens of Shiriti, but Keoratola. Swept along with the plastic bags, rubber chappals, banana skins, dead flowers and other inanimate objects, they had landed up down south, in Mahabirtala.

It seems that regarding this strange and singular phenomenon, whatever the public or the police might think, we should either take up an independent position or avoid any position altogether. The incident happened on 28 October 1999—we need to remember only the date. Those who know it all already, and then smile that insufferably familiar smile when the foretold incident occurs, is there any reason for us to not call them starched douchebags? In the very last hours of this innumerable-skull-adorned century, what exactly did you think would happen? That bulbul birds would bob and curtsy? Shehnai soirees sway through the streets? That level of sadhana, where all the ickering-bickering differences melt away into the aura of the pure essence-driven dawn of un-knowledgeable consciousness—the Bengalis are nowhere near it! Therefore nothing is to be gained from all this weeping and wailing, in fact it might even cause more trouble. At another such moment of the nation's mega-crisis, Sri Kaliprasanna Kabyabisharad (1861–1907) had written a song in Hindi, which was then sung with great pride at the 1906 Congress annual session in Calcutta:

> O brother, our country's in such a hash!
> Mud and ash as good as gems,
> while jewelstones are trash.

Everyone reads 'Hindi song' and thinks it's a Hindi-film song. But this song is not that kind of song. Sri Brajendranath Bandyopadhyay has told us more about Sri Kaliprasanna: 'In the Swadeshi congregations, he introduced a novelty: at the beginning and end of each meeting, he arranged for the singing of nationalistic songs. Even though he himself was not a singer, he had a natural ability for composing such songs. And whenever he attended a Swadeshi meeting, he always had two salaried singers accompany him . . .'. If not exactly this, then we must tune our hearts to a close-enough scale in order to think about the Curious Incident of the Dancing Skulls. Maybe then something might emerge. For now, it is enough for us to know that the dancing skulls are merely a signal. Of an unimaginable phenomenon of mind-blowing magnitude that is yet to come.

Now we will slide back with ease to 24 October 1999, four days ago, and focus on the *Anandabazar Patrika*'s Sunday supplement, Page 12, lower half, near the bottom. This is of course nothing new, as insipid readers we do this often, for we have learnt that it is better to slip and fall than to fall behind. In the five columns of job notices, the second from the left has an advertisement that reads as follows:

### *Travel Far and Wide*

Honoured for 27 years, world-famous Magician Ananda's cultural team requires attractive young men and women, keyboard player, drummer, midget, experienced and sensitive carpenter, licensed persons, manager and electrician. Good wages, education, travel costs to and fro, food and lodging, medical benefits. Contact within the next three days. Time: 9 a.m. to 5 p.m. Address: Magichouse Ananda, C/O Majestic Hotel, Room No. 207, 4C Madan Street, Kol-72 (beside New Cinema).

At the very outset we are amazed not so much by the magic tricks as much as by the magical coincidence. From the 24th, if one takes into account the three days in which to contact, we have the 25th, 26th, 27th ... and then, on the very fourth day, voilà! The day of the dancing skulls! Is this the beginning of the magic, then? We know that the police will turn a deaf ear to our appeal; but is this not enough of a mysterious event? In such matters, who but the police may prove to be the ultimate connoisseurs? Immediately after this, the bastard snag that gradually puts down root in the sceptical mind is: the similarity of names, that is, Magician Ananda and *Anandabazar Patrika*—Ananda within Ananda—is this god's little game or the devil's dirty riddle or the seductive beckoning of a veil-shimmering shadowshape? But no one should mistake this dubious doubt in our minds as an ill-willed attempt to poke a twig up the bottom of an institution as hallowed as the *Anandabazar*. To bugger the great arse of the great establishment that ceaselessly claps the cymbals of news on the one hand and literature on the other would not be productive at all. On the contrary, one could get bamboodled.

A typical case of what such a bamboodling can be like is the life of Mr B. K. Das. Which, incidentally, Dear Reader, bears no connection whatsoever to *Anandabazar Patrika*. Mr Das used to write novels of short length in the English language. He had written only two: *The Mischievous Englishman* and *An Affair with Alligators*. At the time, Calcutta's leading English daily was the *Daily Pleasure*. Its Book Review editor was Mr Panto, and Mr P. B. was the editor of Literary Snippets on that same page. It is impossible to count the number of times that Mr B. K. Das, for the sake of his two self-published titles, had rung the doorbell of the above-mentioned newspaper. A moustachioed thug sat at Reception. His name was Mr Shantu. Rumour had it that there was a murder charge against him. His job was to shoo away unwanted visitors. Mr B. K. Das, on four different occasions, had left two copies of his books with Mr Shantu in the hope that they would be passed on upstairs for the perusal of Mr Panto and Mr P. B. Wrapped in imported marble paper, tied with red ribbon. A total of eight copies of *The Mischievous Englishman* and *An Affair with Alligators* were laid to waste thus. What actually happened to them remains largely unknown. It may be conjectured that Mr Panto and Mr. P. B. threw them away. Or Mr Shantu drew up from his depths of experience the fairly certain possibility of their disposal and thus did not bother to send up the novels at all. Used the patterned marble paper to cover his own pornographic books instead and sold off the novels for recycling, weighed by the kilo—who's to say this isn't the truth? But Mr Das wasn't the fragile kind; his knowledge and determination knew no bounds. Though he quit writing, he next set bravely forth into the jungles of Assam, into the terrifying world of the petrifying python—his job was to capture the babies and supply them to various zoos. And it is in the course of this job that he met his eventual end. While he was ferrying a bear cub under his hat, suddenly and most unfortunately the cub's guardians arrived. Just seven days before this ruthless yet eminently justifiable incident of the bear child, he had written to his poet-friend J. S. Ray in Cuttack. The letter was later eaten by termites. In it, he had written:

> Mr Panto's pantomime can be tolerated no more. Even if it could not be reviewed, at least Literary Snippets could have featured a mention. Who is this PB? I do not know Bengali very well, but I shall rest satisfied by calling him Prehensile Behemoth or Paederast Buccaneer. I have thought of releasing a few pythons on their person. Let it embrace and engulf them.

Not only recently, but novellas have been in currency for quite some time now. Published in 1909, Sri Suresh Chandra Chakraborty's *A Bengali Youth in Kashmir* is an example. But the writer did not drink from this well for too long. He said, 'Only once in my youth was I overcome with the desire to write a few short novels in Bengali, in the form of the English "shilling novels".' Though some people found the novel to be more or less readable, according to the writer, 'who in today's world would like to waste their time either writing or reading such novels?' Sri Sudhindranath Tagore said that he and his wife had liked the book, but that his uncle had made no remark after reading it. The uncle was, of course, Rabindranath Tagore. No matter: the main thing is that, like Mr B. K. Das, it was unique and novel. 'Today's reader is an insufferable jackass. No writer should waste his time on them. Some say that the reader has no time. My foot! I say it is the writer who has no time.' We shall leave to the discretion of the knowledgeable how weighty this one is as a theory, but we have learnt what the Literary Establishment can do to the writer. If today a writer runs afoul of the mighty *Anandabazar*—let us spend a silent moment shuddering at the thought.

Today the practice of reading about the lives of notable Bengalis has all but disappeared from Bengali life. If it lingers somewhere still, then let that gifted reader not confuse the novelist B. K. Das with the aviator Binoy Kumar Das (1891–1935). Aviator B. K. Das' most mentionable contribution is the founding of a factory called Byatra Engineering Works. 1935, 28 April, 10 a.m. Just the thought of it gives us goosebumps. The sky above the village Gouripur, not too far from Dumdum Airport: such is the nature of pig-headed destruction that the aircraft of B. K. Das collides with the aircraft of D. K. Roy. In those days, aeroplanes did not frantically fly to and fro as they do today. The sky was cheaper too. And available in vast quantities. The Bengalis, though, have swiftly recovered from this particular loss. It's a part of their genetic habit to weep and wail in frantic dishevelment one moment and to turncoat and grin from ear to ear in the next. Such a behavioural pattern is not observed among the non-Bengalis, such as the Nagas, Russians, Germans or Africans.

From this point, as Lenin commands, if we take one step forward and two steps back, we will arrive again at the *Anandabazar* discussion. It is best that our deeply deliberated decision is thus: that *Anandabazar Patrika* and magician Mr Ananda are different entities, they have entirely different orbits, their DNA and other such complicated blueprints are so widely dissimilar that the Ganga can flow between them, therefore one may not to be grabbed and cloned into the other. Magician Ananda wanted midgets, ergo 'short people'. Had he wanted 'short writers', then perhaps there could have been room for suspicion. But it will be unfair to not mention that without the *Anandabazar*, the handful of Bengali writers who have turned into moneybags would not have been able to bloat and float so much. They'd be paupers, clutching hurricane lamps instead. Bengalis do not lack in hurricane-holding writers. What 'Rasaraj' Amrita Lal Basu had written about the willies and wenches flocking to the stage during the early days of the public theatre, that applies to the hurricane-holding writers too:

> An irksome presence in the family
> Butt of ridicule and shame to sundry
> With smirks and taunts generally regarded
> By old friends expressly discarded.

Bengali literature's most prominent tragic figure, Rabindranath Tagore, in a letter to Ramananda Chattopadhyay, written from Illinois on 21st Ashwin 1912, had said:

> Upon hearing of the financial distress that the school is
> undergoing, my heart craved to return to the country. But
> my friends here repeatedly assure me that, if my book can
> be arranged to be published, then we can rest assured of
> the school's income. Hence, I wait with hope in my heart.
> But that I will earn anything from the sales of the book,
> I have not that faith any more.

When one sees today the long lines of Bengalis lined up outside Ananda Publishers at the Calcutta Book Fair, one thinks: Ah! If only Rabindranath could gaze upon this breathtaking scene, what absolute ananda he would feel!

We know that many will be furious with us for calling Rabindranath a tragic figure and will aggressively roll up their sleeves even if they are missing their hands. To them we issue a warning right away and right at the beginning: that the maha-thrashing they are about to receive, no shield of station or position can keep them safe from its whiplash.

'Nolen! No-le-n!' Bhodi screams from the terrace. 'You son of a shit-bag, Nolen! Your ears are full of fucking weed or what?' A clutch of crows peck at a handful of rice scattered in a corner. A dead tulsi plant. A broken flower pot. Rotting flowers near the roots. A roof with no railing, covered in moss. Fat snails curled up between the bricks. A banyan sapling struggling to grow. Like any other day, a sticky, dirty, bamboo mat, torn at the edges, laid out in the courtyard. On top of it, an old rusted barley tin full of cotton; an ancient magnifying lens; red-blue pieces of glass; that day's *Anandabazar Patrika* pinned under a broken brick and its eternal attempts to flutter away. Bhodi looks over the roof ledge to the courtyard below. Nolen is plucking tiny white flowers and putting them into a brass basket.

'I'm bellowing at the top of my lungs, fucker, can't you hear?'

'I'm sorry, I didn't. Should I come?'

'Yes, come! When they singe your mouth in Keoratola, only then you'll come or what?! What's Bechamoni doing?'

'Boudi is taking a shit.'

'When she comes out, tell her to finish her bath quickly and bring out the keys. How many rooms are full now?'

'Two. Rooms One and Three.'

'More will come. You finish your bath-beautifications quickly as well. We need to get water from the Ganga.'

'Why? So early?'

'Do what I tell you to. We have to fucking open the disc room today. Ma! Oh Ma! Ma!'

On Sunday morning, 24 October, this is how it was. Bhodi read Magician Ananda's advertisement and received the mystical indication that the disc room would have to be opened. By the Hurricane lamp's ghostly flickering light, this is all that we can see for now.

There's still some time till winter. But the winter poems have begun to sprout. Let us glance at a sample:

Look, yonder lies the sleepy village
    Tiny birds walk now and then on the hour
Blanket-wrapped are the farmer and his wife
    And slumbering snores the cauliflower.

Who is the master-creator of this excellent poem? Who is Bhodi? What lies in the disc room? Why has this poem been suddenly shunted in?

    'Bengal for Pandemonium, China for Craftsmanship'

(*To Be Continued*)

## 2

At the millennial conclusion of the first chapter, four questions had been raised. They have since been put down. Or, since the master of ceremonies must be clear at all times: we have been told that there will be no response-replies for now. This is not a school examination where, for the benefit of the cheaters, the following motto is printed at the top of every answer script: 'Remember, God helps those who rely on their own merit.' But for those who are passionately curious about the Pathans and Mughals, Sri Bimalacharan Deb has explained so long ago the meaning of 'Bengal for Pandemonium, China for Craftsmanship': 'If you speak of panic and pandemonium, then it is difficult to beat Bengal. If you speak of artistic skill, then it is difficult to best the Chinese craftsman.' The State vs Centre war that we are witnessing today is popularly acknowledged to have been started by the Communist Party of India (Marxist), or CPM for short. The maharajas of Bengal had always been the daredevil type. Refused to succumb to the authority of the Pathans or the Mughals. 'One pandemonium would barely stop than another one begin'—such is the great tradition of Bengal. And at the end of 1999, the same scandal continues. The war cries of malignant malaria and the film festival have barely faded and the drumrolls of bus accidents and bus bonfires have begun to sound. Here and there, squeezed into the cracks and crevices, are odds-and-ends programmes, such as kidnappings, poetry festivals, murders and embezzlements. Just as those stutter to a halt, the World Bengali Conference bugles and bagpipes begin to play. Word on the street has it that though the new year has started with an endless cake-eating competition, events will soon take an unexpected turn. Maybe that's why this chill runs down our spine, this feeling of foreboding. At this stage, it's best not to poke and pry too much.

Borhilal has always been compact in size but in no way can he be called a short man. He has a small shop in Haldarpara that sells colourful chalks, sheets of multicoloured marble paper, tinsel, gold and silver ribbons to wrap gifts, pencils, perfumed erasers in many shapes and sizes, rulers, colourful plastic balls, plastic shuttlecocks, imitation Barbie dolls in paper boxes, rough-edged tin aeroplanes, cellphone-shaped pencil boxes, stickers of cricket players, mini cricket bats, Ludo sets, plastic-dinosaur 'Jurassic Park' sets, submachine guns, pistols, water pistols, complete kitchen sets, 'Doctor' sets, plastic lizards, scorpions—all these and so much more. It's not a total flop show, but business isn't that great either. Borhilal is happy with whatever little he makes. He buys the *Bartaman* and reads it from start to finish. He knows that if he stocks lozenges, peanut biscuits, toffee and chocolates, they will boost his sales. Many people have advised him to do exactly so.

'Spare me!' Borhilal says to them, 'And when the ants and cockroaches flock to me, then?! As it is there's a fuck-load of lizards— and they're shitting all over the place.'

'Then do what everybody does: stock them in glass jars with the lids shut tight. Sweets stay inside, insects stay out.'

'Oh, you have no idea—they'll find a way in, they will. Damn fuckers are downright devious. I know them very well.'

'Only you have such silly fears! As if people aren't selling them anywhere else.'

'Why won't they? Yes, they're selling. But they're dying too. Leeches, cockroaches, then spiders, termites. You don't know them. Some are chewing their way through your clothes in secret, you don't hear a sound. And some others lick you and then you're covered in boils or all your hair falls out.'

Overall, the philosophy according to which Borhilal runs his shop may well be called Small Is Beautiful. Borhilal hasn't married. He lives in Chetla, in a one-room portion of his ancestral home. Eats in a hotel. Nothing fussy. But there is a picture of Bajrangbali Hanuman in his room. He offers it small boiled-sugar sweets and water. After watching some police constables wrestle in his childhood, he'd decided to become a wrestler. Even attended Tarak-da's wrestling akhara for a while. The walls of the akhara had pictures of Gobar Guha, Great Gama, Small Gama, Zbyszko and Sandow. Rows of loincloths hung like dead bats from a rope. Cries of 'H-oop', 'H-up'. Then one day it had been only a medium-level blow from one of Tarak-da's rather scrawny-slim students but it had thrown Borhilal's neck into a sprain. So instead of a wrestler, he ended up a shopkeeper. But he didn't forsake Hanuman-ji. Although there is another reason for that: no god but Hanuman has the power to chase away ghosts. In fact, ghosts are such bastards that they can materialize in the form of the very god you're praying to. And you, elated in your gormless glee, think: Oh, I've prayed so hard that my god has no choice but to appear before me! Ghosts are masters of such grotesque games. They turn everything upside down and inside out and then disappear. Then there are those bastards who keep ghosts as pets. Use their ghosts to size up their enemies. Granted, all this Borhilal has learnt via hearsay. But that hearsay can suddenly turn into reality, that Borhilal didn't know. Neither did we. To keep knowing the unknowable, that is how we must proceed. The field of reading is like a wrestling akhara too. Smashing and thrashing is a daily feature here. Because it's often underhand, it's not always perceptible. Be that as it may, Borhilal, ever-vigilant of ghosts and insects, did not suffer from an innate servile-since-birth temperament. Though born quite some time prior to the halfway mark of this first-silent-then-talkie century, Borhilal never displayed the mentality of a servant or khansamah or khidmatgar, never went about slavishly crying out for a master. On the contrary, he could have been a great wrestler, hung a giant lucky charm from his neck and gone for morning walks by the Ganga; or gathered a bunch of the neighbourhood boys and initiated them into the power mantra of nationalism. A small change in the time of birth can cause a huge shift in the universe. Later we shall come to understand how absolutely true this is.

24 October 1999, Sunday morning, Borhilal realized he had three options. He could go to the cinema. He could visit his only sister Korobi at her in-laws' in Belgharia. Or as an exercise in self-reliance, he could go to Keoratola and study the various types of human anatomy. For some secret reason, Borhilal felt a strong pull towards Keoratola. Borhilal surrendered his body to its flow.

The Keoratola Crematorium doesn't have a guided-tour facility. 'Plan a trip to Keoratola this Durga Puja' or 'Come, visit Keoratola with friends and family'—no travel agency has been known to advertise anything of the sort. But Borhilal has observed that some invisible guide seems to shepherd the living spectators straight towards the electric furnaces which, mindful of size and weight, open and close and swiftly swallow dead bodies, one after another. If they are not malfunctioning, that is. All the furnaces working at the same time—no one has ever witnessed such a supernatural occurrence. On the other hand, there is no dearth of corpses. At times there is such a queue that Keoratola is House Full, and the corpses have to be sent off to Shiriti or Boral to be finally freed from their mortal coils. Filled with delight at their crematorium visit, especially at the sight of the electric incinerators, and alerted to the insignificance of human life, the spectators proceed with bold and knowledgeable footsteps towards the food stalls. Earlier, when people died, they were burnt on wood pyres. Electric incinerators are a recent phenomenon. Though now a tiny version of those incinerators, the microwave oven, has carved out a place in so many affluent households. But that one doesn't burn to ash; rather, it roasts, grills, bakes, etc. And that too, not usually people.

Borhilal has never given in to the lure of that invisible guide. He comes down the Chetla bridge, crosses the road to the paan shop on the other side, buys a biri and lights it from the glowing edge of the thick rope that hangs by the shop and works as an improvised lighter for smokers, then crosses the road again and walks into where the bodies are still cremated on wood pyres.

Someone must have been cremated at dawn. He notices a huge heap of ash from which a few embers send out wisps of smoke that curl into the air like the Indian Rope Trick. Close by lies a mattress so old and so black and partly wet that no one's bothered to reclaim it. Borhilal walks along the side of the wood-burning area, enters the gate at the end of the crematorium and then, before crossing the Old Ganga ghat, turns left. Small puddles here and there. A musty smell. Two dogs biting each other. On the right:

Respected
Sir Ashutosh Mukhopadhyay

*Born*        *Died*
29 June        25 May
1864        1924

Alas, Royal Bengal Tiger. Alas, Calcutta University. Alas, Calcutta Corporation. What a state the mausoleums are in. Dirty, paint-chipped, cracked, patterned all over with bird shit. A huge old banyan tree hangs above. A tiny sapling of which has taken root on the ground. Well hidden from human eyes, the inevitably destructive roots of Banyan and Co. approach with stealthy steps. Alas Bengal's Tiger who loved even the meat in sweetmeats. Roar!

Although it is not right to address Ashutosh as Bengal's Tiger any more. Because, as the daily commuters are no doubt aware, at the Lansdowne–Padmapukur crossing, for many, many days, on two legs of bamboo there stood a board that bore the legend:

Bengal's Tiger
Somen Mitra
Zindabaad

Now the inscription has changed:

Golden Bengal's
Golden Son
Somen Mitra Zindabaad

This is called magic. Now he is Tiger. Zap! And he becomes Golden Boy. Today's sinner is tomorrow's saint. It is evident that as far as the fates of Congressmen are concerned, where Lakshmi, Goddess of Wealth, once reigned supreme, now the Lady of Infinite Emptiness has arrived and taken up residence.

To hell with them! Facing Sir Ashutosh is Rajendra Nath Mookerjee. He's not doing so well either. Pot-head vandals have cracked open his concrete tomb, stolen the iron chains. If one is not entirely mistaken, then it is about him that Sri Subal Chandra Mitra had written: 'Among the white man's business community, he is the most respected and influential of all Bengalis.' Forget the white man, leave out the lords and ladies, now even the native brown lumpen have no regard for him. Out of his head grows a neem tree.

Borhilal had to cancel his plans of going further left, because a connoisseur's collection of vomit, moss, shit, etc. would have to be overcome. As a gust of wind blew at him over the opulent heap, and Borhilal decided it was best to move along. He knows what has to be done now. The gate on the right is locked. One key used to be kept in Ma Tara's temple, and a duplicate in the crematorium office. Now no one keeps any key anywhere because of the local louts. So Borhilal has to climb up the dilapidated railing and jump down the other side. Really, sometimes it is so difficult to meet the demands of the road!

There are concrete benches on either bank of the river. On the bench on the left sit three men: one lanky, one short-fat and a third instantly identifiable as a barking-mad type. On the other side sits a rather large chap in a lungi and yellow vest, his eyes closed and smoking a biri. One can immediately tell that he's no small fry. 'Don't bother me and I won't bother you'-type. Borhilal climbed up to the right. The Ganga is swelling up. Now he has to jump. Must make sure not to sprain his groin!

Let us seize this moment to inform you that the three men on the left are Phyatarus who, by the powers of a secret mantra, are able to fly, cause massive mayhem at festivities and in any home and household remotely regarded as happy. There are many Phyatarus. For now, it's enough to know these three: the lanky goods is called Madan; his dentures can be found in his pocket. The short-black-fat one is DS; there is a whiskey by that name: Director's Special; on either side of his dented run-down briefcase are stuck his initials, though it is hard to read them. The third specimen is Poet Purandar Bhat. By and large, they are pleasure squatters.

Suddenly, Purandar bursts out:

So many bouquets of flowery tokens
So many clicks for photofiles
Can never be mended if broken
All embraces remain futile.

Hail Ganga, Hail Ram
Poet Purandar watches
Incessantly the corpses come.

So many lovers separated
So many bangles broken
Both boy and boss are fated
By death to be equally taken

Incessantly the corpses come
Poet Purandar says,
Hail Ganga, Hail Ram.

At this elegiac poem, DS grew stricken and snapped: 'Just as I was dozing off! No warning, nothing, started a bloody corpse concert.'

'What do you expect in a crematorium? Wedding sonnets instead? Cretin!'

Madan's admonishment deflates DS a little. 'No, that's not why I said so.'

'Then why did you?'

'A BJP line is creeping into Purandar's poems—that's why.'

Purandar, so far silent, now mumbled 'Prick!' and lit a biri.

DS heard the biri packet rustle: 'Oh, Bengal Biri! Pass me one!'

On the opposite bench, yellow vest leant sideways, launched a massive fart-bomb and then walked off.

'Uff,' said DS, 'that was as loud as a Burima Chocolate Bomb!'

Madan charged again: 'Must you say something all the time?'

Purandar seized the chance to vent: 'Madan-da, it's not DS' fault. This is normal.'

'Meaning?'

'He was born on the inauspicious side of a half-holiday—this is but normal for him.'

Borhilal stood in front of Sarat Chandra Chattopadhyay's mausoleum. Both Bengalis and Bengali literature are in a similar state. If there were no iron grilles in front of Sarat Chandra's dusty head, someone would have sliced it off and run away with it. As they have with some other heads. There is no end to insult, injury or insensitivity. His gaze turned to the right, Sarat-babu sees it all. Round his neck hangs a dried-up garland of marigolds. From the garland stretches far and wide a spiderweb. The mausoleum is full of garbage, more cobwebs. The facade is mostly broken. Withal is a museum of sorts. Broken bits of bamboo, white feathers off dead pigeons, five dead garlands, leaves, paper, empty Pan Parag packets and thousands and thousands of black ants scurrying to and fro. Even though one side is closed, there are lots of dogs. Let them all be christened Bhelu.

Right beside Sarat Chandra is Sri Sri Vishuddhananda Paramahansa Dev's memorial: Mahamahopadhyay Gopinath Kaviraj's mentor has relatively better luck; Gandha Baba, or the Perfume Saint, seems to still have a few followers because his grille has been newly painted silver. Beside him, more memorials to the uncared for. One after the other. Hemendra Nath Das Gupta. No one can make out who lies next to him. Charuchandra Chattopadhyay. Patriot Krishna Kumar Mitra. Ajiteshwar Bhattacharya. Surendranath Mallick. Surabala Ghosh. Scattered on the ground are an assortment of tinsel ribbons, marijuana bongs, empty sweet boxes, tender-coconut shells, plastic water bottles and glasses and innumerable filthy polybags. And everywhere, that strange smell.

Borhilal walked up to the ghat and saw a fat man glug-glug filling empty foreign-liquor bottles with Ganga water and shoving them into a BigShopper bag while the short-fat one hooted at him from the bench: 'That one, that chiselled one is a Scotch bottle. You'll crack your arse if you want to buy one. Bastards, how much more should I see?! The smell of whiskey hardly gone and he's filling the bottles with Ganga water! That, that one held Hercules rum. Whacked from the Army stores.'

Madan smirked. 'Your master's a big chap indeed. No pint–nip business—only litre bottles. What will you do with so much water? What a fucker-type he is, eh! So much we're saying, but he's saying nothing! Say something, boss. If nothing else, a curse? There's three of us, so you're worried we'll thrash you? Maybe the bastard's mute from birth. Or he's a bone-deep bloody bastard!'

The fat man in the yellow vest, aka Nolen, finished filling the last bottle. Put it into the BigShopper and stood up. So many bottles full of water, but he doesn't flinch. As if a cushion tucked under his arm, and he's on his way to a soiree. But as soon as Nolen climbs up the steps of the embankment, a strange thing happens. Just as a dog faces its master at the jerk of a leash, the three Phyatarus leap off their bench. And then set off, walking behind him. Not a sound from their mouths. A girl appears on the other side, so Nolen veers right. The three behind him dive right too, as if on cue. Now Borhilal begins to follow them all. A glass car draws up with a corpse. Two Tempo vans full of people behind it. Nolen folds his hands in respect. So do they. Nolen crosses the road, scratching his left ball. Madan, DS and Purandar cross the road behind him, scratching their respective left balls. After this lane and that, past a biggish courtyard, over the open drains, keeping the discarded iron-cage-like Haringhata milk booth to the left, Nolen enters yet another lane and goes towards a house that we now know is Bhodi's single-storey home with the railing-less roof. A dilapidated signboard hangs crookedly over the door, the letters blurred and unclear. You have to tilt your head to read them.

Borhilal read the message spelt out in broken alphabets: Rooms on Rent for All Inauspicious Occasions.

'Look, the Nameless One, opening wide its mouth.'

(*To Be Continued*)

*3*

No child today reads *Lal-Kalo* any more. Therefore who can open his enormous mouth in the dark, and why that makes the awful-looking executioner break out with trembling beads of perspiration—such questions do not arise. Girindrasekhar has been exiled from the land of dreams to the land of eternal slumber. As also Dakshinaranjan, Dhan Gopal, Hemendra Kumar, Sunirmal, Khagendranath, Sukhalata and hundreds of other known and unknown litterateurs who wrote for children. Now is the era of the child litterateur. Children read nothing but Feluda or Tintin. Their parents are equally unread. High-protein diets from childhood, supplemented by Branolia, broiler chickens, Kellogg's, etc., has made the kids almost-obese already. Soon they will attend coaching classes in either computers or hooliganism. The Big Bongs' broods are entirely unaware of Hnada-Bhnoda, Nonte-Phonte, Bnatul the Great, clueless about even Chyanga-Byanga. No child in any other land is half as selfish or evil. Think of our next-door neighbour Bihar, if you will. Or Nepal. There one comes across innocent children. Often.

But now: back to Borhilal.

The crooked door made out of wood from old fruit crates, with scraps of biscuit tins nailed all over it, had a hole through which Borhilal could peep and thus witness the scene playing out in Bhodi's courtyard.

Bhodi emerged, rubbing his belly. 'Why have you brought these three fuckers here?' he asked Nolen, back from the Ganga.

'Shooting off their mouths, they were. So I thought: let me take them home. Size them up later.'

'Wait, wait. The case is not so simple. I'm thinking: Why today of all days did they fall into our trap?'

'Sprinkle their heads with water and purify them. I'll chop them off at once. We'll have offered a sacrifice. Bodies and heads can both be used up for sadhana. Nothing will go waste.'

'Not a bad idea.' said Bhodi, 'What ho! Silver-tongued scally-wags! Digging for worms—'

'But discovered vipers!' laghed Nolen, 'All mum now, eh? Ooh, how the curses were popping like corns, back at the river!'

First DS, then Purandar and then Madan burst into tears. Borhilal could hear someone chanting mantras close by. He could smell burning cloth. In the meantime, Nolen has fetched a rather wibbly-wobbly scimitar made of tin which, really, won't be able to slice through anything at all. But even that doesn't stop the three men's tears. Bhodi is pacing before them and intermittently bellowing: 'This way or that, if it has to be done, then it must. If, bastard, there's a hint of scandal, then marry one will. The skulls have danced. The skulls will dance. Uff, such huge disc-size heads, strung up in a garland. This way or that. Heads don't give a twat. Just the bodies, sputtering. Arms grasping. Legs unclasping.'

The Phyataru chorus rises to a heartrending howl. Outside the door, Borhilal is thinking: just the sight of chickens being slaughtered makes his throat tingle, and now, here, three live humans will lose their heads right before his eyes . . . Are these people occultists? . . . Even now one reads in the papers reports of a human sacrifice or two . . . Should he rush to the police station right away and tell them . . .

Bechamoni is enormous to begin with. Now, enveloped in a red-and-gold Benarasi saree, she looks even more bountiful, her shampooed hair . . .

'Again—again?' she chides Bhodi, 'That same old vulgarity?'

'How many times have I told you to stay out of my business!' Bhodi roars back.

'Boudi,' Nolen pleads, 'the scimitar's itching—any moment now, blood will splatter. Please, you go inside.'

Bechamoni smiles like a benign goddess: 'It's an auspicious day. The Phyataru-guests have come. You've given them a scare— OK, good for you. Now boys, come, calm down and sit quietly. No one will chop off your heads. That's just Godi's folly. Nolen, bring them some sweets and water.'

'So you suggest we not sacrifice them?'

'That evil word again! As if you can't see them trembling already!'

'Since you're pleading their case so hard, I'll let them go . . . All right, I'm setting you free this time. But wherever and when-ever, whoever and whomsoever, you've got to stop fingering their arses. This I must insist.'

'What did you mean: Godi's folly?' asks a tearful DS, 'I didn't understand.'

Bechamoni shyly draws the edge of her saree over her head, as Bhodi benevolently explains: 'My name is Bhodi. She's my wife, so how can she utter my name? So she calls me Godi. Now you know what she meant by Godi's folly.'

Purandar and Madan sit down. DS follows suit. Nolen places three clay cups and a bottle of Bangla in front of them.

'You have seen Godi's folly. Now try a bit of Nolen's nectar.'

'We shouted a lot of nonsense at you back by the river. Please forget all that, brother.'

'See, brother, you're a Phyataru. The Phyatarus are doing what they're supposed to . . . and—'

Bhodi waves at Nolen to be silent. 'Let me explain,' he says, 'Today is a day of great conjunctions. The last time such a day came around was more or less a hundred and fifty years ago. When the game of discs commences, then Choktars and Phyatarus form one and the same party.'

'What's a Choktar, sir? I know doctor, lawyer—'

'Arrey, doctors, lawyers, solicitors, advocates, they don't have Phyatarus among them, they don't have Choktars either. We are not the publicizing type. So nobody has any clue we exist. The three of you, for example, how many people know you three are Phyatarus? Not a peep about you lot in the newspapers, the Sunday supplements, the news channels. Same for the Choktars. Nowhere. No one knows. Come, now pour the drinks. Nolen has opened the bottle already. A Chetla brand. Rasa Distillery, might smell a bit. The Farini label's not available this side of town. It's all governmental gobshiting. So, my brother Madan, now will you utter a word or two?'

'I can't help but wonder where I've seen you before—I'm trying to remember.'

'My dear boy, Choktars and Phyatarus have a soul connection. Nothing to wonder at there. It's a bond that stretches way back in time. All right, Bhat Poet, out with the poem you've made up just now.'

'Really?'

'Of course! Spit it out! Poem's not meant for swallowing!'

Purandar clears his throat. 'It's titled "Each Man's Job".'

'Such titles don't work,' says DS almost immediately. ' "Each Man's Job"! Everyone's will just turn the page and carry on.'

'Why?'

'The title's enough to let on it'll be full of advice. The public reads poems for pleasure, no one wants to listen to a truckload of philosophy-buggering bullshit.'

Madan says, 'DS, will you stop? You haven't even heard it yet, and you're arguing against it!'

'Don't hold me back, brother. Pleasure you've had enough of. Now, before you think any more, listen:

'Each Man's Job'

Shashadhar catches rabbits
Mohitosh sends mosquitoes to their tombs
Each man skilled at his task
Right from his mother's womb.
The forest guardian strips the forest of every tree
Saws the branch he sits on, one and two and three
    They weep who nest on leaf and bough
While the Angel of Death claps in glee.

Bhodi's face is aglow with delight: 'Wow! Wow! Superb. This, this is poetry. Feeling, allegory, deep thought, brisk pace. This is what adds up to great poetry. And that pubic garbage they write these days? Makes no sense whatsoever. How did you like it, DS?'

'Need to think about it. It's a philosophical poem, after all, can't comment in a hurry. But I don't think Purandar has understood it entirely. Caught-and-delivered case. What, am I wrong?'

'I'm not saying anything just because Bhodi-da and Boudi and Madan-da are present. Anyway, such scorn is not new to Purandar Bhat's life. Soldiers of war never concern themselves with mosquito bites.'

'I'm a mosquito?'

'Yes, Anopheles.'

'Ah, will you two stop?' says Madan, 'No point bickering. I'll explain the poem to DS later.'

Borhilal, one eye pressed against the tin door, felt something crawling up his leg. Glancing down for a moment, he saw a huge red ant. Trying to shake it off, his knees hit the door with a loud crash. Even though no one else heard it, Nolen pricked up his ears. He was about to get up and investigate, but Bhodi stopped him. 'It's nothing. Witness. Everything needs a witness. A witness is necessary. Ignore it. Now, ask me whatever you want to know but keep it short and sweet.'

'So, sir, what exactly is a Choktar?'

'This question makes no sense. What is a Phyataru? In which case, what is a Choktar? A Choktar is a Choktar. But I can say this much: there's none better at panic and pandemonium. But if the time's not right, then nothing can be done.'

'Not clear enough.'

'How can you expect it to be? It's only the first episode today. That *Janmaboomi* series, it's crossed three hundred episodes, and the public still has no clue about its plot. And you think you can grasp this vast unfolding right away on Day One? And why would I, like an absolute twat, pull my veil so long in the front that my arse hangs open at the back!'

Bechamoni is embarrassed: 'Godi's tongue is like that only! So vulgar.'

'Shut up. Vulgar! It's the sign of greatness to be able to abuse openly rather than plotting in the privacy of a dirty mind. Tell me quickly, what else do you want to know?'

Now it was Purandar's turn: 'Achha, Bhodi-da, the sign on your door says Rooms on Rent for All Inauspicious Occasions. What's that mean?'

'Look, every day, every moment, every second without pause, so many evil rituals are being conducted. In today's world, everyone has at least 10–20 enemies per head. Hard to tell friend from foe. Court cases, frauds, wife burgling, vote stealing, contract cadging, petty grudging, cheating, embezzling, using little thief to screw big dacoit, female trafficking, political pingponging, nominating—to deal with all this, people need voodoo, cheap black magic, hypnosis, binding spells. And so I rent my rooms for the performing of any of these rituals. Weddings, first-rice ceremonies, funerals—all that I don't care for. Just now, for example, there's a cushion-cruising going on in one room, and—what's on in the other one, Nolen?'

'They never said. A bearded chap locked himself in with a middle-aged woman. I'm not sure what they're up to. But I did smell burning cloth.'

'Blast and buggery! Kick the door down, kick them out at once. Take the money and throw them out through the back door.'

Nolen went off. Soon after: thumps and thuds, crashes and cries.

'This is an everyday occurrence. They go away if you chase them. It's because of fools like these that the police get a chance to show off.'

'What's the cushion-cruising case, Bhodi-da?'

'Very interesting. Congress, and all their petty offshoot parties, they sit on the floor, on mattresses and cushions. If a cushion is successfully cruised, as soon as you try to lean on it, it'll slide away. You simply won't be able to sit properly. Therefore, embarrassment.

Therefore, total constipation of your political career. So many more things can be done—crematorium spells, ghost spells, stomach upsets, flying razorblades, burgle spells, cholera or plague spells, poltergeist panics, padfoot activate, diarrhoea, dysentery, whore-gigolo attracting spells. Rooms are needed for all this. And who rents out those rooms? Choktar Bhodi. Got it?'

'No option but to get it! Total champi business, boss!'

'Big customers, all of them. Minister, cinema star, cricket player, doctor, barrister—the whole lot. Have to keep it very hush-hush. Not a soul can know.'

'But the signboard!'

'That's the Choktar cunning at play. If some small fry turns up, let them. There's always the back door. And if need be, a range of burkhas, black robes, false beards, moustaches, wigs at the ready.'

'Don't the police make trouble?'

'Of course they do. Every time a new OC arrives, they huff and puff a bit to start with, then they all come down a size or two. Every land has its laws. Money in your pocket, keep your plug in your own socket. And voila! No more trouble. Sit tight. And keep shoving it, softly, gently. This is Choktar's business dharma. But it's a CPM government, after all. They can get an itch in their groin at any time. And as soon as they do, this signboard comes down and a new one goes up.'

'Which one?'

'For a nursing home. Have a name for it too: Death's Angel Nursing Home.'

'Ooh, daddy! But who'll come to a nursing home with that name?'

'Come?—they'll bloody fly and flock! Everyone knows that no patient survives a nursing home. So, if it's a near-death case, they'll bring it here. That way the family will have done its duty, and the patient dies happy. No problem. I have two doctors ready. Not a single person has lived through their treatments. Besides, there's Bechamoni, Nolen—'

'We're here too, Bhodi-da.'

'Of course, of course. Oh fuck! Baba's come. If we don't get on with things, he'll be very upset indeed.'

'Baba? Where!'

Nolen's smirks and Bechamoni's giggles add just the right amount of eeriness to a moment already grown grim. On the other side of the door, Borhilal too is swaying in a cradle of doubt. Only Bhodi is unperturbed. As he folds his hands and looks up to a corner of the roof, six Phyataru eyes and Borhilal's two swivel up in the same direction.

On the corner of the roof sits a huge, ancient and wise raven, staring at the scene below.

'The disc room will open,' says Bhodi reverentially, 'Spell's in motion, magic's in the potion—everything is adding up. I knew Baba wouldn't stay away at a time like this.'

The kind of Bengali language that can be reclaimed no more, that Bengali had a name for such a bird—Dandakak. It may have been that this type of raven was widely available in the Dandak-aranya forest of yore. No problem even if not. Such ravens are not much spotted in Calcutta. But in the time of Begum Johnson, apparently they were quite a common sight in the city. Since we have no choice but to come to Begum Johnson (1728–1812) even-tually, we may as well sing that prelude now. She lies buried in St John's Church in this very Calcutta, quite close to the graves of Job Charnock and Admiral Watson. It is not unfair to hope that, but for an earthquake or so, she will remain there and thus for the rest of eternity. At the moment though, Bhodi's raven-shaped father has let out a rather hoarse syllable which, whatever else it may be, is certainly not a crow.

'What do you want, Father? An ananda-laddoo?'

This time the Raven spoke—or spake—in clear human tones: 'The day of amazing ananda draws near. The magic and the spell, hand in glove, Ananda at *Anandabazar*, Phyatarus in the Choktar home, the skull's magic dance a mere four days away—when everything's so full of joy, then why waste time?'

'Well, without you—'

'Shut up. I'll slice your tongue in two if you speak again. Open the disc room, bastard.'

Bhodi, without wasting another moment, takes the bunch of keys from Bechamoni. The lock is a product of the early days of the empire; the key could compete with a bamboo pole in length. A buzzing sound on the other side of the door, as if a thousand bees were whirling, sky-diving. As soon as the door is opened, a few small discs, or mini flying saucers, shoot out, screeching like sirens, and disappear into the muddy sky. The large discs spin loudly but stay inside.

'Leave the door open. They'll come and go as they please. You carry on with your work. I'll be back at the right time.'

And the Raven swoops away.

Borhilal was feeling hungry and thought that now was the best time to scoot. He could always come back later and see how far matters had proceeded. Calcutta's winter may not have teeth enough, but it had gums. Now and then, he also felt strangely warm. As he walked home, he noticed a huge bearded head painted on a wall and the words beneath it, as fierce as a cannon roar: 'Marxism is invincible because it is science'. Directly below the damp wall ablaze with these words is an open drain. There, on the stagnant water, clumps of lissom moss sway their dusky hips and thousands of mosquito larvae dance in delight.

> All towards Armageddon! All towards Armageddon!
>> On horseback and elephants we ride
>>> While some others trudge, side by side,
>> Of golden chairs and floral chariots swells a tide
> All towards Armageddon! All towards Armageddon!

(*To Be Continued*)

## 4

This is the Age of the Quiz. In every hamlet, every neighbour-hood, every home, beneath every public-water tap, incessant quiz competitions take place. As every man's armoury of knowledge increases, as every human child's headpiece grows richer and richer in brain cells, the importance of quizzing increases proportionately. When did the first public urinal open on the streets of Calcutta? What is the fine, in Great British Pounds, for taking a shit on a London street? What is the name of Kapil Dev's grandfather? Where in Santiniketan can one buy foreign liquor? Who was the last baby-taxi driver of Hatibagan? Why don't termites eat through cricket bats? Many such questions and their answers are carefully collated, day after day. But who wrote the poem quoted at the very end of the last chapter of this serialized novel? Many quiz masters will crumble before they can answer. Of course, there's no point asking any child. Even their fathers have no clue. The batch before them might have known, but most of them have disappeared into oblivion by now. The poet in question was not a champion bull-shitter like the poets of today. Although the world back then was just as full of arseholes as it is now. Why else would he write:

> A token of love        and words thereof
>      A droplet of tear will I never get!
>    'Tis true this earth        is with monsters gird

The gods of mercy I've never met
On travels vain though I have set.

It is about this great mind that, in 1948, Sri Jogendranath Gupta had observed: '[he] is Bengal's last national poet', and far from being a vain hope, Gupta simply assumed that 'everyone would agree with this claim'. It is needless to state that no one did. Sri Kailashchandra Acharya had probably anticipated this. He was the publisher of a collection of the poet's works for which Sri Gupta had provided a foreword. It is not possible to know what else that foreword had to say, because in his Publisher's Note, Acharya clearly mentions the honest truth: 'Due to a paper shortage, we have reluctantly had to omit a large part of the original foreword'. Historians may carry on debating whether there truly was a crisis in the capitalist paper industry in 1948 or not, but the poet about whom we are making such a fuss, he had a far simpler solution:

Adorned in shit, with thrashing sticks we revel
If Bengalis be human, who pray are the devils?

The Bengalis have forgotten him today. They will not remember him tomorrow. But none of that matters a whit to pucca-poet Gobindachandra Das.

One knows that many objections will be raised. Quite a nice strum we had going there, why did the tune suddenly grow so serious, maestro? But then, had anyone ever guaranteed an uninterrupted flow of frivolity? The writer's will, his skill and swing, his mastery of twists and turns, especially his audacity—if all this be first rate, then in one fell swoop the melody can swan dive from mundane to melodrama. The modern narrative tends to be many-sided, multi-perspectival. Now it ha-ha laughs, now it woe-woe wails. It will be thus, for a while now. Every now and then the writer will snore, for he is drunk on the dream of literature. But the reader is wide awake. The land on which the Pathans fought their battles, that land is now the grazing land of goats. In such a situation, the reader has no choice but to keep vigil. Make sure that from the mighty mountain of garbage called Literature, not one morsel must be lost. If it is, there is no saving us from disaster. Even a little while ago, this was not the case. The Bengali reader treated works of literature in the same way as bolsters or monkey caps— they were essential. But now those days of buying a ticket and going for an elephant ride are over. Gone, forever. Now we don't buy tickets any more, we dig canals instead. And once you've dug a canal, can you stop the crocodile from crawling in? In the grand sprawl-spiralling scheme of things, let this be a tiny whorl.

Not all, but many soap-opera serials do have something called the 'Recap'. By virtue of this, the wise viewer doth internalize the summation of all events hitherto occurred, and even if he bunks class from time to time, like a nectar-drunk bee he cannot be separated from any flower blooming on the countless boughs and branches of the main plot. Similarly, it may so happen that a reader commences perusing this metropolitan novel from this point on, or has perhaps been doing so since its very genesis, right where it began with the chandrabindu. It may also happen that having read *Dawn of Maharashtra* and *Rajput Twilight* immediately before this, and having derived such transcendent ecstasy from them, that same reader found *Madhavi's Armlets* to be utter rubbish. Let us say that out of affection or misplaced mushiness, he has named this novel *Bengali Life-Noir*. In any case, all this is dead beat, for at the very beginning we have the enormous chandrabindu. Shall our serial novel then, O Distinguished and Most Honoured Reader, have a Recap too? If the Last Day of Judgement be not today, O Reader, why then are you silent? At the end of the day, the crocodile will have you. But there is time yet. What's the rush?

About two hours after Borhilal scrammed, the Phyatarus lurched out of Bhodi's house. Albeit with still-functioning brains.

'Uff, how stupid we've been for so long!'

'Why?'

'I thought we were the best. There wasn't a son of a bitch who could take us on. But now I see—'

'See what?'

'I see the difference between the tiger's coat and my short and curlies. Choktars are the real aces. Thank god, they've pulled us onto their team. Just think: if they hacked our heads off and buried our bodies under the tagar tree, nobody or their uncle could have saved us! No trace, no police case!'

'I was worried about something else. I, DS, don't worry about life-strife. But the wife is going on eight months. What if I didn't get the chance to show my son what his father was made of?'

'Shut up. Who was the first one to break down? You! Isn't that so, Madan-da?'

'What's Madan-da going to say? I thought of my son, and my heart wrenched so—'

'Ah-ha, how does it matter who cried first. To be honest, all our asses were curled tight with fear.'

'Uff, totally tight!'

'Whatever. All that fear-sheer is gone now, so no point going on and on about it.'

'No, no.'

'We have to sit down calmly and recap the whole thing. So far, the Phyatarus have been big bosses. But now it seems the Choktars are the top daddies, five levels up. You know the story, right?'

'I know.'

'I don't.'

'OK, DS will tell it to you some other time. All in all, now we have to dance to the Choktars' tune. Choktars leaders, Phyatarus cadres. Choktars are jackfruit, we're lychees.'

'Choktars—you lead the way, Phyatarus will follow!'

'Mongrel pups can bark and spew
Choktars roar and Phyatarus mew.'

'You came up with that right now?'

'Indeed I did!'

'Madan-da, Purandar's the real thing, I tell you. I won't fight with him any more.'

'I thought of another one. But I can't say it out loud.'

'Whisper it, then. Just some maids washing dishes over there at the public tap, so what if they hear?'

'The garden bursts with
            CPM blooms
Sneakily, beneath
            Grows Trinamool.'

'Oye, now those maids are staring at us!'

'Of course they are. This place was a Congress stronghold till just the other day. Then it became CPM majority. Now Trinamool's on the rise. Brawls can break out any time.'

'How do you know all this?'

'Not enough to just be a poet, dear boy. Have to keep our eyes and ears open too. We are what you may call "political poets". We write none of that gormless muck. Only fresh and fabulous. Like a live wire—one touch, and you're dead. Understood?'

'Hah. As if I'm going to boil my brains by letting in any of that poetry-foetry. Already coping with a thousand and one problems! In through one ear. Out through the next. Game over.'

'Of course game over. Between your ears lies nothing but space. How could poetry dwell there? O Lord, such a myriad medley of motherfucks hast thou manufactured!'

Madan could tell another spat was brewing. 'Stop it, both of you! Be happy with whatever brain whoever has. Now, do you remember everything that Bhodi-da said? DS, tell me: who was the founding forefather of the Choktar clan?'

'Oh, I heard that. But I can't remember now.'

'You never pay attention. And that's why you'll land in deep shit someday, I can see it clearly. You heard it just a while ago, and you've forgotten it already?'

'It's all that booze I've drunk, I guess.'

Madan is so angry, he takes off his dentures and puts them in his pocket. 'Bollocks. The ocean of alcohol that I've consumed— you'll never even be able to swim through it. All that booze, eh?!

'All right, all right. I didn't pay attention. I'm sorry. Now, tell me.I promise I won't forget again.'

'I don't know. I hope Bhodi-da can't tell what we're up to at the moment. Who knows what he'll do if he's pissed with us again!'

'I do, I do—here, see, holding my ears and saying sorry, see. I'll never forget anything ever again, I promise.'

'OK. Purandar, you—do you remember?'

'I mean . . . you know, I was looking at Boudi's freshly sham- pooed hair and a poem was coming, so . . .'

'Wow, just wonderful! Tweedledee and Tweedledum, you two! Do you remember what shampoo it was?'

'No.'

'Dog shampoo! The sahibs wash their dogs with it. Ever seen their dogs? Long golden coats of hair. Cold-country dogs they are. They go out to shit in the snow.'

'Then why did Bhodi-da get that shampoo for Boudi? She's his wife, after all.'

'Because. After years of sadhana, Boudi's hair had become so matted that ordinary shampoo couldn't get through. That's when Bhodi-da asked Nolen to buy some dog shampoo. The label's got a dog on it. First, Boudi drenched her hair with kerosene. All the lice-trice vanished, the knots and tangles loosened a little. Then— dog shampoo! And now, just look at her hair! Not hair, it's become plumage!'

What followed immediately after is rare indeed. Truth be told, to even imagine that such an incident can happen today despite the all-enveloping mosquito net of the internet is in itself an act of courage. Lying in his spit of a bedroom, in his ancestral house in Chetla, Borhilal is witnessing this very incident in his dream. His intestines are roiling with the culinary remains of an almost-shut-for-the-day eatery, its chairs turned over on the tables for the night: scraped-together morsels of cold, stiff rice, a curry of over-ripe cauliflower with spikes like the back of a porcupine and the fatty oilskin of an elderly fish-tail—turning and churning in his belly. Though his dream soundtrack was original, the visuals were in black and white:

Jhoon-jhoon jhoon-jhoon, clip-clop clip-clop, swish-swoosh, swish-swoosh, creak-creak-creak. As this shake-rattle-and-roll scene suddenly clatters down almost onto the shoulders of the three Phytarus, they leap to the side of the road with the agile alacrity of alarmed natives. This is Calcutta's famous Hawa Khana or 'eating the air'—the gleaming Phaeton car. Real blinkered stallions run ahead, not arthritic mules. A turban so huge on the head of the coachman, you'd think he was the governor-general's personal chauffeur. An enormous memsahib sprawls in the open Phaeton. This is she, the one we've mentioned earlier, the very same Begum

Johnson. Blinking her big eyes and watching both sides of the road. On the seat opposite sit two lissom lassies. In the ears of one asleep Borhilal and three awake Phyatarus, an invisible soft spirit whispers and flits away: 'The one on the left—know her? Miss Sanderson. Beside her—Emma Wrangham.' All four promptly salute. And—oh boy! Following the Phaeton are two sahibs in breeches and loose-sleeved white shirts. Swaying along slowly on their horses. Both men look up and take the measure of Rani Mukherjee's bewitching body on a movie poster. Then they look at the two young women. This time, the soft spirit commentary is not required. All four of them realize that since one is Mr Sleeman, the other must be Mr Sherwood. In 1971, an advertisement appeared in a Calcutta daily (not the *Anandabazar*): 'To be sold by private sale: Two coffee boys, who play reasonably well on the French Horn, about 18 years of age; belonging to a Portuguese padre, lately deceased.' These two coffee boys had been bought by Mr Sleeman and Mr Sherwood.

This audible Hawa Khana vanishes just as suddenly as it had appeared. Well, this is just the beginning. Such things will keep happening now. 10 Clive Street was Begum Johnson's address. Someday, maybe we'll get the addresses of the other two missy-babas too.

'What do you think? DS?'

'Those two girls are superbowls, boss, but the fat aunty's scary.'

'Listen, be careful what you say about them. If the sahibs get to hear even a peep, we'll be done for. Purandar?'

'I'm thinking, is all this the result of disc-magic? Bhodi-da did say that things were going to go topsy-turvy.'

'Just the eve, brother, it's just the eve. The spectators are still arriving, settling down, taking their places. The musicians are yet to come.'

'You mean there's more?'

'By god, yes. Truth is, once the Choktar summons are sounded, no one can stop what follows.'

After the dream disappeared, Borhilal's slumber grew deeper. It is as pleasurable to get Rani Mukherjee, Ms Sanderson and Ms Emma Wrangham in one dream as it is irritating to tolerate the presence of Begum Johnson and the two lecherous men. For a while now, an anaemic fly had been sucking on the sweets kept in front of Hanuman-ji. Now it settled on Borhilal's nose. Borhilal turned over on his side. A horse race is underway. Borhilal is not bothered with history. Why should he be? But this instructive dream will not leave him alone? This time no more lords and ladies—just horses. Borhilal has seen the horses' water trough. Now he comes to know that though the present-day race course was established in 1810, there was another one at the far end of Garden Reach before that. *Hickey's Gazette* carried reports of race meetings and race balls in Calcutta as early as 1780. The Bengal Jockey Club was established in 1803. It goes without saying that no vociferous claims have been found holding forth on the deep affinity between Bengalis and horse riding. Although who doesn't know that for any Bengali, riding a horse to go take a shit is but child's play?

Borhilal, still asleep, rolls over onto his belly.


'But, one thing. Don't tell anyone a word of what Bhodi-da said. Just keep pretending you know nothing.'

'Mad or what? The one we're pinning our hopes on—not a word about him.'

'Not a squeak. Bhodi-da said he's going to watch us for a few days. Then start us off with a small task or two.'

'Achha, those discs that flew out, what do you think they're doing now?'

'No way to tell. It's a game of mystery. But that Hawa Khana Phaeton that went by, that surely was the disc's doing.'

'Just gave us a preview. Isn't that so, Madan-da?'

'Of course it was. Bhodi-da said, though, that nothing much will happen over the next three or four days. DS, what's our money scene?'

'I have the grand total of four rupees in my pocket today.'

'Purandar?'

'How much do you want?'

'Not much. We can't fly till it's properly dark. So I thought in the meantime we could down some tea and biscuits.'

'Oh, that's not a problem, I have about twelve bucks.'

'Not me.'

'Why?

'Once I've charged alcohol, I loathe the thought of tea. But if you want to charge, then I'm game.'

'With four bucks in your pocket, what are you going to charge? Burnt diesel?'

DS put down his dented briefcase on the road. Then slid his hand inside his pants and took out a finely folded hundred-rupee note from his underwear. When he unfolded it, the note fluttered in the breeze.

'I'm DS, OK? When it's puja season, I always have one or two big notes on me.'

'Oh bastard, what a five-star fuckstar you are!'

'So, then? Madan-da? How did I do just now?'

'Listen, if you weren't a born bastard, would I have made you a Phyataru?'

'I feel a new energy now! Was feeling so slow and soggy all this while.'

'Where will we go? Ganja Park or Garcha?'

'Neither. Both those places have too much shady public. Let's go to the Tollygunge Phari instead. It's larger. And there's less of a crowd.'

'They don't give you the real stuff most of the time, you know that, don't you? They punch it with water.'

'Never mind. I'm not so easy to fool, my man. They know that only too well.'

Sporting a very happy body language, the three Phyatarus jump into the Second Class compartment of a Tollygunge-bound No. 29 tram. The tram, without a moment's delay, creaks and clatters its weary way along its designated shore. Along the tracks are clumps of grass and short shrubs of berry and unknown creepers and many, many looming pyramids of shit. Along the road on either side run innumerable cars. Billows of polluting black smoke envelop everything in a tender cloud of dirt. And whenever there's a gust of unruly wind, plastic bags of various sizes fly about, like so many white doves of peace. Those on the road think of home. Those at home think of the TV. So no one has the time for these little miraculous sights. Only the madmen and bats remain sensitive about this matter. The Calcutta that has been broken, twisted, scorched, melted, pulped and clawed into a monstrous concoction of unknown metals and synthetic substances, the real friends of that Calcutta are the madmen and the bats. Along with a few painted girls, stray dogs, owls, mice, rats, cockroaches, beggars and ants. And mosquitoes, flies and the breath-choked specimens of the last few butterfly species, some moths, sparrows, mynas, crows and eagles. In case anyone has been left out, this space remains open; no fullstop closes this sentence

There is no glory in banging the door shut on anyone's face. Whether one is heard or not, one must keep trying. In writing, in non-writing—everywhere. All the time. Only then can they come. Even the proudest of them all, the blazing furnace that eats everything, even that has to open its doors. If we get a chance, we can of course always return to these cogitations.

That same night, as he bought some peanuts from a shop at the mouth of the lane that led to the Tollygunge hooch shack, DS met a hollow-cheeked, unshaven, middle-aged driver. A pint in his armpit. A plastic glass in his pocket. A burnt-out biri in the corner of his mouth. DS marched him over to where Madan and Purandar were sitting.

This man, they saw, didn't add water to his drink.

'I'm a regular customer,' he said to them. 'I come every day, I drink a pint and I leave. No fuss, no muss. When the pint's done, I'm done too. Don't drink a drop more, not a drop less.'

'Never?'

'Never. You know where I learnt this from? From my boss. Cool as a slab of ice. Never said: "Balai, I'm running late. Overtake that car. Push that one off the road." Instead he'll say: "The ones in a hurry to attend their father's wedding—let them go ahead." So true. You have to go. I have to go. Is there any point in killing each other on the way?'

'This is what most people simply don't understand.'

'As it is, the roads are few in number. Then, there's a new car launched every other day. Young men not old enough to shave are

sitting behind the steering wheel and thinking they're heroes.
Arrey, boss, this is Calcutta. Try any tricks here, and you're dead.'

Purandar dips a finger inside his glass and flicks out a fly.
'Thank god it didn't fall in your glass,' he tells Balai the driver,
'Your neat drink would have killed it in no time.'

'What is in its destiny, nothing can stop. Fate, fate, it's all fate.'

'So you believe in fate?'

'I didn't always. My little boy, four years old. If he'd been alive,
he'd be a young man today. Died of a doctor's maltreatment. Since
then I've become a believer.'

'What happened?'

'He used to suffer from spasms. Something like epilepsy. God
knows what possessed us, we took him to a fancy doctor. He'd just
recovered from mumps then.'

'All fancy doctors are bastards. All they know is money. How
to grab the poor and fleece them through and through.'

'A lot of people egged me on, said I should sue the doctor.  I
said, Can we poor people ever win against them? Lawyers, police—
they're all in cahoots with them.'

'And would you have got your son back in the end?'

'That's true. He fell to his fate. What can we do?'

A little way ahead, a boy is squatting on his heels and vomiting.
The ground has a slope, the vomit rolls along it. Customers jump
into the shack over the stream. Jump out.

'All right, brothers, we'll meet again. Remember my name,
Balai. I never forget a face.'

Balai left. DS lit a Charminar.

'Sob stories, fucker, they piss on my mood. I'll go get another
bottle.'

'Then you'll get too drunk, and the folks on the bus will give us an earful.'

'Who will, eh? Which sodding dick will?' DS is shouting. The people at the other tables turn and stare.

'Oye, stop it! Everybody's looking! Go, get more booze if you have to. But I'm not going to tolerate any chimpanzee behaviour.'

DS takes out a broken-toothed plastic comb from his pocket, runs it through his hair, then stands up on unsteady legs. An almost-smile on his face. 'Can you tell me whom I was swearing at?'

'I can.'

'Whom?'

'That dumbfuck of a doctor.'

The disc room is awhirl with swirling susurrations. Discs of varying sizes are swooping through the air. Some as large as manhole lids, some like dinner plates, some like quarter plates, some as small as bottle caps—all round, of course, but in varying circumferences, big and small. The strange thing is the absence of collisions or inter-saucer tackling despite such apparent pandemonium. Only when they come too close to each other does a slight blue spark flash along their edges.

Since the disc dancing will continue for a while now, we can safely proceed towards the scene in the veranda outside. Our eyes may be afflicted with a pins-and-needles from watching the same scene for too long—such a danger cannot be entirely ruled out.

The light from the dirty, mouldy, 25-watt hanging bulb makes everything in Bhodi's veranda look dull and like a heap of broken shadows. Bhodi sits wrapped in a flimsy cockroach-eaten shawl. Beside him is Bechamoni garlanded in hibiscuses. The garland is fake. Plastic flowers, with clumps of tinsel ribbon in between. Five or so old men and women are seated in front of Bhodi, bowing to him from time to time. A few hands' breadths away, Nolen waves a hand-fan at a clay dhunuchi, prompting forth more plumes of fragrant smoke.

Bhodi one-sidedly blasts his volunteers: 'What did I say to you last year on the day of evil-avenging Mahadwadoshi? What?'

'Lord, you said, when it's time, the Great Spectacle of Discs will begin.'

'What else?'

Suddenly bit by a mosquito, the responder scratches his bum instead of his head. 'O my lord, I don't remember.'

'No, you don't, because you're an areshole. Didn't I say, the day is nigh?'

'Yes, O lord.'

'If you can't remember by heart what I say, you write it down. Understand? Fuckers! I'd read out a poem too. Does anyone remember?'

'Yes, sir.'

'Then let's hear it.'

The old man clears his throat and gets ready to recite but is startled by Bechamoni who suddenly bursts out laughing.

'That's nothing. You carry on. She's getting possessed, it's bound to happen.'

The old man recites:

'Skulls play peek-a-boo
Dark wench says, Coo!
Hail the mighty discs, hail,
Puck-a-poo puck-a-poo.'

'Bah! Bah!' says a delighted Bhodi, 'You'll make it yet, I say. Now hear this: "The ananda-laddoo has an ananda potion, Infidel year ends, and all horrors are in motion."—What did you understand?'

'It's your gospel, O lord,' say the devotees, 'How will we understand?'

'You will soon enough. I won't have to explain. The 7th of next month is Kali Puja. That day not only you but the whole world will understand. Another four days, and we'll have a preview. Now, scram! On the one hand the volunteers and the Phyatarus ate up my whole day, and now the wife goes and gets possessed. My day's just shattered to pieces, pieces! Oi Nolen, No—l—en!'

Pathan, goats, reader, text—it will continue thus. Be that as it may, 'Ananda-laddoo has an ananda potion' makes clear the reference to Magician Ananda's advertisement in *Anandabazar*. Infidel year means 1999; our sacrificial goat goes round and round means 24th October. Then: November and December. Grave horrors will be unleashed. Everybody knows about the skull dance on the 28th. Most Refined Reader, you will certainly not confuse skull dance with candy dance. And what if you do? Whatever is candy is also the skull. At any moment, chaos will break free of its chains and rule the world. Bhodi might bellow 'Bechamoni—i—i!' Now let us see what happens during Kali Puja. Statutory warnings these days have become indispensable in literature too. Therefore:

> Don't go that way, dear man,
> there the pho-ting-tings meet,
> And the headless three chatter
> with the mouths upon their feet.

(*To Be Continued*)

## 5

The kind of writing that concludes each of its outbreaks with (*To Be Continued*) is comparable to a deadly dire submarine, lying in alert ambush. The submarine called *Beggars' Bedlam* floats up once a month in the blue and muddy waters, amid the jellyfish, the sighs of the Titanic and death-dealing magnetic mines and then, soon after, on the orders of Captain Nemo, sinks back into the deep again. Dolphins do the same thing, though they are entirely lacking in periscopes, torpedoes and aggressive intent. All this explaining has but one target: at any moment, the submarine can spring a leak, resulting in instant tragedy and much grief. That moment may not be too far away for us, for the pho-ting-tings mentioned in the preceding (*To Be Continued*) are all too real, and not the stuff of fantasy at all. Not only novels or novelists, but even when entire social structures and empires have dared to muck about with the pho-ting-tings, then whatever ensued can only be described as a full-scale fucking fiasco. Hence not only does the threat remain but also that the danger increases by the minute. Many had been hoping that the limericks and proverbs and myths would all add up to some hefty truth. Such as: Why must the hero fearlessly cross the border and stride towards dangers unknown? First, he'll fail spectacularly, then enrol for a few days in some wizened wacko's coaching class, then bankrupt some dragon or monster's start-up forever and whizz back in a rusted, double-winged aeroplane manufactured by Going and Co., accompanied by a woman who's too good-looking to be true. This same-shit saga has many incarnations across the world. There seems to be no hope of its timely end. But what this tale of ours may or may not mean, we have no intention of coughing that up anytime soon. Through its periscope, we can see:

> In every corner glow bonfires aplenty
> Gathered together are the cognoscenti
>
> (One of Purandar's stunning couplets)

Those are the bastards who'll say whatever there is to be said. They always have. Our task is to irritate them, trick them into corners and then roll them up in a sheet of tarpaulin and thrash them soundly. With a short bamboo stick, if possible.

> How lifeless, how ineffectual
> It must be another intellectual.
>
> (Another Purandar original)

On 27 October 1999, around 9.30 a.m., a half-musical metallic melody began to sound inside the rusty tin bucket hanging in a corner of Bhodi's courtyard, as an ancient fork and spoon, dropped once upon a time by a passing crow, began to dance within, and as soon as Bechamoni smashed a broken plate to the ground in the courtyard, Bhodi came running down from the rooftop to pick up the phone. Indeed, it will be quite difficult for the reader to accept that even in this age of internet and cybersex, such outdated telecommunication still survives and with such gusto. This is the same telephone that Bengali children of yore used to build toy versions to play with. Bhodi held the old and rusted tin can labelled

Bengal Baby Food to his ear; it doubled as both mouthpiece and receiver.

The phone wire stretches across a small, swampy spit of land and all the way up to the second floor of the house diagonally across Bhodi's. The swampy plot is covered in wild yams, underneath which lie rotting four or five generations' worth of trash. Only a thief might dare to walk in, and even that thief will get the fright of his life because chameleons, frogs, scorpions, and every species and subspecies of mosquito sit tight and squat there, creating their very own Jurassic Park. It is directly above this plot of land that the double row of wires crisscross the sky. One slightly loose, the other nice and taut. When the loose wire is pulled, the phone rings. In that house, it's a bell; in Bhodi's house, it's the fork and spoon in the bucket. Absolutely fuss-less, problem-free. This one talks, that one listens. That one talks, this one listens. Both can't speak at the same time.

The word or words that come through do not sound wholly natural. Slightly nasal, metallic, a slight ghost-ghost touch.

Bhodi says: 'Now what?'

'Nothing. All clear.'

'How many went yesterday?'

'Eh?'

'I said, how many went yesterday?'

There are four knocks from the other side. To verify, Bhodi knocks four times from his end as well. From that side, Bhodi's interlocutor says, 'I'm hanging up now.'

'OK.'

Every morning Bhodi is informed about how many bucket-loads of dirt have been moved. This is the arrangement with Sarkhel. Although Bhodi and Sarkhel have no dearth of ambition for their grand and noble project, Bhodi is frequently tormented by the memory of Pramanik's warnings. Pramanik, retired from Oil and Natural Gas Corporation of India a long time ago, had been at once both Bhodi's dedicated volunteer and critic. Even though it's been a year and a half since he's left for his home in the heavens, Pramanik's dream visits to Bhodi continue unabated, exactly as they'd planned. His language has become quite lucid after death. Alive, his every sentence used to be weighed down with a kilogram of courtesy, now he's simply irritable and cynical.

'What's that sisterfuck Sarkhel doing?' Pramanik snaps.

'What he's supposed to be doing. Moving soil.'

'Balls he's moving soil. Only scratching at the top. Like he scratches his armpits. I've warned you so many times. But you and Sarkhel want to do the impossible.'

'I'm going to make it possible. The name is Bhodi, after all.'

'If you do, I'll change my name. I, Anadi Pramanik, will thenceforth be known as Cunt's Brother Pramanik. I'll chop off my ears. Won't be able to wear my glasses. So what if I'm dead?—I still read a journal or two, try and keep myself up to date. Who knows, maybe one day I'll even end up getting married. No end to madmen's fancies, you know!'

'Uff, Pramanik, you lose your temper too quickly these days. When wise men like you die, they should be quiet. As though they're sleeping off the opium. You're the only one I've seen who's so agitated, like a dog in heat. That's not good.'

'You're entitled to your point of view. Here, everything's different. And we don't give two shits about whatever happens in your world. It's just that when I witness such stupidity, I lose my temper.'

'So you're saying that Sarkhel and I are stupid? Who's the one who told us all about it, eh? Did we know anything about it?'

'I shared a factoid, imparted a pearl of wisdom. But before I could finish, you fools rushed in.'

'Shut up! Don't think you own my head just because you're dead.'

'I'd be better off picking up a dried coconut shell from the streets than owning that piece-of-shit headpiece of yours.'

In the throes of such altercations, Bhodi groans and gesticulates, and Bechamoni shakes him awake.

'Eh?'

'What eh? Your stomach's full of gas. Understood? Full of gas.'

'Oh.'

'The things you say—I don't understand a word.'

Bhodi does not answer. He gets up and drinks some water. Splashes some on his belly, neck and shoulders.

Bechamoni lies down again. 'Told you so many times, don't drink so much.'

'Shut up. Does your brain understand what is or isn't happening? All this non-stop nagging. Females should shut their traps.'

'Oh . . . oh . . . as if you've kept me like a queen all these years. Morning and evening, this "female" . . . "female" . . .'

'What else should I call a female, then?'

Bechamoni's soft sobs can be heard in the heart of this utter darkness of Kaliyug. A repentant Bhodi stretches his hand towards her. His fingers seek to run through the reams of her shampooed hair. Bechamoni grabs his hand, pushes it away. Her bangles jingle. Bhodi waits a few seconds. Bechamoni sobs. Once more, Bhodi's hand stretches out towards her.

In the last week of October 1999, a very interesting thing occurred in Calcutta. But the general public, especially the Bengali public, has become so libertine of late that unless something takes place on the television screen, they don't come to know about it all. It's not easy to gather the wisest and the most intellectual Bengalis of the past under one roof. But if such a gathering could be arranged at the Netaji Indoor or the Salt Lake Stadium, this couplet from *Brajangana* (by Michael Madhusudan Dutt, not Purandar Bhat) could easily be posed to them as a question:

> Why did you, my darling,
>> fill your basket with so many blooms
> Is the night sky's starry necklace
>> hidden by a cloudy gloom?

Be that as it may, whatever will be, will be. Even if God has a hand in what ensues, we certainly don't. When an entire race of people is hellbent on self-destruction, it's no use trying to reason with them. Heading to the crematorium, but still holding onto their cellphones. Holding on so tightly that no one can pry open their fingers. In the end, there is no choice but to burn the phone too.

The interesting thing that occurred is this: when the Metro train rolled into Tollygunge Station from the empty station yard at the back, a giant raven was perched pat on the roof of compartment No. 4. This has happened quite a few times. It is apparent that the raven is saving its wings from unnecessary strain. Once in a while, the raven has even got off at Esplanade and Chandni Chowk and Central stations and dirty-danced on the platforms. We have met this particular raven before. He has been spotted not only on the Metro trains but also on the trams, hitching a trip or three, though no one has paid him much attention. Bhodi's father the Raven was a common sight in the Kalighat area not so long ago, swooping about hither and thither. Sometimes pecking at bread on the roofs of the Kalighat sex-workers' shanties, sometimes perched atop Ma Kali's temple, high above the crowds, watching the goats being sacrificed.

Borhilal—after buying a bunch of fake Barbie dolls from the wholesalers at Chandni Chowk—took that same train to Kalighat. But he never realized that the Raven was sitting right above his very compartment. Such barriers help the actors in this tale to become the protagonists of their own narratives. They are just like the barriers we have seen many a time in public urinals. Though public urinals are not above the occasional askance glance. And yet we must clarify that not everyone who peeks so curiously is a homosexual. One may elaborate on such matters in the future. And when that happens, Dear Reader, there will be no holding back, I can assure you.

On the afternoon of 27 October 1999, Comrade Acharya escaped the cruel grasp of a terrible tragedy; whether anyone else came to know or not, he knew only too well how terrible the tragedy and how narrow his escape. On that fateful day, no one else was present on the second floor of the Communist Party office save for Comrade Acharya. A rare occurrence indeed. Comrade Acharya, staring intently at the black-stone bust of Vladimir Ilyich Lenin on his desk, had fallen into a doze. (You couldn't quite call it sleep.) As it is, thanks to the various daily struggles as well as the cold war between the liberal and the conservatives within the party, all the leaders were more or less exhausted. In the midst of all that, Comrade Acharya's situation was a little more pitiful than the rest. Because in the case of the civil skirmish, he could not bring himself to decide which side to be on. The doze grew deeper. The next stage was that particular section of REM slumber where the eyeballs dance around too much. Memory is always sweet. Comrade Acharya dreamt that instead of his usual white pyjama and kurta, he was standing in North Korea's Pyongyang airport wearing woollen pants, an overlong overcoat and a cap made out of Russian wildcat fur. Little flakes of snow were falling all around him. In front of him, a statue of Comrade Kim Il-sung. Dressed in a military tunic. But life is so full of complicated contradictions that Comrade Acharya could not concentrate on the incomparable sight before him, that is, Comrade Kim Il-sung's silent, unmoving statue, as was necessary just then. Distracting him was the super-duper hit song, lyrics and music by Ravindra Jain, from the movie *Chor Machaye Shor*, in the immortal voice of Kishore Kumar:

Like ankle bells, I've sung out too
On these feet, and sometimes on the other . . .

Snapping awake, Comrade Acharya is confused: though Comrade Kim Il-sung has vanished, he can still hear Kishore Kumar's melodic voice—it's streaming in through the windows. Alas, the heartrending pain of those anklets. If one understood everything simply by sitting in Delhi and tinkering with computers, then life would have been so much simpler. The phone rang. Let it. No need to answer. But this stupor? What was he to do about that? Unable to come up with a solution, Comrade Acharya lit a king-size cigarette and finally arrived at the synthesis that a long march along the inner veranda couldn't hurt, could it? That this synthesis was the otherworldly siren call of the sepulchral unknown—could a mind marinated in dialectical materialism ever comprehend such wisdom? Never. Ever. And as one thought, so one did.

Just as he'd started to walk, he heard: 'Watch Out! Watch Out!'

By the time the warning words entered Comrade Acharya's ear, his Kolhapuri chappal had become entangled with the bottom of his dhoti and he was teetering on the step between downfall and dropped dead. Thank god for the railing in front of him. Ah, the crisis was past. In the end, it was the left hand that saved him. Bravo!

But who cried 'Watch out! Watch Out!'?

He was alone. So who was it that warned him? The voice had spoken in a refined Bengali. That language that has so fallen from grace today that certain restless sons of Mother Bangla are agitating for its restoration to former glory.

In that same Bengali, exactly that, sans any Georgian accent, the voice spoke again: 'Think you'll hang up a photograph and be done with me?'

Almost at once, Comrade Acharya found himself choking on a lungful of strong pipe smoke: 'Comrade Stalin!'

'Drop it. I've seen plenty of your kind. You lot think I just don't get it. Quite right. I don't get it but you do?! Pale streak of yesterday's piss! If I'd laid my hands on you at the right time, I would have knocked all this wishy-washy indecision right out of you.'

'Don't I know that, Comrade!'

'You know fuckall. And if you call me Comrade one more time, I'll punch your idiot face. Did you make a revolution? Do you even know what that is?'

Comrade Acharya scratches his head in shame.

'All you do is elections. And I don't think you'll ever be able to do anything else either. And this bunch that keeps moaning and groaning—why're you trying to please them all the time?'

'Not exactly please, sir. As per democratic process, we are allowing them to ...'

'Don't stop, go on—'

'I mean, sir, as per our democratic process, we are allowing them three months instead of the two in order to defend their interest—'

'Why? Is time for free? Anyway, forget about them. Have you made up your mind? Do you know what you want?'

'Why don't you tell me, sir? I just can't make up my mind.'

'And you never will, clearly. I can see that you're also fated to . . . No matter. Pay attention to what I say. In my opinion, this isn't a problem at all. Just as a dog goes back to its vomit, these liberal communists will return to their bourgeois burrows. The question is: Will you join them too?'

'No, sir! It's not what you think . . . I only want that our democratic guidelines—'

'No point whining about that shit to me. Democracy! The titans of the world didn't know how to fuck with democracy and a little shit like you wants to teach it to me? Democracy! Do you really want to know how to get those arseholes in line? Have you got the guts for it?'

'Actually, sir, these days it's the heart that's been fluttering from time to time.'

'Of course it has. Stutter and flutter and then one day stop entirely. A very logical and simple solution . . . Ha ha ha, how does it feel? To hear the man of steel laugh? How many bottles of vodka can you drink in one go?'

'Bottles?! Just one drink and I'm . . .'

'Hah. I know exactly how far you lot can fly. No wonder the world has gone to the dogs. Even now, how deeply I regret my mistake.'

'Mistake? You mean, yours?'

'Whose else? I killed so many. Lists of names would come to my desk. I'd write "For Execution J St" with a blue pencil next to their names. When the army was being purged, I wrote only "The Camps" next to one name. You understand? When other tasks clamoured for my attentions, the lists went to Molotov, Kaganovich, Voroshilov, Schadenko or Mekhlis. They'd simply write "For Execution" so as to avoid any complications. Oh, those were the days. I should have got rid of that fat Ukrainian mother-fucker right then.'

'You mean Nikita Khrushchev?'

'I see you've got some education after all. Read a few books in your time, eh? Not as much of an ass as I'd thought. Though reading too many books isn't good for you either. Trotsky and Bukharin both read so much. But did it help? If you read too much, your mind grows confused. When you need to make a tough decision, you think: it could be this or it could be that. And you lose time. And your lost time is the counter-revolutionaries' gain, they strengthen their hold on you. That's why I now think that I should have been even more merciless. More! Even more! I had thought that sparing no enemies would serve me well.'

'Didn't it?'

'Would I be in this state if it did? Do you know what happened on 24 August 1935?'

The pipe smoke swirls around Comrade Acharya. Some words screamed in Slavic. Gunshots.

'No, sir.'

'Zinoviev, Kamenev and Smirnov were shot. Smirnov's wife and daughter were arrested. In 1937, they were shot too. That same year, Zinoviev's son Stepan Radomyslsky was shot. Within a few days of Kamenev's execution, his first and second wives were executed. In 1939, Kamenev's eldest son, Alexander, was killed.

Before that, on 30 January 1938, Kamenev's other son, Yuri, was executed. He was 16 years and 11 months old. Kamenev's grandson, Vitali, was arrested in 1951, he was 19. He was sentenced to 25 years. He died in 1966. Despite all those executions, all those arrests, I failed. I must have grown soft somewhere, weak. I left holes, loose ends. Now, sit down and think very hard about everything I've said. Show a soft spot and you're dead. Understand?'

'Understood, sir.'

'Anyway, I will be back. In the history of the future, many more Stalins will come. So will many more Hitlers, Tojos, Churchills, Roosevelts, Trumans and Titos. But all of them, dummy versions. The Real Thing is not possible any more.'

'What will happen, then?'

'Some obnoxious otters like you will muddy the waters, what else.'

Thick coils of pipe smoke begin to seep into the glass of the Stalin portrait on the wall. Everything is quiet. The king-size cigarette between Comrade Acharya's fingers has burnt out long ago. His head is spinning. His head doesn't feel much like a head any more, more like a frisbee.

Comrade Acharya slowly walks back to his office. Sits down in his chair. He has a headache. Maybe he should have his head examined by a doctor. Is it depression? Or anxiety? What is the cause?

On the evening of 27 October, an ancient tram (No. 30) was trundling into the Kalighat Tram Depot. On its roof was perched a raven. Then it flew off towards Kalighat Park.

Those hard-working readers who have followed the *Beggars' Bedlam* submarine (I wouldn't use an inauspicious word like 'sinker' or 'shipwreck' here) with utmost love and attention from the very beginning, they as well as every single person in the land know only too well that 28 October was the night of the skull dance (see Chapter 1). Experts feared that this submarine would float up to the surface again on 21 Kartik, i.e. 7 November 1999. For those who cannot stand verbosity or vulgarity, whose ears buzz at bad language, those persons should at this time turn their eyes towards the many harmless and hapless tug-boats lining the Ganga and not wait about for the elaborate events that are about to unfold. Only two small points to note for the moment: It's best not to sit by the Ganga till very late at night. And 21 Kartik, i.e. 7 November, is Kali Puja.

| 22 | 6 | 6 | | |
|----|----|----|----|----|
| 18 | 4 | 3 | | |
| 16 | 4 | 4 | | |
| 25 | 10 | 4 | 3 | 1 |

(*To Be Continued*)

*6*

In the last instalment, or during the dying breaths of the past chapter, the four lines of mysterious numbers that we had arranged are the chemical makeup of ordinary red flares, and the last one of electric-ignition parachute-flare bombs. These days, the toothless Kali Puja that we have to endure thanks to the rulings of the almighty High Court is unmitigated torture. It has rendered even more miserable the already naked institutions of Burima's Chocolate Bomb, Bachhu Captain, Sachhu Captain, Kali Bomb + shell + Dhani Kalkattawali. The rocket, though, was banned long before the 65-decibel furore. And even before that was the ban on QuickFlashes, Mongoose Curlers and Smoke Balls. In the poorer neighbourhoods, we may hear a depressed chocolate bomb or two or glimpse a flare of hope in a rocket burst. That's all. Fireworks are not a Naxal conspiracy. Once a year if you burn some fireworks, you end up killing a number of useful and useless insects such as mosquitoes and leafhoppers. The sulphur smoke strikes terror in the heart of some truly terrible microbes. Besides, that's the one day that Bengalis can smell war in the air. But nothing is to be done. Those who'd trained their baby hands on the Little Cannon tend to graduate quite easily to pipe guns. Tots still suckling at their mother's tits can mix their gunpowder in 72-11-11 parts and make a rope bomb in a jiffy. When this is their first attempt at overcoming the fear of the unknown, how can they stay away from the Molotov Cocktail later? At the very least, they'll hurl a country bomb or two. These days, sadly, from grandson to grandfather, everyone is lighting only sparklers. Or, with amazing courage, setting off rockets set into their father's empty booze bottles. Such Bengalis will in the future mix Lactogen in their rice, and in their adolescence dust their armpits with talcum powder and, on the grounds of the government-sponsored Nandan Film Centre complex, sniff out safe spots in the shrubbery.

And yet these same Bengalis were fighters once. Bengalis, remember Colonel Suresh Biswas' finger commanding the cannons during the struggle for independence of Pele's Brazil? Remember, those revered Bengalis who made machine guns and cannons for the native rajahs? Have you forgotten the sound of a Mauser? Do the names of Lewis Gun, Dumdum Bullet and the Winchester Repeater not tempt you to roar? If not, then may you be sacrificed in the name of the goddess. As many races have been before you. Dispatched to there from where no one returns, because no return visa is available. Of course, this is no reason for you to start thinking you're a special kind of arsehole. Those who are squawking so loudly today will end up in the same hole tomorrow. The hole where, for ages now, the mammoths and dinosaurs have been waiting, holding welcome garlands in their hands. History is but a glittering mirage. Earlier it used to be Gandhi of Arambagh. Now if you say Arambagh, the Bengalis think you're talking about big-big monster-size broiler chickens. Just one leg is enough to frighten you witless. Thank god one doesn't have to see them alive. But yes, one must admit that the Bengali food habit is very progressive. These days the Bengali is cooking Chicken Manchurian at home with consummate ease.

*Beggars' Bedlam* will now get into the events of Kali Puja, 1999. This is a significant stationon our journey. One may call it a junction. Before that, though our train doesn't halt at two insignificant Tikiapara-type stops, we must mention the following:

(1) Unable to deal any longer with the world's disregard, poet Purandar Bhat has taken his own life. Alarmed by the stench from the locked room, the neighbours broke open the door—and found not a dead man but a dead mouse. A portrait of Purandar on the wall. A garland around it. Below, a piece of paper strung on a thread, bearing failed poet Purandar Bhat's last poem. The learned reader will doubtless be reminded of Sergei Esenin and Vladimir Mayakovsky's last poems written before they ended their own lives. It doesn't matter if they don't.

The deceased poet's statement was thus:

'Arsehole World'
Purandar Bhat
(1948–1999)

Why does my life come to no climax
I crawl on my belly through fields of fallen flax
Why does my life have no crown or crest
I'm a lizard only, I eat insects, I lay eggs
My death will not make any headlines
So I piss on temple walls, commit petty crimes
At my death, no pussycats will weep
Lady Canning's name for eternity so sweet
One foot in heaven, one in hell's halls
One cannon, but two cannon balls

After he read the poem, the local schoolmaster turned to the policeman: 'Did you get it?'

'Tremendous!'

'What do you mean?'

'Astounding imagery. But he received absolutely no recognition. I've never heard of him.'

'Purandar Bhat? What kind of name is that? Bengali?'

'Can't quite tell. Could be from Bihar, or the Odisha border. Might have become Bhat from Bhatta.'

'Wonderful, what an interesting point. From Bhatta to Bhat.'

'But where did the man go?'

'Can never be sure of these poets. Maybe he dove into the Ganga. In which case, he's probably at the sandheads by now.'

'Astonishing. May I copy the poem?'

'Yes. I can tell this is a case of suicide. But until it's confirmed, I have to write "Missing".'

'And when you find the body?'

'Then it's over. Case closed.'

(2) Readers who have studied this narrative from the start have surely not forgotten novelist Mr B. K. Das who was killed by bears. He wrote in his diary (subsequently devoured by mice):

> I am a great litterateur, that is why my job is to fool the reader first and slaughter him later. My pen is a knife, if not a sword. The small-fry trash authors turn their readers into mosquitoes, and then die of malaria caused by the same mosquitoes' bites. I've written only two novels. And those trash authors, who's to say if they write with their pens or their penises? They keep producing novel after novel. God is my strength. Now if only the Devil will show me some favour, then I can shake the world.

Everyone agrees that it was wrong of Mr B. K. Das to compare readers to chickens or mosquitoes. The bear cub's sudden startled cries deep in the jungles of Assam, the bear parents' furious growling, Mr B. K. Das' last few desperate screams, the chattering and whooping of terrified monkeys—this tragedy is no less than the death of Hector.

The original Tollygunge Police Station resembles present-day Yugoslavia. The numbers of mafia men, purse snatchers, heroin peddlers, gamblers, skin thieves (i.e. rapists), smugglers and newly bloomed criminals and rowdies are increasing with such quantum leaps that one police station cannot possibly deal with them all. Therefore Tollygunge Police Station has been split in two. The crematorium remains under the jurisdiction of the original Tollygunge PS. Just as Belgrade has remained in one of the last slivers of Yugoslavia. An old elephant is, after all, not entirely without value.

7 November 1999, Ma Kali's Puja. Since the morning, Calcutta's civil society has been conducting its puja peacefully and without incident. All the liquor shops are closed. As they are every year on this day, by law. No one knows how that fucking affects matters one way or another. Because the day before, inevitably, the line outside the same shops is 2 or 3 miles long. A docile, disciplined queue. No sign of any Asian barbarism. Not only that, the hard-working black-marketeers buy gunny sacks' worth of bottles and stock up for emergencies.

In *The Night of Kali Puja*, Premankur Atorthy has painted such a throbbing-alive picture of the Kali Puja of yore that all other descriptions since tend to fade in comparison. Appearing as no more than loosely packed fountain fireworks that wheeze and gasp for a moment or two before collapsing into frazzled farce. In contemporary Calcutta, the state of writing literature and the state of manufacturing fireworks are more or less the same. Saltpetre, sulphur and finely ground charcoal are not enough—so many more materials are required. Once upon a time, even babes in arms knew that for red stars you needed not only potassium chlorate and dry nitrate of strontium but also sulphur and carbon. Such a giant red star shone atop the Kremlin. Green stars? Find some barium nitrate and orpiment. Nothing but a blue star will capture your heart? Brother, you'll need at least 2 grams of Paris Green, or Kashmiri Jangal. So curious, the long and ancient connection that Kashmir has with bombs and explosions. Flower Fiesta, Sugar Spot, Pearl String, Spinning Top, Pineapple, Chrysanthemum, Mughal Gardens, Thousand Petals, Marigold, Jasmine, Nasreen—these are all nicknames for different fountain fireworks. Alas! Alack! In those days, even the grandfathers would say, 'Bomb? Child's play. Make a hole in an empty coconut shell and fill it with gunpowder. Then put a long wick in, and wrap the rest of it tight around the shell. Best thrown into the ponds. On the ground, they can be quite dangerous.' But these days the Bengalis are stupefied by such thoughts. Bengalis did not bomb only White men and natives, you know. When the country was finally free, a contingent of the Indian army went on an expedition to the Pindari Glacier. That expedition included one Sri Hemendra Chandra Kar, MA. He notes: 'The River Sarayu flows right by our path. While we walked beside it, we were seized by the desire to fish. Time was of the essence. So we devised an innovative solution. We threw a grenade into the water. The water began to whip and whirl and fish of all sizes—big and small—began to float to the surface. And we collected them!' But today, this same Bengali tiptoes through the fish market like a timid pussycat, mewling miserably. The Bengali is losing his fur, his tail is wet and tucked between his legs and the bit of moustache that remains is not worth twirling any more.

7.30 or 8 p.m.—must be one or the other—Tollygunge Police Station's most devious informer, Gagan, rushes into the bald Officer-in-Charge's office, highly agitated. Smelling slightly of rum. A startled biri stuck between his fingers. 'Sir! Sir! Uff, they've fucked law and order right in the arse, sir. If you don't take a force there right now, we won't be able to tackle the fucking sister-fucks, sir.'

The bald OC slams his cap down on his head. 'Where? Which bastards?'

'Just cross the crematorium and you'll spot them. In the old days, this side of the river would have rocket contests with that side. Thousands and thousands of rockets, I mean, hundreds at least, set off into the sky. And what cussing, what fun and frolicking! Men, women, jumping up and down, shouting their twats off.'

'Rockets? You mean flying fireworks? That stuff's banned. Where are they getting it?'

'Honestly sir, you do talk shit. Banned! Go and see, no one gives two hoots about that bullshit ban. That side has the No. 9 Jelepara slumdogs. This side has the Kalighat keoras. And the bombs that're bursting! You'll think it's a war front, sir!'

'Hey, you! You, I forget your name! Tell them to bring the car. I'll take my jeep. Should I . . . take the force with me?'

'First you go and see. There's thousands of people. Many more are coming, holding Hazaks. It's all a bit strange. Oiled bodies, and big sticks. I'm not understanding what the case is. Sir, the left-front government hasn't had a fall-mall, has it?'

'What utter rubbish you talk. Absolutely no sense to your words. All that rum down your throat, who knows what you saw.'

The jeep came out of Tollygunge Police Station, turned towards Rashbehari Avenue and then disappeared through a gap in the left.

Neither the bald OC, the stooge or the constable got to know that black-robe-clad Madan and DS were flying overhead, following them.

DS was sobbing. 'Fucking arsehole, Purandar. Killed himself by suicide and just totally ruined my Kali Puja. I'd stocked up on Bangla, had so many plans . . . And now . . . I can't accept this, not in my heart. He killed himself—and we knew nothing?'

'I refuse to believe anything without evidence,' said Madan, 'Failed poet—so of course he can kill himself. Then why not just gulp down some Baygon-faygon? But, no! And now there's no sign of the body. Who knows—I'm just not getting it!'

'It's an unnatural death. It'll be terrible if he turns into a ghost or something. I gave him such a hard time. Never mind now. Look, down there, uff bastard. See how many rockets they've set off all at once?'

'The reflections in the river are making them seem more in number. Vive la Kali!'

At a much higher altitude, flying like a detective satellite, was Bhodi's monstrous father, the Raven. And he was not alone.

'DS, Bhodi-da told us to watch from a rooftop—but all the rooftops are full!'

'Let's go sit on that neem tree. We can see pretty far from up there.'

'Not a bad plan. This side is clear. Overhead is clear. Look left look right both sides tight and drink up all the milk.'

Gagan the informer looked at the welcome committee that rushed over as soon as the bald OC stepped out of the jeep, and now stood before them, shining in the jeep's headlights, and whispered, 'Don't mess with this lot, sir.'

'Why not? They're armed?'

'No sir, they're not people. All ghosts. These are the rowdies who ran the crematorium long ago. But dead now, dead for ages.'

'Eh, what are you saying?'

'Yes, many retired back in the Naxal days.'

'Come, OC-sir, come,' says one of the rowdies, 'Everything is proceeding peacefully. No sign of any trouble.'

'Behind them,' Gagan whispers, 'are thugs from other neighbourhoods. They're here as guests. Joga, Bhanu, Mongla, Bhutni, Tali, London and d'you know who that tall Afghan is?'

The bald OC was terrified.

'That, sir, is Mina Peshwari. Murdered during the Partition riots.'

The earth shakes with the burst of chocolate bombs and the double dooms of the dodomas. One large bottle rocket shot up in the air and burst into the glowing face of Netaji Subhash Chandra Bose.

'Can't find fireworks like these any more, sir. Have to be specially ordered from China Market. Come, sir.'

Meanwhile, a corpse arrived in a glass hearse. The bald OC has broken out into a sweat: 'Is that corpse a ghost too?'

'Could be, sir. Anything is possible. Don't say a word, sir.'

'Am I mad? D'you think I've nothing better to do?'


Sackfuls of bottle rockets on this side of the Ganga and that. Charges from this side here to that side there. If one side slows down its attack, the other side erupts with boos and heckling. Depending on how the rockets are launched, some bounce off the surface of the water and then land on that side. Every now and then, a sparkling chrysanthemum or electric rocket lights up the night as bright as day. By that artistic glow, the beggarly but beatific ghosts can be seen clearly. Most are bare-bodied, wrapped in gamchhas. The women ghosts are the ones who once worked tirelessly to grind and filter and dry the gunpowder in the sun. The baby ghosts are the ones who used their tiny fingers to stuff gunpowder into the whistle-slim shells of red rockets and the Motia shells of electric chrysanthemum rockets, though finishing the job could not be done without the help of senior hands. It is important that the people of Calcutta understand that the stricken children who throng the streets on the morning after Kali Puja, collecting half-burnt half-spent firework shells—those children are not ghosts—they are simply small-size humans. Even if their penises or their bottoms peek through their ripped pants, they are not embarrassed. For those half-naked, skeletal children, here is a gift from *Beggars' Bedlam*:

| SALTPETRE | SULPHUR | CHARCOAL |
|-----------|---------|----------|
| 10 | 3‖ | 3| |
| 10 | 2 | 4 |
| 18 | 3 | 3 |
| 16 | 2‖ | 2 |
| 15 | 2 | 2 |
| 15 | 2 | | 3 |

The ratios above are for gunpowder. The steps that need to be taken next in this matter do not necessarily come under the purview of literature.

The lanterns glow, the sticks swirl and swish, hit and crack. The fighters leap and pounce, bellow and roar.

Now an invisible ghostly radio plays a commnentary in the bald OC's ears: 'These are all Bengali lathials, stick fighters, trained at various akharas. Jogindra Chandra, Harimohan, Krishnalal, Narayanchandra, Motilal and Priyalal Bose's akharas were the oldest. See that lot, flexing their muscles as they come, they learnt their moves at the newer akharas. Nutubihari Das, Gopal Chandra Pramanik, Papri Abdul, Dengo Khalifa, Pocha Khalifa … so many new set-ups. Oh, there goes Professor N. C. Basak. A 1,026-pound rock was placed on his chest and smashed to pieces with an enormous hammer. And that woman there, that's Tuku Rani, barbell expert. She had a cow cart carrying 30 passengers go over her.'

The bald OC leapt into the air as a chocolate bomb rolled over and burst at his feet.

'Don't worry, sir,' one of the dead rowdies assured him, 'Just the young ones having some fun. It's an auspicious day, after all. Please, come this way, sir, come and see our Red Hibiscus contest. It's only just begun.'

'Red Hibiscus contest? You hold a contest for flowers during Kali Puja?—how wonderful!'

Gagan becomes active with his explanations again, and the rowdies of old Calcutta nod along and smile: 'No, no, it has nothing to do with flowers, sir. Listen. There's a big drum. Understand? A big, round, black drum. Everyone pours whatever alcohol they've got into it.'

'Cocktail?'

'Uff, listen, no. Father of all cocktails. Scotch, Bangla, cholai, brandy, rum, vodka, gin, wine—everything in one place. Once it's full, they put a rubber tube in. The tube's fit with a scale. And a red hibiscus is placed on the surface, gently, floating.'

'Then?'

'Then they measure who can take the longest sip through the tube and make the hibiscus sink the lowest against the scale. Got it?'

'Got it.'

'First, Second and Last—they all end up rolling in the gutter over there. All that alcohol mixed together. You can guess the rest. I've never tasted it, but I've heard it's damn deadly stuff. It'll wipe the floor with the best of them.'

'Come, sir. Come and bless the drink. After all it's the Crematorium Kali of Calcutta.'

'No, no, I don't drink-shrink. You carry on competing. I'll clap.'

'How is that possible? Why not have some whisky, sir. Straight from the Navy, the crate's not been opened yet. And a little curried goat to go with it. Won't take no for an answer sir. In the old days, so many important people used to come. What days they were. Whenever Gopal-da came, the women used to burst into ululations.'

'Gopal-da? Who's Gopal-da?

'Haven't heard of Gopal Patha, sir? And what about our very own Ram Chatterjee?'

'Oh of course, of course I've heard of them. Everyone has heard of them. Eh Gagan, what do you say? These fine people, inviting us so nicely.'

'Of course, of course.'

'Then let's have two pegs before we go back. They'll be so hurt if we refuse.'

'Correct decision, sir. Only two pegs. You should go with them, sir. We'll wait here.'

'How can that be? On this night of Goddess Kali, you've all come here with Sir. All of you are our guests.'

When the jeep returned to the station, it was past 11.30 p.m. All of them were quite brimful.

'So Gagan, you finally made me drink with a gaggle of ghosts? Hic! That mutton was so spicy. Hic! Very hot.'

'But the whisky was solid.'

'Did you read the label? Hic!'

'Yes, sir. Whyte and Mackay.'

'Not just any old whisky. Real Scotch. Every company uses water from a different waterfall, understood? Scotland! Scotch! Dammit, what was the name?'

'Whyte and Mackay, sir.'

'Thank you. Hic. What good ghosts they were, eh. Treated us so well. They could have lynched us if they'd wanted to, no problem. No father alive would've come to help.'

'You're right, sir.'

'But it's best we not talk much about this. It'll totally ruin our reputation.'

'I'll lock my lips, no problem, sir. Consider it done. But those bastard constables . . .'

'Pfft, as it is they're stupid. Otherwise, of all the things they could've become, why become constables? How much they drank tonight, they'll remember nothing tomorrow. Hic.'

'Sir, can I say something?'

'What?'

'Sir, I'm feeling a bit scared-scared, you know.'

'Take Ma Kali's name and lie down flat. It's not like we're the ones that called down the ghosts. Hic.'

Unobserved by prying eyes, Borhilal was sitting outside and eating sugar-coated fennel seeds, one by one. Now he got up and began to walk back home. DS and Madan saw, suddenly, everything was empty. The jeep left, and poof!—everything vanished! rockets, ghosts, stick fighters, Professor Basak—all gone. A warplane roared across the sky. They looked up. Four glowing flying discs were playing in the air. The same flying discs whose fancy name is UFO or Unidentified Flying Object.

Bhodi was sitting on the veranda. DS and Madan landed in the courtyard, and by the dead glow of the lone lightbulb, climbed up the steps. Nolen was slurping on a Frooti through a straw. Bhodi was waiting, his bottle and glass ready. Curled up beside him was Bechamoni, fast asleep. A cat sat still a little distance away.

'How did it go?

'Awesome. The bald OC's totally bewildered.'

'Ha ha, son. He'll get it. He'll get it eventually. Do you know what stuff this is?'

'Foreign?'

'Na. This is feni from Goa. Just got it today.'

Bhodi poured a drink. Suddenly the cat got up and ran for its life because a giant raven swooped down beside it.

'Pour one for me. In a bowl.'

'Go, get Father's bowl,' Bhodi told Nolen, 'How's the arthritis in your wing, Father? Did the massage oil work?'

'Fuck-all worked. You're an arsehole, your massage oil is an arsehole. Pour one more glass as well.'

'Who's joining us, Father?'

'Not joining—has joined. He's hiding up there. Oi, enough already, come down now.'

The person who swishes down into the courtyard is none other than poet Purandar Bhat. His face is wreathed with smiles.

DS clutches Madan in fear.

'Owed three months' rent,' grins Purandar. 'So I wrote them a suicide note and split. Now those bastards can deal with the mess. This is my technique: stay somewhere for a bit. Then hand over a suicide note and scram.'

'But the police won't let you go. If they catch you, they'll charge you with fraud.'

'That lot shit themselves trying to catch a pickpocket—that lot will catch me? I am poet Purandar Bhat. Bhodi-da, I'd told you everything already.'

'Yes, I knew the whole case.'

Bechamoni suddenly starts talking in her sleep:

'Om namah kot bikot ghor rupini swaha

Om bokro kironey shire bokhho bhoye maya

Om amrita swaha

Om sarbalok bashankaray kuru kuru swaha.'

The Raven flaps his wings and fans his daughter-in-law.

Bhodi looks furious and downs the glass in one gulp. 'One of these days, I'll shove my foot down her throat! I'm warning you. Or smack that skull with a shovel and split it right down the middle.'

Fanned by the Raven's wings, a gleeful Bechamoni bursts into laughter. She's still asleep, though. Bhodi's father loses his temper.

Clicks and clacks his beak and claws. His eyes burn like torches. 'Talk shit at my daughter-in-law again, I promise I won't stay quiet. Sinning, sinning, then cursing too? Nolen bloody bastard knows everything. But keeps mum. Shall I—shall I tell the Phyatarus everything? Blow your whistle once and for all?'

'Father! You're the head of this family, even if you are a raven. How can you spill the family secrets?'

'I will, if I see any more shenanigans from you.'

Suddenly Nolen screams, 'Look!'

Bechamoni wakes up, startled. 'What happened? What is it?'

No one answers. They're all looking up at the sky. Bechamoni looks up too.

The rocket flies a long way up. Then boom-boom, splitter-splutter, crack and crickle, it bursts into a glowing red hammer and sickle. Then, slowly, slowly, it all falls down.

(*To Be Continued*)

## 7

This episode-by-episode serial narrative about the Choktars and Phyatarus, chugging on like a stubborn steam train, has, needless to say, taken its readers by storm. There's something to be said about this, and therefore it must be said. But before we say so, it is not desirable to let some unsaid matters stand wordlessly in the corner, wiping their tears with their chemises like the tragic heroines of silent films. That is absolutely not what we want.

A firework flew up into the sky and transformed into a giant red hammer and sickle. Instead of staying forever in its ethereal orbit, it came down again to start life anew as a load of ash—but not many people will be ready to accept this. We must admit at this point that, in the last chapter, we smuggled in a bit of Tao philosophy: what goes up comes down and what comes down goes up. If the Communist Party of the Soviet Union can hand over the whole country to the mafia and pimps without setting off so much as a single firecracker (though there is no evidence that the Calcutta High Court's ban on firecrackers is in effect over there as well), then what else remains impossible? Anyway, we no longer give a damn about any more wisdom-wisecracks on this matter. But— Bechamoni! Poor Bechamoni! The sleeping Bechamoni, dog-shampooed resplendent-haired Bechamoni, the spell she'd recited in her sleep that had annoyed Bhodi and caused his raven father to threaten him—that spell had been a bewitching spell. Like a hidden agenda, a paranoia runs through Bechamoni daily—that among his disciples, Bhodi's wandering eye has found a few females he'd like to frolic with. This paranoia is not entirely unfounded. Nor unfamiliar. Though Bhodi can counter-argue that he's witnessed Bechamoni being the target of leery lustful looks, too. Nolen might even support such a claim. But we cannot afford to be drawn into this debate. This is a primordial problem in the affairs of men and women. Even the gods have shown their prolific prowess in this matter. Such affairs will carry on and on, and some middle-aged hacks will produce piles of poppycock on variations of this theme to be published in some arsehole autumn-special magazine issue or another, and the Bengali reader, whether he is in Mongolia or Malanga Lane, no matter where, will indeed read them all. This disease has only one reliable cure—a baby hanuman. But there's a snag there too. The animal lovers will how?-how! harangue us. Blameless little disciples of Lord Ram, bearers of our long tradition, where are you packing them off to? I mean, it's not even a zoo—at least that we would have understood.

Be that as it may, *Beggars' Bedlam* has already, I mean, in its serialized form, even before embarking on its journey of being published in book form, been receiving feedback. Let us test a random sampling. We have, of course, withheld names and addresses:

1.  This unending drivel about Choktars and Phyatarus is intolerable. When can we finally read 'The End'? Is this penmanship or Prattleship Potemkin? A tale told by an idiot . . .

2.  The writing is smart but still gasping for air in the Marxist cage of 'freedom from'. Where is that high thought about 'freedom to' which we can find in contemporary Western narratives . . .

3.  Mindblowing! Superb! Awesome! Only one request: please don't end abruptly, like coitus interruptus. Or a sudden attack of limpdick . . .

4.  A despicable attempt at earning accolades by pimping the unholy nexus of American imperialism and international reformation . . .

Of course, if anyone alleges that no such letters were received, that the whole thing's a fraud, we have nothing to say to that either. Everything is possible. Endless possibilities come together and walk hand in hand with measureless mysteries under a black umbrella on the path of the grand unknown—but where are they going? We can't reveal everything just yet. Right now, we're at the headquarters of Bengal Industrial Development Corporation.

But let the too-clever-by-half not confuse the above organization with the one below:

WEST BENGAL

INDUSTRIAL DEVELOPMENT CORPORATION

(A Govt of West Bengal Enterprise)

5 Council House Street, Calcutta 700 001

| PHONE | 91 33 2105361–65 |
|---|---|
| FAX | 91 33 2483737 |
| E-MAIL | wbidc@vsnl.com |
| WESBITE | www.wbidc.com |

Confusing the two will cause a catchall-catastrophe. Everyone knows, especially industrialists at home and abroad know, that a surge of new industry is flooding West Bengal. And ADDA has a very important role to play in the deluge.

This is not the same adda with which we Bengalis are so familiar. There is no scope for blethering chin-waggery here. This ADDA is the coming together of the Asansol Planning Organization and the Durgapur Development Authority. That is, our, that is India's, Ruhr Valley. Just as Howrah is our Sheffield. The Sundarbans our Africa. Delhi our London.

Our very own Borhilal had once visited Durgapur to eat at his sister's brother-in-law's wife's father's funeral. As luck would have it, a WBIDC meeting was being held right there, right then. Borhilal witnessed something he would never witness again, not in his own or even his father's lifetime. A special train brought down all the bigwigs and behemoths of industry from Calcutta, either corporeally or via representative. At Durgapur Station, a Contessa waited on the platform, as if it too would board the train. Mr Chairman got off the train, got into the Contessa and the Contessa drove away. Borhilal realized at that exact moment that, without delay, West Bengal was going to pinch the world's bottom black and blue. Unlike the innocent fart, the 'Making Things Happen' slogan was not simply noise in the wind.

There must have been a slight chill in the air in the bottom half of December '99 or else why would the taxi that stopped in front of West Bengal Industrial Development Corporation around 11 a.m. spit out one coat-pant-clad and hat-headed Bhodi, one Bechamoni dressed in a mangy long coat like an ancient memsahib and one old white man in shorts and a Sandow vest? It was more than evident that the old saheb wasn't bothered by what passed for winter in Calcutta.

Mr Chairman received a card. It said:

| |
|---|
| **A.Ku. 47** |
| (A Bengali Institution) |
| PROPRIETORS |
| Sri Bhodi Sarkar |
| Srimati Bechamoni Sarkar |
| BUSINESS ADVISOR |
| Mikhail Kalashnikov |
| ACCOUNTANT  Sri Nolen |

The day before, a local newspaper published in the Salt Lake area, the *Daily Grind*, published an article along these lines: innumerable flying discs have been spotted flitting across the Calcutta sky. Many questions have bobbed up in people's minds. From whence have these flying discs arrived? What do they want? How long will this spinning be spun? Why is the government silent? Why are the scientists not saying a word? This rather voluble presentation by an in-house reporter was accompanied by an editorial addition: 'If we are to believe Western psychoanalyst Karl Jung, then what man sees in the skies is the Eye of God. This eye lies dormant in every man. Why this must occur at the start of the millennium, we do not know. The West is proficient in their study of UFOs. The East is wary. If any of our readers has studied UFOs in secret, then they may contact us, and shed some light on the matter. But without any remuneration. Your name and address will be kept confidential.' This editorial failed to have any effect on the wider public because the *Daily Grind*'s circulation has increased to seven this year from last year's five. Calcutta is home to several eccentrics and madmen. It has always been. You could even say it's a tradition.

As soon as the three of them walked in, the rather revolting chairman stood up. He had a hoarse voice: 'How do you do . . .'

Bhodi cleared his throat and said: 'No haa-doo-doo. I'm Bengali. My better-half Bechamoni: Bengali. Mr Kalashnikov: Russian. But no matter. You are Bengali. We can all banter in Bengali.'

'Yes. Of course. Tell me, this man's a Russian?'

'Spasiba. Dobroye utro!'

'You don't know him? He's so famous! Heard of Mr Kalashnikov, haven't you?'

'Can't place him right now. Though the name sounds vaguely familiar.'

Bechamoni snaps opens a crocodile-leather handbag and brings out a photograph: 'Take a look. Does this look familiar?'

'Eh, but this is a gun!'

'Yes. An AK-47.'

'My god!'

'The K in the AK is Mr Kalashnikov. Mikhail Kalashnikov. This is his invention.'

'Oh god! But madam, you look familiar too. I think I've seen you somewhere.'

'Impossible. I don't go anywhere.'

'No, no. I think we met at Heathrow once.'

'You're mistaken. It wasn't me, must've been someone else. I think you're confusing me with Mrs Pochkhanewala in Bombay. Lots of people do.'

'Maybe I am. Sorry, madam.'

At this very moment Mr Chairman might have suffered a heart attack because Mr Kalashnikov exclaimed quite suddenly, 'Kharasho! Kharasho! Rabindranath my favourite. Raj Kapoor. I love India. *Awaara*. Jan-gan-man. Mithun. *Disco Dancer*.'

'Wow, your Bengali is really so good.'

'Kharasho. Ochin kharasho. Mr Vodi, please present your proposal. Much time has been spent on persiflage.'

'Yes, Mr Bhodi, please continue.'

'I will. The matter is too secret. No babbling or bellowing. We'll have to do it softly softly, on the sly. If we can pull it off, then we'll be rich overnight.'

'Mr Vodi, please refrain from overmuch badinage. Come to the point.'

'Yes, Mr Kalashnikov.'

'We're going to build a rifle factory.'

'Rifle factory! Where?'

'Anywhere! Haldia, Durgapur, Asansol. The front will be something else, a decoy. Underneath will lie the real deal: AK-47—ti-gig, tig-tig-tigitigitig . . .'

'What on earth do you mean?'

'Listen. People will be told we're making canned juice or tomato puree, or PVC bags and specialty polymers. But under that cover—lock, stock and barrel . . .'

'Interesting—'

Bechamoni said: 'Now, tell him about the product.'

'Very simple. Whether it's your regular army or any guerrilla group, everyone loves the AK-47. I'm not saying so because it is my invention, but it is indeed a delicious assault rifle. The American Armalite doesn't come anywhere close. Truth be told, the AK-47 is an advanced submachine gun capable of firing a medium-power cartridge. Do you know anything about weapons and warfare?'

'The less you tell me, the better. Especially about guns and bullets . . .'

'OK, OK, say no more. I understand. What we need today is rapid firing power, or one should say, marching fire.'

Mr Chairman swallowed, 'But whatever will we do with such a thing? The military is not in our hands.'

'Shut up! Why do you need the military? Everywhere, all around you, guerrilla action is taking place. And the AK-47 is everyone's favourite.'

'Fiji, Seychelles, Nepal, Burma, Bangladesh, Sri Lanka, Bihar, Assam, Medinipur, South 24 Parganas, Chechnya, Philippines, Indonesia, Pakistan—have you thought of the demand? You'll never be able to supply enough. Just by selling guns, West Bengal will mint millions. Every Bengali home will have bundles of cash and carbines—can you imagine?'

'That's all right. But . . .' Mr Chairman looks at Bhodi's card, 'The card says A.Ku 47? Sounds more like acupuncture to me.'

'First: what's in a name? Second—'

Bechamoni interrupts Bhodi: 'You stop, darling. Let me explain. This name has a deeper significance. 1947 is the year of Indian independence. And A.Ku. stands for Aakash Kusum—a dream, a fantasy, a chimaera.'

'What?'

'Exactly. Not a nightmare at all. Since 1947, Bengalis have not had a taste of gunfire. First the Revolutionary Communist Party of India, then the Naxalites—all unprepared struggles. But the dream does not fade away. Today, we can finally give that gun, deliver that dream into every hand, every household—'

'Mr Chairman, I made the German MP-43 and MP-44 that fired 7.92 mm Kurz ammunition . . .'

'Please, Mr Kalashnikov, I'm entirely unable to understand that kind of technical detail!'

'Nyet. If you want, I can even make an AK-74. They can be fitted with NCP night-vision and cutter knife and bayonets too.'

Mr Chairman breaks out in a sweat and rings a tabletop bell.

'Sir?'

'Bring four cold drinks. Or should I just ask for beer?'

Bhodi puts on his hat. 'Don't. We don't drink beer.'

'Then Scotch?'

Bechamoni says, 'I'll have some Pepsi.'

Mr Chairman excused himself for a pee, went into the en-suite luxury toilet and sprayed some cold water on his bald pate. Looked at himself in the mirror. He was all alone, yet a ghostly radio sang in his ears: 'The new plastic magazines can take 30 rounds of ammo. Every bullet weighs 53.5 grain, travels 900 metres per second. On a flat trajectory, it can travel 400, even 500 metres . . .'

'Oh my god, what will I do with all this information?'

'Piss.'

'All right. I am.'

'Yes, piss properly and listen carefully to what I say. All models of Kalashnikov assault rifles are gas operated.'

'So?'

'The gas generated when one round is fired goes from the middle of the barrel to the gas chamber above.'

'I don't want to know.'

'No one does, but they have to. The gas expands in the cylinder and pushes back the piston.'

'I won't listen.'

'I'll bash you in the face. "Won't listen!" Bloody babe in the woods! The piston is attached to the bolt, which gets pushed back with the piston. So the empty shell passes through the ejector and the firing hammer is cocked. The bolt when it moves presses a return spring which in turn—'

'Fuck this shit. I'm putting my fingers in my ears.'

'Good. Put them in your ears. Put them wherever you like. The return spring brings the bolt to the front and a new round of bullets are released from the magazine into the chamber. The bolt then locks into firing position—'

'Help! Help!'

Mr Chairman flings open the toilet door and stumbles into his room. The plastic covers of the water glasses are spinning a few feet up in the air. The room is empty. The computer screen shows the blueprint of an AK-47 from different angles. The TV turns itself on, and a man with a strip of black cloth tied around his mouth points an AK-47 at him. His cellphone rings, and when he answers it, his ears are filled with the sound of gunfire. The waiter who enters with various bottles of drink, glasses, ice bucket and tongs, he too has a AK-47 slung on his shoulder . . .

Even though not a bullet touched him, Mr Chairman fainted flat on the floor. Flat out, but not foolproof—Mr Kalashnikov's famous Russian laughter floats around the room along with the smell of Stolichnaya vodka and the sound of Joseph Stalin slapping someone's back, creating a wondrous kaleidoscope . . . tig . . . tig . . . tigi . . . tigitigitig . . .

Just as all these events are totally true, so three times true is the fact that when these events were unfolding, Bhodi and Bechamoni were in Kalighat and Mr Mikhail Kalashnikov was in Moscow. We swear, by god, we have no hand in this caper. But our critics won't listen. Don't want to listen. Because each and every one of them is an arsehole to the very last man.

An almost-dark veranda. Save for the ghostly-ghastly hanging bulb that feebly glows. Needless to say, this is Bhodi's house. It would be wrong to say it was about eight-ish. The cold wind from the north blows in so many emails from lost civilizations—one cannot keep count. What messages they may bear is a mystery not only to mere mortals but even to Lord Shiva and His father. And it must be specially mentioned here that there is absolutely no effort to comprehend them. When everyone has laid themselves back to sleep, why should we alone keep ourselves awake?

A rickety stool. Three-legged. On it sits the enormous Raven. Among the devotees sitting before him, we can spot Bhodi and Bechamoni and almost everyone else. Even Borhilal has wrapped himself tight in a shawl and slithered into the crowd. Baby Gopal bears witness in every household. But how about our witness Borhilal?

Also on the stool is a bowl of Bangla moonshine for the Raven. He dips his beak in the bowl. Turns his head up to swallow. Then he starts to talk: 'This bloody bastard Bhodi, trying to be a guru despite the dreadlocks round his arsehole, I told him, Bhodi: Don't take on too many devotees if you know what's best. But he's a greedy fucker. Just so he can drink every day, he's grabbed just about anyone he could. Look, whether you supply the alcohol or you bribe Nolen, you can't hide anything from me, I know exactly which arse still has shit stuck to it. Bhodi doesn't know it yet, but he'll understand one day. I'm telling you straight: If you betray me, I'll fuck your arse so wide that it's a river.'

Voices rise from the front: 'No, no, O lord, please don't.'

'We won't betray you.'

'If we have committed some small scandals, O lord, please forgive us.'

The Raven takes a few more sips of moonshine. Lifts a leg and scratches his neck with a claw. Then starts to talk again: 'To those who are new here, I speak to you. We're the descendants of Atmaram Sarkar, understand? In Subal Mitra's *Simple Bengali Dictionary*— I bet you lot've never heard of it—I'm quoting from memory here— it says: Atmaram Sarkar is Bengal's most accomplished magician.

His origins are not known to us. In the magazine *Bharatbarsha*, Ganga Gobinda Ray writes that Atmaram was born in Bana Bishnupur District, Prakashchhilim Village. But Atmaram's descendant Jiban Krishna Sarkar has written in the same publication that Atmaram was born in Hooghly District (present-day Howrah), Kamalapur Village. Atmaram's father was Madhabram Sarkar. Madhabram had four sons: (1) Banchharam (2) Atmaram (3) Gobindaram and (4) Ramprasad. Other than Banchharam, none of the brothers have descendants. The above-mentioned Jiban Krishna is Banchharam's elderly great-grandson. This family belongs to the Kayastha caste . . .'

The Raven drinks again. Puffs up the feathers on his neck.

'Quoting again—seen how good my memory is?—It is believed that Atmaram studied magic in Kamrup Kamakhya, and when he came back to the country, he began to befoul the magicians' tricks because of which they heaped abuse upon him. Many fantastic stories about Atmaram abound even today. He could make a sieve carry a palanquin. In the end, it is believed that the very ghosts he ruled ended up killing him. Unquote. Therefore, beware. You've all seen Bhodi's bottle trickery. But what does he keep in the empty bottles, eh Bhodi? Beware! They'll spill right out if you open their mouths. And oh, the thrashing you'll get—'

An uproar begins again: 'Please, please don't open them.'

'Long live Bhodi-da. Long live the Raven. We won't tolerate betrayal, never, never.'

'Shut up. All this shouting will expose everything. Silence. Now, it is our dynasty's tradition that we will unleash the dance of the flying discs once in every lifetime, let fly the grand game of the multiverse. Bhodi's flying-disc carnival is proceeding exactly as per that plan. Understood? Today that bastard chairman's gone off to the nursing home. Wait and watch what happens next. Not a single lying arsehole will be spared. At least 50,000 factories are either shut down or gasping their last breaths. No one gives a shit about those, fuckers, the whole lot's jerking off downstream. Formula One racing! Hotel! Car-parking plaza! Now deal with the flying discs, OK?'

Again, the voices rise: 'The dance of the discs, long live, long live.'

'Downstream, die die.'

'Sister Bechamoni, long live, long live. Comrade Nolen, long live, long live.'

'Down with all chairmen, down down, die die.'

Already Purandar Bhat has produced a two-liner and whispers it into DS' ears: 'Hail, hail, Atmaram, Chairman's little anus jammed.'

'Bah! Wonderful. Will you publish it?'

'I might.'

At the end of the speech, the Raven said: 'Listen to the words of a great man. I'm quoting this from memory too. Words of a saint, after all. They always bring a tear to my eye.'

He wipes his eyes with his wings. Some devotees cry out in anguish, some burst into sobs. A sniffling snuffling sound all around. The Raven opens wide his wings. It is ... it is as if an advertisement for an ethereal paradise: 'Children! I've forgotten the Almighty and made you my all—so whom among you can I forget? If I forget you, what will remain of me? You are all canaries in the Eden of my heart. If morning and evening my heartstrings don't strum with your songs, I grow restless. Even when you are sad, I am joyous. I live mesmerized and immersed in you.'

Who spoke these words? Witless Reader, do you know? The chances are very slim. Be that as it may, you can always bugger a try. Even if you are wrong, there're no guillotines in sight. Perhaps it is that which the pundits describe, or will describe, as—Globalization's Clusterfuck!

(*To Be Continued*)

## 8

In the last instalment, a direct challenge was issued to the readers via the so-called saintly quotation. Even though we knew all along that the Bengalis have turned away from the gods and hence will not possibly be able to counter this attack. At the very least, a feeble effort or two had been hoped for. But the embers of such expectation have now burnt to ash. We find this moral decay to be despicable. These days, at the drop of a hat, Bengalis spout Bakhtin and Foucault at seminars; recite Gramsci's theory of hegemony while decrying the eminence and authority of the Punjabis and Gujaratis who now rule the Bhabanipur area; from the Big Bang to the smallest tadpole, everything dances at the tip of every Bengali finger but the sermons of the 108th Paramahansa, Sri Nigamananda Saraswati, about them those jackasses know nothing. We can do nothing about this sorry state of affairs. If calculations are ever made, then it will be clear that no other race has produced so many saintly paramahansas. Nor so many uncountable innumerable criminals. Nor is any other race so adept at self-destruction.

The great British sahibs had a plan to improve the lot of the Bengalis, which could be called: 'From Baboon to Baboo'. It failed. Some remained baboons, some scrabbled halfway to Baboon-Baboos and Baboo-Baboons; only a handful ascended to the Baboo stage. The next blueprint for the Great Bengali Remodelling was

Swami Vivekananda's. He said: Throw all the sacred books and scriptures into the Holy Ganga, and play football instead. In the beginning, the Bengalis had dutifully obeyed him. If they hadn't, then Mohun Bagan couldn't have defeated the all-white eleven in 1911, nor the Islington Corinthians face such a humiliating defeat in Dhaka. But who can save a race whose every pore oozes arse-holery? Today, as in most every other sport, the Bengalis have entirely lost their footing in football, and because there is so much more money in cricket and tennis, Bengali parents are yanking their children from their beds and forcing them to attend training camps. Delivering them into the hands of huge hulking coaches who per-haps would have been better suited to be carriage coachmen.

The next plan belonged to the Indian National Congress which imagined that the Bengalis would open decorator's offices and mint their millions by supplying cushions at various Congress confer-ences. Did the Naxalites have any grand plans for the race? Well, even if they did, they all died too soon. Then came the CPM. Its plan was noble indeed. Advice from distinguished luminaries in the fields of education, literature, business and real-estate develop-ment was blended with the precepts of the exact sciences and the model that thus emerged may be described as: 'From Monkey to CPM'. The meaning is quite clear: first a monkey, then a troglodyte. And from there to Neanderthal, Australopithecus, Ramapithecus, Peking Man and every different flavour of the Homo Brigade to at last, a glorious CPM: Bengali men and women walking shoulder to shoulder towards an unknown but alluring, rubicund future. The plan was noble. Just as noble as choosing to call the state 'Bongo' and the city 'Kolkata'. But what the CPM needs to understand is: these Bengalis will simply not be able to work that hard. And two, no matter how obsequious their obeisances on Rabindranath Tagore's birth and death anniversaries, Bengalis are inherently vul-gar and obscene. Where even the palest shadow of vulgarity cannot fall, even there the Bengali shines brightest. Otherwise, when the bus stops in front of the Indian Statistical Institute, why should the conductor shout 'Testicle! Testicle!'? Why else would the conductor (inevitably Bengali) of a Balikhal-going bus scramble his alphabets and yell 'Khalibaal! Khalibaal!'—Only pubes! Only pubes!—and cause so much environmental pollution? Why indeed would the Bengali bookseller cycling through the posh neighbour-hoods, selling horse-racing booklets, roar, 'Hole Race' or, fur-ther abbreviated, 'Hole! Hole!' Really, I just don't know what will happen or how. Trinamool must also have an equally attractive plan for the Bengalis, but the time is yet to come when we may air our well-considered opinions about it. And whatever whoever might say, a bit of puffed rice with one's tea is absolutely nothing new. In fact, if one adds a fried snack or two, it may well be considered an effective preliminary to that enjoyable tête-à-tête known as the adda. Now, since we have come this far, why should the BJP be left out? Radhanath Sikdar made a name for himself by measuring Mt Everest. Another ever-smiling Sikdar, first name Tapan, has a plan of action that's simple, smooth and straightforward: 'From Man to Hanuman'.


31 December 1999, the inevitable occurred. Dang! To understand the gravity of this event, it is enough for one to understand that, on the last night of the Gregorian calendar, when Bhodi's followers came in droves, flocks and floods, bearing various kinds of alcohol, spicy snack mixtures, fried split peas, crispy gram-flour cakes, flat-roasted chickpeas, peanuts and cashews—they, alas, did not find Bhodi. Nolen was blasting the FM radio at high volume; and Bechamoni, wearing a vintage ball gown like an old-style mem-sahib, was dancing something ballet-like with amazing adroitness, and from the empty curve of her outstretched arms it wasn't at all

hard to fathom that her dancing partner was the invisible ghost of some long-dead sahib. Plunging the supplicants into despair and gloom, Nolen informed them that: responding to urgent summons the night before, Bhodi had, with military haste, hurried away.

'Leave the gifts here,' he told them, 'and best you lot go back home. Try any tricks, and you're dead. He said he'll see you all in the new year. He also said . . .'

'What? What?'

'He said: Little kicks from a little calf can be forgiven. But if the big bulls try to rush each other, then I'll break their horns and shove them where the sun don't shine.'

'Our lord disappeared on the last day of the year? Why didn't you hold on to him tight?'

'This is why I'm tempted to call you lot dumbfucks. He who ascends to his spirit body from one moment to the next, how can anyone hold on to him tight, you fool?'

Bechamoni bursts into trills of laughter, and twirls round and round with her ghostly partner, dancing the waltz. This is a Great Atamaram–blessed special magic item (not magic realism) known as Gilligilli Pump. No researcher will ever discover why it is called thus. Be that as it may, but the sluggish and sickeningly sweet theory through which *Beggars' Bedlam* is dragging its feet, that no longer remains a secret stratagem nor a hidden agenda. Dear Witless Reader, do you know that fried-dough delicacy, the luchi? And the deadly decadence of downing layers of sweet milky rabri wrapped in the blistered skin of a piping-hot luchi, have you ever experienced that? After such an evening repast, what is mandatory is a visit to a brothel. In the next chapter, you will see how effort-lessly our witness Borhilal has mastered the art of visiting brothels. You will also see how some children of man frolic in the elusive mysteries of eternity, even as their feet are firmly planted in our mundane world. Never forget, not even for a moment, that the world rests in the hands of lunatics. At any moment, it can all be bamboo up the bottom. Later, O Witless Reader, when you have ripened rosily into a delicious, incredibly inedible bitter-apple fruit, then you'll understand that the necromancy of literature is nothing but a divinely planned deception, behind which, in the Katyn forest, 13,000 Polish officers, killed by the NKVD, are listening with solemn faces to the 'March to the Scaffold' in Berlioz's *Symphonie fantastique*. Behind which, Ali Sardar Jafri is reciting 'The Call of the Blood' and a blood-drenched Peshawar Express is ferrying corpses ceaselessly. Writer, reader, publisher or critic, no one will be spared. But for now—dang! For those Bermuda-shorts-sporting writers who have vowed to splash about in the swimming pool of commode-cleaning acid, let us leave a few prophetic lines from Purandar Bhat:

> Dutiful slave, O my dutiful slave
> All your life you made posies
> From your pubic shave
> Duteous slave, O my duteous slave
> Dutiful slave, O my dutiful slave
> Look hither-thither, or in reverse
> What's here, at the end of our universe,
> Bamboo Villa's recto-killer
> A ring'ed stave
> O my dutiful slave, my dutiful slave!

Dang! Sarkhel's shovel hit an obstruction but Sarkhel kept on digging though the outcome was that his shovel grew blunt, his hands grew blisters and not much else. That's when Sarkhel called Bhodi via the telecom system described earlier, and Bhodi instructed Sarkhel to pause operations:

'Stop the digging.'

'Then?'

'Then nothing.'

'I say, and then?'

'Stand down. I'll come.'

'When?'

'Early morning. When all the fuckers are asleep.'

'OK.'

As it is, winter. On top of that, the crack of dawn. By the banks of the Old Ganga, in the thick of a snail-rotting fog, a band of nearly naked men are industriously employed. They are not spirits from the other world. Not Phyatarus. Not Choktars. Just people. Their job is to pick out small worms from the numerous crevices—drowned tyres, bricks, shoes, old coconut shells and discarded clay pots—along the river, and supply them to the aquarium shops that sell red and blue fishes. Sometimes they find locks, timepiece watches, rusted Nepali daggers and gun chambers. They are clever folk. They know they can cut open their feet in that water. So they make sure they wear slippers carved out of car tyres, or something equally tough. Some of them may even be wearing Adidas, Lotto or Nike sneakers. How do such expensive shoes land up on their feet? Actually, goods are exchanging hands at all times, moving hereabouts and thereabouts. Fake, real, stolen, smuggled—the market is flooded with goods. This was expected, after all, it's all been foretold for a while now. And it has finally happened. So deal with it. The public's idea of all prophecies is this: the elephant will fart, the elephant will fart. But then—a whisper at most, certainly no bang. When the opposite happens, the jackasses even then don't open their eyes.

But none of this will harm even a hair on the Great Cat's furiously furry back.

At the crack of dawn, Sarkhel is surprised at Bhodi's outfit. Full military dress. Olive-green pants. Hunter boots. A camouflage commando vest topped with a military jacket that is a common sight on the Siachen glacier.

'No hanky-panky. No whining. What's the problem?'

'I can't understand it. I dug about five arms' length, and there was a loud dang!'

'Blow it with a shovel, like a depth charge. Just how submarines are taken care of.'

'Shovel itself is blown to bits. Look, look at these blisters on my hands. I've put some Boroline on them.'

'This Boroline-foroline doesn't work on the battlefield, dear Sarkhel. Wherever you're wounded, amputate. Hand, feet, head—leave it all behind. Just keep marching on.'

'You can keep marching if you want. I can't do it any more. I've run out of strength. Plus, I'm afraid too.'

'Afraid? Afraid of what? Afraid on the battlefield! You make me laugh, Sarkhel!'

'I can shoot off some of those *Sonai Dighi*–type dialogues also, you know. Enter Messenger. To the King: "Maharaj! Maharaj! The enemy has breached the castle." Maharaj, to Messenger: "Fuck me, I'm screwed." Prompter prompts from the wings but can't be heard. Hence King: "Come Queen, let's withdraw within and take a piss."'

Bhodi laughs. Rolls on the floor, laughing.

'Top! Top! Oh, Sarkhel, that was a solid one. Now, finally, I've warmed up. Tell me, why're you afraid?'

'I'm thinking: it's a fat, iron pipe. Either there's electric wires inside, or it's a shit-and-piss sewer line laid by the British. If I try to break it, I'll either be electrocuted or become a manure martyr like Nafar Kundu.'

'Listen, a whole lot of enquiries and headaches had to be endured before that spot near your house was settled upon. A line can't go through there—not water, not electric, not shit, nothing.'

'Then what made that dang?'

'A cannon!' said a voice in the waning darkness, startling both of them. It was the Raven, cloaked in shadows and thus invisible to the human eye.

'Father!'

'Yes, my little Bhodi darling.'

'So early in the morning, so cold, and not even a shawl . . .'

'Never mind. No need for such shows of filial fondness. Now listen carefully: Suddenly, my eyes got night vision. And I saw clearly: that's a cannon down there.'

'So now what?'

'Don't be afraid. It's not big, it's small. You could call it a wiener cannon.'

'Sir, any chance of any wham-bam?'

'That fear of yours will kill you. No cannonball inside it, no gunpowder. Only dirt. Leave about an arm and a half's length on either side and start digging from the left. Then you can bring out the little fucker.'

Bhodi starts digging with the shovel. Sarkhel shifts dirt with a bit of broken pot. Bhodi starts to sweat and takes off his military jacket. Then lunges and plunges with the shovel. The dirt was loose on his side, so it didn't take long. When he pushed the shovel in again, he could tell that one side of the cannon was free.

'God has put everything into your skulls except intelligence,' snapped the Raven, 'The shovel's job is done now. Shove the cannon with an iron rod or two and shake it loose. Then get down there and haul it up.'

Sarkhel is thin, so he gets down into the ditch. But even after he has tried the rods, he cannot move the cannon.

'Oh, this is most annoying. The damn thing won't budge!'

'And it won't. Slide a rope under it. Then the two of you come up here, pull from two sides. Even if it doesn't come up, it'll stand up right. Then you can bring it up.'

After some more struggle, the two-arms-length-long baby cannon comes up on level ground.

The sky is full of colour. It is like this every day.

Sarkhel scratches and scrapes off the dirt. At the back, it's shaped like a dome. The mouth is shaped like a lion.

'Do you know who this belongs to?'

'After we wash and clean it, maybe we'll find something written on it.'

'Maybe. But I'll tell you anyway—this belonged to the Portuguese pirates. In those days, the Old Ganga flowed elsewhere. A lot of ships sailed on it too. The Portuguese pirates and slave traders had cannons like these on their ships. One cannonball was enough for small boats. Don't scoff at it because it's small. Made in Lisbon, don't forget.'

'Can we still use it?'

'Why not? You'll have to love and look after it. Get hold of gunpowder. Cannon balls.'

'Then should we hold this thing in stock?'

This question comes from Sarkhel. Because the arsenal that Bhodi has been amassing in secret—Sarkhel is its chief armourer.

'If we sell this to a museum or to a sahib, we can make some good cash. Antiques are heavy hot in the market right now.'

'You'll get some money. But you won't get this iron, this crafts-manship. I say, wash this thing and polish it with kerosene. Let it stay in our stock. If we can charge it properly, it can blast the testicles off police vans 200 feet away.'

'When Father is saying so, Sarkhel, let's not argue. We will hold it in stock.'

The Raven flaps his wings: 'You two take care of the cannon. Fortune favours those who do good on the last day of the year.'

'You're going away, Father? Who will guide us, then?'

'My dear, I have to go to Eliott Road now. Eat some burnt cake at the bakery and then fly to the sahibs' cemetery. From there to Neemtala Crematorium. I have a busy day ahead of me. I'll come again later. All you have to do now is clean it. The bang-bang's all for later.'

The Raven spreads wide his vast wings and flies away. Crows, sparrows, mynas, etc., have all begun to sing. Dawn is a very aus-picious time indeed.


Bhodi and Sarkhel bring the Portuguese cannon up to a room on the second floor.

'Father's right. Who knows how long this was buried under-ground, but see, not a hint of rust.'

'Must admit that the Portuguese were jolly good cannon builders.'

'That they were indeed. What a sliver-small country so far away. And then—sailing across the seven seas they land up here, on the Old Ganga, blasting cannon balls everywhere. Money, jewellery, women—looting everything in sight. Just the thought of it sends a chill down my spine.'

'I know the name of one Portuguese thug.'

'Who?'

'Carvalho.'

'Rubbish! That's just some fellow in a play. Once upon a time, Bhumen Roy played Carvalho on stage and made a big name for himself.'

'Maybe.'

'Not maybe—he did! Anyway, here I am worrying that if the digging goes bust, what are we going to fight with?'

'I've been thinking the same. After all, it's going to be such a great war.'

'Whatever it is, God is with us. Understood? Otherwise, out of nowhere, nothing anywhere, we end up finding a Portuguese cannon, eh? Uff, wham-bam and what a grand slam we'll have. Just let them provoke us—just once.'

'We have to make a list of everything we've collected so far. But, I have a doubt.'

'What doubt?'

'We haven't been able to do much with guns. One double-barrel shotgun, that too ancient. And two cheap pistols.'

'So? How is that any less? Cannon, shotgun, pistols. Then we have knives, scissors, and then we have the shovel. Think of them all as one.'

'But according to our plan—'

'Wait, Sarkhel, wait. No military force can be built in a day. Today if people see our armoury, they'll say it's as laughable as Queen Razia's beard. But when they see submarine periscopes peeping out on the Old Ganga, mines floating at every shore, and every hand holding a six- or ten-round revolver, what then? Their arses will shrivel up in fear. And, and one more thing: you must remember the most important thing.'

'What?'

'Run such an aggressive campaign about your military and armoury that when word of it reaches the ears of the enemy, they will start to tremble. We have to set off the rumours. But only when the time is right. Such as: Army, Navy, Air Force? We have it all.'

'Navy? Air Force!'

'Yes, why not? If you think about it hard enough, anyone can build a submarine. It's nothing. Boat + Underwater Swimming = Submarine.'

'But the Air Force?'

'The discs are flying, after all. And with such force! On top of that, the Phyatarus can drop a few bombs from a high altitude! And don't forget, Father's with us too.'

'Right. I forgot.'

'That's the problem, Sarkhel, you have to know your own strength. This is a fundamental fact of warfare. If you don't, you die. Then comes the plan. Maybe the enemy has breached your walls. Come, baby, come—you're letting them inch closer and closer. And those arseholes are thinking: Amazing, we've almost taken the castle. Then suddenly you enforce the Scissor Stratagem and surprise-attack them from either side and slam-bam-bam the daylights out of them. Something like that. The main thing is: you need some grey cells in your head-pot. In history, you'll see so many

superpower nations—huge army, with all those fighter planes—are
suddenly fucking with some tiny-small country. But then, suddenly,
those superpowers are shitting themselves. Shitting so hard and
fast, they've no time to wash or wipe their butts.'

From the slant of such conversations, is it not gradually becoming
evident that the Choktar plan involves military action, or something quite like it? But does the reader want to know right away
which way *Beggars' Bedlam* marches—towards positional warfare
or a guerrilla struggle? Mao, Lin Biao, Tito, Giáp, Fidel, Che—
which variety of military tactic will be followed? Will both sides
be Bengali or will foreign mercenaries join the fight? And if a
bloody brawling brouhaha does indeed break out, then which side
will the reader support? Each of these questions is very valuable,
very venerable and utterly urgent. But on this dewy dawn, the discovery of the cannon is such an event that even those with the least
sense of military tactics and strategy will understand its plausability
in the theory mentioned above. If such understanding dawned in
every house and home, then we wouldn't need to grovel and gasp
for a Bengal Regiment. The Bengal Regiment would have practically formed itself, and its bravery would have made everyone else's
heroics pale into insignificance.

A famous Bengali from Chandannagar once wrote:

Haran Chakraborty was very strong. One day he felled a
large lychee tree in Udaychand Nandi's garden without
using any implements whatsoever. Even while two men
squeezed his throat tightly, he could swallow a whole
banana. Gaganchandra Banerjee once lifted a galloping
horse up into the air. Almost forty years ago in Palpara, in
Birchand Boral's home, arrangements had been made to

entertain the French governor by showcasing feats of physical prowess. The governor had praised profusely Bengali's strength and courage.

Who is this writer? Who, my dear heart? Who indeed? The only answer from the Bengalis is their uninterrupted silence. Oh, how much lower must we sink in our shame?

(*To Be Continued*)

*9*

Now, the suspicion that will poke its head in from time to time and softly give a laugh or two is this: Is *Beggars' Bedlam* a quarrelsome quiz for the penniless or another kind of enquiry entirely? The company that set up this bullshit business is either mute or running on a loop. Why did this happen? Is this another trick of the flying discs? Is anybody out there? Radio silence. This is like a desperate knock-knock on the toilet door. Who's there? Silence. This cock-up is not going to be resolved so easily. And the process that Bengali boys and Bengali girls need to implement so that they may resolve it is as rare as it is easy. As Chapter 8 was wheezing its last, an excerpt from an extremely serious piece of writing by an eminent Bengali of Chandannagar had been cited, unless the press forgot to include it and it's been left out. We can imagine that Bengali smiling at us from behind a dark window, enframed by fairy lights. He is or was Harihar Seth. And will remain so in the future. As will dinosaur eggs, pictures of Bankim Chandra Chattopadhyay wearing a fruit-basket on his head and time capsules tucked into craters across the world. No complaints or excuses will be heard or heeded. And in the middle of all this, that familiar 'waa waa' cry rings out again.

If the drink delirium dissipates, if the jamboree in the garden draws to a close, then one might gather up courage and interrogate the reader about the abovementioned 'waa waa' cry of which we have been forewarned, but where? No hands go up in the air because they're all busy scratching. For shame! Shame! In the last week of October '99, did we not learn from DS that his wife is eight months pregnant? Pregnant for eight months, or maybe the eighth month has just begun. In fact, even the tenth month and ten days, if you don't believe me, see the mark of the umbilical round the neck, to be a mother is no small matter—to make the shoe fit, this must be so. And so it is.

In January 2000, as arranged, at Shisumar Maternity Home, Dr Gajendrakumar Roychowdhury (or as he is better known: Gyno Gaja) delivered the millennium's first real or fake (the debate continues) Phyataru Junior by Caesarean surgery from the belly of DS' dark-skinned, fat, slightly moustachioed, frog-like wife. If one went by the name of the nursing home—Shisumar, or Slay the Child—one would think it specialized in killing children, and not delivering them to life. But that is not so. According to the dictionary, 'Shisumar' refers to the Ganges river dolphin. As a child, Gajendrakumar had watched from his father's lap the dolphins leaping up and falling back into the heart of the Ganga. A group of dolphins rising, falling, over and over again. The scene left a deep impression on Ganjendrakumar's infant heart. And thus grew his sense of obligation to the dolphin. And thus the name, Shisumar Maternity Home.

Outside, with trembling hearts, wait DS, Madan and Purandar Bhat. There are more members of the public around them. The three are clad in winter clothes, but hot with excitement. Purandar gets some tea from a footpath stall. He doesn't bring it himself though. A swollen-belly child labourer brings it over to them, the cups held in a cage-like wire basket. In Purandar's hand, wrapped in a discarded lottery ticket, are three biscuits.

'Going to be a father for the first time. But you're looking like a sacrificial goat.'

'Ah Purandar. You didn't go the family way, after all. It's easy to say things like that. You'd know if you were in DS' situation.'

'Get married, if you dare. Let's see how brave you really are!'

'I'm not going to fuck myself in the arse just to show you up, my darling. And it's different for poets. Everything happens in the heart.'

'Eh?'

'I'll explain later. Now eat your biscuit.'

'Oh, I clean forgot I was holding them!'

'Soon enough you'll be holding only a hurricane—and not much else.'


Just then, Bhodi was sitting on his haunches, peering into a black-stone bowl full of water. Nolen was arguing with the sweeper about cleaning the drains. Bechamoni, after her bath, head tilted to one side, was slap-drying her long, wet hair with a towel and Bhodi's father, the Raven, was watching from a corner of the rooftop how droplets from his daughter-in-law's hair suddenly fly up into the air, and the sunlight is rainbow-lit one moment, and in the next moment, it's all gone.

'Thank god, it all went well.'

Bechamoni whispers in a sing-song voice to herself, 'What went all well?'

'DS had a baby,' snaps Bhodi, 'What else, your last rites?'

'Is that any way to talk, my dear?'

The Raven bristles, 'That's what happens when you don't wash your mouth properly. Is it a boy or a girl?'

'A boy! Nice round-bellied bubby!'

Bechamoni chortled, 'I knew it!'

Bhodi starts to snap at her again but remembers his father's presence and holds his tongue.

The Raven flaps his wings.

'Are you leaving, Father?'

'Yes, a bonny baby is born, I should tell Begum Johnson. In an earlier age, there'd have been an orchestra playing, happy hijras dancing.'

The Raven flies away.


The bald OC's desk phone begins to ring.

'Hello.'

'Waa waa!'

'Hello?'

'Waa waa!'


At the CPM party office, Comrade Acharya's phone also begins to ring. But Comrade Acharya is not there, so the phone rings and rings and then finally falls silent. Comrade Acharya, you carry on crafting your devious proposal for the next party conference. While here, events are unfolding, one after another. You have no idea. But you'll have to pay the price. Whether you want or you don't, the Choktars will bedazzle and the Phyatarus will multiply. The discs will fly. Begum Johnson will throw a grand party. The Maharaja of Patiala will parade through the city once a year, stark naked but for a breastplate made of 1,001 bluish-white diamonds. John Stuart

Mill will come to the conclusion that India has become 'a vast system of outdoor relief for Britain's upper classes'. Churchill will say, 'I hate Indians, they are absolutely beastly people with a beastly religion.' Once in Kapurthala, a swarm of locusts descended on the fields and decimated all the crops. Today the same decimation continues but without the locusts. At that time, in response to the weeping and wailing of his subjects, Kapurthala's great philandering Maharaja had said: 'Let the locusts dance, we are going to dance in Paris.' Comrade Acharya, please carry on writing your devious proposal. We will carry it out to the letter. You can depend on us. We are as compassionate as quicksand.

Parting her light-pink-lipsticked and lively lips, trainee nurse Miss Champa whispers, 'Who is Mr DS?'

'Eh, what?'

'You're Mr DS?'

'Yes.'

'Dr Roychowdhury wants to talk to you. Please come with me.'

DS, sweating profusely, follows Miss Champa to the doctor's room and discovers a very distraught Gyno Gaja. Legs stretched out on his table, he's sprawled, exhausted, in his chair. A wet towel on his head. Senior Matron Mrs Porhel is massaging his left hand.

'You?'

'What?'

'No, I mean that baby boy—are you the father?'

'It's a boy?'

'Superficial examinations seem to tell us so. Now, tell me, you, and your wife—what exactly are you?'

'What do you mean?'

'I mean, simply, are you people or ghosts or something?'

'Why do you ask?'

'Why? All newborns cry, sir. But your son, he was cackling with glee, and as soon as we snipped his umbilical cord, he began to fly about like a bird!'

'How are they?'

'Good. The mother will come round soon. But—'

Before DS can respond, Purandar and Madan burst into the room: 'No ifs and buts. If the mother or child are harmed in any way, we'll torch this gyno business to the ground.'

'Who the hell are you?'

'Shut up! Don't try any funny stuff. You're right, we're human but we're also not. Want to see a trick, just a little one?'

In front of Dr Roychowdhury, Mrs Porhel and Miss Champa's astounded eyes, the three Phyatarus take off and hover five feet up in the air, like helicopters. Their hands flapping by their sides, like wings. Their mouths grinning from ear to ear. The three down on the floor are on the verge of a frightened fit. Before six stunned eyes, the Phyatarus land back down again.

At a signal from Dr Roychowdhury, Mrs Porhel and Miss Champa bolt out of the room.

'How long will it take?'

'At least a week. The mother, I mean . . . is a bit older, so I am thinking—'

'Oh, you can do all the thinking you want. We have nothing to say. We're not poking our noses into any of that medical stuff.'

'Doctors do doctoring
Lawyers do lawyering

Phyatarus tumble in the arsehole sandpit
While Choktars do choktaring.'

'What did you understand?'

'I don't need to understand. Yours is the last word.'

'That means you surrender unconditionally?'

'Listen,' says DS to the terrified doctor, 'don't take this the wrong way. But my money situation is tight. We were fucked over backwards even before you came into the picture. Your operating fees, operation-theatre charge, bed fees, nurse—we can't pay for all that!'

'Even if we could, we won't:
Those who loot the beggarly
Phyatarus shit on them eagerly.'

'Oh, please, don't do that. I haven't said no to anything. Pay me whatever you want to, I have nothing to say.'

'We have nothing to say either.'

'Do you drink?'

'Who, me?'

'Yes, who else? Us?'

'Yes, I mean . . . a peg and a half of brandy maybe, at the end of the day.'

'Very good. We'll bring you some fine booze, foreign stuff. Take good care of the mother and child. And then you'll see, we'll be ready to lay down our lives for you. Won't let nothing stand in your way. One of these days, we'll even take you to Bhodi-da's place. Then just watch how your fortune takes off. You'll have to hire a truck to cart your cash. Everything that is happening, it's all by Bhodi-da's grace.'

'I must visit him! Does he live in an ashram?'

'No, no, he doesn't babysit no children of no gods. Bhodi-da is just like you and me. But replete with benediction.'

'I must go. Please, come and see your family whenever you wish.'

'No, don't tell us to break the rules. Bhodi-da has forbidden it. We will make sure we come only during Visiting Hours. Why would we bother you otherwise?'

'If we come during non-Visiting Hours, the guard at the gate will scold us. We'll get angry, kick the shit out of him. In the middle of it all, your nursing home's reputation will suffer. We don't want any trouble.'

'We'll be on our way now.'

'All right. I'm so fortunate to have met you. Please convey my deep reverence to Bhodi-da. Perhaps if he could bless me a little. I've been thinking of opening an AC ward on the third floor. Rich Marwaris want AC rooms, political leaders too.'

'It'll happen. If Bhodi-da cracks a smile, just a little, there's no big daddy in this big wide world who can stop your luck from turning.'

The baby Phyataru flaps and flies up into the air, somersaults in space. DS' wife regains consciousness, but unlike most Caesarean mothers, there are no moans and groans nor a face creased with pain. The new mother smiles and raises her arms. And the flying baby swoops down towards her milk-laden breasts.


The Positional Astronomy Centre in Calcutta spied through its telescopes innumerable discs flying through the air. The director, Mr Sikdar, saw quite a few of them with his own eyes. But he refused to believe it. Because Real Science doesn't believe in flying saucers. The surprisingly successful conspiracy aiming to destroy Real Science by polluting it with fantasy and pseudo-science—Mr Sikdar roars against it in protest. We've been fortunate enough to be startled by his roaring at various seminars and debates and TV panels. But does this aforementioned 'we' also include the scientific-minded readers? Do any of our little friends know the answer? Come to think of it, who are these 'little friends' anyway? Can we find everything we need from our friends? Is storytime grandpapa truly married to storytime grandmama? Featuring 2,000 other unsolved riddles such as these, a few copies of the 14th edition of *Tell Me Why* still crouches like a dark horse beneath the ashy ruins of old books. 'Putting this inside that, the bitch and her lover lay down flat'. The meaning of this is not what may instantly leap to the mind. The meaning of this is a door latch. The tangles of a riddle are complex indeed. Like a Rubik's cube. Let the great men traverse those paths, slowly, slowly. The night grows deep. Where does Borhilal go on this winter's night, his shawl wrapped around him tight? Why does he go? Since the chance of scandal lies this way, let us turn our minds to that same way at once.

Walking out of the blind lane behind the temple, Borhilal stops abruptly. A cold breeze, reeking of fish, blows in from the direction of the Old Ganga. But that is not why Borhilal has stopped. The sound of a big car is growing louder, drawing closer. It has only one working headlight; the light therefore falls on only one side of the pavement, and as luck would have it, it's the very side on which Borhilal is standing. Rumble-rumble, rattle and clank, there is only one kind of car that can make that sound. A Kolkata Police van, which if sold without a moment's delay by the weight for scrap would certainly bring home some money for an otherwise destitute and deprived state government. Inside, the bald OC sits next to the driver. In the back sit three drowsy constables. In this part of town, novice brothel-goers end up getting mugged twice. First the street thugs clean them out, then the police come along and dissipate what's left. Even though Borhilal is free from such elemental fears, he stands stock still like a statue and lets the one-eyed van roll away to a safe distance. From his shawl-wrapped shoulders hangs a threadbare tote bag, the kind favoured by intellectuals, inside which is a newspaper-wrapped pint of rum. Except for extra-special occasions, Borhilal does not touch booze. But when he does drink, he doesn't drink like a cheapskate lout. A section of our readers will surely think Borhilal's calculated self-control is worth emulating. But this proposal will raise no waves of consideration in the hearts of the alcoholics and the dedicated dipsos. This is not because of any ingrained arseholery on their parts. Those who drink a lot and all the time, their cerebrum and cerebellum undergo vital changes. Their neuron clusters may be compared to those brass bands who'd rather sit idle than work for pay. The result is impaired judgement, forgetting the hula-hoopla of the night before, etc., and numerous other such syndromes that we don't need to analyse anew. But yes, science is not unanimous yet about marijuana. Thus far and no farther, no one knows any more. And what the fuck will we do with knowing any more anyway?

A handful of houses, the whore-street cringes in the winter cold. Not every prostitute is lucky enough to have a brick house. The house that Borhilal stops in front of is a mix of brick and mud. Fractured shafts of detective light from various sides and scattered thief-like shadows meld together in an indescribable chiaroscuro. Borhilal knocks on the door twice, and calls softly, 'Kali, Ka—li.'

It doesn't need to be said that the one who opens the door with sleepy eyes is Kali.

'Come in. I thought maybe you won't come today, after all. I fell asleep sitting up for you.'

Kali turns up the lantern's worn-down wick. As a result, Borhilal's monstrous shadow suddenly rears up and falls on the pictures of the gods and goddesses hanging on the narrow walls.

'Give me some soap, a clean saree.'

Borhilal goes out into the backyard, washes his hands and feet and face with a laundry soap worn down to a sliver, then comes back in, making sure to wipe his feet on the improvised gunny-sack-doormat laid outside. Then he takes off his tired, workaday clothes and drapes Kali's clean saree around his waist like a lungi. The cloth is soft and tender, it smells of the moon.

Meanwhile, Kali has set out two glasses, a small plate full of deep-fried shrimp heads and a big bottle of water. Borhilal combs his hair with Kali's comb. Then half-lies down on Kali's bed laid out on the floor. Rests his head on his hand, so his biceps swell.

Kali says, 'Your arm will grow sore. Take that bolster instead.'

Kali measures out some Old Adventurer rum. Picks up the bottle of water.

'Why're you staring at me? See how much water you want.'

We know that the thinking sections of our society are often divided over debates and discourses and disputes about whether or not we may call Kali a sex worker. Both parties are so belligerent that if they could, they would fuck the other in the arse. It's not as though we can't catch a fish or two in these muddy waters. All we need is one wide net.

The light in Kali's lantern slowly grows dim. Waa waa cries from Shisumar Maternity Home rend the air. Even though it is everybody's responsibility to maintain the current state of peace in the kingdom, it is more the king's than anybody else's.

Recognizing this truth, Rabindranath Tagore wrote to the Maharaja of Tripura, Sri Brajendra Kishore Deb Barman Bahadur, from Almora:

You must be supremely patient for the sake of the betterment of your state. In many instances, injustice and inequity will rear their heads to assault you. Do not let your natural righteousness make you forget yourself. You must endure much anguish in silence—do not think of yourself, but only of your duty. So that no weakness assails your kingdom or its king, you must, slowly and surely, and with great care, endeavour to eliminate all the wicked undergrowth. You must be especially careful to not cause a sudden revolt to assail your kingdom.

Waa waa!

(*To Be Continued*)

*10*

*Beggars' Bedlam* had set out with the mission of gladdening the heart of the nation and its people, but since the last chapter's, or episode's, publication, we have come to truly understand what it means to be entrapped in the embrace of the supernatural. The whole matter shows absolutely no sign of a human hand! When the first proofs arrived, we noticed that where it says (*To Be Continued*), there instead it said (*Not Continued*). Even after corrections, that disheartening 'not' remained. Neither the computer's mouse nor cat—none of them were misbehaving. They are pure and virus-free. Neither was any tomfoolery attempted by the junior editors at the magazine where a chapter is just about published before it's blasted into oblivion. Instead of (*Not Continued*) if it had said anything else—such as (*Not Moved*) or (*Not Subdued*)—we could still have saved face, but (*Not Continued*) is most insulting. The thought occurs to the author, as inevitable as the call of nature, that this must be the editor's arseholery. And maybe it could've even been proven to be so. But while they were bickering over the issue, the editor hurled a photocopy of the manuscript at the author and said 'Is that my father's handwriting, then?' No, it was indeed the author's own! The same script, sans any error—(*Not Continued*). To paraphrase the editor: continued or not continued, he doesn't give a shit. The author thinks the same thing. All arseholes, in the end, are similarly constipated. Mysteries, like petticoats, are by their very nature enigmatic. No one knows the truth. The supernatural often uses automatic writing or other similar subterfuges to point a finger in the direction of a foreordained future. But the nature of man does not allow him to readily accept the guidance of ghosts. Inexorable fate thus guides the wandering traveller's footsteps towards the will-o'-the-wisps, and delivers him to the adroit thugee waiting in the darkness beyond the desolate marshlands. Therefore let us assume that this time too the inevitable will occur, but until we can actually catch it red-handed . . .

Perched on the top spires of the Second Hooghly Bridge, the world's third longest suspension bridge, the Raven surveyed the various distinct neighbourhoods of Calcutta: Khidirpur; Watgunj; the docks by the Ganga; rising like a posy of pubes—the Millennium Park; Eden Gardens; Maidan; the obelisk of the Black Hole Monument; the chaos of Chowringhee; the daily dazzling market of virgin college girls on Free School Street; Bhabanipur; North Calcutta, enfolded in the monstrous arms of a thick black fog; those areas of Ballygunge from where, in Jibananda's short stories, characters such as Hemen, etc., took their fat wives on buses or taxis to Firpo's and devoured fried croquettes and cutlets; or, shifting his gaze slightly, the Eastern Bypass, Salt Lake, Kasba Connector. The Raven turned his head this way and that, and looked, and cursed constantly under his breath:

'That bloody sisterfuck Bhodi needs to be taken to the cleaners. A city like a honeycomb, full of pigeon-holes—he should be launching a guerrilla attack. But no! That peckerhead's planning army-style positional warfare! Positional warfare, with a baby-dick cannon! Fucking pilgarlic jackass! Told him: fight later, do some research first. Even told him where to look. Mao, Giáp, Che,

Marighella, Tito—look at their work, only then take your note-
book and pencil and flop down on a mat with your arse in the
air and draw up your own strategy. War's not child's play, after
all! Got to keep the elephant and the howdah and the mahout all
in your line of sight. But no, the bastard keeps blustering. Unlimited
blustering! Anyway, I don't care. If anything goes wrong—in plain
English: I'm out. If you've got the balls for it, then sit with Begum
Johnson and listen to the stories of the old wars. What Tipu did,
whom Hyder Ali pricked, how Siraj-ud-Daulah fully fucked Fort
William—but then could he counter the British? They'd already
dropped anchor in the heart of the Ganga and were merely biding
their time. Run, hide, and only when you see the enemy swimming
in fountains of wine and women, that's when you swing into action,
*Sholay*-style, the iron's hot, put the hammer to it! But no! Only
bombast and bluster. Uff, it's quite cold up here. Should I flap my
wings? High altitude, after all, and an English breeze. Oh, what a
race they were! Left this land so many years ago, yet their memory
so fresh, so fragrant.'

The Raven flaps his wings. One feather falls off, and swirls
through the air. It won't be right to think of this feather as an
ordinary crow feather because, spiralling down to the Ganga, it
stuck itself like a sticker onto a Silver Jet and sailed off to Haldia,
free of charge. If you want to understand why Haldia Petrochemicals went bankrupt, you must keep this incident at the forefront.
This contains the vital clue. We are forbidden from revealing any
more. Because if news of the revelation reaches the CPM party
office in Alimuddin Street, it might prompt even our usually supine
state government to stir. And *Beggars' Bedlam* just doesn't have the
balls to take on that brouhaha. Of course, by now, it must be evident
to one and all that we don't want to ruffle any feathers, whether it
be *Anandabazar*, CPM or Trinamool or even the headless Congress.
Although if on their own steam, entirely unprovoked, someone

takes it upon them-selves to be incensed—well, we can't do any-thing about that. These are but lightweights. Even the British—who ruled the world—experienced great crowning ecstasy only to eventually drown in the depths of despair. Wandiwash, Arcot, Plassey, Buxar and Seringapatam—oh, the exhilaration of each victory! And yet after the Black Hole (not to be confused with the deadly phenomenon in outer space) of Calcutta or the Patna Massacre, such angry tears, kicks and curses rained upon the punkhawallah. In order for us to awaken to this tragicomic aspect of history, we must journey again and again, led by an odious Englishman by the name of Ivor Edwards-Stuart, to the boudoir of Begum Johnson, for Begum Johnson is that incredible woman who, in the cracks and crevices of time between four marriages, witnessed Siraj-ud-Daulah in the flesh, conducted casual conver-sations with such illustrious men as Colonel Robert Clive and Admiral Charles Watson and watched with great delight how the Holkars, the Scindias and even the fearsome Marathas curled their tails in front of John and Co. and said 'yessir, yessir'. This is why we must always bow low before Begum Johnson—we have no choice.

'Hail Ma Ganga,' said the Raven and took off into the ether and at that very moment noticed a flock of discs flying past, towards Howrah. It would not be an exaggeration to say that they frolicked their way along rather than flew. The dance of the discs is comparable to that of flies in the market, buzzing around slabs of meat and fish. But while we may be able to predict what the flies may do after they have dizzied themselves with such sport, about the intention of our flying discs even the father of Lord Shiva may not hazard a guess. They may charge at a ferryman singing a doleful ballad, or pause mid-flight to stare at the young women bathing along the banks. No one can say which of these will happen. Not only in the world of quantum—Werner Heisenberg's uncertainty principle applies everywhere.

From his position high up in the sky, the Raven shits with strategic precision. And even though the shit flies lightly for a moment, gravity inevitably pulls it downwards until it falls, of all the places in the world, on the sunglasses of a seasoned traffic sergeant. The sergeant says 'Shit!' and stops his motorbike. The shit sticks to his thick eyebrows, runs down his RayBans. The sergeant's next utterance is: 'My nice handkerchief—totally fucked.'

A mischievous smirk glints on the Raven's long, obsidian beak as he carries on his way and then, after a short flight, executes a perfect landing next to the bronze angel atop the Victoria Memorial. Just then, a gust of wind blows and the angel, heartbroken at being left alone for so long, turns her face away. Readers of Bengali literature will not be unfamiliar with the scene. Though not many present-day specimens bother to read the works of Trailakyanath Mukhopadhyay any more. Atop the Memorial's dome, the angel and the Raven.

Then, suddenly, the Raven noticed the following: taking advantage of the public-toilet atmosphere of one-sided globalization, a group of British tourists are walking around the grounds of the Victoria Memorial with an assortment of cameras. Standing on the gravel path in the garden, the Memorial's curator is lecturing them on the paintings of the Daniells, Zoffany and Verestchagin. This man is not only the curator and director of the Victoria Memorial, he also the foremost among all the heavy-duty authorities on Calcutta's short history. At many twists and turns along his own ascent towards glory, he has been heard to say—sometimes openly, sometimes secretly, depending on the situation—'By the grace of Charnock!' Today was no exception either. The idiot tourists bid goodbye with many laughs and smiles and the curator walked back to his office thinking that much writing on ancient Calcutta's brothels was scattered across sources far and wide, why could he not compile and edit and publish a volume of all those texts—would the book be written in Bengali or was a concurrent English edition also necessary?—how much work was required to make it a hefty tome?—At the end of such complex thought processes, and back in his office, he reclined in his chair and sighed, 'By the grace of Charnock.'

Almost immediately, an answer came from the window, 'Why? Why not by the grace of your father?'

This is a fairytale scene. Inside the room, a scholar, and outside, on the narrow ledge of the window, the city's oldest raven aka Bhodi's father.

Having fired his arrow, the Raven scratches his beak.

Was it the Raven who spoke, then? Or a ghost? The curator thinks for an instant that he may have died without his knowledge. Alive a moment ago, he is now dead and been granted entry into the world of the Great Beyond. In that world, not only ravens but even mosquitoes, frogs, lizards, all of them can effortlessly utter intelligible sentences. But then, his devious mind led him to another thought: had he simply projected his own imaginary idea onto the raven outside and caused this amusement? In which case, there was no harm in pushing things a bit further. So the curator said again, 'By the grace of Charnock!'

The raven blinks: 'One peck and you'll understand whose grace is keeping you alive. Fucking varmint. Here, I curse you: in your next life you'll be born a dung beetle. That too, not in Calcutta. Maybe in Burdwan or Mankundu, out in the sticks. A dung beetle in a vat of dung. You'll eat shit, wear shit and one day die in shit.'

The curator thought he'd hurl a paperweight as hard as he could, but couldn't muster the courage. Instead, he said: 'I see you've learnt to merely parrot some words. You know nothing about the tide of evolution that carries man towards superman. Obviously, crows and jackdaws are not supposed to know such things.'

'Crows and jackdaws, eh! Know this—this raven's the only one who can tackle a dozen of your Aurobindos and Nietzsches. Throwing superman at me! First become a super dung beetle, then a super pube and then we'll see about superman. The fewer conniving dirtwads like you are born, the better. "By the Grace of Charnock!" I'll cuff you round the lughole if I hear that name again. Charnock! Fuck Charnock!'

'Charnock was a great man. Would Calcutta exist without him? Would horse-drawn trams have run for its tricentennial celebrations? Would so many magazines and journals have published so many special issues? Would so many seminars and conferences have taken place? And would my august presence and I have attended them all? Sometimes chair, sometimes keynote speaker, sometimes chief and sometimes special guest? Tell me, would all that have happened? Rubbing shoulders with so many ministers and important dignitaries?'

'Charnock was a great pube. That arsewipe came, shat on the banks of the Ganga and founded Calcutta. Without shitheads like you, how could that marauding philanderer be touted as the father of our city? In a country of sheep, whatever a ram says is irrefutable logic. And your government is a piece of work, I must say. Celebrating Calcutta's birthday, my arse. The same goes for your moron ministers. Same goes for you. Keynote speaker at a conference of asses. You're a jackass!'

'You can say whatever you want, it won't tarnish the greatness of Charnock one bit. I'm only upholding the truth.'

'Shut up! Truth does not need to be upheld. Truth isn't a flying broomstick. Teaching me truth! Have you heard of Joseph Townsend?'

'I may have.'

'Don't lie. Townsend was a skirt-chasing Ganga pilot. A mate of Charnock's. Both die-hard womanizers.'

'I protest. You've said this before. Charnock rescued a helpless window from the sati pyre and married her. And here you are, maligning—'

'Don't squawk so much. No pot to piss in, and you're espousing elegies. Rescuing widows, huh! Then, listen! A vital historical document. In poem form. Write it down. What? You want to record it? All right. A bodacious babe like that, those come-hither ways, was Charnock going to burn such a peach in the fire? A woman's not a matchstick, after all.'

'What historical document?

'I'll tell you. You read it, and then think about it. I'll tell you, and then be on my way. I'll come back after three days. Then you'll tell me. Now: press Record. Eight lines, written on Joseph Townsend's grave. The language is a bit archaic but a rank charlatan like you will have no trouble. Right, here we go:

> Shoulder to shoulder, Joe my boy,
> Into the crowd like a wedge!
> Out with the hangers, messmates,
> But do not strike with the edge!
> Cries Charnock: Scatter the faggots,
> Double that Brahmin in two.
> That tall pale widow is mine, Joe,
> The little brown girl's for you.'

The Raven flies away. The curator presses Stop. Rewinds. Presses Play. The Raven's voice recites Townsend's epitaph. The curator swallows hard. Drinks some water.

'Astounding!'

At the very next moment he remembers that, in his next birth, he will be a dung beetle born in a vat of dung.

Bhodi stops in his tracks when he hears the dismaying news from Nolen: of their four rooms, only one has been rented today. That too by a complete crackpot who's brought his own bowls and bottles.

'Uff, that stink of burning hair! What's that arsehole doing?'

'Must be black magic, what else. Collecting hair-burnt smoke into bottles. Should I go look through the peephole?'

'Go, look. It's all right if he's only burning hair. Don't want him setting himself on fire!'

Nolen sticks his eye to the peephole and squats outside the door. And perhaps because of his assumption of this special posture, an aggressive fart explodes out of him. And at once the crackpot shouts from within: 'Fucking farting while spying on me? I'll show you when you come asking for the rent. Fucking scumbag.'

Nolen leaps away. Looks terrified.

Bhodi smiles sweetly at him: 'Auspicious customer. Not an entirely cracked pot, after all. Did you see anything?'

'Just what I'd thought. He's filling little bottles, like the ones for homoeopathy medicines, with smoke from burning hair and corking them tight.'

'Do you know what they do with the smoke?'

'Black magic, what else?'

'A special kind. Release that smoke into a window's room, and in three nights she'll be drawn to you like a pin to a magnet. He's going to make a killing with every bottle. And there's no shortage of buyers. Thousands are targeting widowed chicks every day.'

'Pulling close is one thing, but bewitching entirely? That's hard. There's even a saying about it, "Like a garrotte's knot, a widow when she's hot".'

'That's their problem. Earlier, they ate herbal sweets, ruby-coloured desserts, and went to the hakim. Now I hear they're importing some kind of tablet from America. You'll go broke buying just one box. But if you've got the money, then all you have to do is swallow just one. Kolkata has a monument—you'll have one too. And once it stands up, there's no sitting or lying down.'

Nolen's mouth hangs open. 'That's dangerous!'

'Dangerous on top of dangerous. Super dangerous. Anyway, don't mess him Or he'll make a fuss about payment later.'

'Oh, I'll cut him down to size soon enough.'

'Do that. I'm going out. Hail, hail the Raven. Hail the flying discs.'

Bhodi is about to leave when Bechamoni calls out, 'Ei Nolen, call him back!'

'Oh,' Bhodi snarls, 'you had to get in the way. That's just what I was afraid of.'

'Wives can get in the way, that's all right. Isn't that so, Nolen?'

Nolen nods like the jackass he can be sometimes.

'Stop that drama. What do you want, tell me quick.'

'It's growing colder. My skin's so dry, my cheeks feel like they're burning. Bring back a glycerine soap with you, don't forget.'

'Why? Oil is not enough for you? Oh my Marilyn Monroe, can't do without glycerine soap, eh! Everything costs an arm and a leg, and that stuff is for White people anyway. Do you know how much it costs? And here, only one room rented today.'

'I don't want to know how many rooms you rented. I've seen rooms enough. Don't say when you kiss me later: Bechu, why is your cheek so rough?'

Nolen titters. The smoke from the burning hair is making all their noses sting. Bhodi's face looks like he's taken a hit on the wicket.

'Can't you mind your tongue? Who'll say you are a respectable housewife?'

'So what will they say? Huh? Ask them. What will they say? A prostitute from the streets? All this temper just because I asked for a glycerine soap!'

Bhodi hadn't anticipated that Bechamoni would burst into tears. Moreover, there's the fear of his father flying within earshot. He might peck at Bhodi's head or slap-flap him with both wings.

'Aah, you're becoming like a child with every passing day. Did I say I won't bring the glycerine soap? Can't you tell when I'm joking?'

Bechamoni carries on sobbing.

'Stop it. No need for such tear-jerking melodrama. Nolen, I'm off. Keep an eye on this little girl. And don't let the hair-burner get away either. Here I was, setting off on an important errand, but no, I must deal with tantrums and tears instead. Glycerine soap! Seen so many fucking glycerine soaps come and go!'

After Bhodi leaves, Nolen mock-admonishes Bechamoni. 'And you can carry on so, Boudi. You know he's got such a mouth. But his heart? You should know that those who have a sweet tongue, no one can tell the poison in their hearts. But Bhodi-dada is the very opposite. He'll sting you with his tongue, but fill you with honey otherwise.'

'I know. Or I'd have left for my father's a long time ago.'

'God forbid! Don't even think such a thing!'

Amid this intimate, transparent and touching exchange, a door is slammed open and the deranged crackpot-type comes out, loudly clearing his throat, a cloth bag hung from his shoulder. At the sight of the hirsute stranger, Bechamoni pulls the edge of her sari low over her head and walks away, the silver bells round her ankles tink-clinking with every step. The crackpot-type survey's Bechamoni's backside out of the corner of his eyes. But this is done routinely by non-crackpot-types too.

The crackpot takes out some cash from his greasy breast pocket. Counts out two twenty-rupee and six ten-rupee notes and hands them to Nolen. From his cloth bag comes the muted screech of glass bottles gently rubbing against one another. Nolen gives back a twenty-rupee note.

'What?'

'That's a taped-up note. It won't work.'

'Where?'

'What's that in the middle? The piece of tape shining right there.'

'Oh, that happens. But it still works.'

'It might. But not here.'

'OK, fine, I'll change it. There's a fight between the master and the mistress, isn't that so? I could tell. Here, take this, it's a fresh note. So, am I right?'

'You see that wooden club leaning against the tagar tree? When I shove that where the sun don't shine, then you'll know what's going on between the master and the mistress.'

'Oh fuck. I said one thing, and you understood something else entirely!'

'I understood all right. You know what happens with the smoke from burnt hair?'

'I don't need to know.' The crackpot leaves without further ado. Nolen bolts the door shut. The airs hums simultaneously with aeroplanes and flying discs. A Boeing-747 pilot is astonished by the frenetic frolicking of the discs in mid-air. He contacts Ground Control at once.

Across this inexplicably supernatural space that frequently overwhelms us with thoughts of endless ephemerality and beckons lightly, 'come, come', just as the Boeings have the right to roam, so do Bhodi's flying discs. If not to make this exact point, still, the poet has written:

> Water and air, earth and fire and sky
> Five elements make up you and I

Not satisfied with this, he went a few furlongs ahead—martyring himself at the altar of equality and writing this so long before Operation Barga:

> Sky and light, water and air.
>     —If every man has the right
> To these, how can Earth be ruled
>     By only a handful's might?

The title of this poem, replete with a militant sentiment, is 'Sabai Bhoomi Gopal Ki'. 'All the Land Belongs to Gopal'. But what is the name of the poet? Can anyone identify that specimen?

(*To Be Continued*)

*11*

If an identification parade for Bengal's poets is ever organized, then, from the vantage point of the flying discs, it will look like a mega procession of ants. A procession so long that when its head is crossing the shadow of the pyramids in Egypt, its tail will still be in front of Thanthania Kali temple in North Calcutta. So many poets have neither been nor will ever be born in any one land again. In that procession march Kanhapada and Bhusukupada as do Rabindranath, Hemchandra, Bishnu De and everyone else. You will also find the poet who wrote 'All the Land Belongs to Gopal'. But in all that pushing and shoving, no one will be able to identify Bijoylal Chattopadhyay. Maybe you'll spot Michael Madhusudan Dutt, or think another looks very like Nazrul, but who will identify Bijoylal? Where is there such a scholar or lover of poetry? They are as endangered as the armadillo or the snow leopard.

Life will increase its tally of mistakes
'Wanting and receiving' unfairly relate

Now tell me, dear child, who wrote that? Can you recognize him? You can't? He is Gopal Lal De.

So many new creations—in the blues of the sky and sea
The poems you wrote
in the stem of the tuberoses' lonely motion

Show me those poems, yours and numberless
You're a poet, I am a poet—and my desire is bottomless

Who is this poet? Alas, alas! It is A. N. M. Bazlur Rashid.

Grab any intellectual of your choosing and ask them: 'Baul breeze blows madly in the mahua forest' or 'the koel's day is long past, now the peacock's cries pierce the skies'—Can you tell, by the scratches of whose pen these lines were etched? Mr Sailendra-krishna Laha has said that this poet's poetry 'does not have the pungency of alcohol but the tranquillity of cool water'. Who is he? This poet whose verse does not have the kick of rum but the tender bubbles of Pepsi? The poet Kalidas Roy did not realize in his lifetime that the title of 'Poet Supreme' would not suffice to keep him alive in the hearts of readers.

Let the mega procession of poetic giants march towards the dentured maw of eternity. We're on duty elsewhere. We better head that way.

Like every year (except the year of the fire), the Kolkata Book Fair in the year 2000 contained no end of ananda and bazaar, ananda and commerce, ananda and ice-cream, etc. If the flag of religion flies on this side of the fairground, then the other offers the intimate biography of a giraffe. Though it is a lamentable loss that despite all that is available, we cannot find *The Mysteries of London* anywhere. The row of policemen on guard at the fair can easily be mistaken for a set of encyclopaedias. Of late, the fair has transformed from a bookfair into a cookfair. Which is what resulted in the blazing circus where fire and smoke performed a clown and trapeze act, respectively. Aided by a fire-brigade truck, complete with a long nozzle and a faulty pump. The eyewitnesses to this incident are divided into two groups. According to one, it was a tragicomedy. According to the other, it was a comi-tragedy. But we cannot afford to lose ourselves in this demo-republican dumb-fuckery.

From the year that *Beggars' Bedlam* embarked on its cursed journey, from that very 1999, the bookfair has been under the hawk-eyed surveillance of Lalbazar's Detective Department. Because, national or international, there are many kinds of scoundrels. Knowing they exist, that they go forth and multiply, one cannot leave a bookfair of this magnitude unprotected. (It goes without saying that such care and surveillance is due to one particular minister's anxiety and fear.) Different detectives perform different duties at the fair. Among them, Golap Mallick—named after the rose—is always assigned to the male urinals. Big and  small posters and notes are stuck to its walls every day, differing in shape and content. It is Golap Mallick's duty to collect samples of them all.

In 1999, on the fourth day of the bookfair, Golap Mallick was astounded by a certain photocopied poster. To the left of the poster, it read:

*The great poet Rabindranath Tagore's words on Sri Ghee*

On the right, it said:

*Santiniketan, Bengal*

Adulteration of ghee as well as that of the liver has now become commonplace and inevitable in Bengal. May Sri Ghee obliterate this anguish and aid Bengalis in staying alive—this is my wish.

Rabindranath Tagore
1 April 1937

Golap Mallick wets the edges with water and peels off the poster with much care, takes it back to police headquarters at

Lalbazar. There, Chief Inspector Daw studies it for a while, then sends it onward to Detective Taraklal Sadhu.

Sadhu tells Golap: 'Look, Mr Rose, this city of Calcutta you have before you, it contains at least 100,000 nut jobs. They themselves don't know that they are nuts. The people who live with them don't know either. They eat and sleep with them daily, and still don't know. They're that stupid, get it?'

'Yes sir. I'm thinking that would make the number of nuts close to 500,000.'

'Of course. And then there are the cretins, the pilgarlics and the complete arseholes. It is our job to smell out which among them are dangerous or agents of a foreign power. Your poster is interesting. This text is not in Tagore's *Collected Works*. But why photocopy a poster? This one must be truly nuts.'

'But, sir, I was thinking, what if it's a coded message? A secret instruction? It could be, sir.'

'I didn't think of that angle. Well done, Golap. But you've put me in a spot now.'

'I mean, there are some smart nuts, and there's the reactionaries too.'

'That's true. I won't take the risk. What do you say? I'll send this upstairs with a note.'

'That's best, sir. In case there's any trouble later.'

Taraklal sends it upstairs with a note. In a file. The file came back a day later. On it, someone had written with a felt pen: 'Pubes'.

After this incident, Golap arrives at the decision that since upstairs does not worry about possible conspiracies or impending attacks, then why should he, Golap, dig up snakes in pursuit of worms? Even a detective as weathered and cunning as Taraklal understood the gravity of the poster. But those above him?

'What's it to me? Whatever I see next, I'll just hand it over. Then the sisterfucks can do what they like. These foreskins are running the country! Had they worked for the British instead! Would've shoved batons up their bottoms and made them dance!'

This realization made Golap very melancholy and morose. It is with that same desolate air that he aimlessly ambled from one urinal to another at the 2000 bookfair. His steps were slow and slothful. At dusk, he had a cup of tea and showed his police pass to the tea seller in lieu of payment. Then he lit a small Capstan cigarette. Just as he blew out the smoke, a toothless man said: 'Got you! Can't slip away now.'

'Eh!'

'Gopal! In front of Tollygunge Police Station. On the concrete bench. Naxal time. Nearly 30 years, but no change!'

'Sarkhel!'

'Yes!'

'Just one mistake. Not Gopal—Golap.'

'Twenty-year gap. Minor mistake. Can happen to anyone.'

'Have you retired?

'Long ago.'

'But your hands . . . those scratches, calluses . . .'

'Oh, that's from digging—' Sarkhel holds his tongue in time.

'Digging? Why are you digging?'

'Oh, gardening. Gardening in earnest. The size of my marigolds, you'd think they were tiger heads!'

'Oh, right. And your missus?'

'Oh she . . . in 1986 . . .'

'Oh!'

They each had another cup of tea. Sarkhel paid. Then he took out a piece of paper from the bag hanging from his shoulder.

'Keep this. I haven't printed many. I'm only giving them out to a select lot. It's free. Read it when you have the time. But—don't take it lightly.'

'So, did you buy anything at the fair?'

'What will I buy? Is there anything worth buying? Only rubbish. Oh, yes, I did find something. I was missing three from my ghost series. Managed to pick them up.'

'Let's see.'

Three books, none more than 40–50 pages. *Man-eating Ghost*, *Thug Ghost* and *Ghost on the Train*.

'Have the ghosts finally caught up with you at this age?'

'You could say that. It's the subject I'm studying now. You must be on duty?'

'Yes.'

'OK, I'll be off then. There are about ten left. When I'm done handing them out, I'll be gone. It's so dusty here too. Remember, don't forget to read it!'

'Of course I'll read it. But when will I see you again?'

'Soon. At this same place. You must read it, brother. I worked very hard to write it.'

When Sarkhel left, Golap Mallick opened up the sheet of paper folded like a grocery list and began to read:

### The Ants Grow Wings
#### K. G. SARKHEL
(Retired clerk, Geological Survey of India)

Everyone knows why the ants grow wings. To fly. When exactly these wings began to grow, that I cannot tell. But based on cladograms developed by eminent palaeontologists, scientists have arrived at the firm conclusion that birds have evolved from the Theropoda suborder of dinosaurs. John Ostrom says that Theropod dinosaurs such as Ornitholestes, Deinonychus and Ornithosuchus, etc., bear a great resemblance to the ancient bird, Archaeopteryx. Palaeontologist Gregory Paul says that once the Compsognathus began to hunt the Archaeopteryx, the latter was forced to take to flight. But I do not agree with this conclusion. The reason being that ancient birds such as the Archaeopteryx (evolved 150 million years ago), etc., became extinct 65 million years ago. What they did or didn't do is impossible for anyone to know. This boundary of death is called the K–T extinction, which means that this apocalypse happened at the boundary between the Cretaceous and Paleogene periods. Brother Reader, you are doubtless aware that you are living in the early period of the Cenozoic era. The wild and flying birds of the Cenozoic era—Archaeopteryx, Apatornis, Paleocarsonis, Hesperornis, Sinosauropteryx prima and the renowned Pterodactyl—were not songbirds like the myna or the cockatoo. Nor were they eagles or vultures. Those unknowable birds were not the kind to flit in and out of our hearts like favourite melodies.

Everything I have said by way of introduction is at once relevant and irrelevant. Relevant, because from this introduction you will understand that flying is an ancient matter. Irrelevant, because why should we worry about when prehistoric birds started or stopped flying? We want to prove instead that humans, without any exhaustive evolution, can fly too. No fossils have been found of flying humans. Nor will they ever be. But there are humans alive who can fly. Not only do they exist, they exist all around us. You must be astonished! I won't reveal everything in this essay. I will only hint at the truth. This is because I don't want the flying humans to be discovered. Or bothered in any way. I only desire that the country and the honourable government (state and centre) be aware that humans can fly. They go by a special name. I even know some of them personally. I do not want this essay to lay it all bare before you. But I, K. G. Sarkhel, am talking about them for the first time here. I will be relieved of this duty after saying a few more things. But Dear Reader, the desire to fly will haunt you like a hungry ghost. You'll look up at the sky time and time again. You'll see the clouds fly past. And you'll want to fly too. Apart from some unfortunates like ostriches and chickens, you'll see so many insects and birds delirious at their ability to fly. Aeroplanes are flying. Satellites are flying. Rockets. Balloons. Even the smoke from the crematorium. And there you are, standing on solid ground, biting your hands in regret. What a great similarity you bear to the dragon-like monstrous lizards of Komodo island! They're on four legs and you, on two. This is why poet Purandar Bhat has written:

> The bees fly, the wasps fly, the hornets fly too,
> If they find your bottom bare, they'll sting you.
> From above, shit-eating vultures shit on your head,
> Bengalis are not only jackasses but also unprotected.

In a country where such magnificent poetry and poet is uncelebrated, where these four lines are not included in MA exams for detailed literary analysis—there, surely the majority of Bengalis will remain land-grazing mammals. How many of us can hope to travel or graze in the realms of ether? Moreover, the realms of ether are not safe. Especially, since the threat of sky-buying is hanging above us like the sword of Damocles. Be that as it may, we have nearly lost our way in the throes of emotion. Let us resume our cannonfire upon the headquarters of the central matter.

I know scholars will raise a ruckus: Humans can't fly. To me, that argument is nothing more than the howls of foxes and jackals. Because K. G. Sarkhel has not entered the boxing ring without evidence. It is not easy to challenge a man like me.

The *Shiva Samhita* says, 'He who masters the elements, and sits in meditation friendless and with a heart devoid of desire—when he focuses on the tip of his nose, his heart is emancipated and he is granted the ability to move freely in the ether.' The *Gheranda Samhita* mentions the Vayaviyedharana Mudra, which grants the ability to traverse the skies. But why go so far? While meditating in his jail cell, our very own Sri Aurobindo once floated off the ground.

This has also happened in the land of the sahibs. Fioretti de San Francesco tells us Saint Francis levitated while meditating atop the mountains in La Verna. This also occurred in the life of Saint Teresa of Avila (Imbecile Reader: this is not Mother Teresa of Calcutta) and in public too. She instructed the nuns to not spread the news. Saint Joseph of Cupertino not only flew but also carried with him a heavy iron cross. The same can be heard of Saint Alphonsus Liguori and the Blessed Thomas a Cora.

But the flying people of my acquaintance are neither monks nor saints. In fact, it will be no exaggeration to state that they are quite the opposite. I've talked about them here because those were my orders, ignoring which would ensure that I would not spend in peace the rest  of my time in this mortal realm. The aim of my freely distributed essay is to give ample warning to the government and the executive powers: an apocalyptic conflict draws ever nearer. No one can stop my acquaintances from jumping into this affray, yelling bloody bedlam. In this faction, there are both flying and non-flying champions. There is black magic. There are illusions. And baby monkeys who can slip into holes of any shape and many sizes. If the government and authorities choose the path of conflict, then I will implore them to remember the title of this essay. If those wings grow, they will not do so for flight. But for death.

*The End*

That this 'The End' is the end of Sarkhel's essay and not that of *Beggars' Bedlam*, does that need to be spelt out any more clearly? Of course, some readers may choose to read this 'The End' as the final death and stop reading the whole thing entirely. They may even issue threats to that effect. One essential feature of the contemporary fashion of writing substandard stories is that every story must have the ability to counter any kind of situation. Whether or not *Beggars' Bedlam* has that ability will be proved soon enough. Wrestling-fan Borhilal's red briefs are drying on the line. The wiener cannon is ready. It is important to warn the readers at this time for their own good. It will be no use squawk-squawking later.

After reading the essay, Golap's first thought was that he must pass it on to big boss Daw the very next day. But then he paused for a moment: Sarkhel was a friend, after all, and written some simply silly nonsense stuff. All his teeth have fallen out, he's an old man. It won't be fair to get him into trouble. This was the decision he was veering towards when he left the fair, but a sudden desire to check out the new, and maybe nubile, girls on the market lured him towards the vast open space of the dark Maidan.

A little way through, Golap thinks he may have miscalculated. Not a saree nor a salwar-kameez, nothing in sight. But the cold has grown more intense since he stepped onto the grass, and in that emptiness, all alone, he is beginning to feel a little scared. He lights a cigarette and plans to get back on the streetlamp-lit road that runs alongside. He is just about to walk that way when this line uttered from a tree above him turns him into a statue: 'Submit Sarkhel's essay to the Detective Department tomorrow, understand?'

Sarkhel gulped and began to chant 'Ram Ram' but that didn't help in the slightest.

'Do you think I'm a ghost that the name of Ram will ward me off? Go show your Ram to Advani. We're much harder nuts to crack.'

'But, sir, who are you? If you're not a ghost, then why are you on top of a tree?'

What swoops down with a whoosh may well be dangerous but is not a ghost. It is a giant raven.

'If only ghosts are allowed to live on trees, then what will birds and bats do? Rent rooms at Lalbazar?'

Golap is rigid with terror. His tongue feels like lead. Beads of sweat dot his forehead.

'Cat got your tongue, eh? Think I haven't seen your dick-swinging and muscle-flexing elsewhere? Drinking tea for free every day, eh? Now, what did I say you have to do tomorrow?'

'Submit Sarkhel's essay.'

'Yes, and not just submit. Tell that Sadhu to write a strong note and send it upstairs.'

'I'll tell him, sir.'

'Why sir? Is this Lalbazar? Also: you're too old now. Quit the whoring. You've whored enough. Got grandchildren at home now, after all.'

'Won't do it again, sir.'

'Again with your sir! If it was the Calcutta of my time, you'd be dead meat by now. Tell me why?'

'What do you mean, your time?'

'You don't need to know. A bunch of thugees came from Burma. Crouched in ambush in dark fields like this. Come a traveller or a stupid pilgrim—and pounce! Pull the lasso tight until the prey is foam-frothing-at-the mouth finished. Then grab whatever they've got and run. Murder a few on nights like this and then—back to Rangoon! Pagoda. White elephant. Now, walk away quietly and go home.'

'I'm going, but I don't know who you are.'

'You can see, can't you—I'm a raven. Older than the trees and rocks. Don't muddle for more. Get out of here. That's best for you, and saves me busting my arse in this cold.'

'I'll do as you say. Please bless me. I can tell you're a great personality.'

'You're right. OK, I bless you. After all, a friend of Sarkhel is a friend of ours. If any arsehole pulls at even one off your pubes, you just let me know.'

'Where will I find you?'

'Very easy. For two consecutive nights, go up to your festering, rat-infested roof and think of me with love. Think of my face. These mad eyes, scabby feathers, these claws that can rip out eyeballs. If you close your eyes and think of me, I'll come right away. Your signal to me will be activated on the first night itself. This is not like your cellphone signal. It's the father of all signals. It's possible I'll be far away when you call. Say, on top of the Bandel Church. In that case, I'll download your signal and come the next day. If I happen to be closer, then I'll come at once.'

'OK, let me take your leave then.'

'Go.'

Big Boss Daw is absolutely alarmed by Sarkhel's essay.

'What is this, Golap, what have you discovered? This is a straight-out declaration of war! Do something. Take it and go to Mr Sadhu. I'll call him and warn him as well. I don't like this, I'm telling you. I don't like this at all.'

Golap takes it and goes to Taraklal Sadhu. Mr Sadhu was busy comparing bullets from a corpse with bullets test-fired from a country-made pistol found at the crime scene.

'Oh-oh, a Golap is blooming in my room today! What's the matter?'

'You don't have to worry about blooming Golaps. Just wait and see what's really blooming. Look at this.'

Sadhu starts to read, and his lower lip begins to droop.

'Interesting! I've got only as far as watching *Jurassic Park* on TV. All this gobbledegook makes no sense to me.'

'Just read the last paragraph.'

Some time passes. Sadhu begins to frown. His forehead creases. His eyes pop.

'What does he mean? A conflict, again? A bloodbath? Is this Sarkhel fucker a Naxalite? No matter, whatever happens will happen. The government and administration have been challenged. I won't take a risk—I'll send it upstairs with a note.'

Two days later the file came back. On top, someone had written with a felt pen, 'Crazy Fuck'.

Begum Johnson hears it all from the Raven. Scratching at the prickly heat on a nearby slave-girl's back, she says distractedly, 'But Mister Magician, this West Bengal government, they are not mature. The jerks received such an important document but did not comprehend its gravity. I am really sorry. The fate of Bengal is overcast with cyclonic depression. Why sadden yourself? Damn it! By Jove, has anyone ever seen such imbeciles who, witnessing a spear charging after them, do not remove their rectums? I am at once bewildered and amused.'

Saying thus, Begum Johnson kicks the slave girl affectionately. And she, in response to this caper, bursts into peals of laughter.

Is this what is referred to as tit for tat?

Does anyone know?

(*To Be Continued*)

## 12

In the preceding squall, i.e. Chapter 11, one matter must not have gone unnoticed by any type of reader, whether the reader be hawk-eyed or weed-eyed. And that matter is the iron-fist-in-a-velvet-glove-style declaration of war by the Phyataru–Choktar strategic alliance. It is as innocuous as a nail sticking out in a shoe, but just as dangerous. However disparaging the comment (Crazy Fuck), made by Lalbazar's detective department about Sarkhel's declaration, the matter wasn't harmless at all.

That this warning would be issued had been decided in a core-committee meeting attended by the Raven, Bhodi, Bechamoni, Sarkhel, Nolen and Madan. The great witness Borhilal had been outside the door, listening to the rise and fall of their discussion with great admiration and recording it all in his head. In the course of that protracted deliberation were mentioned many alluring phrases and topics, such as 'insurrection', 'down with them', 'parliamentary arsebuggery', 'Chittagong armoury raid', 'Tigray', 'Tupamaros', 'death of Carlos Marighella in 1969', 'FARC's guerrilla tactics in Colombia', 'Ashu Majumdar', 'Régis Debray's *Revolution in the Revolution?*' and 'Sushil Dhara's silent march', etc. Since the meeting is a secret, it will not be seemly to divulge further. In fact, it is best that one assumes a 'we know but we won't tell' demeanour. This has double benefits. In the formally declared impending war, *Beggars' Bedlam* may borrow Borhilal's red wrestling briefs and jump into the ring, or, if the wind changes, may start to sing 'I'm a little wildflower . . .' and sidle away into the sidelines. We don't have to move in every direction. But we must preserve the possibility to move in strange directions. In this context, one may examine the douchebaggery of Bengali intellectuals, writers and artists. They do not sing 'Ole, Ole' in the famous yam-filled jungles of Santragachi. They don't even want to be trained in the art of playing 'doctor doctor' like the naughty teenage couples in the shadows of Nalban park. All those jerks are gunning for a large house in Santiniketan, to hang a Gujarati swing-seat in the yard and swing their fistula-ridden, blister-dotted, blackhead-stippled, much-buggered backsides thereupon. Every weekend, all the dumbasses head to Bolpur. Then of course there's also the Poush Mela in the winter, Holi, Tagore's birth anniversary aka worship-the-beard festival, the singing of broken songs to the banging of bloated drums—had Tagore ever realized that the possibility of a full-moon night would be entirely ruined by such a pack of cretins crashing into the forest and polluting the place? Can we do nothing about this? Yes, we can. We can agitate and mobilize the Santhals who are still standing despite years of oppression, use body language to pause the music, then open the bags and set the wild cats free. Even feral ship rats will get the job done. What started with the best of intentions has now devolved into ball-scratchery. Hence, the correct medicine must be applied. A majority of highly conservative Bengalis will be pissed with *Beggars' Bedlam* for this stance. Agent Orange will be released into the air so that *Beggars' Bedlam* does not detox the readers' hearts like a beneficent bacterium. But darling, the dealers of magic discs don't worry themselves over paltry threats from pubes. Thus now will begin the literal decapitations. Long live Mikhail Bakhtin (1895–1975). The uncrowning of false kings is the true revelry of all carnivals and the carnivalesque.

Some plunge to their ruin swiftly,
    some others are slow in their fall
At the end of the road, Hiroshima awaits us all
All our fates end in the crematorium fire
The one constant is You, O Lord of the Pyre
From the heart of darkness, a new creation you will recall

Long live the crematorium. Long live the flying discs. Long live Choktars and Phyatarus. Long live Kumud Ranjan Mullick.

Now let us touch lightly on a delicate intellectual problem. We're not agreed on who is behind it, whether it be ghosts or spirits (not methylated) or cow apparitions, but *Beggars' Bedlam* is increasingly refusing to be governed by earthly time, matter, gravity and fuck-trons. Star German physicist Werner Heisenberg's autobiography is titled *Physics and Beyond*. Due to its ghostly fate, *Beggars' Bedlam* too is being pulled more and more towards this 'beyond'. It no longer wants to be subject to the laws of physics. It wants to break free of the written or printed word and escape into the ethereal. It used to be a housewife, but it may become a harlot. Therefore, Innocent Reader, beware! You need to know the proper rates before you visit those neighbourhoods. From Dhara to Mandu, let the pilgrimage of dunces continue. Our path and destination lie elsewhere.

The glorious and beneficent role played by Lal, Bal and Pal in India's salvation is similar to that played by the nagarpals in the case of Calcutta. That is, the police commissioners. Earlier, they beat up pickpockets; used mysterious balloons to foil opium-trafficking plans in Arakan; sicced violent constable-thugs onto the communists in Taltala and elsewhere and watched the thrashing with glee (especially in the Ranadive era); in the Naxal days, they studied the secret torture manuals of the Israelis, South Africans and the CIA and then instructed their men in those methods. These days, they also find time to attend dance dramas, half-naked orgies, contemporary music programmes, poetry soirees and lie-down-and-draw competitions by sex workers. Some have progressed a few steps further. But we shall not stir the pot lest we find ourselves slapped with a petty case of slander. Readers may grow suspicious about the efficiency of their commissioners. Some wealthy reader may even start to think of themselves as a self-appointed police commissioner. Just as for every post office, there is also an unofficial courier service. There was a time when couriers were only used by terrorists and out-law political revolutionaries. Now, there is a courier service in every home. The more thuggish of them shit regularly on the shoulders of the official post.

A half-burnt, mid-sized carp. Smeared with vermillion from head to tail. One large curved fish-blade, set in a block of wood. A last coil of revolting smoke curling up from a dhunuchi. Eight pairs of eyes—the Raven, Bhodi, Sarkhel and Nolen—awaiting eagerly.

Bhodi's father speaks first, shattering that hellish hush with an otherworldly voice, 'Bob's your uncle! Now, slice the dice!'

Bhodi yells, 'Long live! Long live flying discs.'

All the voices join in. Except Borhilal standing silently with his eye at the door.

Bechamoni decapitates the fish in one sweep, alienating head from body.

The night has just begun.

In that half-bloomed night, in his spacious, second-floor veranda, whiskey glass in hand, Calcutta's police commissioner, Mr Joardar, was wondering if he should hand over the West Bengal People's War and the Maoist Communist Centre's secret infiltration report to the chief minister the next day or if he should keep mum for a little while longer. Suddenly, he saw, like a bolt from the blue, or by way of a more difficult phrase, like a cloudless precipitation (not premature ejaculation), a flying saucer, making non-Bengali noises, dive in a Z pattern onto his beloved lawn. In the interests of safety and security, the lawn is illuminated by halogen lights. By their glow, the commissioner watches the flying disc madly massacre the late-blooming dahlias, hollyhocks and petunias and all his other wonder-flowers. The idea flashed across his experienced, police-trained brain that this must be a remote-controlled toy sent for his cerebral-palsy-struck only son by an uncle in Hong Kong. Is that what it is? Or is it some kind of drone? There is not time for this dilemma to be resolved. For the flying disc, after butchering the lawn and garden, sweeps up to the veranda with a nonchalant whoosh, and with the same silent efficiency with which laser rays accomplish grand tasks, severs his head and disappears into the ether. Dr Guillotine (check correct French pronunciation) would have admitted, if he had been there, that it was indeed very high-quality work.

When such incidents, that is, beheading ceremonies, happen in some Arab nations, we see the head lying stupidly to one side. It is usually the body that flails about. Though once severed from the body, the head may choose to open its mouth, stick out its tongue and make a silly face. The beheading that Uttam Kumar, with his U-shaped haircut, witnessed that fateful, foggy morning on the Maidan, that had involved a police firing first. Many years later, a headless skeleton was fished out of the Manohar Das water tank.

It was 10 p.m., the *Tonight* show on FM radio was just starting to play. Today's topic was homosexuality. But first, a song: 'On this bank I stand, and on the other are you . . .'

The commissioner realizes, astounded, that even after the beheading, everything written in the above paragraphs are in fact his own thoughts, and that he is listening to the radio programme with his own two ears. He's even holding his whiskey glass. He tries to take a sip but the glass slides smoothly to and from the empty space where his head used to be, like a ballerina. Then Joardar puts down his glass, picks up his head and puts it back on in the correct position, and holding it with one hand, downs the rest of his whiskey. The whiskey goes down too. Without any difficulty. But as soon as he lets go, his head falls down. And oh such cruel coincidence, at that very moment Mrs Joardar walks out onto the veranda. She missed the first beheading. But not the second. Needless to say, confronted by this grotesque and macabre sight, she falls to the ground in a faint.

'Loli! Lolita! Uff, fainted. Really, there should be a limit to being dramatic. I'm the one that's lost my head, yet she's the one who's senseless. Look, honey, I'm perfectly normal. I just have to hold on to my headpiece, I mean, my head. Loli! Lo—li!'

Some readers may be reminded of Vladimir Nabokov's *Lolita* (1955). Especially those middle-aged male readers who may unknowingly be a victim of the 'Lolita Syndrome'. Maybe, or may not be or may as well be. Who's to stop them? Is there such a person who can?

Be that as it may, we're talking about Lolita Joardar here. Wife of the police commissioner. These wives are creatures of an entirely different kind of maker. They've spent so long listening to talk of bodies, heads, dacoits, choppers, knives, chopped-up women stuffed into sacks, kidnappings and disappearances that they're no longer fazed by much. In no time, splashes of ice water and a large Patiala peg restores her. She comes to terms with her two-piece husband in a jiffy. Perhaps this is why the Raven had said: Slice the dice!

It's dinner time. Downstairs, the bawarchi sounds the gong. Mrs Joardar is the first to descend. She's wearing an English house-coat. And Japanese grass slippers. Behind her is the commissioner in an embroidered silk lungi and a translucent vest.

But—what's that?

The commissioner is coming down the stairs, holding both his ears with his hands. As though a headmistress is taking a naughty child on a tour of the school. The bawarchis are terribly alarmed at the sight. As they should be. They've often seen the commissioner get a tongue-lashing from his wife. But they'd never imagined such a scene, not even in their nightmares. And what happened just after is bloodcurdling. As the commissioner, spoon in his hand, bends over his soup, his head nosedives into the bowl. A headless body sits in the chair. Two bawarchis and one cook crash to the floor, unconscious. On the carpet land the serving tray, cutlery, roast chicken and gravy.

Mrs Joardar barks: 'What stupidity. You have to adjust your head with your hands! And only then take a sip. Forget that you once used fork and spoon. You can't let go of your ears for even a moment. Tomorrow I'll see if we can manage something with a hat and some string. Deal with your own mess. Spilling soup, scaring the staff—disgusting!'

'Sorry, Loli! I didn't think the head would topple like that. I don't know what's happening! No provocation, no prior report—and I was beheaded!'

'Whatever has happened, has happened. We can't do anything before tomorrow, so there's no point in pointless conjecturing. Hold on to your ears and sit up straight. I'll feed you.'

'You will? That's best. The soup's very bland today. Put some sauce in it.'

'Wait, let me wipe your mouth first. I already have to feed and bathe our son. Now there's one more. My life's been spent in mothering everyone. Never had a moment to think of myself.'

Mrs Joardar said this affectionately, but the police commissioner silently thought: 'You want to think of yourself? Eyebrows plucked to within an inch of their lives, face as round as an egg. And then there's all that stuff you put on it. Face creams from Taiwan! With a butterfly on the jar. And the stink, my god! Fucking beautification! Just the other day I saw Tabu at Taj Bengal. Oh, what a thing! What lips! And look at this one! A cushion. Exactly like a cushion. At least earlier she was younger. It was OK. Bunty, Mrs Sen, the home secretary's wife Himani Shome—ravishing! Even now! Even now. You have to know how to age gracefully. But here—applying kilo after kilo of age-defying cream. Well, all you're going to have is this headless husband. Get it? Bloody cow!'

What he finally said out loud was: 'Ah, you have to cut the fish kebab into smaller pieces—you can't put the whole thing into my mouth! The neck connection is unsteady, don't you get it? Who knows what will go wrong again!'

'I'm sorry, darling.'

'Not even a five-star restaurant can beat Abdul's kebab. I eat it every day and it still never gets old.'

'Just like me. No, darling?'

'Um ... mmm.'


That same terror-filled night, Madan dreams he is being chased across the market by packs of biting fish heads and severed heads of broiler chickens. Catfish, carp, snakeheads and other ferocious fish gape at him, their mouths lined with row after row of sharp teeth. Anchovy heads too. Pecking at his feet. Madan wakes up. Gropes in the darkness for the bottle and gulps down some country liquor and only then feels as though his soul is back in his body. As it happens, on that fateful night, poet Purandar Bhat, clad only in a gamchha and having drunk quite a lot, was sleeping in Madan's room under an improvised mosquito-net tent. Even fast asleep, he doesn't stop writing poetry. Madan brings his ear close to Purandar's mouth and hears, in the style of a devotional song:

> Round Kali's neck a garland of heads
> No clothes upon her, yet glorious, bedecked
> To adore you in the lines of my verse
> I bring you baskets of many more heads.
> Mother Kali laughs with glee:
> I love these heads you bring to me
> Purandar's heart sings
> Five hundred hues sway and swing.
> From the heads you cannot divine
> which the robber, which the swine
> which the saint and which the felon
> which the father and which the son
> I bring you baskets of severed heads …

Madan thumps Purandar a few times. When he realizes Purandar won't stop, he goes back to bed.

That same terrifying night, sleeping next to his fat wife and new-born baby, DS dreams of the film star Helen, dancing, and has a wet dream.

Borhilal sleeps with his underwear across his face because the streetlights stream into his room. He doesn't have a wet dream.

Trembling from the fervour of that restless night, when the moon's spotlight falls on her eyes, Mrs Lolita Joardar sees the commissioner's severed head on the pillow, snoring, while the body has rolled over on its stomach. The body farts. When a mid-curtain of cloud is drawn over the moon, Mrs Joardar sinks back onto the stage of sleep.

After this, the inevitable will occur. Some small fry will no doubt raise the question, 'What is the mystery of the five hundred hues? Or that of the severed heads?' Is it all mere drunken tomfoolery? The first answer to this question is a smirk and a zipped lip. The second answer is: since your parents didn't throw you into the gutter after you were born, and spent money on giving you an education, then why don't you spend 2 rupees and 50 paise on Dr Mahanambrata Brahmachari's *World-Mother Kali's Postulate*, tuck it under your armpits and go home and read it? Out of these two possible answers, which one should we use? If we minus the few small fry, what do the rest of the readers think?

The next morning at 11.22 a.m., the chief minister, via his personal assistant, sends for the police commissioner. He wants to discuss the ISI's terrorist plans for Calcutta. Since these agents frequently set up their hideouts in the jungles and operate guerrilla-style, like that dacoit Veerappan, Forest Minister Bonobihari Ta, the home minister and our old friend, Comrade Acharya, have also been asked to join.

Just donning the uniform won't do: the head needs to be attached to its rightful place. This time, it's Mrs Joardar's acumen that saves the day. It takes just one bellow from her, and the tall motorcycled sergeant hands over his STUD-emblazoned helmet and scarpers. With the helmet on, the commissioner's head stays in place, and moreover, he can freely move his hands. That is, though beheaded, he is not disabled. Just before he leaves, at the doorstep, Lolita gives the commissioner one pink rose and a small envelope, sealed.

'All right, a pink rose. But what's in this envelope?'

Mrs Joardar smiles sweetly. 'After the meeting with the CM, when you're on your way back to Lalbazar, open it then. Not before.'

'What the fuck.'


The CM is shocked when he sees the commissioner. 'What's this? Have you started motorcycle racing or what?'

'No, sir. My neck hurts, I need a medical collar. But I have no time. I've failed to show up for two doctor's appointments. So I'm making do with a helmet for now.'

'How odd you look . . . like those people who go up into space and such?'

'You're right, sir,' Bonobihari Ta pipes up, 'like a pilot.'

'Why must you comment on things you don't know?' snarls the home minister, 'Sir is saying that Mr Joardar looks like a cosmonaut.'

'Same thing. Pilots fly, cosmonauts fly too.'

'Will you two stop? I'll meet the deputy general later. First, I want to hear from you, Joardar. You've roamed the jungles plenty. What's your reading of the situation?'

'Then, sir, let me go into some detail. Ever since the hijacking of Flight IC814 from Kathmandu, I'm observing that—'

The phone rings. The chief minister picks up the off-white receiver. 'Hmm? Union home minister wants to speak to me? Ask him to call later. I'm busy.' He hangs up. 'Nonsense. Go on.'

The commissioner clears his throat to continue, but the bell rings and the personal assistant to the chief minister, Mr Ghosal, enters: 'Sir! Sir! The Miss Calcutta Contest was held yesterday.'

'Not Miss Calcutta,' roars Comrade Acharya, 'It's Miss *Kolkata*!'

'Ah, you interrupt too much. Go on, Mr Ghosal.'

'Sir, all the beauties from the contest have come to meet you.'

'Me? Why? What do they want?'

'Nothing, sir. Today, sir, as they say, is Valentine's Day. They want to present you with some flowers.'

'OK, bring them in. After all, a group of young beauties. Beauty is truth.'

Like a flock of chirping birds, the naughty beauties walk in. The one holding the bouquet of roses is the winner of the Miss Kolkata title—Rosa Kapadia. They give the men flowers, and small smiles, like flower buds, begin to bloom on the ministers' grim faces.

'Joardar, you didn't take off your headgear? It's minimum etiquette. Just because your neck hurts—'

'Yes, sir.'

Joardar clicks his heels, stands to attention and takes off his helmet with his left hand. His head rises up with it while his headless torso extends its right hand for the bouquet. Rosa and the rest of the beauties wilt at once like roses. As though chloroformed, they roll their eyes and, one by one, start dropping to the floor.

'No head, sir!' screams Mr Ghosal, 'Sir, no head! It's a ghost!'

As the head starts falling out of the helmet, Joardar grabs it by the hair with his right hand and puts it back on his neck: 'No ghost, sir. A minor adjustment will fix everything.'

The CM loses his temper: 'Why are you on duty in this state? Beheaded? I'm not going to tolerate this.'

Joardar drops the helmet. Holds his left ear with his left hand, keeps his head in place. Salutes with his right: 'Head or no head, Joardar never falters in his duty.'

'Spoken like a brave policeman but . . .'

Ghosal had left the room, that is, had run for his life. Now he returns with the deputy general in tow.

Comrade Acharya exclaims: 'What's going on? I want a full report!'

He demands a report without actually looking up at the deputy general. The deputy general, just like the police commissioner, is also wearing a helmet.

In the police commissioner's shirt pocket lies Mrs Joardar's sealed valentine's card. A red heart and beneath it, two blue lips. And the signature: 'Love you, Loli'.

(*To Be Continued*)

## 13

13—since the inauspicious and irrelevant 13th chapter has arrived in utter disregard of our will, we may as well welcome it with the skull-splitting dhin-chak-koor-dhin-chak-koor cacophony of a brass band. The intimate reader of history already knows, that be it in the days of dinosaurs, the aeons of amoebas or the epoch of *Homo sapiens*, whenever a noble endeavour has been undertaken, a section of dinos, amoeba or *Homo sapiens*, with no provocation whatsoever and aided and abetted by a few troublemakers, have conspired to ruin it. Therefore, who can doubt that kith and kin of the same kind of misinformation would not be unleashed upon the Choktar–Phyataru–Common Man Combine? In answer to this, valiant Bengalis would have once proclaimed: 'If people are talking, then by Jove, I'll marry.'

That is a bygone era. Now, as the poets say, we live in 'poisonous times'. If poet Bishu Datta had retired after composing only this title, even that would have been enough. But poets never do that sort of thing. That's why he went on to write:

> In the heart of the prison, whose eyes evade sleep's capture?
> We must accept this age, when with its poisonous hands
> It engulfs us all. O poet lost entirely in rapture
> There is no release for us from its demands.

It is not easy to elucidate on this poetic fragment. We cannot mistake a cable fault for a minor load-shedding. After viewing Rabindranath Tagore's paintings, Sri Bimalchandra Chakrabarti had written: 'If I were to try and discern some meaning from his paintings, I would be disappointed. He painted out of joy—there is no other reason for him to pick up the brush.' But not only the experts, even the imbeciles won't agree with this assessment. Why would Rabindranath Tagore set out to paint a truckload of ghostly paintings, as if he had nothing better to do? Paintings that made small children wail in terror? Why? The answer is a simper-smirking mystery hidden deep in the whirlwind of a vortex. Like smoke curling up from a pyre in a long-lost cremation ground. Who can stop the ghostly snapping of necks? Be that as it may, let us not be distracted by such discussions on off-sprouting topics, but firmly grasp instead the muddied game of denouncing these poisonous times. An incident of these times. From not even that long ago. Congress leader Abha Maity, driven by noble intentions, was distributing Milo among the starving people of Medinipur. And snap, the anti-Congress Communists issued a song, to the tune of 'A little girl wanted . . .'

> When Abha-didi's Milo
> Everyone did swallow
> The diarrhoea laid them low
> (repeat) Abha-didi's Milo

That tradition of defamation will not spare anyone, least of all Choktars–Phyatarus. That's why we must be on high alert. We must also broadcast our preparedness. Just as Sarkhel has done before. Bob's your uncle, after all.

It has been a long time since spring has come to Calcutta. Just as Middle Asia, by the grace of the Soviet Union, bypassed capitalism and welcomed an evident and 'true' socialism, so too, if we discount a handful of stupid cacophonous cuckoos, we can assert that, in Calcutta, summer bypasses spring and comes right after winter. And during such a stifling summer, that is, in the heat of March, one poster is seen plastered all over the city. After swallowing up Delhi–Bombay, a half-Afghan sex doctor, for whom nothing is impossible, has landed in Calcutta. This is what the poster says:

```
                SEX DOCTOR!
                SEX DOCTOR!
        Kalifa of the Hakeemi Gharana
                of FarGhana
           Barbaak Kamaal Kabuli
                In Calcutta!

            SEX DOCTOR! SEX DOCTOR!
      After Kabul, Peshawar, Delhi, Bombay
        Last Stop! Last Stop! In Calcutta

             Room 37. HOTEL GOPAL
               95-A Lucky Lane
                 Calcutta 16


          MORNING: General Audience
             EVENING: Special
```

Advertisements with the same message also catch the public's eye in the various Bengali (except *Anandabazar Patrika*), English, Hindi and Urdu dailies. The police have to struggle to contain the enormous crowds during the General Audience. The full responsibility falls on the shoulders of the Park Street Police Station. Total fucked-up case. The Park Street OC breaks out into a sweat just narrating the whole affair on the phone to our old acquaintance, the bald OC in Tollygunge: 'I was doing just fine. Pimps, johns, customers. Catch four or five of them. Knock them around a bit. Catch three or four drug peddlers. Thrash them soundly. One or two pickpockets. Kick arse, lock up. Then out of nowhere this arsehole sex doctor lands up. And everything's fucked. Every morning, masses and masses of people. And the people—fucking pubes—have nothing better to do either. Wizened old bags, barely a heartbeat, but still angling for some action. It's like someone's thrown chilli powder onto my life, I swear. And here I was thinking, us brothers could go hang out at Oly Pub one of these days.'

'But brother,' says the bald OC, 'I've heard the man's a miracle worker. He's giving out a pastry or some kind of preserve! And the results are fantastic. In just one night, the clients are turning into wild cocks. All time on!'

'Is that right, brother!'

'Damn right, and right from a horse's mouth too. I'm wondering if I should pay him a visit late one night.'

'You will? If you say so, I'll make arrangements. Maybe the two of us, quietly . . .'

'Go ahead and set it up. How long's he going to be around?'

'Can't tell. The hotel owner's a Grade-A arsehole too. Even if he knows, he's not telling. If I ask, he says: Look, sir, these are Bedouin people, sword-swashbucklers from the desert lands. Now you see them holding court in a cloud of perfume, sitting on the carpet and smoking a hookah, but then if the mood strikes, they'll pop and fizz and vanish without a trace.'

'Then let's not wait.'

'I won't. But there's a huge rush. All the bosses are coming and going. Bosses from everywhere. If you see the list of names, you'll faint. Who's not on it?'

'We have to find a gap somewhere, and slide ourselves in.'

'Oh, I'll manage that.'

'Yes, and then.'

'What then?'

'What else! Then Bob's your uncle.'

And at both ends of the telephone, peals of laughter bloom. That same bloom of laughter that can wither in a trice. With just a little tap.


The curator of the Victoria Memorial Museum is elated. Because the headless commissioner himself had called to say that tonight, 13 March, he has an exclusive appointment with the Afghani sex doctor at 10.30 p.m. and he is loath to go without his childhood friend, the respected Mr Curator. In their boyhood, sitting atop a dilapidated wall in a burnt-out Shiva temple, they had shown each other their magic sticks. Those sticks had just about begun to twitch, not been firm enough to wrestle in the gladiatorial arena of life's challenges. Oh, those tremors, that warm, fuzzy memory, that innocent homo-play—can that ever be forgotten? It cannot. Thinking of this and many other things, Mr Curator calls his middle-aged professor lady-friend who, despite being a teacher of geography, has entwined herself around the curator through their shared love of literature.

'Am I interrupting you?'

'A class was cancelled and I was just sitting quietly. So all's well.'

'What's well?'

'You won't understand.'

(The sound of deep sighing on the other end of the phone.)

'I understand.'

'Good.'

'Listen, the reason I've called. I've just had an idea. The problem of literature is one of class. If you arrange them on opposite sides, all conflict disappears. No one knows this. I'm telling only you. Because you'll understand.'

'If I don't understand? If it goes over my head?'

'It won't. The way I am thinking about it, it's all happening much lower than the head.'

'I think you're being naughty now.'

'No, no, no naughtiness. I went to a wedding. The food was served as a buffet. And that's where I got my idea. We can look at literature in two ways—veg and non-veg.'


Wearing his red wrestling briefs, small-paunched Borhilal was in his room, doing push-ups before Hanuman-ji's picture, two bricks placed one arm's length apart in front of him. Borhilal does two sets of push-ups every day. Twenty push-ups in each set. That's enough to keep the upper body taut. Then he does two sets of fifty Patiala baithaks each. Jumps ahead, squats and jumps back again. In the old days, this kind of squat was especially popular among wrestlers and bodybuilders. Now it's the age of straightforward squats: sit, get up, sit. After each set, Borhilal takes a sip or two of sweet sherbet and mutters to himself: 'Sex doctor! No upper-body strength, no calf strength, no thigh strength—one chop and they're down—and everyone's rushing to his den. All of them will die of heartburst. Go, take a look at Manohar Aich. Bam, bam, bam, he can smash your rib cage into four. Can you? Even at this age, he can knock the heads of two Afghans together and make them see stars. Can you? Nothing but gimmicks. Like those gyms sprouting up in every neighbourhood. All new-fangled nonsense.'

While he was muttering, a large gecko came out from behind Gobar Guha's framed photograph and went behind Sandow's. Borhilal didn't notice. The cockroaches come to lick the sugary treats Borhilal offers Hanuman-ji every day. That's when the herds of geckos stream out from behind the framed photographs of Gama Pehalwan, Gobar Guha, Eugen Sandow and the female wrestler Hamida Banu. The geckos divide up the cockroaches among themselves by wrestling, both Graeco-Roman and freestyle. If one zooms into this scene, one will understand how dinosaurs settled their differences in prehistoric times. Cinema needs the help of fight choreographers. Without him, all fights are dull. But the choreographer of the gecko fight is God Himself. And the most miraculous thing is that, in this materialistic world, He is doing this without any hope of compensation. He doesn't even wait for applause and accolades. He makes the geckos fight and exults in the joy of his own sport! The tributes that are due to Him, I doubt if they will ever be forthcoming from a race as fucktwat as the Bengali.

In this inauspicious 13th chapter, on the evening of 13 March, Madan and Purandar Bhat grabbed DS from either side and burst onto the scene in a style reminiscent of a few truly great tragedies. Nolen was then cleaning the kerosene lamp. Bechamoni, in a salwar-kameez, was practising her Kathak in the courtyard and Bhodi's father, the ancient Raven, was explaining the ta-ta-dhei-dhei, lochketa-mochketa and suchlike accompaniments and rhythm schemes. Nearby, Bhodi and Sarkhel were talking on the veranda but in such low tones that no one could hear a word. Amid these normal, everyday and rather mundane goings-on, some of the flying discs were sliding back into the room while some others were flying out and disappearing into space with a whir. The big discs make a humming sound. The ones the size of small coins, or bottle caps, or a carrom striker—they screech for a second, then either spin around the room or zoom out and away. Was there any fuel powering the discs? If there was, what kind was it? We will never know. Just as we will never know if anyone, bar Kaliprasanna Bidyaratna, ever compiled the 108 names of Goddess Kali, and even if they did, why is that volume not available today? If Queen Chandraprabha truly killed King Raghunath for being madly in love with Laal Bai. If the builders of the pyramids carried with them any photo identification. Even the veg and non-veg lot most likely don't know the answers to these mysteries, and if they did, they probably won't reveal them in our language. So there is no point in thinking about them.

DS' sudden entrance and loud wailing as if turns the Raven, Nolen, Bechamoni, Bhodi and Sarkhel to mute characters of history. Did Gerasim Lebedev's famous theatre ever create such a moment of absolute stillness?

Everyone is startled. Then Bechamoni wails, shattering the lachrymose silence: 'Oho, who beat you up like that! Your back, all covered in welts. Nolen, bring some ice!'

Bhodi gets angry, 'Ice will do nothing. It's too late for ice. Father, please fan him with your wings. The right cure for the right ailment.'

It must be Atmaram Sarkar's magic! As soon as the wings flap against his back, DS stops wailing. Slowly, the snivelling sobs die down too. A smile even begins to bloom on his freakish, pocket-watch-like face.

The Raven roars, 'Who did this to you? Which arsehole?'

'Po . . . po . . . police . . .'

'Why? All those thieves and robbers and sex traffickers, and they had to thrash you?'

'Ah, I went to the sex doctor from Kabul.'

'What did that whoreson say?'

'What will he say? It was the General Audience, as crowded as a fairground. All the traffic was gridlocked. The officer-in-charge couldn't deal with it, so he ordered a lathi charge. And I was right in front. The more I said, don't hit me, the more they hit me. The more I cried, the more they hit.'

Madan speaks next, and Purandar nods in agreement: 'When I came to know, I said: are the wheels falling off your cart that you're dying to go to a sex doctor? You have a formidable wife at home, just birthed a son the other day, and you need a sex doctor? If it was me, at least that would make sense.'

Purandar says: 'Even if it had been me. Bhodi-da, would that have been wrong?'

'Nothing wrong. Whoever needs it can go. He's come because people go to him. Father, what do you say?'

'I say, why raise a hand against our man? Though DS, you didn't do the right thing. Of course, if you don't consult me, you'll have to suffer being stuck in such holes.'

'What hole, Father? He's a famous man. A hakim from Kabul, after all.'

'Stop spewing words. Kabul is now full of Taliban. This arsehole isn't a doctor from Kabul. Full fake. He's pure Indian.'

'What!'

'I went to Begum Johnson early this morning. One sahib started talking about the sex doctor and Begum broke down, giggling. Do you want to hear what Begum said?'

'Oh, please tell us. This sounds most interesting.'

'She said the arsehole's a total fraud. He's actually an arms dealer. From Rajasthan. Smuggles arms over the border. He's heard that with the election due next year, West Bengal's currently got a great demand for arms. Medicines, those pastries, those preserves—it's all bullshit. The real stuff is Czech revolvers, Chinese rifles, Russian rocket launchers, grenades—he's taking orders, and collecting advance payments. The goods will come later in big trucks, delivered to the right addresses. Understood? There's no way to tell when you see from the outside. He was jailed in Nepal for two years. Then he went to Bangladesh. When he was wanted in Bangladesh, he ran off to Myanmar. From there to Sri Lanka.'

'Begum Johnson knows all this?'

'By heart. And you know what all those potions are?'

'Whatever they are, I've not heard one bad report from his customers.'

'Hmph! There's an Indian version available of Viagra. It's called Edegra or something, and there's a few more too. That's what he's handing out, mixed in with dough. And with it, a combo of Okasa-Mascul, .303 rifles and Silajit. He's calling it yakut halwa. Apparently, it's a Mughal formula. Well, the main ingredient in yakut halwa is the brain of sparrows. And is it so easy to catch that many sparrows, eh? On the highest peak of the tallest mountains, Silajit oozes out of the rocks, like sweat. Crazy monkeys in heat scale those rocks to eat that Silajit. When they've scratched it out of the rocks and are about to put it in their mouths, that's when you shoot them from below. The dead monkeys roll and roll all the way down, and you prise out the Silajit from their claws. Understood? Collecting all this is not a matter of joke. Heritage preserves, yakut halwa—people hear these names and start jumping up and down in a frenzy. Whatever. Since DS was beat up because of him, we need to cut him down to size. Work him over so he never brings his gimmicky arse back to Calcutta.'

With a serene smile, Bhodi says: 'Don't fret and fume over it any more, Father. Please carry on teaching dance to your daughter-in-law, as you were. I'll take care of the sex doctor. What say, Sarkhel?'

Sarkhel chortles.

'Should we arrange something for tonight?'

Sarkhel tilts his head to one side and acquiesces.

'Nolen, the boys have come, make some tea. And quickly, get us some snacks.'

Bechamoni says, 'I'll have a potato croquette.'

The Raven prefers something else: 'Nolen, four batter-fried eggplant fritters, piping hot! Not the cold ones.'

'You don't have to tell Nolen. You carry on keeping time, just like the boss said.'

Nolen walks away, memorizing and muttering the list of snacks under his breath. Bhodi and Sarkhel return to the veranda and resume whispering. Bechamoni wipes her forehead with her dupatta. Then stands with one hand on her waist and the other stretched high above her. Both her ankles are wrapped in little dancing bells. Madan, Purandar and DS sit on one side of the courtyard to watch.

'I like this dance a lot,' says DS.

'Do you know what it's called?'

'Yes, Kuchipudi.'

'Fuck off. This is called Kathak. If you don't have strong legs, this dance will pop them out of your joints.'

'Will you lot shut up?' the Raven snaps.

Then, the lochketa-mochketa—the timekeeping for the dance. Ta-ta ta-dhei, dhei-ta-ra, dhei . . .

On 13 March, at 10 p.m., police knuckles tap on the door of Room 37 at Hotel Gopal . . . knock . . . knock . . . It's the police commissioner and the curator. The door is opened by a severed hand. The commissioner is unnerved but not alarmed, because he himself is wearing a helmet for his severed head. But the curator? How will he endure this hair-raising scenario? A torso is sitting on the couch. The hand that opened the door is sailing effortlessly towards them for a handshake. On the table, the sex doctor's turbaned head is smiling widely.

'Come in, come in, please do take a seat . . .'

Another hand is taking out a spoonful of yakut halwa from a glass jar. Two feet clad in curly-toe shoes walk about the room. The commissioner shouts, 'Ah! Those discs—they're here too! That damned disc devilry again! That cruel flying saucer! Oh god!'

The curator first thought that the room had been turned upside down, that he was afloat in the middle of it, like a balloon. That is not so. As he slowly loses consciousness, the door is pushed open and the officers-in-charge of Park Street and the crematorium-adjacent police stations burst into the room. Both are very drunk, their eyes half-closed. Which is why they don't recognize the helmet-wearing police commissioner.

'Scoundrels! You've even forgotten to salute. How many bottles have you two had?'

The bald OC recognizes the voice and is deciding whether or not to salute. The Park Street OC—thick-headed at best, and now sloshed—shouts: 'Who are you, arsehole, that I have to salute you?'

'What? Who am I, arsehole?!'

The police are quite often involved in occult happenings. Such as making a hale-and-hearty person disappear. The police never claim to know magic. Yet everyone knows that the police are the greatest magicians of all. Then again, sometimes, the police them-selves are subject to magic. About that kind of magic, poet Haribar Sakar has written:

When Lochan Goswami to Jaipur went
The police there a new law did invent
No one is to defecate in the water
Else: jail, or a fine your pocket will slaughter
Goswami wakes up and sets off on his mission:
Proceeds to shit in front of the police station
The officer starts to shake with fury
Roars, 'Grab that man and bring him to me.'
The constable says, when he gets to hear,
'It's stinking sky-high, I cannot go near!'
The officer goes himself, he's hellbent
But is astonished to be greeted by sandalwood scent.

Dear Reader, can you tell who is this Lochan Goswami? Wherefrom did he acquire the magic of transforming shit to san-dalwood? Ta-ta-dhei-dhei . . .

(*To Be Continued*)

## 14

Thanks to Marxism's extensive expansion and proliferation, most readers today are atheists. Religiosity has almost disappeared from the country. Hence, instead of causing further abashment to atheists, it's best to spit it out that the revered Lochan Goswami is a great saint of the Matuya faith. His miracles are innumerable, impossible to record. This is how cynicism is banished. Devotees test their gurus. Gurus allow themselves to be tested. Next is the poet's task of documentation. Which, here, Haribar Sarkar has done and earned our eternal gratitude. Though the question does arise as to why he ever bothered. Nothing should be done for this ungrateful and globalized race, i.e. Bengalis. Let us take the example of *Beggars' Bedlam*. If it had been written in Pashto or Coptic, it would have caused an uproar by now. Even if it were composed in Pali or Magadhi, the result would not have been different. Of course, the writer writes with one intent. But something entirely different happens. Just as it did with the *Communist Manifesto*. We can elucidate this point at a later time. Now, let us turn our attention to the important conversation taking place between Bhodi and Sarkhel on the telephone:

'I called twice. Was wondering what happened.'

'What will happen? I was taking a shit.'

'Ah, I see. Any news?'

'Yes. One rusty sword and two kukri knives.'

'Very good. But no real stuff.'

'No.'

'Baby-dick cannon, sword, kukris! We'll fuck their arses.'

'Whose?'

'Whoever messes with us. Did you soak them in kerosene?'

'Soak what?'

'The sword, the kukris?'

'Why?'

'It will clean the rust.'

'There's no kerosene.'

'I'll bring some tonight.'

'OK.'

'Don't worry, we'll catch them one by one and bugger them all.'

'I'm hanging up.'

'OK, tonight then.'

'OK.'


Almost one Sarkhel worth of dirt has been dug out. But who can say how many Sarkhels worth needs to be excavated for the real stuff to emerge? It may even be that the digging will be all for nothing, and what remains in hand is the shovel. As soon as the beads of anxious sweat break out on Bhodi's forehead, Bechamoni wipes them away with her saree's end. 'What are you so worried about?'

'You won't understand.'

'Whatever I say, it's the same answer: you won't understand, you won't understand.'

'Oh-ho, this is men's business. If I tell you, you'll tell everyone.'

'Do I tell your business to everyone?'

'You don't. But how long till you do? Women can't keep secrets, that's a fact.'

'O my great alpha male! Have I told anyone you keep ghosts in jars and bottles?'

Bhodi realizes that the situation can suddenly slip out of hand. For one, Bechamoni can start bawling. And even if his father the Raven is not around now, he'll hear of it for certain and then there'll be no end of trouble. Why does his father have such a soft spot for his daughter-in-law? It's not as if Bhodi has never wondered about it. Now he changes the subject: 'Did I say so? You went to see your sister in Dumdum. If I was the suspicious type, would I have let you go? I let you go because I trust you.'

Bechamoni swallows the bait: 'Do you know what my brother-in-law said?'

'What?'

'Oi Bechu, how does your man Godi or Bhodi drink sahib-brand booze every day? I've heard he rents out his rooms for all sorts of dirty business?'

'Son of a whore! So what did you say?'

'I said: Brother-in-law, I'm only a homely housewife. What our menfolk drink and what business they get up to, we don't think about that. But yes, if he neglected me or betrayed me, then I'd know. My sister said: See, how you had to be slapped back into place by your sister-in-law? It's not for nothing people call you a shit-eating scumbag.'

'Good! Well said!'

'My own sister! Doesn't she know that he cheats on her twice a day? Your son is married, soon there'll be grandchildren and there you are—'

'Ahaha, don't bring up all that now. You should know, above all vices is the Vice of Woman. If that virus gets you, you're as good as dead. It'll bankrupt you, make you sell off even your mattress. My stomach feels gassy. Can you put a poultice on it?'

'Does it hurt? You gobbled up all that spinach and prawn curry ... I knew right then ...'

'You know nothing. Sarkhel and I are going to open a big business. That's why I'm so gassy. Once it takes off ...'

'What's going to happen when it takes off?'

'When it takes off? Say, you suddenly want to go to Bally or to Puri, or to Vrindavan and Mathura. Then you won't have to go to Howrah Station and board a crowded train.'

'Then?'

'You'll go from your own rooftop. Get dressed and go up. You'll see a large grasshopper-like thing. Waiting for you. A helicopter. All the ministers and politicians use them to fly about.'

'Yes?'

'Yes! When Bhodi Sarkar starts playing the game, then all those bastards will run around, trying to hide their arseholes. I'll bugger any that comes before me.'

'Is that any way to talk?'

'That's the whole truth. If you're afraid of being fucked, then don't come to the fight. You're good, I'm good too. Long live the world. Mix it up, O Mother! Just once, mix it up real good.'

At the time of this conversation, Calcutta's famous jeweller V. D. Dutta had arranged for a star-studded soiree. This eye-popping event was taking place at the Kala Mandir auditorium. That auditorium has a baby auditorium in the basement. Where a musical programme of Tagore's songs was currently underway. In the auditorium upstairs, the stage was packed with luminaries from the worlds of football, history, cinema, journalism, cookery, fashion design, pedicure, philosophy, politics, dog breeding, etc. Three or four television channels had their cameras rolling. Just then, a man walked on stage wearing a freshly pressed silk kurta and a fine dhoti. It was DS. Grabbing the microphone from the anchor, the mysterious Miss M, he began to speak: 'I've arrived. The flight from Mumbai was an hour and a half late. The flight had a bomb. The dog sniffed the bomb out. A whole lot of trouble. But where's the chair for me to park it? Chair! Bring a chair, bastards! Cha—ir!'

A chair arrives with astonishing speed. Everyone's stunned. Miss M smells Rasa-brand country liquor on DS' breath. And bam! it hits her right in the ego.

'This stage is full of heavyweight honchos. At least, that's what you lot think. But they're all riffraff. Hacks. That one that's come to bugger history, he's the curator of the Victoria Memorial. Look at his face! Gulping down that acid reflux. Why, you ask? He's worried I'll show you just how much shit is stuck to his arse. What, shall I? What were you doing yesterday afternoon?'

As the curator slowly collapses in his seat, the others around him start to grow restless with fear. The audience begins to rumble and roil. The police approach. The Park Street OC shouts: 'Who are you? Have you been invited?'

'My name is DS. Foremost authority on sex studies. I piss on invitations. Anything else?'

Utter chaos erupts in the auditorium. Only the TV cameras remain focused on DS. The lights go out. Pandemonium. A woman screams. Some people start fighting. Sounds of slaps and punches and kicks. They're breaking the auditorium seats. The police and ushers' flashlights come on. And by those beams of light, they see DS flying high up in the air. Via the cordless microphone he's holding, DS' stereo voice booms out of the sound system: 'Now you arseholes know who I am? I am DS. Everyone, buy a copy of my book *Kokh Shastra* at once. You'll learn what the Koka Pandit told the king of Kashmir about males and females. It will change your life. There are four types of Kaminis, or female sexualities. Every woman is one type or another. Each type needs a different treatment. Oi arsehole OC, what are you going to do with that flashlight—catch me?'

The lights turn back on for a few seconds. Not only the foremost authority on sex studies but also two other men, that is, Madan and Purandar, are flying, and a gigantic raven. The lights go off again. From above, in that unfamiliar darkness, three streams of warm liquid start to trickle down, splashing, splishing, drizzling, indeed pissing down, and the lights turn on and off, on and off again . . .


This time, the story of Calcutta's regime change was not relegated to the gossip column of an obscure Salt Lake daily. Even the chief minister had to stir, take note. The beheadings of the police commissioner and the deputy general were not unknown to him, nor the tragic tale of the sex doctor's many bits and pieces. It is true that he did not give these incidents as much importance as he should have. Future historians will perhaps point to this as one of the distinctive features of his time in office. Some others might say that there was no organized attempt to bring the various events of this time within Marxism's inevitable orbit. If there had been, history could have perhaps used the stairs to climb up instead of a rickety ladder. It's far easier to run away with a ladder than it is to move a set of stairs. Some may even ascribe blame to a genetic deficiency inherent in the Bengalis. The incident is one, but the explanations are many. One solution to this multiplicity of explanations and excuses is: cloning. If all historians could be killed off and only one cloned, then all this trouble would end. But neither the state nor the centre has that kind of unlimited power. It is this realization that prompted Goebbels to say that the state should have the power to break its own laws. Culture—apparently this one word was enough for the gentleman to start twitching for his revolver. The man was a total scum-type. But let no foolish reader calmly talcum powder their armpits, safe in the knowledge that all such men have left the world. The game's still afoot. After the first tremor will come the aftershocks of Kashi-Mathura. Of Treblinka, the concentration camps at Buchenwald. Of the gulags dotted around Siberia. What did you think, darling? That life would go on with its Son-in-Law's Day and little male-female play and the sweet milk pudding at baby showers? Destination: 1960s Belgharia, where Inu Mitra rules as Congress muscleman? That prospect is as ruined as jaggery dusted with a sprinkling of fine sand.

We'll cast a glance at a few random occurrences at Writers' Building and then leg it towards the permanent exhibit. Any major (or major general) novel's novelty lies in its pacing. A ready example, being passed from hand to hand, is Milan Kundera's *Joke*. But that too contains an interesting fact. In the foreword, the one whom Kundera calls the great novelist, that famous poet Louis Aragon has been read by very few. Go figure!

A white, bullet-proof Ambassador car was coming out of Writers' Building, the chief secretariat of the state government. In it were the chief minister, the home minister (we've previously seen him being heckled by Stalin) and the chief minister's personal secretary Rakheykeshto, whose only job was to record the minister's every waking moment on a handheld camera. The Ambassador was proceeding fairly slowly, when suddenly a slim, RayBan-wearing sergeant held up a hand. The car stopped. Everyone was astonished. A very annoyed Comrade Acharya lowered the car window and roared: 'What's the matter, Comrade Sergeant?'

Comrade Sergeant turned. A young sahib. His lips still reeking of fresh milk from the cows of Derbyshire. His moustache sparse, like a young lad's. This is what he said: 'Native, sit quietly. First goes the white man, and then the chattel, yes? If you are naughty, you will get the baton, do you understand, you filthy scumchild?'

On this sensational scene, the volume is slowly turned up; ring-ring ring-ring, clip-clop clip-clop, whip-whoosh whip-whoosh, creak-creak—just like a horse-drawn carriage. Begum Johnson. Miss Sanderson. Miss Emma Wrangham. Mr William Sleeman. That infamous kick in the punkhawallah's arse. That mating season for missy-baba's dogs. Those pig-headed sahibs' duels and their near-misses. Mutty Lall Seal's bottle-and-cork trade. The cacophony of torch bearers, grass cutters, khansamahs, khidmatgars, hookahbardars, gardeners, water bearers, dhobis and ayahs. The threats from Bhutanese and Afghan Rohillas. And in the end, a white Ambassador car. Bullet-proof.

When the mighty nation stirs, then even the most lifeless of objects must stir too. The state coming to its senses is no different. If the central government doesn't see fit to stir, the regions cannot afford to follow suit. That's why Golap Mullick is told that the two files he had sent upstairs a few days ago and a year ago, which had been returned with the words 'Pubes' and 'Crazy Fuck' respectively, need to be unearthed, the two remarks either erased or blotted out with dark ink and sent upstairs again and that this order is of the utmost urgency. Golap takes this order to Sadhu and the following conversation takes place:

'See sir, what full-fuckery! Remember those two files? Then those arseholes didn't give a shit, but now they want them again!'

Taraknath Sadhu was at that very moment engrossed in a book titled *Death by Poison: Then and Now*. He smiles and tells Golap, 'Not potassium cyanide, not even phytotoxins—just an overdose of saffron is enough to finish someone. What do you think, Golap?'

'But they put saffron in biryani!'

'Correct! You hog it every chance you get. Don't have any more ever again. Maybe the cook adds a bit too much by mistake. No motive for murder, but you pop off anyway.'

'Fine, I won't have any. But what do I do about the files?'

'Which files?'

'Oh, the one with the Tagore advertisement and the—'

'One with madman Sarkar's nonsense, right?'

Golap realizes that even a seasoned investigator like Taraknath can slip up—he meant Sarkhel when he said Sarkar. And by way of the tail-end of that realization, a tragic thorn pierces Golap's heart—poor Sarkhel! Widowed, toothless Sarkhel. Sarkhel whose marigolds are bigger than tigers' heads. Now the police will beat him to a pulp.

'Yes, sir.'

'From the time you took to say that, I can infer that you're really worried. Don't be afraid. Take your time and find them. Since the big boys have asked, they must have it. But it's also true that files don't grow on trees. Buried in dust, and such huge stacks of them. It'll take some time. But since they have asked, best get started.'

'That I will. But tell me, they sent them back like that! I can guarantee they didn't even look inside. Is that fair?'

'The more I read, the more confused I am about what's fair and unfair. Everything is tangled up. Saffron in biryani—can't trust even that. How many more years for you?'

'For what, sir?'

'Retirement, what else?'

'About five more.'

'You'll suffer. I'm out next year. Whatever—get on it. Let it take time, I'll deal with it.'

Taraknath Sadhu returns to *Death by Poison*. Golap thinks he should go up to the roof and summon Father Raven. Why not even go to Kalighat and warn Sarkhel?

The next day, Golap found both files. Blotted out the remarks with black ink. Sadhu sent the two files upstairs.

But the trouble started when they were opened.

One file had contained Tagore's famous words on Sri Ghee. It goes without saying that those words were not there any more. Instead, there was a poem, or rather, a fragment:

. . . all that remains in sum
In the posy-filled park
In the greedy, hairy heart
Is a mega-bashing of the bum.

And in the second file, that used to have Sarkhel's essay, there was a photocopy:

(5 March 1838)

Delhi. We have learnt that when news of Raja Rammohun Roy's demise reached the court of Delhi's badshah, every courtier was dismayed. Notably, Mirza Silling and his coterie stated that the three hundred thousand a year increase they had been hoping would come through the good works of the Raja would not materialize. But they further vouchsafed that they would not despair, for the government had sworn to the Raja that it would pay the aforementioned monies, and the death of such an illustrious man would surely not deter the government from keeping its word.

The rattled bosses of the Detective Department were not just nervous, they even suggested to Sadhu that since the arrows of their suspicion had landed on Golap, they would like to grill him. Taraknath, in answer, sang the lines 'Then why doesn't the murdered rose get justice ... No bite to your bums but want to shit on the world? I'll see how much fur each one of you has down there! Just touch Golap once and see what I do. He's the one who found it all: Tagore's ghee company, Sarkar's ultimatum. Yet who wrote "Pubes" and "Crazy Fuck" on those files like a prize arsehole, huh? You lot! Grill him, huh! Spent my life messing with murders and corpses, and now a few fuckheads pop up from nowhere and say they'll grill Golap. I'll raise hell. Lalbazar, Ministry, Intelligence Bureau—I'll bring down the apocalypse. You want to see? Should I tell the Association your plans?'

'Ah, Mr Sadhu, you are needlessly excited. Actually, we didn't mean that exactly.'

'Listen, let me be clear, I am Taraknath Sadhu. When you were drinking baby formula, I was scratching my armpits with a .303. Be careful! If anyone touches so much as a hair of Golap's privates, I'll set this place on fire!'

'Fine, so be it. Let Golap be as he is. No one will tamper with him. But the original content is gone from the two files and new content come in—what do you have to say about that?'

'I'll say magic and mystery. Till I have evidence to the contrary, I'm going to keep mum. But Golap knows nothing about it. Poor man. All the files were in my office. Why don't you blame me? Grill me instead?'

'How many heads on our shoulders do we have, Mr Sadhu?'

'I used to think you had one, but I can see you're growing one too many these days.'

Taraknath slams the door on his way out, and the heads of the Detective Department sit with faces like rudely rejected tomcats. If they had survived an encounter with Dumdum bullets, their faces would not have looked any different.

The shadows gather. Through every bush and hedge slithers the winds of endtime. The moon, like a half-eaten cake. The moonlight, black with grime, wilted. The tropical jungle hums with insects. Golap Mullick arrives on Sarkhel's doorstep. He can hear a faint 'clop clop' sound. His experienced ear tells him the sound is worldly, not supernatural.

Softly, Golap calls: 'Sarkhel? Sarkh—el?'

At once the clop-clopping stops. Golap takes two steps forward. And stops in his tracks, a harmless statue. Because something is poking into his back. Not moving an inch. And now a warning: 'Don't move. If you move, you die. Put your hands up . . . up!'

Golap puts his hands up. A flashlight shines into his eyes. Behind it, the blurred outline of a figure.

'Arrey, brother Golap! Oi, you, put down the sword! Couldn't you hear, he was calling me by my name? He's my friend. You haven't poked-foked him, have you?'

'Not yet. But if you'd been any later . . . My hands were shaking. Maybe I would have—'

Golap finally speaks: 'Why was your hand shaking? Aren't you used to swords and scabbards?'

'Of course I'm used to them. I'm used to everything. But this one's from the Mughal era. That lot used to be six, six and a half feet tall, more than ninety kilos heavy. This stuff wasn't made for our hands.'

Sarkhel takes Golap into his room. Sarkhel is wearing only his underwear. His skinny body is covered with sweat and dirt.

Golap says, 'Were you gardening?'

'You remember? I was gardening and also preparing for the rebellion. Did you read the essay?'

'Didn't I? Very clear-cut. So you're certain there's going to be a war?'

Bhodi says: 'What do you think? All these swords, baby-penis cannon, rifles—for nothing?'

'Baby-penis cannon?'

'Portugese cannon. Small-sized, you can even call it small-fry cannon. Very effective between ships.'

'Shut up. So, tell me, brother Golap, why are you here?'

'I came to warn you. That essay you wrote . . .'

'Understood. I gave it to you precisely so you could pass it on to the bosses. So, what did the jackasses say? Their bottoms must be shrivelling up with fear?'

'At first, they didn't even bother to read. Can you imagine that? Now, suddenly, they sent for me. I gave them the files. But it's not the same stuff any more. Some nonsense about Ram Mohan Roy dying, etc. . . .'

'How can it stay the same? If you open the file now, you won't find Rammohun either. It'll be some other stuff. If you close it and open it again—again new stuff. I'll mess with those motherfuckers so much, they'll forget to wash their butts after a shit.'

The Raven's voice. He sits by the broken window and flaps his wings. Once.

'Dear Lord? You?'

Golap walks over and respectfully touches his forehead to the Raven's claws.

'What's up? My beautiful Golap-flower is looking a bit wan.'

'It's nothing, O lord. The bosses at the department were jerking me around. Now they're quiet again.'

'So they are. You're under our protection. Whoever fingers your arse, we'll blast theirs wide open. Speak.'

'O lord, I'd come to warn Sarkhel. But if you indulge me, I want to tell you my heart's desire.'

'Speak. Bhodi, listen carefully. You're too distracted.'

'No, Father. I'm paying attention. You didn't mind, brother Golap, did you?'

'No, brother Bhodi, such things often happen in rebellions. What is there to mind? O Lord Raven, I too want to join your team.'

'Join? You have already joined. If you were not one of our own, why would Sarkhel give you that essay?'

'The goings-on in Lalbazar, who's plotting what—I'll report everything. I hate the whole damn lot of them.'

'Of course you will. You are, after all, our very own Golap. Bhodi, Golap has enlisted with the rebellion. Won't we entertain him a little?'

'Oh Father, does that even need to be said? Brother Golap, what will you have? Country or foreign?'

Sarkhel pipes up: 'Don't be shy. Everything's free and frank here. I'll go wash up. Gardening all day ... not easy.'

Golap joins in with gusto: 'Foreign, then.'

'Sarkhel, tell Nolen on the phone.'

'OK.'

'One day I'll come and see Sarkhel's flower garden.'

The Raven chortles. Bhodi says nothing. Sarkhel comes back, all cleaned up. Nolen brings a bottle of rum, glasses and fried black peas. Such a warm and intimate air envelops them all.

Before the Great Revolt of 1857, was the country's mood also so warm and intimate? That is, right before the First War for India's Independence? O Marxist Reader, have you read *Bengalis in Rebellion*? Oh, do tell!

(*To Be Continued*)

*15*

Why should you read *Bengalis in Rebellion* at all? If you do, you might come to know how diligently the Bengalis brown-nosed the British during the Great Revolt. But no, you'd rather read Foucault, who, in a manner of speaking, has saved us. There-fore, the great responsibility of awarding punishment and teaching discipline to our readers has fallen on the shoulders of the great and powerful *Beggars' Bedlam*. But *Beggars' Bedlam* is no rebellious bull that, red-eyed, will drop its yoke and join the revolutionary coachmen in their manic pre-capitalist dancing. That's why, we (that is, *Beggars' Bedlam* and its readers) only need to know the mystery of the wax paper; let that 318-page manuscript remain unknown as it has thus far. It was the work of British spies. 1857: 'Lest the young men are arrested midway on suspicion of being spies, they secrete the letter within their bodies. Even stripped naked and their clothes turned inside out, the letter will not be found. Of course, the letter was not hidden in their mouths. The letter was wrapped in wax paper and slid up the anus. When required, the young men could slide out the package, relieve them-selves and then put it back in the same place. It is horrible indeed, but in the time of the Great Revolt, such horrible courage was the mood of the times.' Through a certain lens, Bhodi's business is also one of revolt. Therefore, philosophers may find resonances. There is no one to stop them. Durgadas Bandyopadhyay (author of *Bengalis in Rebellion*) has written at the end of his autobiography, *The Great Story*: 'Once again in Bareilly the English rule. My heart is stunned. Thus today I end my life's story here. The rest of it is not worth committing to paper.' What a great realization and such a candid admission. What control! Many fuckwit jackasses secretly harbour a desire to write their autobiographies. Some of these geniuses have indeed written them. Even had them printed and published. About that, there's really nothing to say. The road that great men ride on elephant back, the jackasses want to take a howdah down that same road. But these days we are a little short on the supply of elephants. Oh, if only Netaji Subhash Chandra Bose was still alive!

The pocket watch that DS took to Radhabazar to be fixed ended up flummoxing even the most seasoned of watchmakers. No one had any parts for that grotesque watch, much less the spring.

'So you're saying you can't fix it?'

'I'm not the one to fix it, everything depends on the Almighty. But chances are slim. None of the parts are available any more.'

'Belonged to my grandfather, should I just throw it away?'

'No, no, why will you throw it? Keep it as a souvenir. It's an antique piece, no one understands the value of these things now.'

'But the damn thing's not working. Can't you suggest something, anything?'

'There's nothing to suggest. Though yes, middle-aged, crazy white men sometimes come to buy such antiques. You'll see advertisements in the paper. Old toys, gramophones, clocks, pens . . . that kind of thing. You can make big money if that happens.'

'Do they advertise in the Bengali papers too?'

DS steps out of the shop and slips the watch into his pocket. Purandar says: 'You know you'll never sell it. Won't fix it even if it can be fixed. You really can blather on!'

'What's the time?'

'Was 2.30 p.m. in the shop.'

'Right. And Golap will come at 3.15. We have to pass the time. Forty-five crisp minutes still to go.'

'What's the point of walking all over town? My legs are killing me. Let's find a tea shop to sit in.'

'If the palanquin is yours, so must be the bride. You pay for tea, then.'

'Fine. You're becoming more of a skinflint every day.'

'It's not that. Just running low on cash. You never had a family, children. Spent your whole life writing poetry . . .'

'I don't write poems any more. Did you know.'

'What do you mean?'

'Means I don't write poetry any more. I gave it up.'

'What?'

'No fuckers read it. No fuckers want to print it. What's the point of writing that crap?'

'What will you do then?'

'I'll write songs. Songs are very popular now. Don't you see the heaps and heaps of cassettes? Any arsehole these days is farting out an album. That's why I'm going to write songs. There's a ready market. I've written one already. Do you want to hear it, over tea?'

'Are you going to sing?'

'No, no, I'll read. The tuning comes later. Then the music for the start and end. When the thing's ready, the singer will sing it.'

The tea shop Purandar and DS are sitting in has a giant framed photograph of Goddess Santoshi Ma. Talat Mahmood's mellifluous voice wafts out of an FM radio. People are drinking hot tea from dirty cups and eating cold nimkis. Drivers are smoking biris and abusing the hell out of their employers. An old man, hunched on the footpath, is wearing black surgical sunglasses and sipping tea. His pockets are full of greasy papers and a single ballpoint-pen refill. Purandar and DS order two teas and stand a little distance away from the old man. Purandar takes out the song from his pocket.

'What kind of song is it?'

'Folk. Just listen to it. The lyrics are enough to convey the mood. All right, all right, I'll tell you anyway—it's a song for fisherwomen. It's night, and a flock of fisherwomen are going hunting for fish.'

'Unbelievable!'

'Yes. Now, listen:

In the backwaters of the snakehead, the carp dives for its kill
We're going fishing, O brother, in waters deep and still
She drops her veil, her bodice she rips
The chameleon starts to paint her lips
Salmon hogging, hilsa noggin, carp as big as crocodill
We're going fishing, O brother, in waters deep and still
We're the ghouls who wait in the shadows
Feet turned around, heels in place of toes
We fry our fish in their own fat and eat them with such thrill
We're going fishing, O brother, in waters deep and still.'

'Fan—tas—tic! Fantastic, boss, but towards the end it sounds like they're ghosts.'

'Not ghosts. It's a metaphor, a feeling. They're calling themselves fish ghouls to emphasize the aquatic ambience. Understand?'

'OK, but who's going to sing it? Oh, Asha Bhonsle would have sung it so well, and added some of her trills of laughter too!'

'No point thinking about that. It's my song, so its future is inevitably dark. Some chit of a girl will sing it, who else? In this market, without some support from CPM or Trinamool or at least some big-belly benefactor holding you up on a stick, you've no chance.'

'I don't believe your future's entirely dark.'

'Why not?'

'Well, you've become a Phyataru, haven't you? Made friends with the Choktars. Then there's the talking raven, the flying discs, Bengal liquor in the a.m., English liquor in the p.m.—how many people have so much?'

'I hadn't thought of it like that.'

'You're getting it without asking for it. That's why you're not thinking of it. That's why my wife says no one cares for something if it's free.'

'She's right. Good you said so. I promise I won't think this way any more. Uff, just now a song's sparked in my head.'

'Is this one also about fisherwomen?'

'No, no, it's your college-going, urban young woman's song. I've got only the beginning. Do you want to hear it?'

'Go on!'

'Neither a sister-in-law, nor a wife
Rather be a government ayah for life . . .'

'Hot stuff, boss! Now you still have knife, rife, strife and house-wife to rhyme with.'

'I won't need the housewife, unless a bed or sofa enters the scene.'

'Look, there—over there!'

'What?'

'The paan shop across the street!'

Its Golap. He buys a paan and puts it in his mouth. Bites off the end of the betel stalk and spits it out. A small ball of paper falls to the ground.

'Golap will now go back to Lalbazar. I'll pretend to scratch my leg and grab that paper. You'll guard me.'

'Should I scratch my leg too?'

'Are you crazy? If they see two people scratching their legs, all the spies will be alerted. They're everywhere. Let's go. Otherwise, some son of a bitch will kick it into the gutter. Many people see a lump of paper and think it's a ball.'

Spies share a close-knit, secret world. A world that is the playground of many spy agencies across the globe. CIA, KGB (currently FSB), MI5, Mossad, the extinct Stasi, ISI—no one knows how many of these toddlers are horseplaying in their knickerbockers in this mysterious sandpit. That the Choktar–Phyataru faction is not far behind in this innocent game cannot have eluded the reader. Bhodi unfolded the lump of paper. Written on the back of a printed handbill is: ALL M AND CT UNDER I

'Hmm-hmm, brother, the name is Bhodi, after all. Mess with me, will you? Where's Nolen? No—len?'

Nolen thuds down the stairs from the roof.

'Set this paper on fire. Watch till it burns completely. Then make a large peg of Bangla and rum punch. I knew the plot would thicken. Thicken to yoghurt, in fact.'

That night itself, Bhodi, the Raven and Sarkhel convened a special core meeting. Lalbazar detectives have started keeping a keen eye on the prostitutes and country-liquor joints. It turns out that Sarkhel doesn't quite grasp the gravity of this.

'We don't go to brothels, we don't even drink country liquor. We aren't beset by that particular lice. So why would they bother us?'

'You utter so much bullshit right at the beginning that it makes my head explode. Hitler must have had a major general like you by his side, that's why he lost his headpiece! Unthinkable! There should be a limit to this dumbfuckery.'

So far, during this strategic discussion, the Raven had been standing on one leg and scrawling in the air with the other. Sensing that Bhodi was on the verge of rage, Sarkhel changed the subject and addressed the Raven instead: 'What are you writing, my lord?'

'Oh, nothing. Doodles. Whenever I feel that war is looming, I doodle. Stalin did too, he drew foxes.'

'And you?'

'No subject in particular. Sometimes ghosts, sometimes turtles, sometimes fighting scenes. Bhodi's wonderful, but he's got a short fuse. His grandfather was the same. It's popped up again in the third generation. Have you heard of Gregor Mendel?'

'No, sir.'

'He discovered it, in 1865. Eight years after the great Indian revolt. Some day I'll tell you all about it. A jackass called Lysenko tried to fuck with Mendel. Stalin also got overexcited and finished off Nikolai Vavilov. And voilá, shit hit the fan. You know nothing. And how would you know! In the country of asses, the jackasses are the leaders. Just like your leader is Bhodi. If both your arses could be polished four times a day with some of that fine sand from Magerhat, maybe you'd grow a bit smarter.'

'No, no, O lord, please don't punish us so hard.'

'OK. I won't. Now, say what you were going to say. But if I see you bickering again, I'll really lose it!'

'Hand on my heart, won't happen again.'

'Fine, go on then.'

Just then the sound of an explosion outside the gates startles them all.

'Who? Who's there?'

'Me, Nolen.'

'Why? What do you want?'

'Boudi said: "The generals are scheming and strategizing, Nolen, go give them a bottle of booze." That's why.'

'Good, come in.'

Nolen enters with a bottle of Bangla and three small glasses on a plate. One large jug of water. Shrimp fritters.

'What burst outside? Did you fart?'

'No, sir. I stepped on a cockroach—it burst.'

'Oh, I thought it was a toy gun. Close the door behind you and tiptoe out just as you came.'

Nolen tiptoed out just as he had come.

'Father, listen. Sarkhel, pay attention. It's only the start of our rebellion, but we have fucked them over. The fear of death has entered those sons of bitches' arses and messed up their brains.'

'Elaborate.'

'One, the flying discs have played havoc with their heads. They can also tell that Sarkhel's ultimatum is not to be taken lightly. Add to that the AK-47 factory, the dickhead curator—all together, it's a helter-skelter case. They can tell something's coming but they don't know what. They're fatheads, after all, their grey cells are on strike inside those headpieces . . . they think common criminals are ganging up on them, that's why they are monitoring the P and the CL—that is, prostitutes and country-liquor joints . . . that's such a low-level response . . . if only that was enough to stop a rebellion. Fuckwits, pure fuckwits. But hats off to Golap. He's a true spy.'

'Uff! Now I finally understand. O lord, we have indeed chosen the right leader. Don't you think so too?'

'As a father, I can never praise my son. That kind of fuckery is not part of our family tradition. But since they've taken a step, I want us to take a counter-step and show them that we don't give two pubes about them. Bhodi will decide that step. I just need to down one stiff peg and get out of here.'

'Why, O lord?'

'I shouldn't say, but you're as good as little babes in arms. It's all right if you know. Today, at Park Street Cemetery, Mr Sleeman and Mr Sherwood are going to duel it out. I'm refereeing.'

'Well, sir, what is the master race fighting about?'

'That same age-old fad: Miss Emma Wrangham. The same bickering all over every page of history. And every street in every land. All the dogs barking over one bitch. If by chance an old dog passes by, he'll also whip out his gun and join the fight. This will happen in the future too. No way to stop it.'

'O lord, your Mr Sleeman, and then, what's his name, oh yes, Mr Sherwood—they've been dustified for centuries. Yet their bhoots are still fighting?'

'You can't call the sahibs bhoots—you have to call them ghosts. Am I right, Father?'

'You are, though these days if we call them white bhoots, I don't see them minding too much. But it's getting late, and the pistols are ready. Miss Wrangham is fainting frequently. How will Begum Johnson cope all alone? Goodbye.'

Raven spreads his giant wings and flies out of the open window into the ghostly darkness to referee a duel. Reader, with an open heart, look outside the window where things are beyond earthly rules. You too shall see the same dewdrops falling like the notes of a piano, as they used to fall then. Small flowers blooming in the grass. As they bloomed then. Lose yourself in this scene. Look, little cloud girls are flocking down from the sky, running across the fields, their laughter pealing through the air. Skipping in slow motion. What beautiful golden hair. What milky white necks. What flowery chests. Go deeper, as if you are in a lift, climbing down the cloud-maiden's belly. This lift won't stop. It'll stay with you till the inevitable nightfall. O Nabokov, if all the filth from all the kitchens in the world was brought together, it still wouldn't come close to the filth in your writing.

'Sarkhel, I'll be off too.'

'What? That counter-step—what's your plan?'

'That's why I've got to go now. Do you know what's going to happen tomorrow?'

'What?'

'The top capitalists of West Bengal are going to meet the chief minister.'

'So why should we twist our pubes into a knot?'

'You'll see. By which I mean you'll read it in the paper. Might even watch it on TV.'

'Give me a hint, please. This is too much suspense!'

'Lots of booze left. Drink it up. I'm going into the disc room. The doors will be closed for a couple of hours. I can't say more. Goodbye.'

When Bhodi stands up, Sarkhel looks at his shadow cast by the light from the lamp's kerosene flame, how it was aglitter with a phosphorescent glow. Earthworm oil is also rumoured to emit such an otherworldly light. This is what Walter Benjamin called the 'aura'. In Bengali, we say abha. But, Dear Reader, do not mistake this abha with Abha-didi of Milo fame. That would indeed be a catastrophe.

That night, at Madan's house, Purandar Bhat completed his second song:

> Neither a sister-in-law, nor a wife
> I'd rather be a government ayah for life
> With the building's super
> I'll frolic in the bower
> To find love's biggest delight
> No modesty or shame in sight.
> This way
> Or that way
> The world will see love's true light.

Madan says, 'In both your songs, you're trying to give women a bad name. Has your wife run away too? Like mine?'

'I'm not even married! Wife run away, huh.'

'Ah, jilted lover. Understood your case. It's late. Go to bed now.'

'That's best. Once you're asleep, you're free of all troubles.'

There's still quite a bit of night left. Kali and Borhilal lie naked in the darkness on Kali's floor. Borhilal coughs.

'Can't sleep?'

'I almost was. But something seems to be slithering about on the roof.'

'Nothing to worry about. Just the house snake.'

'Eh?'

'No need to cry. He lives up there. Sometimes, at night, he slithers out for a bit. Frogs, mice—he grabs a bite and then comes back and falls asleep again. All good. Now go back to sleep.'

'After what you've just told me, sleep's not coming anywhere near me!'

'And I heard that someone used to be a wrestler? A champion wrestler, that too?'

'Wrestling takes place between humans. Snakes, insects, ants—I can't stand those things.'

'Stop it. None of them will do anything. The ones who will have already came by.'

'Who?'

'Police. They went to every house, told every girl.'

'Told them what?'

'They said: Look, girls, who's coming to whose room, what they say, what they do—you report everything. Big boss' orders. Don't hide anything. Or the female police officers will come and skin you alive. Not just anyone, it's the big boss' order.'

'You'll tell them about me?'

'Yes.'

'You will?'

'Stop it. The night's nearly over and you won't stop your foolery. Why should I say anything? Is the big boss my lover? Police, hmph! Every month, don't they come and take their cut from us, counting every note? As it is we're a shameless lot. Never know when we'll say something that'll make their pricks curl up inside them.'

'What if they see me?'

'So?'

'They'll say: Oi Kali, you dirty whore! Borhilal, the toyshop owner, comes to you. Why didn't you tell us?'

'I'm not the kind to stay quiet and take their shit. I'll say I took a loan from Borhilal-babu once. But how will I pay him back the cash? Instead, I'm paying him back in kind, with my body. So why does it sting your private parts, dumbfuck? Let them come.'

'Well said, paying it back with your body. Come, come close to me.'

'Why, who's stopping you from coming to me?'

'As if I'd care if there was!'

Beloved Reader, do you want to fall in love with the Kalighat whore called Kali? If you are a female reader, you may bow your head before Kali. Or let us all come together and praise Kali the whore, let us sing together, let all the gods hear, all men:

Slowly she takes up arms     Ties her belt, knots her charms
                Wears every weapon with care
A golden band                round each hand
                And then a silken cloth above there
On her back a quiver she throws     fills it with silver arrows
                Her spears and blades are ready to swirl
Flowers ablaze in her hair        thus the queen doth prepare
                And then sets foot upon the world

When Kali's hymn from Sri Chandandas Mandal's *Maha-bharat* was resounding everywhere, just then, while there was still some night left, the door of Bhodi's disc room burst open, and unlike what we have seen before, countless fine and near-invisible discs twirl-whirled out and vanished into the sky.

(*To Be Continued*)

# *16*

It is only by holding the hand of poetry that nubile Bengali literature took its very first steps, no matter what its direction. The beginning of this episode therefore also begins with a poem. The poet is no famous fruitcake, nor a brooding banana. It is but our very own Purandar Bhat:

> Bengal's got everything—wife and ayah and whore
> Then why, O my brothers, are you sad so?
> Nishinath, Abdul—why do you cry?
> Let us eat the rum-birds in the sky.

No matter if no famous personality points out that this poem lacks the suspense of 'the dark drums beat doom, doom, doom'. We need not despair. No matter if such finer points remain forever unknown to us. In the prevalent atmosphere of communal harmony, whatever we get—is that not enough, after all? O Selucus, why beneath the skirt must you focus? How dramatic . . . how sublime. This is how we must proceed. So what if we lag a few steps behind? An abyss lies before us. Why not run the other way? From the talkies back to the silents?

'Strategic retreat!'

Who shouts? The Führer or Yahya Khan? Or is it Marshal Zhukov? None of the above. Clad in a military-tunic it's Bhodi;

he shouts, and then stands as still as a picture. His eyes are closed. His disciples are dumbstruck. The light from the lantern strides about everywhere. Not a cough, not a murmur. And now, who breaks this mesmerizing silence? It is Major Ballabh Baxi. His Bengali, alas, is not quite up to the mark: 'Don't quite understand . . . strategic retreat? If you expose a little—'

'Expose? OK, exposing. Government on high alert. A spy at every street. Maybe a few here too, to bungle our plans. Can you guarantee, Captain, that there's not a single mole here?'

Ballabh Baxi used to be a Major but Bhodi always calls him Captain. Before Baxi can twirl his moustache and talk his shit, the disciples chorus: 'No, O lord, no, no, we are keeping an eye on each other.'

'If there was one, we'd have identified him.'

'Just give us a name, O lord, we'll bring you his head.'

'Shut up,' Bhodi roars, 'be quiet! I just say a word, and the lot of you start shouting. O little darlings, could any whoreson lurk in these shadows by pretending to be my disciple? Just one look at his face, and I'd have known. What do you think I was learning during my deep meditation in Aghor-baba's den? These things I must say now and then to the Army's head. It's called heating the air. Understand? Pushing up the temperature. He who masters this technique can never fail.'


Borhilal could hear everything from outside the tin door. Make no mistake, reader, Borhilal is no spy nor a Kim Philby–type. As stated already, Borhilal is the witness. Whatever happens in the world, there is always at least one witness. But there is no government rule that the witness has to be human. The witness could be anything— a pot or a ladle, a bell-metal plate, a fart-smelling plant or a one-eyed tomcat. The person-in-charge of the universe has, with much skill and cunning, braided people together in such inscrutable and unknowable ways that we will never be able to comprehend. It's best not to talk too much about it. Many think they know how and when the case will turn, and shout it about like a fatwa. Then, after making an absolute fool of themselves, they either spend the rest of their days in hiding or make a name in the neighbourhood as a teller of tall tales. But telling tall tales is a tall order. There is a town called Amta in Howrah. And within the Amta jurisdiction there may still be a village called Khila Baruipur. There, Gopimohan and his wife, Birajmoyee, had a son. The fashion in those days was for massive-mouthful names. So they named him Surendramohan. But the toddler Surendramohan, aged a mere two, fell prey to a mysterious illness, broke everyone's hearts and finally kicked the bucket. The family took the infant corpse and, according to custom, began to dig a grave for its burial. But lo and behold, the infant corpse started blinking his eyes—and was alive once more. Gopi-mohan's mother had said, that the ailing or 'ela' child should not be given medicines but holy water—that was the only thing that could save him. So people started calling the child 'ela' (pronounced ah-la), and thus Surendramohan became ah-la mohan and then, at last, Alamohan. The pride of Bengal, Alamohan Das. Even after knowing this real-life story, if the windbag smartasses don't give up pretending to know it all, then we must speak-ty not. Just like the Dass Bank, they will fail and ruin a lot of people in the process. Das Company, Dove Company, East India Company—no company will survive. Two out of the three are already non-existent. Now we wait for the last, the red-eyed Dove Company, to call it a day.

At this point, we may find it pleasurable to listen to a bit of Bhodi's lecture: 'The government has stirred a little in its seat. Its blowing the dust off its guns. Sunning its ammunition so it's not all damp. Heating up the public. But we've spotted the bastards' game. No one or their father can size us up that easily. That's why our plan is now a strategic retreat, slowly roll back the line. Roll it back so much, that it's almost about to be exposed. And then, then we'll open. Full-fledged exposé. Rat-a-tat-tat-tat, rat-a-tat-a-tat. Got it?'

'Yes, O lord.'

'Everyone's got to be careful, batten down the hatches. One eye cocked and alert all the time. On the other hand, pretend to be as innocent as a cowherd who doesn't know his ass from his molass. This is the plan. Potol?'

'Yes, O lord?'

'Did you release what you were supposed to into the Ganga?'

'Oh, that I did yet last Sunday. They were so happy to be free. Wagging their claws and chasing one another.'

'Good, good, this is how it should be. I gave an order. And it was done. Nolen, make Potol a nice glass of tonic.'

Potol went off to have his tonic. Bhodi doesn't usually share details of his military plans, but today was an exception: 'I thought about it—submarines cost a lot. Build the shell. Shove in an engine. Put a periscope. Even after all that, there's no guarantee of safety. Might get stuck in a pile of mud during low tide. Then what will you do? There's nothing you can do. That's when the idea flashed across my mind. And I understood at once that it could have come only from the mind of Baba Banchharam Sarkar himself. Like a radio. He's talking, and I'm picking up, while the rest of you are listening to music or quiz programmes. So: as advised, so executed.

Potol's a third-generation fishmonger. He's the only one who can do it. So I said, Go, Potol, go to the salt-water fisheries, get about 40 kilos of those monster baby crabs, set them free in the Ganga. The water's high in protein. Every day at least a hundred dead dogs and cats are thrown in. Sometimes dead people too, in sacks. They'll fatten up in no time. And then—you've got the father of all submarines. As soon as the police set foot on the water, the fat crabs'll get them.'

'But O lord, if we get into the water, they'll bite us too.'

'There lies the limit of your imagination! We'll trick the police down to the water. But we'll only go as far as the bank. Then— they'll find out the rest. Even if they somehow crawl-sprawl out of the water, how will they survive? Maybe a crab's dangling off their dingle? Those monster crabs, they're like turtles. Once they bite, they rarely let go. The sahibs' bulldogs were like this too. Hardly see them any more. In any case, which shitty Bengali can afford to feed a bulldog? Daily, 1.5 to 2 kilos of beef. Flat but furious face. Enough to make the bottom drop out of your stomach. Huh, keep a bulldog, eh? No wonder all I see these days is these bastards and bitches walking about with little white things, like baby foxes. Making them shit. They all look the same. Like chickens in a poultry farm.'

Borhilal sees out of the corner of his eye that a shadow from the end of the alley is coming closer. It's almost at the corner now. Now it's turned the corner. Borhilal pretends to zip his pants up after a piss, and starts to walk away. Golap and Borhilal pass each other. At a glance, each man sizes up the other's battery power. In the shades and shadows, this is how battles are fought. Golap understood that the bloke is short, but stacked. Borhilal in his turn could tell that though the other fellow had a bit of a belly, he was no stranger to push-ups and squats.

Golap had trained eyes. And with those eyes he can spot neither piss stream nor pond near Bhodi's door. He knocks, and Nolen opens. The congregation had just begun the customary swaying at the end of the service.

'What are you doing, Nolen? The enemy's doing minus to his water right at your door, you're doing nothing?'

Nolen runs out to see. But there's nothing to see. A cat was crossing the road. He winked at Nolen. And with a ripple in his whiskers, he grinned such a grin that World Poet Tagore may have been prompted to say 'munchkin'.

'Golap! My rose garden, come, come to me.'

Hugging Bhodi close, Golap whispered something in his ear.

'Sarkhel,' shouts Bhodi, 'Golap says the game's afoot. The plot's thickening—to pudding, no less.'

Sarkhel hurries forward. 'Really?!'

Immediately after, an utterly delighted Sarkhel and Golap and Bhodi enter a room (not the disc room) and lock the doors. And Nolen stands outside, like a Kremlin guard. Causing temporary excitement among the congregation, the Raven arrives with a flap, and Nolen cracks open the door so the old Raven can garage himself inside.

The disciples were leaving, after taking a boiled sweet each from a housecoat-clad Bechamoni. Before he takes his share, Major Ballabh Baxi snaps a salute. The courtyard is empty. The plateful of sweets whirls away from Bechamoni's hand and swirls up into the air. The wind plays the jasmine tree like a violin, and so melodiously that the courtyard is transformed into a Viennese ballroom. The *Blue Danube* starts to play. Oh, how rhythmically Bechamoni moves her feet to and fro. Nolen's eyes, as though they're made of glass. His feet a little apart, his hands on his waist. A military bearing indeed, and on top of that clad in only a thin cotton towel.

We could hear from Golap himself about the successful, top-secret Operation Lobotomy that he was sharing with Bhodi, Sarkhel and the Raven. But perhaps only a mysterious, third-person narrator could do the incident justice.

That morning, the representatives of Bengal's commercial sector were supposed to meet the chief minister. The topics were, as always: the workers' increasing agitation and desperation at Haldia Petrochemicals and elsewhere; a joint venture with Papua New Guinea in the hosiery industry; etc., etc. There could have been some talk about the incredible progress in the bread and savoury-snack industry, but where did they get the chance? Whenever a discussion is ruined, somehow it seems that a tragic tune begins to play. Do we have the right to debate why a silent and continuous seminar cannot take place on the ruination of discussions?

The leaders of commerce had drawn up a plan that was nothing short of alluring. After a breakfast at Peerless Inn, and some jokes and jests and banter, a select few industrialists would board an electric bus which would take them to Writers' Building. The electric buses were meant to signal to the rest of the world that West Bengal was well on its way to pollution-free industrialization. Black smoke from chimneys would no longer decimate Bengal's iconic vultures, eagles and herons. A chemical warrant would be issued on all its rivers and water bodies to prevent the further destruction of Bengal's gourami and guppy and barb fishes and save them from vanishing into oblivion. It is to be hoped that a habit the Bengalis have mastered—of passing terrible-smelling gas—will abate as well. Luckily, Mr Bilimoria had a brainwave which he whispered to Mr Sen-Barat. And Mr Sen-Barat passed on to Mr Neota. The electric bus could break down at any time. So their own cars should be ready at all times. Thank god for Mr Bilimoria's scepticism. It was proved once more how keen is the foresight of the industrialists. For right in front of Great Eastern Hotel, the electric bus grunts and groans and grinds to a halt. A lot of police were present. So many that one could even have thought, mistakenly of course, that they were marching off towards Writers' to give someone a thrashing.

Anyway. Mr Neota got off the bus and into his own Toyota Qualis, Mr Bilimoria into his own Mercedes and Mr Sen-Barat into his own Daewoo Cielo. Following their example, the rest of the industrialists got into their Tata Sumo, Opel Corsa, Volvo, Maruti Supreme, Ambassador, etc. A cavalcade of cars and police carried on, and the pollution-free electric bus remained where it was. An excited audience was watching from either side of the road and abusing the whole lot of them soundly.

'So, bastard, wanted to ride an electric bus, eh?'

'Fucking pube. It doesn't work, piece of shit.'

'Brother, how many batteries does it take?'

'Two. Same as you.'

'Great, now they've fucked up traffic. As it was there was a huge jam.'

'What damned dumbfuckery. So many mouths to feed, and they want batteries in their buses instead!'

'Fucking shit! What a fucking mess, man!'

The public will always say such things. Let it. We can't afford to stand like fools beside the stuck-still electric bus and listen to such unpleasant talk all day long. The pallbearers must move on with their corpses. As must we.

The chief minister had asked Comrade Acharya to be present for this meeting. But Comrade Acharya had protested: 'Uff sir, why do you want me around these class enemies? All those Neotas and Fyeotas . . . you know how it is. I almost have an allergic reaction.'

'Stop it. Neota is neither an egg nor shrimp that you'll break out into an allergy. You're just too orthodox about everything. Therein lies your downfall. You've got to be present for tomorrow's meeting. I need you there.'

'I'll see you in the evening anyway. We can finalize things then.'

'What do you mean you'll see me in the evening? Where and why?'

'You're inaugurating the theatre festival in the evening.'

'What?'

'Drama. Theatre festival.'

'Oh yes, I can't remember anything these days. Theatre, drama—why do you involve me in all that nonsense?'

'Ah, but you can't get away from it, sir.'

'Look, those performances really make me lose my temper. Oh, the performances I've seen . . . ! John Gielgud as Hamlet, can you imagine? Then Olivier. And then this local stupidity? Intolerable. I'll go, cut the ribbon—that's it.'

'No ribbon-cutting sir—you'll light a lamp.'

'Whatever. It's all the same. I'll light the lamp and then I'm out of there. Not possible.'

The CM slammed down the phone. Comrade Acharya realized that he simply could not skip the meeting tomorrow. Where's the relief? Comrade Acharya looks at the wall, to Comrade Lenin. From behind the framed photograph of Lenin ran out a small cockroach, with a pair of giant geckos in pursuit. 'Discovery Channel,' mumbled Comrade Acharya, 'just like Discovery Channel. Marvellous!'

Among the police constables posted outside Writers' Building, only Nakshatra Nath Hawladar noticed that the industrialists, clutching their bouquets and moving ahead with serious and perspicacious steps, did not look all right at all. Each one's eyes wasn't seeing what was in front of him but seemed to be focused on that which was invisible, never to be seen. At once, Hawladar jumped to the conclusion that whether dawn broke or not, that old sipping-sipping drinking-drinking must have started. But most historians are not in agreement with Hawladar. They hold instead that among the liquids consumed by Bengal's apex industrialists that morning were Ayurvedic gooseberry water, tea, coffee, Horlicks, lemon water and apple juice. Perhaps the historians are right, but our perverted sympathies tend to lean time and again in Hawladar's direction. The Bengalis' hunt for truth has thus historically derailed itself many times. Not everything is, alas, in our hands.

In the chief minister's room, the chief minister is of course present, as is his personal secretary, Comrade Acharya, the finance minister, the labour minister and the fish and poultry minister, with whom Comrade Acharya's relationship is not at all an amiable one. The inspector general is out of station. Gone to Scotland Yard, to study anti-terrorism. So the chief minister has bypassed the officers next in charge and called upon the police commissioner to be present. Joardar is wearing his helmet; or his severed head may fall like a ripe grapefruit from a tree and create an atmosphere of terror.

Mr Bilimoria gingerly hands over the bouquet of red roses to the chief minister, because the thorns are poking out of the silver foil wrapped around its base. The chief minister has accepted many bouquets of roses in his lifetime. It makes his blood boil, but there is no choice. His face bears a smile he has perfected many years ago, a smile that comes back to his lips every now and then. Then Mr Neota presents his bouquet, followed by Mr Sen-Barat. The plan was for them to present their bouquets one by one, but suddenly, from the back, jute baron Mr Dholakia's booming voice roars: 'Today's not the day to play with flowers. You have to concede that dumdum bullets will be fired upon militant workers—rat-a-tat-tat rat-a-tat-tat, one dead body—boom, one more, boom, more and more, fire, fire, rat-a-tat-tat rat-a-tat-tat—'

The chief minister is aghast, astounded.

Joardar's face is pale.

'No pasarán!' roars Comrade Acharya, 'Firing on the peaceful workers' struggle, and that too with Dumdum bullets! Do remember where you are and to whom you're talking, Mr Dholakia!'

Mr Dholakia smiles an angelic smile. His raw-silk safari suit shines in its light. 'Do you understand property? Property is theft. Labour power is a commodity. Wage-slave labourers sell this commodity to capital. Why? To live. How long will you disenfranchise them, oppress them? No to tyranny!'

The rest of the capitalists roar as one: 'No to tyranny! No to tyranny!'

'No to despotism!'

'No to despotism! No to despotism!'

The finance minister is highly educated. No coarse language ever crosses his lips. Nevertheless, he whispers: 'Oh fuck!'

The chief minister says: 'What's going on? I don't understand.'

Comrade Acharya pats down his dishevelled hair: 'Very strange! Weird! Bizarre!'

Mr Bilimoria says in a sober voice: 'Please say what you have to say logically. Peacefully. Don't forget, we have a grave social responsibility.'

Mr Dholakia narrows his eyes at Mr Bilimoria and spits: 'Bloody capitalist pig!'

The chief minister is forced to intervene: 'Ah Mr Bilimoria, let the discussions proceed.'

Bilimoria is famous in the industrial world as a tea magnate: 'The daily reports I am getting from Darjeeling and its surrounds are very alarming indeed. Workers are damaging the imported machines—the drying machine, for example. Managers have no voice. With so much disruption at the production level, how can we accept the big export orders?'

The fish and poultry minister is quite young: 'The Russians are still buying your tea?' he quips, 'Even after the counter-revolution?'

'Some, but not as much as before.'

The chief minister does not relish the young minister's inter-ruption: 'Whether the Russians drink tea or not, we don't give a fig. Why do you bring up such irrelevant things? Mr Bilimoria, please continue.'

'Yes, sir, but I think I first need to educate your fish and poultry minister. Fucking about with the Russian counter-revolution eh? Do you know the history of the Russian revolutionary struggle?'

'Of course I do.'

'I'll give you such a thwack, you'll find yourself inside a tea bag. Who first understood the danger of capitalism in Russia?'

'Lenin.'

'Lenin? In 1874? A little boy of four? Neither Herzen nor Bakunin gave it much importance. Tkachev was the first to understand—have you heard of him? You haven't. Have you read his debate with Engels on the quick call for political revolution? Even Plekhanov had to debate with Tkachev. You have to give a man his due. Look son, there is only one history and that is the truth. Read, read, read everything. You look like a facetious and flippant young man, nothing more. Anyway, sir, about the futures trading thing that the forward markets commission is thinking of—'

Some of the industrialists scream: 'Comrade Trotsky, red salute! Long live the red army!'

'What India demands today!'

'A red flag on the Red Fort.'

Mr Neota suddenly breaks into song, terribly tunelessly: 'Oh those black-black eyes, those light-light cheeks . . .'

The chief minister yells, 'Rogues! Stop it, stop! Call the forces. Joardar, why are you standing there like a fool? Call the forces, let them take these away.'

Sen-Barat booms away: 'Capitalists of the world, unite!'

'Unite! Unite!'

'No governmental dictatorship on industries!'

'No dictatorship! No dictatorship!'

'The black hands of capitalists—'

'Break them! Grind them!'

(*To Be Continued*)

## 17

Gentle Reader, have you heard that the thing called the novel that is available in the market has begun to sing in a lovely lighthearted three-beat tune? Let us pretend that *Beggars' Bedlam* is a young Hindu widow. Let us further pretend that after spending the day flooding her bosom with tears, at the magical hour of twilight, when djinns, houris and goblins come out to play, she begins to sing:

> I do not know, sister, for which crime by which mister
> Into this family of doom
> Fate has sent me, and impaled me,
> On a giant spear of longing and gloom.

Such is the tragic state of *Beggars' Bedlam*. There's simply no one to offer it a spot of comfort. If there was, then instead of this song, it may have burst into 'My name is Chin-chin-chu . . . Chin-chin-chu . . .' or 'In the wind flies away my red headscarf' . . . But we're helpless. Hence, this song cried out, selected from the treasure trove of melancholy that is *A Widow's Lamentations* written by some dickhead religious zealot. The pages and cantos of that volume drip with the weeping and wailing of two widows named Sarala and Tarangini. These two, though, have no connection whatsoever to Buddhadev Basu's famous play *Tapasvi and Tarangini*. Just as there is no connection between *Anandabazar Patrika* and the ad that ran on its pages in which Magician Ananda announced his need for a 'short person'. But, how far does our intelligence, our imagination, stretch, after all? Overwhelmed and overcome by this conflicted world, we have begun to think that market power, the state government's power, the central government's power, East India Company's power—they are the greatest of all. The most powerful. But above them all operates another power. One may start talking about its scandals, and never finish. What use is the news of ships to a little man? But what kind of ship is it? Not a sea-going vessel, nor a flying one. So? What is it?

The police forces arrive as per the chief minister's orders and take away the delegation of industrialists. Needless to say, there is no question of frogmarching men as powerful as these to the Lalbazar lock-up and beating five kinds of shit out of them. No, it was all done under the chief minister's astute leadership. They were taken to hotel FFort Radisson, at Raichak. Where they were first examined from head to toe by the famous Dr Khetri. Who declared them all to be normal. Normal pulse, normal blood pressure, normal stool, normal urine. Perhaps they were all a bit mad. But that was not within Dr Khetri's purview. Then came a team of specialists from Bangur Medical Institute. Along with four distinguished psychiatrists, carrying a range of complicated machinery. Then an aggressive-type arrived with a lie-detector. The tireless work of all these people finally resulted in that success that turned the key and unlocked the mystery, but what it revealed was totally terrifying. No one is capable of reading that enormous report to its end; the thing needs to be cut down to size.

To that end, the chief minister snapped, 'No beating about the bush, no hedges of any kind, what's the main point?'

The report's conclusion: in some entirely unknown manner, and overnight, all the industrialists have been lobotomized. And not only that: things that were never supposed to be there, such as radical thoughts and theories, have been put into their brains via suggestion or some other technique. Therefore, even though they look like one person, there are two camps within each man. One is capitalist, the other is revolutionist or something of that ilk— Marxist, Stalinist, nihilist or anarcho-syndicalist, Trotskyist, or Bernstein-type, Dubček-aligned, Titoist, Maoist—there are many strains.

But what is lobotomy?

The kind of surgery that divides the brain in two is known as lobotomy or leucotomy. These men have had a prefrontal lobotomy. The connections between the prefrontal part of the brain, as well as its connection with the thalamus, have been severed. In the 1940s and early 50s, this kind of surgery was performed in America in order to rehabilitate criminals. These days, it's almost unheard of, because very effective medication is available. W. L. Jones' book *Ministering to Minds Diseased* (1983) contains much information on the subject. If this book doesn't satiate one's thirst for knowledge, then one may leaf through Sperry or Ornstein's work on split-brain research. They recorded the strange activities of a husband who had been thus operated upon: with one hand he pulled his wife close while with the other he pushed her away. Though it must be acknowledged that many Bengali husbands tend to act similarly conflicted without having undergone such surgery. This kind of horseplay by such whoresons is even alleged by some to bear philosophical relevance. Everything happens because of a deep-rooted complex. Everything is trauma. A good thrashing with a stout bramble branch will in no time at all drive away much of this arseholery, if not all of it.

Be that as it may, does the Reader remember what happened at the end of Chapter 15 or 16? Let us quote: 'The door of Bhodi's disc room burst open, and unlike what we have seen before, countless fine and near-invisible discs twirl-whirled out and vanished into the sky.' Now, can you hazard a guess as to who may have performed such a series of infinitely delicate surgeries? And now do you understand what Golap meant in the last chapter when he was telling the others about 'successful top-secret Operation Lobotomy'? Earlier we have observed how the large discs so easily and bloodlessly slice off heads, legs, arms. Now we discover that the finer discs are adept at operations as amazing as brain surgeries. There are even finer discs, they are entirely invisible and make no sound. They can slice and dice in the dreamworld, and create such astonishing collages that are entirely beyond compare. The discs' ability to carry out all kinds of detachment and division truly beggars belief. A significant feature of our modern lives is considering the warmth of the artificial glow of floodlights as our first and our last truth, and that it all lies within our grasp. Just as a corpse sleeps peacefully, knowing that the coffin is its final resting place and reality. Even its own impending rot seems entirely natural to it. But that coffin rots and mingles with the earth, and that earth seeps into the water and flows over the rocks, and over them all— the endless and incessant crash-fall of celestial lightbeams; all of this is a joyous, ecstatic circus, somewhere in it a grasping and unclasping trapeze, somewhere the waiting souls of writers in clown costumes, the iron-ghosts of dictators, the graceful whirl of dancers and the silent and grim-faced march of all kinds of insects in and out of the Afterworld—is this not a miraculous gift? Is this not filled with *that* possibility that we are still incapable of expressing in words? There is no such thing as a savant, or a genius. Only a varying degree of fool. And worse. Far worse.

In the middle of all this, Bhodi is possessed. On the one hand, the state government's preparations for war, the sleeves being rolled up in every nook and cranny, frequent requests for meetings with the General Officer Commanding-in-Chief (GOC-in-C) of the Eastern Command. On the other hand, Sarkhel's eternal digging, random incidents of mess and mayhem caused by the Phyatarus, a light romantic air rippling between Begum Johnson and the ageing Raven, the rising excitement of Bhodi's disciples, Golap's counter-intelligence, the fledgling hopes of the CIA, MI5, ISI and FSB outposts in Calcutta—somewhere between these two opposing powers and assorted third-party agitation, Bhodi becomes possessed.

A naked Bhodi stands on the roof of his one-storey house, slaps his massive belly over and over again and floods the air with a variety of vulgarity, among which, admittedly, there was mention of some other things too. We will consider only those non-vulgar and non-objectionable portions of his unspeakable ravings that will be deemed relevant and dignified and thus receive the all-clear from the publishers, because a peculiar novelty of the modern novel is to create a congested web of a welter of facts, most of which is facetious frippery. And at times, instead of facts, there is that non-stop philosophical windbaggery that readers think is valuable and by which they are needlessly awestruck. *Beggars' Bedlam* will stick a leg onto this boat as well as that. If its end lies in a watery grave, why should it attempt otherwise?

What the possessed Bhodi said:

(1) Yes, yes, carry on ... no day no night, just turn on the TV and watch the flocks of bitches swaying their behinds from side to side ... no one will cry when you die, no one will do your last rites ... the arse swings ... aha my Bengali grandfather's pubic chandeliers swing ... oh no, the roll-chicken's running away ...

get some air every now and then, turn the fan on, get some air, the pendulum swings . . . oh the festival of swings in my ancient palace, O Ma, the hot milk burns my little Gopal's mouth, whole race, hole race, hole! Hole! . . .

(2) They'll loosen the bungholes, they'll screw the poor so hard and split those arseholes wide open . . . they can't stand the swagger of the poor folk but the poor are so dear to me, O my beloved Uncle Pussy Cat . . . look left and right and slurp the milk bowl dry . . . the government's found a honey hive stuck to the bums of the poor . . . they'll fuck the poor as wide as Bhuto-mullah's creek . . . they'll raid all the hideouts, the bottles of Bangla, the pots and pans, they'll kick everything to the streets, recto-killer . . . recto-killer . . . renting videos so late at night . . . recto-killer . . . recto-killer . . .

(3) O my toerag, whereforth art thou! Where did you run off to, O toiling toerag? Toerag yells: Gundichas, I'm at the house of the Gundichas. Halwa! Halwa! Yum yum gobble gobble halwa! Halwa! Four annas for a quarter. Four annas for a quarter. Halwa, halwa!

(4) O barren wife, barren wi—fe! Who's going to fill your womb? The gambler king. Who's the gambler king? The gambler king's a beggar. What does the gambler king eat? Puffed rice and water from the municipal water tap. What kind of rice can you boil with that water? White-white grains, fat and plump. Who's going to give the gambler king some gold? Bhodi will. What will Bhodi's barren wife give? Bhodi's barren wife will give her breasts. Round the gambler king's big belly, above his cock, what is that tied on a black string? A coin with a hole. What's that? Oh, but this coin is made of gold? Yes. So the gambler king has gold in store? Yes. And then? What're those two things on Bhodi's barren wife's chest? Two packets of

Mother Dairy Toned Milk! Go, catch the arsehole Nolen, catch. Catch . . . catch . . . Nolen-shitter . . . catch. What's up mister pot-turtle? Why're you going glug glug glug? O mister pot-turtle! O fuck. The gambler king's pissed all over the place!

Bhodi's father, the old Raven, watched Bhodi's raving rampagery for a while, then sat under the nearby municipal tap that gets water twice daily and flapped his wings and washed himself vigorously. Then he said, 'Daughter, please massage the crown of my head with some oil. Begum Johnson was being a bit playful, she's messed up all my feathers. Can't seem to locate  my natural parting. Put a little oil, and then get the comb. But be gentle— you're too strong.'

Nolen was squatting on his haunches near the jasmine tree, picking up ants and crushing them one by one; Bhodi, naked, was running up and down the stairs like a battery-operated gorilla.

Bechamoni began to comb the Raven's feathers.

'Ah, that feels so good. It's been so long since my feathers had some care.'

'Father, may I ask something?'

'Of course, my child.'

'Who's the ghost that's possessed Bhodi?'

'Oh, that's just Neshu. He'll be gone by tomorrow.'

'Neshu? I've never heard that name uttered in this house.'

'It's never come up. He was an old man. An absolute arsehole. Wore black surgical sunglasses. And snorted something or other from dawn till dusk. Did nesha all day long. That's why he was called Neshu. But yes, people used to come to him for tips on horses. He was their wonderboy. Whichever horse he chose was sure to win. Jackpot, Quinella, Triple Tote, Placing—he helped so many win millions! And in exchange for what? Two small packs of ganja or one large bottle of booze. Neshu was as famous for racing as he was infamous for a scandal in his youth—he'd married a maidservant. He had the guts for it, I must say. These days, they throw the phrase around at the drop of a hat. But Neshu said it first: If there's gossip, I will marry. This time of year, he feels the urge to possess. But where is the vessel into which he can pour? Whatever he's making Bhodi say, keep in mind, there'll be some things that are bound to come true even before three nights are past.'

'Father, you know everything that will happen and that won't.'

'That I do, daughter. But, alas, I can't say a word.'

Nolen is an unalloyed arsehole. Just to take a dig at the Raven, he muttered as though to himself: 'Ooh, all the pundits are shitting themselves but a crow's the wisest of them all!'

'If jerk-off jackasses like you don't start shooting their mouths off, how will the dark ages truly arrive, eh? You'll see, in time, you'll see. Then when you cry for your uncle, we'll see who comes to help you.'

Nolen is truly dedicated in his jackassery: 'Why will I cry uncle when you're there? I'll call for you instead. And then, are you sure you'll be able to stay away?'

By way of an answer, Raven's face lit up with a beatific smile. The same smile that has been a source of such constant reassurance for us all. Although more often glimpsed in a photograph rather than in person. The whole world is rocked by unrest and agitation. But the Bengali is entirely unperturbed. Because he knows that the photographs that cover his walls will undoubtedly save him from all evil. And no matter what happens, the *Anandabazar* will be published tomorrow.

How long this total tomfoolery will continue, even a super-computer cannot predict.

Borhilal went to Barabazar and bought five boxes of 'Puppy House' (puppies pop out of a plastic house and grab things with their paws), three toy-duck families that laid eggs while walking and a helicopter that flutters its wings and lights up when you pull a string. All these toys are from Chinamen Land. No one knows if this toy-export or toy-smuggling business is motivated by some 'catch them young' dirty ploy aimed at Indian children. But no matter how much pleasure the Bengalis derive from their mocking cries of 'Chinaman chang chung a vat of butter', it is a truth universally acknowledged that what the Chinese are thinking behind their inscrutable smiles is not at all easy to fathom. Sooner or later everyone finds out that they don't use those little sticks to only eat their rice.

When *Beggars' Bedlam* took its first few steps, it was revealed to us that Borhilal had some kind of a phobia about insects and ants. Thus, he was now lying in the middle of the floor, on a makeshift bed, surrounded by lines drawn with insect-repellent chalk. A breeze was blowing in from the Chetla side, the kind that arouses unmarried Bengali men and makes them impetuous with their affections. However, it wasn't supposed to affect Borhilal. And it didn't. He was sleeping like a log and watching in the virtual reality of his dreamworld how his married life with Kali had become so humdrum that the two of them were squatting in front of her room, picking out insects from a heap of old rice, and the flailing insects scurried off here and there, chased away by the broad stripes of sunlight. Kali has finished her ablutions while Borhilal was away at the market. This Kali has never been a prostitute. In the courtyard, Borhilal's freshly washed red briefs are drying on the clothesline—a wire, strung across two bamboos stuck into the raw earth of the courtyard. Red pants, give me the key. Open your lock wide open for me. Thus goes an inscrutable riddle. Why wrestlers derive such wholesome joy from bandying about lewd jokes, that we will never know. Both Kali and Borhilal look up at the sky. Even in broad daylight, someone has set afloat paper lanterns. And there, over there, who let fly those paper balloons? Somewhere, new fireworks are being tested; their tails of smoke can be seen, slowly fading away. The whole sky is ablaze with joy. Oh, look at the long tail of a candle kite! The higher it pulls at its string and soars, the more its smoke tail curls and coils, like a magic ribbon. And to one side of that same sky, a black heron flies away. There is not much sky between here and the Zoo. How small the window of respite. To see the sky.

But that small window is enough. A red light burns bright at the tail end. The blades begin to whir. The toy helicopter lifts off, circles Borhilal's room twice. And then flies away.

That same night, after coming back from the scene of a double homicide, the bald OC and his two constables were savouring a bottle of Old Smuggler rum—a gift from a real-estate developer—along with some kebabs from the Punjabi dhaba. In the OC's room, a dirty wire, from which hangs a surly lightbulb. The tubelight's dead. The helicopter flies in through the window. Starts circling the bulb so rapidly that a peculiar moving shadow shimmers on the wall.

The OC loses his temper: 'Wanted to relax and enjoy a drink but no, those fucking bats have to barge in. Hit them, take my baton and give it a thrashing!'

In response, the helicopter lands on his table. Its lights flashing on and off. Its blades spin round and round. One of the constables reaches out, but the OC yells: 'Don't touch! It's remote-controlled.

Can burst any moment. Do as I do. Lie flat on the ground. Even if the building's blown to bits, we'll survive. Dear god—'

Their chairs topple to the ground as the constables leap out of them and fling themselves to the floor, cover their heads with their hands. Exactly like the man on the street does during a lathi charge. The helicopter is skittering about on the table. The bottle of rum crashes to the floor. The helicopter flies up. Its madly spinnning blades shatter the lightbulb. The room is plunged into darkness. The whirring of the blades. Then silence. The room stinks of rum. A minute passes. Still, silence.

'I think that damn thing's flown off, sir.'

'I think so too. But who's to say it's not hiding? The light's out.'

'There's a torch in your drawer, sir.'

'Oh, yes. Uff, what a situation! I've broken out into a sweat!'

What can be seen by the light of the torch is as follows: the helicopter has destroyed the bottle of Old Smuggler. The glasses have overturned, all the files and papers are soaking wet. And after this mini mayhem, the helicopter's flown the coop.

'Fucked the booze in its arse. But we're lucky it didn't explode. Pure terrorist attack.'

One of the constables swiftly slams shut the window.

'Well done. Tomorrow I need to report this to Lalbazaar. Not just us—the whole station's had a lucky escape.'

The other constable lights a candle.

'Sir, can I say something?'

'Say it. Why're you suddenly acting so coy?'

'I mean, the good booze is all gone. I have two bottles of Bangla saved up. Should I bring them?'

'Ah, what? Yes, yes, as quickly as you can. My life was spared today. Now finally it can find some comfort too. Uff, you're a good man, you are.'

'But sir, it was such a small helicopter. Even if it burst, at most it'd be like a firework ...'

'You fool! Those sisterfuckers aren't throwing homemade bombs at us any more. They're using these little jelly things instead. RDX. Semtex. Can blow up a whole building in a second. Don't you read the papers? You see a radio. Playing your favourite songs. But if you pick it up—finis! Know this for sure. Only I know how narrowly we've survived today. Otherwise, I can't bear to think of my poor wife's face.'

The phone rings.

'Hello, yes, OC speaking. What? Two bodies dropped this evening, but that wasn't enough? What? Both sides throwing bombs at each other? Let them. Maybe that will wipe out some of them. What's the point of me going? I'll go, fire two rounds, they'll stop. Let them carry on instead. Even if they don't die, there's bound to be some injuries. No, no, all fucking and getting fucked over just doesn't work for me any more. I'll see, maybe tomorrow. But if I tell you what just happened here, you'll throw a fit! Here a terrorist attack, there a gang war—I can't tackle everything on my own. No, no, why would I keep the body here? I've sent it off. Who's that groaning beside you? Oh, the radio. Fucking FM. Night and day, just nonstop nonsense. Never mind, let it be. You've gone on long enough. What am I doing? One booze session was destroyed, so I'm arranging another one. Goodbye.'

Borhilal wasn't dreaming then. Just sleeping like a log. The toy ducks suddenly set up a chorus of quacking. The puppies came out of their houses, showed their paws and went in again. The helicopter flew in through the open window. Circled the room once, and then gently landed back in place, as if it had never left.

(*To Be Continued*)

*18*

That these shindigs and shenanigans are proceeding towards war—
or shitting it's way to war according to haters—is by now obvious
to all but our dear readers. That includes various species of birds,
impertinent cats and runover dogs—but it doesn't end there, and
since no one knows whose father will have the last word, the universe of spiders, the microcosm of microbes, etc., the ones as small
as grains of snuff but not at all fond of being snuffed out—they too
follow along. Just before a spell of heavy rain, an unprecedented
agitation ripples through the ant colonies. The humans of course
notice nothing at all. Though in the end they pose and posture such
as though they knew it all along. The modern reader is exactly like
this. If the books being written in Bengali today (Bengali, because
the writers don't know English) are not as pleasurable as the 'my
penis–your penis' games of one's childhood, then just forget about
it. O my dear dickhead, even if every writer isn't paid a fixed salary
every month, doesn't have a series of running debts to be paid back
in kind, never has the chance to publish a thick wad in the Durga
Puja special issues every year and doesn't receive a 'free packet'
whether they write or not (straight from the accountant's room on
the 24th or 25th of each month)—some of them still shove the
Mother of Recognition onto the path of the oncoming train, still
shrug off the rate of interest on their debts, and still write, or at

least try to. Darling Reader, when will you understand this? If literature was a corpse, we could have shaved you lot off to lessen the load. But since you have no weight, nor heart, nor gravity, nor status, the Real McCoy–pedigreed writers won't blunt their nibs trying to do away with you. The Bharat blade/India blade should stay sharp, stay shining. The sniping will continue. The shouting too. But now, at this moment: war. Cross-border terra shelling shilling pound dollar—ah oh, wah, bhok, pooi, pawk, pong, lih lih

( )

Fritters, fritter-flirt, flirt-meister Chobilal, oye oye, oye oye ah!

(>)

In flagrante, uff darling, dish-washing woman.

(<)

Oh, what a move!

(Δ)

One face of the pyramid or one-dimensional

Attribution

(=)

Bhangra + Salsa + Lumping-Jumping

Or

BB

Not Beautiful Baboon nor Ball Bearing

Then what?

This my friends is—

*Beggars' Bedlam*

'This heart wants more!' That's what Purandar or Madan thought they'd shout at DS, to startle him. Then get down to talking business. But the scene they saw instead would cancel every public channel's broadcast licence if it was ever aired. DS' wife and baby chortling and flying about the room, and DS, in his underwear, with a yellow datura flower stuck on each finger, pretending to be a monster and running after them. DS has even stuck a flower at each corner of his mouth, so he looks like a yellow-toothed Dracula. DS' naked Phyataru infant is smoothly somersaulting through the air like a seasoned cosmonaut and twisting himself at such angles as would make Nadia Comaneci quit gymnastics. DS' fat, dark, toad-like wife is in her nightie, and her flying style, while not very adventurous is nevertheless quite playful, much like the old carps who frequently cavort in the darkness of deep ponds. And alongside these visions is DS' ghostly TV, the one that shows four of everything. Broadcasting four chief ministers, with four microphones, speaking in one voice and giving a speech at a (four) film festival. Flanking him are four of the same old film director, a has-been hero who's now an old geezer, that once-upon-a-vamp who's lost it all except the Kamasutral habit of bludgeoning her crossed eyes with smudges of kohl.

After studying this scene for a while, Madan barks: 'Stop it. Will you stop it?'

DS sang, 'No-oh, no no no, no-oh!'

'No! If one person is going to constantly break discipline like this, then I, at least, cannot continue with my duty. I'm going to tell Bhodi-da right away. Someone else might be able to carry on, but not I.'

DS does something that everyone thinks he can't do: he retorts and repartees: 'DS doesn't care about Bhodi or Todi or anyone else. Had my lunch of rice and goat-head curry, and now for some fun and games with my family—what the hell's that got to do with Bhodi-da? Finally, the game's getting somewhere, we can't stop now.'

Thus far, Purandar Bhat had been smirking silently on the sidelines. Now he shuts his eyes and delivers an instant poem:

'At the gates, the enemy erect
Inside, a poor prick, society's reject
Not a clue, fucks around with wife and ball,
But alas, suddenly the guillotine falls
Behind the clouds, bombers buzz
A deathly warship, killer of arse fuzz
Yet, no one answers this call, direct
Inside and outside, the enemy erect.'

'Bravo, Bhat, bravo!' says Madan, 'If only such explosive poetry can bring DS back to his senses. I'm disgusted, I tell you.'

'All right, all right,' says DS, 'I'm sorry. Enough playing, OK? Can't wait to run to Bhodi-da and complain, can you? You're such a tell-tale, I tell you.' One by one, DS pulls the yellow flowers off his fingers.

'Your wife and child are here, so I'm going easy on you, all right? Anyway, fuck it. Have you got any booze in stock?'

'Why should I tell you?'

'Uff, again with the drama!'

'All right, all right, I've got some. Open that trunk, take out the deer-print glasses. After all, we're serving guests.'

'The special glasses, eh? Guess it's not our usual bottle of Bangla, then?'

'Only poor people drink that crap. This is pure country-made foreign stuff. Officer's Choice.'

'Your pocket's pretty hot these days, eh?'

'No, no. My pocket's cold. This is a gift. You know my brother-in-law? Perhaps Purandar doesn't.'

'Why won't I know Jona? We've had so many gatherings in this very room.'

'Oh, sorry, I forgot. So, Jona's managed to sell a villa, in this economy—imagine! And get a fat broker's fee.'

'What? That villa finally sold?'

'It did. The agreement's done. Since then, he's been telling me: Brother-in-law, no more Bangla-Tangla. You've damaged your liver enough. From now on, only English for you, only English for me. After all, just the one son-in-law in the family.'

'Such a generous brother-in-law. You're a lucky chap, I must say.'

DS' wife flashes a set of brilliant white teeth, and says: 'After all, whose brother is he? No one's talking about that.'

'We know, we know. Enough, now. Don't you have any of that brain curry left over from lunch? Why don't you bring it—it'll go nicely with the drink. Now, tell me, what's the job?'

'Yes. In short, and in English, it's called an aerial survey. But it can't be done in daylight. Party till twilight, then the aerial army'll take flight. How did I do with the rhyme, Bhat?'

'Brilliant. Actually, everyone's a poet. My studies have led me to this conclusion. Though everyone always says the opposite. There was a mad poet called J. Das. He said it first. And it's not been disproved since.'

'Bengalis are all a bunch of parroting pricks. They'll learn one thing, then keep repeating, keep repeating. Bhodi-da's walloping such a big one after another. But from the way they're behaving, do you think they can tell?'

'Always been a bastard race. That's devolved to bloody bastards now. Anyway, let them go to hell. And pour a large one for me.'

The drink is poured. Water too, with a glug-glug sound. Bhat is wary of too much water in his drink. It makes him pee.

'No more, no more.'

'Don't have it so strong. Your liver will rust.'

'Good. If poets live too long, they inevitably suffer disgrace. But if they can manage to die young, then everyone sighs: Oh no, if only he'd lived!'

'And if you grow old?'

'God forbid! Your poems will be taught in school. Right from childhood, the public will hate you. So when they grow up, nobody wants to read you.'

'OK, stop all that crap theory and recite a good poem. But none of that farting fuckery about the rich and the poor, please.'

'All right. One afternoon, by the Lake. Uff, such a scorching hot day it was. I'd spent a long time sizing up a woman who was sitting there, all alone. But it didn't work. Stupid cow. As soon as a rich bastard came along in a car, she hopped in beside him. I thought: Yeah, bitch, you'll see soon enough. And I was so het up, that I wrote this:

The umbrellas open, their crooked ribs
Pierce the breast, the wood splits
Suddenly I spy the bathing shore

All the ladies sway their pots
Swim and dip and oh so hot
How luscious the bodies, aft and fore

They did not give the thirsty water
Now you know who's a heartless daughter
The alcohol is full of venom vile

The sun scorches the bathing bank
The scissors are hot that trim the pube shanks
Open the umbrellas, their crooked ribs.'

The recitation is over. Madan is looking very meditative indeed. The evening darkens. Bhat takes a small sip and clears his throat. Madan tells DS, 'High thought. Understand?'

'I'm only thinking of that callous cow. Should be strangled.'

'Ahaha-ha, but why? No strangling-wrangling! Bhat, my heart is soaked and wilting. Such a great start you've got there. An umbrella with a crooked handle, opening. So what if I can't write, that opening, the mood—I feel it, you know. But those whose hearts haven't been broken, they won't understand this poem.'

'I don't care. My job is to write it. So I have. If the world is an asswipe, that's not my headache.'


Here is a verbatim presentation of the conversation taking place between Sarkhel and Bhodi at this very moment:

'The water's flooding in! I'm emptying bucket after bucket. But the water's not stopping!'

'Of course it won't. The Old Ganga's just next door. Seen the colour?'

'Blackish. And such a bad smell.'

'Naturally. Only a few hundred years' worth of rotting corpses, shit, dogs and cats. What did you think? It'll smell like cologne from Paris? Or perfume from Baghdad?'

'Look, I know you're the leader. But I can't not say this: please don't joke about Baghdad. So many bombings. But still they're holding out against America.'

'Really, Sarkhel! You also have to stop bringing international politics into everything.'

'That's a big mistake on your part. If word of what you're doing gets out, you'll become an international figure yourself. Day and night, the TV cameras will chase your arse.'

'Really? You think that'll happen?'

'How could it not? Even ten planning commissions could not have come up with your plan!'


Evening slopes into night. That famous twilight gold dazzles its way towards darkness. This is the time when flocks and flocks of Asian birds, such as crows and mynas, sparrows and herons, treepies and cormorants and snipe, etc., all fly back home. No one can tell for how long they have been finishing their work at the office and coming back home on time. Some of them form a 'W' in the sky. Some form a 'V'. Sometimes you can spot one lonely bird, or one tired couple. It is such a surprising notion, and perhaps even a melancholy one, that this used to happen in the time of the British, and in fact even before them, in the time of the Pala kings too. Neither Hunter nor Majumdar have made any mention of them. Bird hunting finds mention in some of the best civilian memoirs. But there are no tender observations about this daily avian commute.

Be that as it may, along with the birds, discs of various shapes and sizes were flying back home too.

'It's time.'

'For what?'

'In five more minutes, the Phyatarus will take off.'

'Why?'

'For the aerial survey. I have no doubts nor questions about Golap's report, but I do want to see for myself. The enemy still doesn't know that we have a strategic air command. By the time it does, our birds will have flown far, far away.'

'Sometimes I wonder why you set in motion such a big event. I can't quite fathom it.'

'How will you? I don't understand it myself. Look, nothing is in our hands. That mysterious advertisement in *Anandabazar*—that wasn't us. Father might know who it was, Begum Johnson too. But they'll say nothing. Only talk in riddles. Once every hundred and fifty years, the discs come out to play. No one knows why. Our fore-father Atmaram Sarkar, what could he possibly want out of this bedlam? I don't know—I'm only following orders.'

'A very tumultuous affair.'

'Tumultuous of the first order. Long Live Disc Father! Love Live Disc Mother! You know the only thing that we need? Bless-ings. Nothing else. If we get just that, this life will be complete.'

'Uff, I feel almost dizzy. Such a big affair. And Sarkhel's a player on that team too!'

'Don't think so much. The more you think, the more your head will spin. Nolen was spinning a riddle the other day. I liked it a lot.'

'A riddle?'

' "Let the world yell and holla, this puja I want Coca Cola." Isn't that great?! And we—we don't even want cola, we only want blessings.'

'Right! Absolutely right!'

'That's my point. We've talked a lot of serious stuff today. Want a drink now?'

'Just the one. I'm still in a daze.'

From the sky, Lalbazar looks normal to the naked eye. It is not so. Madan says: 'What do you see, DS?'

'White and blue clothes drying in the air, what else?'

'Balls. Look closely. The Rapid Action Force is doing target practice.'

'You're right!

'Keep looking closely. Do you know that dick?'

'Wearing that half kurta?'

'Yes.'

'Who's he?'

'Son of a whore. Hunted the Naxals, stamped them out like lice.'

'Why's he limping?'

'Stroke. Whoreson had a stroke, got paralysed on one side.'

'Should I charge?'

'What?'

'I have a 200 gm weighing stone in my pocket.'

'Not yet. We have no instructions to bomb.'

From higher above, a rough voice rasps through the clouds: 'Good! Good!'

Madan, DS and Purandar look up and see, eclipsing Orion with his ginormous wings, the preternatural Raven flying above.

'Oh god, you?!'

'Yes arsehole, it's I. Look below. It's begun.'

'What?'

'A parade in Lalbazar.'

'Do you understand?'

'A parade!'

'Fuckwit! The government's making sure its penis can still stand. Do you know why?'

'Why?'

'So it can fuck the poor in the arse.'

Purandar is drunk on Officer's Choice. He says, 'Your reading's wrong. This is a leftist government.'

'If you want to swallow those lies, go ahead. The world's being run by the World Bank, and this ass is still holding on to the left.'

'What do you mean? This is a leftist police!'

'Dumbfuck. The police belongs to whoever pays their wages.'

'Never mind. Don't argue any more.'

This last warning is from Bhat, but DS is fearless and blunders on: 'What's happening in that building over there? The one with the lights on?'

'The *Anandabazar*'s being printed. What else do you want to know, little fucker? Seven hundred thousand Bengalis will read it tomorrow morning, and then scratch their balls all day.'

'So be it. But what are those, then?'

'Same case. The lights of the media, English, Hindi, Bengali … But all those other lights below, do you know what those are?'

'I can hear shouting.'

'Eviction. Forcible removals. Quit Calcutta movement. All those fuckers living by the sewers, living on the footpaths—get out, all of you. Only all that sparkles must remain. Get out, fuckers: come on, hawkers, prostitutes, no hanky panky now—get out, eat our boots, feel the teeth of our dogs—come on, come on, keep walking—The God of the Road smiles and says, O Apu, does the road ever end? Come, let's keep moving. The wandering life! The wandering life!'

'O Father, O Raven!'

'Go on.'

'They're streaming in through the borders too.'

'Yes, they are. From Bangladesh. They're getting chased out over there, and rushing in here.'

'Who?'

'Hindu Bengalis, for the moment. I know what happens after this, but I won't tell you. Take away their land. Force them out. They're a minority. If the situation was reversed, then it would be the Muslims who were pushed out.'

'And those bright lights over there? The sound of music?'

'When will you ever know anything? That's the literature festival. Some or other brouhaha is always going on over there.'

'Literature festival! But why all those policemen, then?'

Purandar's surprise annoys Madan: 'Does any festival, even a wedding, happen without a minister these days? And ministers mean police.'

The Raven said: 'Heavy preparations. Even the British police did not bother so much during the historic coachmen strike of Calcutta.'

'Coachmen strike? I've never heard of it.'

'How will you? Do these two-bit intellectuals know anything? I'll tell you some other day when we have time. Oh, what stories. All about the old communists. So very different from the upstarts of today.'

How should the relationship be, between property developers and local-level leaders? Comrade Acharya was making some notes on the subject by way of preparing for a top-secret meeting. He was at his table. Watching the cigarette burning between his fingers, the thought suddenly occurred to him that capitalists do make good commodities, after all. Once he'd a cigarette manufactured in the erstwhile Soviet Union. The cigarette was as awful as the packet was crude and ugly. When he'd lit up, it had smelt as a pile of burning wet wood. Alas for Brezhnev; in the desperate attempt to save him, even a shaman had been sent for. Alas for Gorbachev. In a bid to understand the alchemy of politics, he dissolved away in some mysterious liquid . . . Then, suddenly, he snaps out of it. Before Comrade Acharya can identify the military-tunic-clad man in front of his table, a gust of Georgian tobacco smoke obscures everything.

'Have you read *Das Kapital*?'

Like Hamlet's father or Macbeth's Banquo, Stalin's ghost disappears swiftly.


Begum Johnson was playing underhand cricket with her slave girls in the garden. The ball rolls along, and comes to a stop near the hedges. Begum Johnson hears the rustling of leaves, and looks up at the ancient banyan tree.

Not ghosts, but bats. All day long they've hung upside down and observed a Hegelian universe. Now that evening approaches, they prepare to fly out into a Marxist world, looking for fruit.

Begum Johnson gathers her slave girls and walks back to her villa. There, every room is aglow with candles.

(*To Be Continued*)

## 19

The way Bechamoni burst into tears, one would be tempted to imagine that some Bengali soap opera had arrived at its climax, but it is not so, it is rather a heartfelt howl, signalling the death rattle of *Beggars' Bedlam*: 'What have you done, O god! Is this what lurked in your heart? . . . how cruel you are . . . O god!'

'Marshal Bhodi,' roars Major Ballabh Baxi (Retd), 'if you order it, I shall send my commandos. Tat for tit. Or the enemy will think we are cowards!'

Bhodi's disciples bellow in unison: 'DS' blood will not be for nought.'

'Long live DS!'

'Immortal martyr DS, long live!'

Peeping through Bhodi's tin door, witness Borhilal is shocked. DS is dead! Dead?! Even though Borhilal was a strongman, his heart feels as though its being wrung . . . the courtyard is awash with loud lamentations . . . and in this critical situation even Bhodi isn't sure what he should do, so every now and then he's scratching his crotch and keeping an eye on Bechamoni—in the middle of this mess, if the bitch faints or something . . .

And the person responsible for this frantic furore, that Purandar Bhat makes a few heroic attempts to stop this bedlam, but his head is fucked up because of all the yelling and weeping and wailing . . . and on top of that, he's black-out drunk . . .

Bhodi was lecturing his disciples on the upcoming and inevitable war when Purandar, smashed out of his wits on Bangla, hurtled in and began to sob: 'Bhodi-da! DS is khatam-killed! Police action in Hazra Park.'

'What? Finished?!'

'Yes. They surrounded us.'

'Then?'

'Then finished! I escaped. I saw, they held him by his hands and legs, loaded him into the van. Heavy body. So they were struggling. But in the end they had him.'

'Madan? Madan wasn't there?'

'No, only me and DS.'

Bechamoni whispers, 'God, how cruel you are! How cruel!'

'Boudi!' Nolen howls, 'Boudi—i—i!'

Instead of staying stuck in this tragic scene, if we change the channel via our remote control and catch Madan at this very moment, then we'll see him in his room, a towel round his waist, sitting on his haunches, waiting to drain the water from a pot of boiling rice—but what will he hold the pot with? So he takes off the towel he's wearing . . .

*Beggars' Bedlam* now presses another button on its remote, this is not Zee TV, Akash Bangla or Sony TV, definitely not BBC or CNN, instead let us imagine it is the BB channel—and on it we now see a giant red mansion. It's night. Oh, an enormous mansion, filling up the screen. A red mansion. How large is the front yard, my goodness! And look, pots of huge marigolds line the driveway.

Row after row of brass nameplates. Dear Reader, if we stand in front of the mansion, on our left will be a gate marked 'In', the same one through which we have entered and which leads to—Lalbazar! Understood? The second building, on the left, is the Detective Department. Flower fairies flitting about on every floor: Bomb Squad, Homicide ... Come on, DS is going in ... We are going in too. It's too early to know whether we'll eventually be able to use the right-hand gate marked 'Out' ... Come on ... *Beggars' Bedlam* may be faltering a bit, but it's not over yet. This evening will roll on a little longer.

But first, a little break. Who hasn't heard of the famous critic, Pisach Daman Pal? Apropos of this, let no reader confuse him with the poet P. D. Pal. Poet P. D. Pal has recently cyclostyled one of his poems and distributed it here and there, although for obvious reasons, the poem has not been able to rustle up even a single cyclone.

'P. D. Pal's Cyclo Poem'

When the world was destroyed
In the nuclear war
The whole of human civilization
Became a heap of ash no hand could gather
Every land turned to dust, to poisoned grime
The autumn issue of *Desh* was still released
With a posy of unpublished rhymes:
*'To little Ranu, from Bhanu-dada'*

Who will not condemn poet P. D. Pal? The critic Pisach Daman Pal simply cannot be the poet P. D. Pal. After reading the last, that is, the 18th instalment of *Beggars' Bedlam*, he said in a TV interview: 'Fuck! If I was German and *Beggars' Bedlam* had been published in 1930 or 31 or 32 in Germany, then I, yes, I, Pisach Daman Pal would at once register as a member of the Nazi Party and make sure the mega-blast that took place on 10 May

1933, i.e. the burning of 20,000 books, included, without fail, *Beggars' Bedlam*.'

Needless to say, we will not bother ourselves with the seeds of provocation strewn within Pisach Daman's startling statement. We will, instead, follow the Dalai Lama's advice: Let people say what they will, you must imagine it's nothing more than the whisper of the Tibetan wind blowing through the Nathu La Pass. Be that as it may, five days after that interview, Pisach Daman was sitting in his study, in his 11th-floor apartment, and in the warm light of a reading lamp was concentrating on *Deconstruction in a Nutshell: A Conversation with Jacques Derrida*, when he heard a rustling at the window. A giant raven, and in its beak, a smoking cigar.

The Raven blows out a large smoke ring. Pisach Daman is incredulous. The Raven holds the cigar in his claw, and coughs lightly. Then he says: 'This is what happens.'

'What do you mean?'

'I mean, this is what happens to all arseholes. Especially your type.'

'What?'

'Those who forget their childhood nicknames, this is what happens to them.'

'Who the hell are you?'

'Your father Kaliya Daman used to call me big brother. He's the one who gave you your nickname. Remember?'

'How strange! How bizarre!'

'Stop that nonsense orchestra. Your nickname was Pedo Pal. You've forgotten that. And you've read so much rubbish in the meantime, you think you can get away with it. I'll tell the public your name is Pedo Pal. Then you'll see, you damn dumbfuck.'

The Raven flew away. The smell of cigar smoke. On the windowsill, a line of ash, like a turd. Pisach Daman had sent his valet downstairs, to bring him some soda. Along with the soda, the fellow brought him the day's post. And each letter was addressed to Pedo Pal! Pisach Daman felt, slowly, his legs turning ice cold. No mistake. On every envelope, it's his nickname: Pedo Pal, Pedo Pal!

The little non-commercial break that *Beggars' Bedlam* was lucky enough to catch, is now ended. The end is nigh is a cry that may well be raised, but that is not something we need to heed right now.

Commissioner Joardar. The helmet keeping his severed head in place is gone. It's been a while since he was beheaded. After a special consultation with the laboratory assistants who handle corpses at NRS Medical College, he's had an aluminium hatch made on special order from Chandni market that can hold his headpiece in place. It looks a bit like a cage. But his head doesn't dive-swoop into his bowl of soup any more. And despite its money troubles, the contraption was paid for by Writers' Building. When he was first told that the government wouldn't pay, Joardar had lost his temper: 'I was beheaded on duty. If you won't consider that, then I'll make do with the helmet. It's only a matter of two more years. Then when I'm swinging in my Santiniketan garden, I'll be free as a bird. I can keep the head beside me, on a stool.'

Lolita Joardar said: 'We'll worry about the future in the future. Don't worry about that now. Like your plan to swing in the garden, I've got a plan too.'

'What? A garden?'

'Oh, the gardeners can do the gardening. I'm thinking of starting an NGO. Doing some work with the Santhals. Blacks! Poor niggers.'

'Sometimes you say things that just make my blood boil. There I was, hoping to spend my last days enjoying the Tagorean ambience. But no, madam's off to catch Santhals. Do you know what a Santhal is? Extremely violent. At the drop of a hat, they can become fire-furious! . . . They've always been like that. Read, read . . . Santhal Rebellion . . . mysterious drum beats . . . poisoned arrows . . . They screwed over even the British, and here you are . . .'

Now we need to know what happened to DS. Of course, first we need know why it happened at all. The capture was a consequence, not a cause.

When Purandar met DS at Jadubabu's Bazaar that afternoon, he'd noticed right away that DS' mood was rather sour. DS stubbed his toe in front of a fruit stand, and immediately started a quarrel with the fruit seller. The paanwala was preparing a custom order, so he was a few moments late in giving DS his five small Charminar cigarettes, so DS started a quarrel with him too: 'Just because you're working on a rich man's order, your arse got too juicy, eh?' The paanwala was a smart chap. He pretended he hadn't heard a word. It would have been nothing for him to give DS a sound thrashing. But good businessmen don't get involved in small scuffles.

Then DS and Purandar went to the hooch shack in Ganja Park. The place was jampacked. It always is. And most of the customers are Punjabi, as broad as the hills. Elbow your way to the counter, pay your money and pick up your glasses, if you don't get a place to sit, find a corner somewhere and squat on the floor—in one word, a lot of hassle.

'What's the case with Madan-da? He hasn't come for two days.'

'Who knows. Maybe Bhodi-da's given him some task. And he's not allowed to talk.'

'Maybe. But last year, this time, I'd noticed he was a bit morose-morose. I think it's the same time his wife ran away.'

Purandar doesn't answer. Sighs into his glass of Bangla. He is reluctant to talk about the subject. So he says: 'Haven't seen your son in a long time. How big is he now?'

'Not very big. But a real rascal already.'

'Have to see who his father is, after all. This pint didn't quite cut it—no?'

'One pint between two? That's a joke, really. Wait, I'll go get another.'

DS went to get another. Purandar was thinking that when he'd first started drinking, one file used to be enough. Then a line for a new poem flashed across his mind: 'Once it opens, it will close again, but this isn't that kind of a file'. But he could proceed no further: a huge commotion had broken out, near the counter. And a roaring could be heard, which was clearly DS. Purandar leapt to his feet and rushed in. Complete chaos. DS was fighting with a man in a dhoti and a long-sleeved cream-coloured shirt. Coming back from the counter with their drinks, one had bumped into the other. Purandar knew as soon as he saw the man—he was a plain-clothes constable. A specimen from Bihar. As broad as he was tall. While some others were trying to pull them apart, the chap kept saying: 'Did you see? He raised his hand first! And now, he's making the abuses too!'

'So far it's just been my hand,' bellowed DS, 'After this, it won't be hands, just machines—rat-a-tat-tat, rat-a-tat-tat.'

'Bastard, showing machines to police? Let me go, I'm going to take him to the station. Give him a good massage.'

'Huh, showing me police, eh? We shit on the shoulders of the police. Massage? I'll massage you back. You know halwa? Pudding? Turn you into pudding!'

Purandar somehow drags DS out of a mess that's growing increasingly interesting. DS is grunting, fuming and sweating.

'What's the point of such a bullshit brawl? We're here to drink, get a bit high, enjoy, and then go home . . .'

'I wouldn't have hit him. But the sisterfucker suddenly grabbed my collar, that's why . . .'

Later, standing against the Ganja Park railings, that is, on the pavement leading to the pissing alley, they shared a pint. Ate some shrimp fritters. The shrimps were so spicy that they both broke out into hiccups. Then they began to walk down the main road, along the left.

Meanwhile, the police had strict instructions to size up anyone involved in the flying- disc business. Full-sleeved cream shirt had a strong suspicion that anyone who could threaten the police with machine guns must be no lightweight. Maybe the capture of the short one could win him a medal or two. Thus, full-sleeve cream shirt starts following Purandar and DS but on the opposite pavement. On this pavement, DS was in a state of imminent follow-on, much like the frequent fate of the Indian cricket team.

Meanwhile, what had also occurred was the prompt action of the detective department. On the one hand, preparing for battle (guerrilla and positional), and on the other, gathering intelligence. Some special codes were formulated as well.

DS and Purandar walked past the horse-carriage crossing at Chakraberia. They were both lurching along in a zigzag fashion, so the women coming out of the cinema eyed them with alarm and gave them a wide berth. This has happened in the past as well. Humming a tune, along this very footpath have strolled Saigal, Robin Majumdar—and now on that same footpath walk DS and Purandar. Full-sleeve cream shirt walked over to a scowling man, showed his ID and used his Motorola mobile to call Bhabanipur Police Station.

And thus, we can hear a little of the special code in use:

'Hmm, yes, hello.'

'Mukaddar.'

'Sikander.'

'On the rooftop the crow dances.'

'Dances the heron.'

Having delivered the message, full-sleeved cream shirt tells the scowling man: 'You didn't hear anything, did you?'

'No, no, only something about rooftops.'

'Forget it. Walk away quietly. The times are bad.'

The scowling man uttered not a word more and disappeared.

DS and Purandar walk past the Purna Cinema crossing.

Purandar says, 'Want to eat a chop? A little to the left, they fry some damn good . . .'

'Hic.'

'Never mind, some other time.'

'Awk.'

'Do you want to throw up?'

DS smiles and shakes his head. Then slurs: 'Woo—ooo—zy. Boo—oo—zy!' Then he takes a few steps more, then stops.

'Why did you have to drink the stuff neat?'

DS staggers, straightens, and staggers again. 'All that . . . neat-sheet . . . doesn't do . . . anything . . . to . . . DS.'

'That I know. You're DS, after all.'

They're on the pavement outside the cancer hospital. The smells of Sri Hari Sweets Emporium are behind them. Just then, a van marked KP sidles up to the kerb, whistles are blown, boots hit the ground. From some secret reservoir, Purandar pumps strength into his feet and begins to move. After two Ronaldo-style feints to right and left, he suddenly sprints ahead with the ball, as it were. The people around him are dimwits. They begin to run too, helter and skelter and this way and that. DS is captured, though he continues to struggle.

We know what happened after this.

The crying and commotion in Bhodi's courtyard rises to such a crescendo that Bhodi can't control the uproar any more. Purandar had flown off to give Madan the news. Madan got so agitated, he rushed over without putting on his dentures! Bechamoni, between her sobs, keeps looking up at the sky and muttering. Major Ballabh Baxi (Retd) roars: 'Charge! Charge!' Nolen jumps up and down, waving a flimsy tin scythe. The reader will well remember this scythe, once proposed as an instrument for beheading the Phyatarus. This is exactly the kind of situation when leadership can change hands. At least, that's what history says. That is also what happened here, but only momentarily. Suddenly, Bechamoni was not whimpering or murmuring—but letting forth loud peals of laughter.

'Is this a playhouse or a circus?' snaps Bhodi, 'Nolen, has your Boudi totally lost her mind?'

Bechamoni smiles coyly, pulls the edge of her saree low over her head. And gives her hips a little shake.

'Nothing to worry about any more. Father's on his way.'

Really, if the Raven hadn't landed up just then, perhaps *Beggars' Bedlam* would have remained immortal as a serialized tragedy.

'Father! Father! Everything is ruined! DS is dead!'

Everyone is silent. The Raven cackles loudly.

'But Father, DS is dead and you—?'

'Why? What's not to laugh at? What's happened to DS?'

'Purandar was with him. Police attack at Hazra Park. DS killed in action!'

'Pubes.'

'What?'

'Pubes means pubes. Pubic hair. Curly.'

'Curse if you must, but to do so in English . . .'

'Shut up. Nothing's happened to DS. First, half pint with water, then two-thirds pint without water or soda or Coke or Pepsi, etc., etc. Then a punch to the spy-policeman's belly. Then almost passing out on the street. What say, Purandar?'

'Father!

'You thought only you were there, only you were drinking, all alone?'

'You? Were there? I didn't see you!'

'I was there, and I was not alone. Begum Johnson was there too, but in her spiritbody. How would you see?'

'Tell us more, Father. Uff, I feel so relieved, as though the life's seeping back into my body.'

'All right. Nolen, get some water. No booze mixing—pure water.'

A glass of water arrives. The Raven dips his beak into the glass and shakes some water over his head. Then dips each claw in, and washes it carefully.

'They took a blacked-out DS to Bhabanipur Police Station first. The OC informed Lalbazar that an important conspirator's been captured. Now they've taken him to Lalbazar. The beheaded Joardar is apparently going to interrogate him.'

Bhodi is somewhat calmer now: 'Interrogation in Lalbazar? What's going to happen now?'

'I've already fit a plan in place. I was thinking along one line. But Begum Johnson's idea is much better. Everything will be all right. DS is safe and sound. But he's still in a daze. So let him be.'


DS is hauled into the van, laid out on the floor. A hideous snoring fills the air.

Bhabanipur OC tells Joardar on the phone: 'One piece caught, sir. Threatened to fire guns at the police, sir. Rat-a-tat-tat. Another piece was there, sir. But that one escaped.'

'What was in his pocket? Machines, as in machine guns?'

'I checked. No weapons. Only a comb.'

'Good. What's he doing now? Crying? Complaining?'

'No, sir. Totally flat out.'

'What? Doesn't sound like a very important element, then.'

'No, no, sir. Very important. Rammed such a hard blow into one of our men. Right in the belly too.'

'A blow to the belly?'

'Yes, sir.'

'Understood.'

'What, sir?'

'No need for you to know. Send him over right away. I'll see to the rest.'


While DS was being transferred from Bhabanipur to Lalbazar, Joardar took a moment to let Comrade Acharya know that one suspected mutineer had been captured. Comrade Acahrya said, 'What a relief. Thus it begins.'

'What begins?'

'The captures, what else. And here I was thinking, you lot must be busy with your usual pastime: sleeping in peace.'

'No, no, sir, not at all.'

'No matter. Congratulations. Now be quick and capture the rest of them. End the whole affair. But yes, be careful. Trying to get information out of them, don't do anything that will make the Human Rights Commission come after us.'

'Uff, that's a new pain in our arse, sir. We can catch them, but we can't work them over. How can we do our jobs, then?'

'Never mind. Now that you've caught one, you'd better get cracking. I'll hear all about it tomorrow. Good night.'

'Good night!'


Even if anyone has the slightest inkling of where this night is headed, they cannot bid goodnight to this darkness, not yet. That is a matter for later. For now, we merely need to remind the reader that, in the 16th episode, we had been introduced, albeit briefly, to a lowly Lalbazar constable by the name of Nakshatra Nath Hawladar. Thus far, he has endured abandon and neglect and lain as a needle atop a haystack so high that even seven elephants will not be able to eat it all. Nakshatra Nath is a sleeper. Now he will wake up, and by the tender touch of Choktar magic, be transformed into a sword. We must elaborate: because of his association with Golap, Detective Taraknath Sadhu became a 'revolutionary'. Taraknath Sadhu in his turn converted Nakshatra Nath Hawladar. Taraknath had ample reason to be incensed with the system: he'd been the one they'd asked to grill his beloved Rose. He'd seen how a loyal servant of so many years was so easily turned into the prime suspect. And who knew, the lot that wrote such vulgarity on the covers of those files—'Pubes', 'Crazy Fuck'—maybe one day they would as easily target him too. Hawladar had great respect for Sadhu. The last name—'Sadhu', 'saint'—is what had attracted him like a magnet. That same Sadhu-baba had taken him to a restaurant close to Lalbazar, fed him omelette and toast and said, 'Hawla, you turned your pubes grey working for the police. If a terrorist or a dacoit pops you off tomorrow, do you think anyone or their uncle will shed a tear? Did you see the Karar case? They garlanded him, then cremated him, and then? His son wanders about on his own, shell-shocked, and have you seen the state of his wife?'

Karar had been a close friend of Hawladar. His eyes fill with tears, and the lines on his forehead tremble.

'And what about what happened to Bashir?'

'Oh, Bashir! Such a man! So alive. Don't cry, Hawla. Those whoresons have seen a lot of crying. Crying won't do. They need a different treatment.'

'Is there? Such a treatment?'

DS is carried into Lalbazar.

Bhodi's courtyard. Everyone has left. Only the Raven, Bhodi, Nolen, Bechamoni, Madan, Sarkhel, Purandar and Major Ballabh Baxi (Retd) remain. The Raven is looking into a black bowl full of water through a magnifying glass: 'There! There! They're at Lalbazar. My god, that body!'

'Father! You said body? Has he—?'

'Shut your gob. What's with the cock-coquetry when I'm looking into the bowl? Yes, body. A living body. They're taking him now. Where will they go but to Joardar's office.'

Though the intercut method has been used here, this is no ciné-roman.

Joardar's office: DS is laid out on the carpet. Joardar is excited: 'Who are you?'

'Sir, I am Hawladar.'

'Good! Good! Wait outside.'

'Sir?'

'Yes?'

'Passed out from drinking but he's still dangerous. Can you handle him alone?'

'Well, Mr Constable—I am Joardar, after all!'

'Yes, sir.'

Nakshatra Nath Hawaldar takes up his post outside the door, and lights a bidi.

The Raven, with a sharp eye on the bowl, says, 'Moving! It's moving!'

'What's moving, O lord?' asks Major Baxi.

'Your instrument, you goatfuck.'

This last curse cuts Major Baxi to the quick, and he falls silent. Such is the nature of the military. They calmly tolerate the curses that are deserved. But when they are undeserved, they whip out their guns.


At first, DS thought he was sleeping on the grass in Hazra Park. But Hazra Park is bare. When did all this grass grow, then? In the middle of this thought, the large carpet in Joardar's room becomes to DS his own bed back home. A fuzzy light shining in his eyes, Joardar's head encased in an aluminium cage, the smell of room freshener, the sound of the air-conditioner, and in the middle of all this, a phone rings.

'Hello ... Why do you bother me with such things ... I'm on a crucial assignment. Fuck your mushroom soup. Yes, yes, hog it all yourself and for God's sake, don't disturb me any more ... yes, my god, good night ... if you're sleepy then sleep ... good night ... uff, pest! Shameless cow ... so much drama ... should take the belt to her ...'

DS sat up suddenly. Saw Joardar, saw his head stuck inside an aluminium frame. 'Come down?' Joardar beamed at him, 'From the high? The smell says country liquor. Am I right?'

In response, DS delivered a total of three dialogues. That is perfectly possible, and perfectly all right, but why all three of them were in Hindi, we shall never know.

'Kya?'—'What?'

In answer to this, Joardar said in a stern tone of voice, 'You'll soon find out what. Dead drunk, and still so much attitude? Now, cough it up, come clean. According to our intelligence report, the rebels have two parties. Choktars and Phyatarus. Which one are you?'

'Pehley maal bulao!'—'First, send for booze.'

'What? You want booze in Lalbazar? There should be a limit to this tomfoolery. Tell me, are you Choktar or Phyataru?'

Now DS begins to tug at the zipper of his dirty terry-cotton pants, 'Mutey-ga kahaan?'—'Where do I piss?'

On the other side, the Raven flaps his wings in joy. Everyone else looks at him excitedly. 'Solid answer. Now, go on, answer that! If you try any funny stuff, he'll piss a flood down on your carpet . . . Carry on, DS . . . bravo . . .'

Joardar screams: 'Constable! Constable!'

Hawladar enters: 'Sir.'

'Take the prisoner for a piss. Hold on to him. Don't let him escape.'

'Escape from Lalbazar? What are you saying, sir! Come on, let's take you for a piss. Boss' orders.'

Staggering up to his feet, DS notices Joardar's baton. Held in his left hand, and being smacked softly against the palm of his right. DS and Hawladar open the door and step out onto an enormous veranda. There are a few other constables standing about. Hawladar is holding DS by his collar. But an invisible supernatural order makes him loosen his grip. It looks like he's holding tight, but in fact it's a gentle clasp, no more. Suddenly, DS starts humming the Phyatarus' great flying mantra: 'Flap, Flap, Fly, Fly!' And wobbling a little, he takes off—shoots up 9 feet into the air. And then, flapping his arms, he flies out of the veranda.

Hawladar had been certain that something would happen. But that it would be so easy, so simple—that had been beyond his wildest imaginings. He and the other constables ran to the end of the veranda. The sky was shrouded in the mysterious cocktail of moonlight plus diesel-burnt smog. DS flew straight up into that sky, and then higher and higher, almost Dracula-style.

Joardar was thinking it must be a marathon piss. But for so long? Joardar presses the bell, shouts: 'Constable! Constable!'

Hawladar and all the other constables rush in, howling and mewling. Looking like frightened crows, terrified herons.

An hour after this, as Joardar takes but two sips of his coffee, there is a call from Bhabanipur Police Station: 'OC Bhattacharya speaking, sir. There's bombardment on the station, sir.'

'What do you mean? Bomb or shell?'

'None of those, sir. Big bricks, pots full of mud, cauldrons, shit, broken buckets. Stuff like that. Absolute carpet bombing, sir.'

'So why call me? Catch them bastards and throw them into the lock-up.'

'Whom to catch, sir? The stuff's being dropped from the sky. We can see a flying figure or two, but visibility's so poor, and it's dangerous for the fellows keeping watch! Things are crashing down nonstop!'

'Are you saying it's an attack from outer space?'

Bam!

'Did you hear that, sir—that sound?'

'What is it?'

The OC's screams ring out: 'What fell? Oh, sir, a planter . . . with a tree still in it.'

'Let me see what I can do.'

Joardar was in no position to do anything but hang up the phone and gulp down the rest of his coffee. A prisoner fled from the fortress of Lalbazar! Not even fled, but flew! What explanation will Joardar come up with tomorrow, at Writers' Building? As it is, the chief minister was temperamental, on top of that . . .

The phone rings again. With a quaking heart, Joardar picks it up. The voice on the other end is quite forceful: 'You're the police commissioner?'

'Yes. I mean, who are you?'

'I'm Major Ballabh Baxi (Retd). Kindly hold the line. Marshal Bhodi will speak to you.'

'Marshal Bhodi—who's that?'

Bhodi speaks: 'Who am I? I'm me. Marshal Bhodi, current scion of Atmaram Sarkar. Do you remember the flying discs? Off goes the head? Remember?'

'How can I not? On-duty beheading, I remember it well.'

'That flying-disc company is mine. I am Marshal Bhodi.'

'Namaskar, Bhodi-babu!'

'Namaskar. Today you captured one of my men.'

'Couldn't keep him. He flew away.'

'No matter—I'm declaring war.'

'At Bhabanipur Police Station . . .'

'That's just the concert. Next is the real battle. Tomorrow itself, we'll rip your pants off!'

'Marshal! Marshal Bhodi? Marshal!'

The phone is silent. Joardar hangs up. It is ten past midnight. From the sky above Lalbazar, boom bam boom the bombs start raining down. A most terrible sound. The doors and windows are trembling. The coffee cup and saucer are dancing above the table.

Someone from the Bomb Squad rushes in. Says that none of the recovered bomb bits seemed to contain the usual homemade stuffing, no ball bearings, no bullets, no pieces of scrap iron.

'Strange!'

'But they're damn loud, sir.'

'I'm absolutely amazed! Calcutta was bombed by the Japanese back in the Second World War. And now, this is the second time!'

(*To Be Continued*)

## 20

The Rapid Action Force, along with a unit of the police, was advancing from the direction of the Kalighat Tram Depot down both sides of the street, that is, along the tramlines. There were at least 10 vans marked Kolkata Police. This army began to march around 10 in the morning. Slowly . . . slowly . . . it advanced . . .

Close to the Rashbehari crossing, from up on a rooftop, behind a giant billboard advertising cellphones, wearing a faded military jacket, hat and pants, Major Ballabh Baxi watched their approach through a pair of opera glasses. Between two pillars on the rooftop, waited the made-in-Lisbon Portuguese baby cannon. Ready with gunpowder and cannonballs.

The line of control was a wall covered with a Shahrukh Khan poster, against which tired pedestrians usually took a piss. The police did not know that this was so. Inside one of the vans of the advancing army sat the bald OC from Tollygunge Police Station.

Major Ballabh Baxi was counting under his breath: 10 . . . 9 . . . 8 . . . 7 . . . 6 . . . 5 . . . 4 . . . 3 . . . 2 . . . 1!

Then Major Ballabh Baxi yelled: 'Fire!'

And the baby cannon roared: BOOM!

Thank god, Calcutta has no mango groves! And though the main Ganga wasn't disturbed, the Old Ganga definitely trembled, as its murky waters could testify to only too well. Some readers may even have noticed a ripple. That morning, this novelist set a boat made out of a folded postcard on those waters. It toppled over at once, and dirty water rushed into its hull. And soon afterwards, a flock of crabs grabbed it in their claws and capsized it entirely. This is a common fate reserved for writers. And the fate of *Beggars' Bedlam* is unlikely to be different. In the heat of war, these minor details don't catch anyone's eye. They didn't this time either. Therefore, we can ignore this for now.

Old cannons such as this are not like the Bofors gun, that you can load and fire, load and fire. You need to pack in the powder again, cool the gullet, and only then the lighting and eventual discharge. The first cannonball landed on the roof of the bald OC's van and then, like a ping pong ball, jumped about on the tops of the other vans. As it bounced about, it made a boom-boom sound that the police mistook for giant drums.

Major Ballabh Baxi bellows: 'Water!'

A skin-and-bones soldier called Gaja pours water from a plastic mug, nicked from the toilet.

'Why are you watering the arse? Damn civilian dog! Water the body!'

Gaja trembles and pours water on the cannon's body. Just as it used to in the era of brave zamindar Kedar Ray, the cannon smokes in delight.

'Stuff it with powder. Put a shell in. Fire . . .'

This time, an even bigger display. This shell explodes in mid-air into innumerable smaller marble-sized shots, and following their larger predecessor, they too drum and dance on the roofs of the vans.

The roar of the baby cannon, the whistling noise of the shells as they approach, their non-stop dancing on the roofs—all this creates a panic among the force. The men jostle each other as they vie to crawl for safety under the vehicles.

'Enemy scattered. Hit them again. Fire—'

This projectile plays a new trick. Discharged from the cannon, it floats gently in the sky for a while until it reaches the vans. Then it simply floats, suspended above the heads of the policemen. And creates unprecedented suspense. The few policemen who hadn't crawled under the vans, they start running away.

The bald OC takes off his cap, scratches his bald head and calls Lalbazar on the wireless: 'Heavy shelling, sir. Case is curdling.'

'What are you saying, brother? Shelling?'

Boom! This time the noise is ear-splitting.

'Did you hear, sir? They hit us again.'

'How could I not? My ears are ringing! What are the casualty numbers?'

'No casualties, sir, but the force is scared stiff.'

'Do something: there's no use fucking with cannons. So: retreat. Immediately.'

'Thank you, sir!'

The bald OC pokes his bald head out of the van's window and shouts: 'We're going back. Everyone, get in. There's no use fucking with cannons.'

All the policemen who had crawled under the vans, hidden in nearby shops and homes, all of them run out and clamber in. On the roofs, the big cannonball and the small shells are still happily banging out a loud concert.

The police force retreats.

Major Baxi slaps Gaja's arse in triumph and offers him the opera glasses: 'Look, my friend, the enemy is running away. Go, get some more water. To celebrate our victory, we'll have a round of rum.'

Goja runs off again, clutching the plastic mug nicked from the toilet.

Dear Reader, it's not a bad idea to use this momentary military lull to revise a little. This re-vision is not a re-casting, hence not related to welding in any way. Although the thing about welding will be clear shortly.

Karforma—the owner of a wood storehouse in Garcha—dreamt last night that he was sitting at one end of an oval table. The room is enormous, the furniture old-fashioned and grand. On one side of the room is a British fireplace. A fire has been lit, a pile of logs is ablaze. But the punkha is being pulled as well. And the breeze from the punkha, like a giant blower, is fanning the flames over and over again. A giant candle glows on the table. A ghostly ambience. On the left wall, paintings of naked cherubs. Roly-poly, bewinged. Hanging under the paintings are two enormous, crossed swords.

Karforma is spooked, he mutters under his breath: 'I was no trouble to anyone—but what the hell have I got into now?'

As soon as he spoke, a giant raven landed on the table, noisily flapping its wings. Karforma was terrified.

'Did you get scared? But you're not supposed to get scared.'

'Yes, sir?'

'Of course, you don't remember what happened four births ago. In this very room, there was a grand ball, a mehfil. It's slipped your mind, clearly. All the sahibs danced. The booze flowed like a fountain. So much eating, drinking. Do you remember now? Lamb roast!'

'A little! The rumble of a coach, the tinkle of dancing bells!'

'That's it! Your duty was to procure a high-class native courtesan for Mr Sleeman.'

'I remember now!'

'How can you not? That's the same girl that murdered you later.'

'What?

'Yes, she poisoned you. No matter, do you recognize this place?'

'No.

'This is Begum Johnson's bungalow.'

At the speed of magic, across the oval table and in the chair across him materializes the enormous shape of Begum Johnson. So that Karforma can look at her properly, the Raven hops aside.

Begum Johnson is not a believer in small talk: 'Tomorrow morning, Karforma, you have two duties. I won't tolerate any hanky panky. I will also tell you what will happen if you do not follow orders.'

'No, no, of course I will. They're your orders, after all.'

'Good. This paper has Marshal Bhodi's address. As soon as you wake up tomorrow, send your driver Bolai to this address. He will pick up Marshal Bhodi, Bechamoni and Sarkhel. You will arrange for them to go underground.'

'And the other duty?'

'That's like a good boy. You next duty is to call Commissioner Joardar at Lalbazar and give him Marshal Bhodi's address. You must know: the rebellion's afoot.'

'I'm struggling to simply keep my business afloat . . . all this rebellion-shebellion . . .'

'Silence, naughty boy. You've kept a woman too. A rakhail. Last month you even bought a colour TV for her. If you disobey my commands, that same woman will poison you to death. Just like last time.'

'No, no, I'll do just as you say.'

Karforma wakes up, soaked in sweat. His wife is beside him. Snoring loudly. Karforma looks down and sees a piece of paper clutched in his hand.

Meanwhile, the Raven is telling Begum Johnson: 'This contradictory step of yours is not clear to me.'

'I shall explain. Bhodi has declared war. Now the final showdown needs to happen on a fair playing field. I've seen Tipu fight. An open war. And truth be told, at the end of the day, we're the ones that built that Lalbazar, after all. You may call this evenhanded justice. But the police will not find anything in Bhodi's house. Instead, they'll be trounced further. If Lalbazar doesn't have Bhodi's address, the spectacle cannot be complete. And you know only too well, I can't live without fun and mirth.'

Now, Dear Reader, do you remember Driver Bolai? Sunkencheeked, unshaven Bolai. Before he bid the Phyatarus farewell at the Tollygunge hooch shack, he'd said, 'OK brother, we'll meet again. Remember my name, Bolai. I never forget a face.'

Bolai's appearance and disappearance occurred in Episode 4. O Great Reader, have you ever fed catfish to the seals at the zoo? If you have, then remember, by that same technique, *Beggars'*

*Bedlam* is not feeding you forgotten catfishes but gifting you vanished characters, like Nakshatra Nath Hawladar. Like Bolai, etc., etc.

At the crack of dawn, a thump-thump-thump on the tin door. Bhodi thought it was the police. Clad in an ill-fitting military tunic, Bhodi had been fast asleep, an enormous rusty Mughal-era sword laid across his belly. Nolen opened the door. Not the police! But Bolai, with an ancient, dented black Landmaster.

Shortly after, the phone bells in Sarkhel's house ring out.

'Yes?'

'Come quickly.'

'Why?'

'We've got to go underground.'

'I haven't taken a shit yet.'

'Me neither. It can wait.'

When the Landmaster set off, bearing a cloth-wrapped arsenal of one sword, one kukri, one trowel, etc., and the four absconders, Borhilal was standing a few houses away. He turned, and began to leg it towards the Ganga. After his morning walk, he needs to eat his black grams with sugar and do his push-ups. To each his own. Just as Sasadhar must catch rabbits and Mohitosh kill mosquitoes.

Two hours after Bhodi and his team have left in the Landmaster, IPS Officer, Deputy Commissioner of Police Pitambar Singh surrounds Bhodi's house with a group of rifle-holding policemen. A portable microphone is used to announce that if there's anyone inside, they should surrender immediately. Armed resistance will be absolutely no use at all. But, what the fuck! The house is empty! Only a raven perched on the roof. (Begum Johnson was there too, sitting beside the Raven, her feet dangling over the roof's edge. But since she was in spirit form, the police couldn't see her.) The doors to the flying-disc room had been left open. When some of the other rooms were opened, they were found to contain only old flowers, straw mats, coconut shells, dead cockroaches, half-burnt bundles of hay, etc.

Even though Pitambar's origins are in Darbhanga, he is a Calcutta boy. Studied in St Xavier's. 'Looks like they practice witchcraft over here,' he said, 'Interesting. But no rebels.' Just then he notices the Bhodi–Sarkhel telephone wire: 'Mysterious! Seems to be a primitive speaking arrangement. Let me see.'

Following the wire, the police force arrive at Sarkhel's house. And there they discover the enormous one-man wide and deep hole, from the depths of which had been hauled up the Portuguese cannon and a handful of rusty Mughal swords. Pitambar shone a torch into the darkness. Deep down, a pool of black, stinking water. And a cloud of mosquitoes. And that's when disaster struck! In a small store-room-type space on Bhodi's ground floor, one of the constables had spotted four or five bottles. Sealed tight. Filled with liquid. Thinking they may be full of booze, he had opened one. Whether ghosts are kept in bottles or not, whether they can be or not—our job is not to come to any well-considered conclusion on the subject but rather to merely report events as they occurred in this instance—the constable suddenly felt an invisible but hefty pair of hands grip him by his hair and drag him out to the court-yard. Then they thwacked him a solid blow across his face. As soon as he put up a hand to his cheek, he felt himself kicked in the arse. Begum Johnson and the Raven chuckle and chortle in glee. Not even the most famous mime artist could perform so well! What the other policemen saw was: exit, a screaming constable, pursued by a bucket.

Even though Pitambar didn't witness this scene, when he came out of Sarkhel's house a minute later, the visible dejection among his men was as tragic as it was worrisome. The flying bucket had by then gone back to the house. The doors had slammed shut, even though there was no one home. The askew signboard proclaims, 'Rooms on Rent for All Inauspicious Occasions'. On the roof, a giant raven.

Back in his jeep, for a sudden moment, Pitambar fancies that beside him is an enormously fat, laughing, gown-wearing memsahib. Her face like a frying pan. The very next moment: no memsahib. Only the massive raven.

Pitambar mutters: 'Mysterious! Stuffed to the gills with ghosts or what!'

Comrade Acharya practically bursts into flames: 'Cannons firing, cannonballs dancing on top of police vans, no casualty and yet widespread panic among the force, have you considered what the chief minister will say when he hears all this?'

Joardar thought there's no point in being meek and mild: 'Look, I'm telling you straight. This is not an ordinary enemy. This is not your SUCI rally, that we'll just do a lathi charge and beat them black and blue. Explain the situation to the chief minister. I was beheaded on duty—could you do anything about that? Now they're fighting with cannons. What if they lose their temper next, and shoot off a weapon of mass destruction? What will you do then?'

'Don't be angry, Comrade Joardar! Don't be angry!'

'Fine. And don't call me Comrade—stick to Mister. I hate communism and the reds.'

'Do something, please. Something to save face. If Marshal Bhodi continues to heckle us like this . . .'

'Let me see. Now hang up. Let me think.'

Pitambar's report depresses Joardar further. Flying buckets beating up policemen. The mysterious hole in Sarkhel's courtyard. The aerial bombardment of the night before. Plus the attack on Bhabanipur Police Station.

Joardar came up with a new plan. Not from the Kalighat–Hazra side—this time, a massive force will proceed from the direction of Deshapriya Park. But first, they need to determine which rooftop has the cannon.

On the rooftop with the cannon, Major Ballabh Baxi had just finished a working lunch of tarka dal and roti. Accompanied by Hercules rum. Goja had drunk some bhang during last year's Durga Puja. He was very fond of the taste of military rum. After a while, he could hold himself back no longer: 'Why don't you pour us a small one too? It will help set the mood.'

'That I can set, but what if the enemy makes a surprise attack? Have you stuffed the gunpowder?'

'Fully ready. You say the word, and I'll light it up.'

'Good! Very good! Go, bring the water.'

Goja takes the plastic mug and goes off to fetch water.

Major Baxi thought he'd take a two-minute short nap. But the growing-ever-louder buzzing sound in the ether entirely ruined his siesta plans. As they also ruined the plan for the forces to advance from the direction of Deshapriya Park. That great whirlwind of noise was caused by countless flying discs. Flying in formation, flock after flock. And even though it is broad daylight, above the flocks of flying discs fly a team of Phyatarus. This time, it's not just Madan and DS and Purandar. DS' wife, child, brother-in-law Jona, and so many other Phyatarus about whom nobody knew. They all wave at Major Ballabh Baxi. Baxi whistles the famous *Bridge on the River Kwai* tune and dances with joy. It's more than evident that the Phyatarus are flying above an impenetrable shield of flying discs. This is exactly how bombers are protected by fighter planes.

In the clear light of day, the people of Calcutta had not only seen this beautiful scene, but they had also admired it. Whatever happens in the sky, be it a total solar eclipse or an overnight meteor shower, the people of Calcutta will not miss it for the world. And this scene is positively heavenly—flying discs, and above them, flying humans!

The war cries of the Phyatarus rend the sky as though they are divine deliverances:

'Oye oye, oye oyo ah . . .'

'Layla, O Layla!'

'Li! Li!'

'Chhaiya-chhaiya . . .'

An ear-splitting explosion. BOOM! Ti-DOOM! The target: various police vans, both moving and stationary. The bombardment begins. With homemade explosives. And plastic-bag balloons filled with mud and slime. In these clamorous conditions, a new magnitude is added by Calcutta's numerous rowdies and hooligans: the vast reserves of chocolate bomb firecrackers that are maintained at all times, to celebrate the victories or defeats incurred by Mohun Bagan, East Bengal, Brazil or India—those were thrown into the mix as well.

The bald OC was sitting in his jeep, his hands covering his ears.

On top of the vans, the cannonballs rattle and roll.

Evening falls slowly on this explosive Calcutta, though the darkness is lit up every now and then with flashes of light.

Major Ballabh Baxi says: 'Marshal Bhodi's masterstroke is not yet complete. The air attack is underway. Now, it'll be a different game. Send up a flare!'

A rocket is placed in the upturned mouth of the cannon. The rocket flies into the sky, bursts and becomes a circle of light.

From Karforma's rooftop, Bhodi watches the rocketburst and slaps Sarkhel's shoulder: 'Hit them from the skies, don't spare them on land either. Let's see what they do now!'

The rocket that bursts into a glowing circle—that is the ultimate signal. Soon, be they big or small, all the manhole lids in all the roads, lanes, bylanes begin to open, one by one. And the beings that emerge from the depths wear metal helmets with holes cut out for the eyes, gleaming body armour and carry many kinds of deadly weapons, though it's hard to make them out clearly in the dark. Rather like the savage army of Rome, or the knights of Ivanhoe. The appearance of this particular legion terrifies the police further. The barrage of homemade explosives and other liquid and non-liquid missiles has already caused them no end of terror and grief. A closer inspection of the underground army would have revealed their armour to be nothing more than a layer of coal tar painted on old tins, tins for oil, tins for biscuits . . . The plan to have these frightful knights emerge out of the manholes had been Major Ballabh Baxi's. Another one of his innovations had been to weld a pipe to the garbage collectors' old, falling-apart carts, and make them look like tanks. This is what is known as psychological warfare.

Since the morning, the cannon's attack had shattered police morale. The little that remained had been wiped out by the relentless attack from the skies. And the little that remained even after that—every last drop was wiped out by the portentous arrival of the knight-horde and tanks.

Nonstop bombing. And the buzz-whirring of the discs.

Comrade Acharya called Joardar in the middle of this mayhem: 'What do you think, Mr Joardar?'

'No hope. They've buggered us all right.'

'So you're saying the mutiny can't be stopped?'

'We'll be lucky if we can get through the night. Hang up the phone. I can't tolerate your fits and farts any more.'

Comrade Acharya hung up.


The night that Joardar was so afraid of, that same night something happened that ultimately became a reason for the situation coming under control. Who is not familiar with the fact that whenever and wherever anything important happens, Bengal's intellectuals, without wasting a precious second, collectively issue an announcement, an appeal or an empty threat that everyone from the big and the small, the old hands and the younglings, writers, artists, singers, dancers, theatre actors and film artists sign in order to save their own hides and to mess with the rest? Simply by signing such an appeal or protest letter, many have claimed themselves to be writers. No one wants to be left out of signing such things. If they are, they go red with rage. Often, they'll enquire over the phone: Are you sure my name will appear on the letter? And then there are those who don't need to be told anything at all. Has there been a proposal to collect and publish all such appeal and protest letters till date? Has someone researched this subject, or is willing to?

Whatever. After the night that Joardar feared had passed with many more bim-bam boom-booms, almost every newspaper the next morning published an appeal:

8

The bloodless struggle between the forces of the government and the Choktar–Phyatarus is causing much disruption to our sleep. We came to the conclusion a long time ago that staying awake is fruitless. Hence, we have fallen asleep. And when we see in our dreams all that is happening around us, we think our decision was correct. That's why our unanimous appeal is: both parties come together for peace talks. And arrive at such an arrangement that kills the snake yet breaks no stick. Struggle is necessary, as is rest. We need the latter rather more than we need the former. With our blessings—

Kaliprasanna Kabyabisharad, Brajendranath Bandyopadhyay, Mr B. K. Das, Mr Panto, Mr P. B., G. S. Ray, Suresh Chandra Chakraborty, Sudhindranath Tagore, Rabindranath Tagore, Binoy Kumar Das, Amrita Lal Basu, Bimalacharan Deb, Ashutosh Mukhopadhyay, Subal Chandra Mitra, Sarat Chandra Chattopadhyay, Vishuddhananda Paramahansa, Gopinath Kaviraj, Hemendra Nath Das Gupta, Charuchandra Chattopadhyay, Krishna Kumar Mitra, Ajiteshwar Bhattacharya, Surendranath Mallick, Surabala Ghosh, Girindrashekhar Basu, Dakshinaranjan Mitra Majumdar, Dhan Gopal Mukerji, Hemendra Kumar Roy, Sunirmal Basu, Khagendranath Mitra, Sukhalata Rao, Jogendranath Gupta, Kailashchandra Acharya, Gobindachandra Das, Michael Madhusudan Dutt, Hemendra Chandra Kar, Premankur Atorthy, Atmaram Sarkar, Ganga Gobinda Ray, Ali Sardar Jafri, Krishan Chander, Radhanath Sikdar, Harihar Seth, Bankim Chandra Chatto-padhyay, John Stuart Mill, Brajendra Kishore Deb Barman, Joseph Townsend, Kanhapada, Bhusukupada, Hemchandra Bandyopadhyay, Bishnu De, Bijoylal Chatto-padhyay, Kalidas Roy, Shailendra Krishna Laha, Mikhail

Bakhtin, Kumud Ranjan Mullick, Werner Heisenberg, Bishu Datta, Harihar Sarkar, Michel Foucault, Durgadas Bandyopadhyay, Chandandas Mandal, Alamohan Das, Vladimir Nabokov, Carl Gustav Jung, Nigamananda . . .

The above appeal will cause a difference of opinion among future historians and social scientists. One group will say that such an appeal was never published. The opposite faction will claim of course that it was. Neither party will win, because no newspaper with that date will ever be found.

But it was this appeal that entirely changed the war. The next day there was no battle. After 4 a.m., even the bombing began to slowly let up. In the morning, it was observed that every manhole cover was tightly back in place. Knights, tanks—all vanished. The sky so fresh and clear too.

The rest, in short, went as follows: both parties conducted what is known as 'hectic parley'. Golap, Taraknath Sadhu, Nakshatra Nath Hawladar and Borhilal were also involved in these efforts. In truth, the abovementioned appeal had not only touched everyone's hearts but also wounded them deeply.

Begum Johnson quoted from the Bible: 'Just as there is a time of war, there will be a time of peace. Like the day following the night.'

The Raven said, 'Everything is Atmaram at play. Every hundred and fifty years, the discs will dance. It was a damn good show this time. Now, let's wrap it up.'

Bhodi had protested: 'You're saying wrap it up, so I'll wrap it up. But in all this wrapping up, we have to be careful not to expose our balls.'

The Raven laughed: 'Didn't get much of the family traits, but certainly got the mouth. Got to see whose son he is, after all!'

The same thing happened to Comrade Acharya. He was given a dressing down by the experienced, and older, chief minister: 'Read the history of the Brest–Litovsk Treaty. Bukharin wanted to carry on the guerrilla war with the Germans. Lenin understood that would be tantamount to death by drowning. Trotsky had to listen to Lenin that day, understand? If you need to go dressed in a petticoat so be it. You remain as stupid as ever.'

The historic discussion had taken place in the heart of Calcutta, in the Parish Hall of St Paul's Cathedral. Pepsi and Coke—an endless supply of both. Nothing interrupted the peace talks. No party will mess with the other, this had been the gist of the signed peace treaty.

But at the very end, that is, at the penultimate moment of the discussion, Commissioner Joardar intervened: 'That's all very well, Marshal Bhodi. But the mystery of the black hole in Sarkhel's courtyard as per Pitambar's report still remains. It's the second one in Calcutta.'

'Sarkhel, you want to answer? No? OK. I'll let the cat out of the bag. Sarkhel was the one who came up with the idea. In the 60s or thereabouts, some Soviet academic called Kalinin or something had said that Calcutta is floating on oil. That all of Calcutta is Iraq. That's why Sarkhel and I were digging—for oil. There must be one condition here—no squabbling!'

Comrade Acharya said, noting down Bhodi's statement: 'What do you, Marshal Bhodi, mean by condition?'

'This oil will be sold and extracted by a corporation, a company. I, Marshal Bhodi, will be its chairman.'

A few moments' suspense. The whole thing's been captured by Star TV and other channels.

Comrade Acharya said, 'All right, Marshal Bhodi.'

'It will have permanent jobs for all Phyatarus, all Choktars, plus Bolai, plus Borhilal.'

'Yes, I give you my word, Marshal Bhodi.'

That's when the CNN reporter hurled his question: 'Marshal Bhodi, what's the guarantee that you won't become another Saddam Hussein?'

(*To Be Continued*)

*21*

The show's over. But the money isn't.

Borhilal and Kali's relationship continues uninterrupted. All Hail Lord Hanuman! Joardar's head has mended itself. The police commissioner himself hadn't noticed. Lolita Joardar surprised him one morning by kissing him, 'I've sold off that cumbrous frame of yours to the garbage man.'

'What do you mean?'

'Simple. Sold it. Because your head, beheaded on duty, is attached now.'

'Attached?'

'Yes, my love!'

Major Ballabh Baxi has gone underground. No one knows where. It's been rumoured that he may grant an interview to Al Jazeera.

Galas are being held regularly in Bhodi's courtyard. A veritable fountain of alcohol! Nolen is farting frequently, fetching this and that. Bechamoni has grown even more radiant, even more voluptuous.

Sarkhel is digging, hauling up bucket after bucket of soil.

The Phyatarus visit the hooch shacks regularly. Annoy one another.

Let it be known,

The skulls danced.

Magician Ananda advertised in *Anandabazar Patrika*.

So what didn't happen?

Waa . . . waa . . . !

If the intelligent reader or reader-ess, goat or goat-ess hasn't yet discarded this variegated half-baked hotchpotch cacophony at its beginning or middle, then their final catharsis is now complete. It's been wrung out. No nightbird sings alas, 'Don't go, don't go . . .'

Yet engulfing everything is a morose-melancholy feeling. That is the feeling that stays. Why, my dear?


The old Raven was sitting atop the Shaheed Minar. The west of Calcutta awash with the colours of sunset. A beam of that golden glow focuses on the enormous, ruffled wings. The Raven says to himself, 'Finally! *Beggars' Bedlam*'s been published! I should let Begum Johnson know.'

And he flies away.


(*Not Continued*)

# Translator's Notes

**p.1. Old Ganga** | Also known as Adi Ganga, Gobindapur Creek, Tolly's Canal. One of the most significant streams of the River Ganga in its lower course between the 15th and 17th centuries; ran dry due to natural causes in the mid-20th century. Now more of a drain that runs behind the Keoratala Crematorium in South Calcutta, it is still considered by many to be part of the sacred Ganga and hence used for immersing the ashes of the dead.

**p.2. nation's mega-crisis** | The Partition of Bengal (1905), a territorial reorganization of the Bengal Presidency by the British Raj, separating predominantly Muslim eastern areas from largely Hindu western areas. Announced by Viceroy Lord Curzon, it aimed for administrative efficiency but was seen by nationalists as part of a divide-and-rule strategy. Due to protests and the Swadeshi movement, Bengal was reunited in 1911 by King George V.

**p. 2. Kaliprasanna Kabyabisharad** | (1861–1907). Editor of *Hitavadi*, a weekly literary journal. Famous for his satirical writings, which attacked Bengali luminaries such as Bankim Chandra Chattopadhyay, Keshub Chandra Sen and even Rabindranath Tagore in poems composed under the pseudonym Rahu. To protest the 1905 Partition of Bengal, he, alongside Surendranath Banerjee, led a boycott of British-made goods. His 'swadeshi' or nationalist songs were very popular in their time.

**p. 7. 'Rasaraj' Amrita Lal Basu** | (1853–1929). Playwright and actor; one of the pioneers of 19th-century public theatre in Bengal. His acting in *Gajadananda o Yuvaraj*, a play written on the occasion of the Prince of Wales' visit to Calcutta in 1921, satirizing flatterers, incurred the wrath of the British authorities; he was arrested along with the playwright-director, Upendra Nath. His plays, critiquing the follies of both urban and rural societies, include *Tiltarpan* (1881), *Bibaha Bibhrat* (1884), *Taru-Bala* (1891), *Kalapani* (1892), *Bimata* (1893), *Adarsha Bandhu* (1900) and *Avatar* (1902).

**p. 8. shield of station** | Nabarun has indulged in one of his brilliant puns here; this phrase in the Bengali reads 'Jhapater Dhal'—a railway station at Sankari, Purba Bardhaman District, West Bengal. It is one of the stops for the trains running to and from Calcutta and Bolpur. Following the mention of Tagore in the previous paragraph, it is a snide allusion to the rich urban Bengalis frequenting—often by train—their 'holiday homes' in Tagore's university town of Santiniketan. 'Dhal' is also the Bengali word for 'shield'.

**p. 12. Gobar Guha** | Ring name of Jatindra Charan Guha (1892–1972); Indian professional wrestler trained in pehlwani wrestling. Spent most of his career wrestling internationally and defeating champions such as Władek Zbyszko, Renato Gardini, Ad Santel and Joe Stecher. First Asian to win a World Wrestling Championship in the United States. See also Sandeep Balakrishna, 'The Superhuman Diet and Demonic Workout Regime of Pehlwan Gobar Goho', *The Dharma Dispatch*, 13 January 2023. Available at: https://bityl.co/QqB5 (last accessed 2 July 2024).

**p. 12. Great Gama** | Ghulam Mohammad Baksh Butt (1878–1960), commonly known by his ring name 'The Great Gama', a pehlwani wrestler and strongman in British India and later in Pakistan. His extraordinary strength, agility and tactical brilliance earned him the title 'Rustam-e-Hind' (Champion of India). Undefeated in a career spanning more than 52 years and over 5,000 matches, he is considered one of the greatest wrestlers of all time.

**p. 12. Small Gama** | Not much is known about this person, but reports suggest he was a wrestler patronized by the Maharaja of Baroda in western India around the middle of the 20th century. Was meant to fight Hamida Banu (*see later*) in 1954, but pulled out, saying he refused to wrestle a woman.

**p. 12. Zbyszko** | Władysław Cyganiewicz (1891–1968), better known by his ring name Władek Zbyszko; Polish wrestler and strongman. Began his career in Europe but emigrated to the US in the 1910s, where he was billed as the 'Youngest European Champion'. Wrestled the Great Gama twice; after being defeated in the second fight in 1928, he retired and dedicated his life to recruiting wrestling talents.

**p. 12. Sandow** | Born Friedrich Wilhelm Müller (1867–1925); German bodybuilder and showman from Prussia, using the Bulgarian name 'Eugen Sandow'. After a spell in the circus, studied under strongman Ludwig Durlacher. In 1901, organized what is believed to be the world's first major bodybuilding competition at London's Royal Albert Hall. Judged the event alongside author Sir Arthur Conan Doyle and athlete-sculptor Charles Lawes-Wittewronge.

**p. 14. Sir Ashutosh Mukhopadhyay** | (1864–1924). Renowned Bengali educator, jurist, barrister and mathematician. The first to earn a dual degree from Calcutta University; served as its vice-chancellor for multiple terms between 1906 and 1923. Founded Bengal Technical Institute (later Jadavpur University) in 1906 and University College of Science in 1914. Widely known as 'Bangla-r Bagh' or Bengal Tiger. The reference in this section to Calcutta University is evident from Sir Ashutosh's bio; the Kolkata [at the time Calcutta] Municipal Corporation is responsible for the upkeep of the city's memorials and mausoleums.

**p. 15. Somen Mitra** | (1941–2020). Leader of the Indian National Congress party for five decades and briefly of the Trinamool Congress in West Bengal; represented the Sealdah constituency in Central Calcutta from 1972 to 2006. At the time of writing, i.e. the late 1990s, was president of the West Bengal wing of the Congress and widely lionized as a local leader.

**p. 15. Rajendra Nath Mookerjee** | (1854–1936). Pioneering Bengali industrialist and engineer. Beginning his career as a contractor; co-founded Martin & Co. and the Indian Iron and Steel Company. Projects included some of the most iconic Calcutta landmarks, such as the Victoria Memorial and the Howrah Bridge. Also founded the Indian Statistical Institute.

**p. 15. Subal Chandra Mitra** | (1872–1913). Bengali writer, biographer, lexicographer, journalist (editor of *Sahitya Samhita*, a monthly literary journal) and publisher (proprietor, New Bengal Press, Calcutta).

**p. 18. Sarat Chandra Chattopadhyay** | (1876–1938). Prominent Bengali novelist and short-story writer whose works depicted various aspects of Bengali life. His best-known novels include *Devdas* (1917) and *Srikanta* (1917–33). Ardent supporter of the Indian freedom movement, he remains a significant influence in Indian literature as well as cinema.

**p. 21. Girindrasekhar Bose** | (1887–1953). Known as the Father of Indian Psychoanalysis. First president of the Indian Psychoanalytic Society. Engaged in a 20-year dialogue with Sigmund Freud, disputing the Oedipus complex. Established Asia's first general hospital psychiatry unit in Calcutta in 1933. Remembered as author of *Lal–Kalo* (1957), a jewel of early-20th-century Bengali children's literature, about the escalating conflict between two ant kingdoms after the black ants seek retaliation against the red ants for insulting one of their own; a saga of spies, intrigues and strategies. Available in English translation by Sukanta Chaudhuri as: *Red Ant Black Ant* (Calcutta: Jadavpur University Press, 2020).

**p. 21. Dakshinaranjan . . . Sukhalata** | Series of Bengali children's writers mentioned includes **Dakshinaranjan Mitra Majumder** (1877–1956), author of iconic fairy-tale collection *Thakurmar Jhuli* (1907); **Dhan Gopal Mukerji** (1890–1936), one of the first successful Indian man of letters in the United States and an early luminary of Indian English writing, best known for the children's book *Gay Neck, the Story of a Pigeon* (1927); **Hemendra Kumar Roy** (1888–1963), one of the pioneers of Bengali detective and adventure fiction, creator of popular fictional duos Jayanta–Manik and Bimal–Kumar, best remembered for the novel *Jawker Dhan* (1930); **Sunirmal Basu** (1902–1957), writer of numerous poems, short stories, novels, travelogues, fairy tales and comedies for children and young adults; **Khagendranath Mitra** (1896–1978), author of more than 100 books for children as well as founder of *Kishor*, Asia's first literary journal for children; **Sukhalata Rao** (1886–1969), writer and social worker who hailed from one of the most illustrious cultural families of Bengal—she was the sister of author Sukumar Ray and aunt of filmmaker Satyajit Ray.

**p. 21. Feluda** | Fictional detective created by filmmaker and writer Satyajit Ray in the 1960s; became rapidly popular among Bengali youth through novels and stories that regularly appeared in literary magazines *Desh* and *Sandesh*. Ray adapted two of his Feluda novels—*Sonar Kella* (1974) and *Joi Baba Felunath* (1979)—for the screen in the 1970s, both of which remain popular to this day. New film and television adaptations of the stories and novels continue to flourish. Feluda narratives, while entertaining, are marked by a Wetsernized and sanitized sensibility typical of the strictly moralistic, urban Bengali middle class of the mid-20th century. Here Nabarun makes a distinction between the earlier, indigenous and often more complex and diverse children's literature of Bengal and the later, anglicized Feluda- or Tintin-style entertainment.

**p. 21. Branolia** | Popular Ayurvedic 'tonic' advertised as a 'memory enhancer'; especially targeted at children and youth under pressure to succeed in their school and college examinations.

**p. 21. Hnada-Bhnoda . . . Chyanga-Byanga** | Once-popular indigenous Bengali comic strips, mostly serialized in youth magazines such as *Shuktara* and *Kishore Bharati*. Hnada-Bhnoda, Nonte-Phonte and Bnatul the Great were characters created by Narayan Debnath (1925–2022) in the 1960s. While Hnada-Bhnoda and Nonte-Phonte are pairs of mischievous children, their humorous adventures set in urban and semi-rural locales, Bnatul is the first Bengali superhero, with a well-built, broad body, an exceptionally large chest and god-like strength. Chyanga-Byanga is a hare-and-frog pair created by well-known children's author Bimal Ghosh (1910–1982).

**p. 33. Jogendranath Gupta** | (1893–1964). Historian and litterateur from Vikrampur, Dhaka. Edited journals like *Pathik* and *Kaishorak* and authored over a hundred books in various genres. Also wrote biographies, plays and novels. Girish Lecturer at Calcutta University, and recipient of the Bhuban Mohini medal.

**p. 33. Gobindachandra Das** | (1855–1918). Satirist and translator from Jaydevpur, Dhaka; adept in Sanskrit and Bengali. Wrote on sensuous love and natural beauty as well as the poverty he saw around him; his patriotic poems were a source of great inspiration for the Bengali freedom fighters. Translated the *Bhagavadgita* but is best known for the satirical poem *Mager Mulluk* (1893).

**p. 34. chandrabindu** | A diacritic sign in the Bengali alphabet used to signify the dead; similar to the use of 'late' in English.

**p. 36. Grows Trinamool** | In the late 1990s, West Bengal had been ruled by the Left Front, led by the Communist Party of India (Marxist)—referenced throughout this novel as CPM—for over two decades. But political opposition was growing, especially in the form of the Trinamool [Grassroots] Congress party, founded in 1998 by Mamata Banerjee. The Trinamool Congress often gained power by covertly attracting CPM cadres—hence Nabarun's reference to 'sneakily grows'. He also plays on the imagery of Trinamool's party symbol—wildflowers amid blades of grass—to foreshadow the eventual change in power in West Bengal that occurred in 2011.

**p. 46. Mahadwadoshi** | In popular Hindu practice, the eleventh day of the lunar cycle, termed Ekadashi, is observed through ritual worship of deities and fasting. Sometimes two lunar days coincide on one (solar) day, making it a Mahadwadoshi, which is considered particularly auspicious.

**p. 61. the toothless Kali Puja** | Kali Puja, which coincides with Diwali, has traditionally been an occasion for bursting firecrackers. In 1997, to reduce noise pollution, the Calcutta High Court ordered the West Bengal Pollution Control Board (PCB) to set permissible noise levels for fireworks. The PCB set 90 decibels as the upper limit, which made many popular noisy firecrackers, such as chocolate bombs, illegal. It has since been revised to 125 decibels. The '65-decibel furore' that the author mentions refers to the permissible limit for loudspeakers in West Bengal.

**p. 62. Suresh Biswas** | (1861–1905). Born in a middle-class Hindu family in Bengal, he converted to Christianity at 14. Worked as a tourist guide before stowing away to Rangoon. Travelled to England, where he became a circus-animal trainer. Later, migrated to Latin America, the first Bengali to do so. Achieved fame with his tiger performances in Brazil; then joined the Brazilian army, rising to the rank of lieutenant (but not 'colonel' as the author suggests) and playing a key role in quelling the Brazilian Naval Revolt of 1894. Died in Rio de Janeiro at 45; his widow and children received pensions from the Brazilian government. Despite limited records, there is renewed interest in his life after the recent republication of his 1899 biography: H. Dutt, *Lieut. Suresh Biswas: His Life and Adventures* (Calcutta: Jadavpur University Press, 2018).

**p. 62. Arambagh** | Town in Hooghly District, West Bengal; adopted hometown of Prafulla Chandra Sen (1897–1990), Indian freedom fighter and once chief minister of the state. For his Gandhian views, simple lifestyle, selfless work and lifelong emphasis on khadi, he earned the sobriquet 'Gandhi of Arambagh'. Beginning in the 1970s, the town became the headquarters of Arambagh Hatcheries, which has since gained great popularity in West Bengal for its broiler-chicken breeding and meat processing.

**p. 65. Premankur Atorthy** | (1890–1964). Novelist, journalist and film director, working in both Bengali and Hindi cinema. Edited *Nachghar*, one of the first performing-arts journals to take cinema seriously. Best-known literary work is *Mahasthabir Jatak* (1944), a fictional autobiography in four volumes, noted for its irreverent portrayal of Calcutta's early-20th-century elites.

**p. 66. Pindari Glacier ... Hemendra Chandra Kar** | Pindari Glacier, located in the upper reaches of the Kumaon Himalayas in the Indian state of Uttarakhand, is a popular trekking destination. Hemendra Chandra Kar (b. 1915) was a lieutenant colonel in the Indian army who authored an exhaustive *Military History of India* (Calcutta: Firma KLM, 1980).

**p. 67. Hazak** | Or 'Hijack'. Petromax-style paraffin lamp; possibly a brand name.

**p. 67. Baygon** | Brand of insecticide used for extermination and control of household pests.

**p. 69. Naxal days** | Following the Naxalbari Uprising in North Bengal in 1967, the ultra-left insurgency led by militant leaders known as Naxals or Naxalites spread across the rest of the state. Naxalites recruited students and initiated widespread violence in West Bengal, including urban centres such as Calcutta, targeting 'class enemies' such as landlords, businessmen, university professors, police officers and politicians across the political spectrum. In response, in 1971, Prime Minister Indira Gandhi launched Operation Steeplechase, a large-scale anti-insurgency military operation that resulted in the deaths of hundreds of Naxalites and the imprisonment of thousands. These bloody years—from 1969 to 1973—are usually referred to in Bengal as Naxal times or Naxal days.

p. 71. **Bengali lathials . . . trained at various akharas** | Lathials were a distinct social group in rural Bengal before and during British colonial rule, known for their skilled wielding of a bamboo stick called a 'lathi', often reinforced with iron rings. Lathials were usually hired by landholders to settle disputes and enforce authority. Their role diminished after the 1860s with the reorganization of the police system under British rule and the introduction of village police. By the 20th century, professional lathials had largely disappeared, though they were once prominent in social and cultural events, having trained in indigenous Indian gymnasiums known as akharas. Lathikhela, or stick fighting, has survived only as a rare form of performative martial arts in eastern India.

p. 72. **Gopal Patha** | Gopal Chandra Mukhopadhyay (1913–2005); earned the nickname 'Patha', or billy goat, because of his family's goat-meat shop in Central Calcutta. Member of the Anusilan Samiti, a group of fitness clubs that supported secret societies of armed revolutionaries against British rule. In August 1946, when riots between Muslims and Hindus broke out in Calcutta, leading to the Great Calcutta Killing, Gopal formed an armed group with Bengali, Odia, Bihari and Punjabi Hindus from his neighbourhood; they played a crucial role in defending Hindu areas and retaliating against violent Muslim rioters.

p. 72. **Ram Chatterjee** | (1922–1986). Strongman in the town of Chandannagar, West Bengal; participated in local communal riots in 1950, which led to widespread killings, especially of Muslims. Later, leader of the Marxist Forward Bloc political party; member of the state legislative assembly from 1967 until his death.

**p. 75. 'Om namah kot bikot'** | A Sanskrit vashikaran mantra, believed to exert pressure on or control people.

**p. 82. Raj Kapoor . . . *Disco Dancer*** | After India gained independence, it developed a strong political, military and cultural relationship with Soviet Russia. Here, the Russian character Mikhail Kalashnikov (1919–2013) utters terms that bear witness to this relationship. **Jan-gan-man** is a reference to 'Jana Gana Mana', the Indian national anthem composed by Rabindranath Tagore. **Raj Kapoor** (1924–1988), a pivotal figure in Indian cinema, was heavily influenced by socialist ideas and explored socialist themes in his early films, including *Awaara* (1951), which achieved immense success in the Soviet Union, making Kapoor an international star and instantly recognizable figure in Russia. **Mithun Chakraborty** (b. 1950), dancing star of 1980s Bollywood, also made a significant impact with the 1982 film *Disco Dancer*, whose rags-to-riches narrative and iconic disco music by Bappi Lahiri became a huge hit in the Soviet Union, attracting 120 million viewers and earning over 60 million Soviet roubles in ticket sales.

**p. 84. Revolutionary Communist Party of India** | Founded by Saumendranath Tagore in 1934, breaking away from the more mainstream Communist Party of India. On 26 February 1949, the RCPI, then led by Pannalal Dasgupta, initiated an armed revolt, attacking multiple sites in West Bengal, including the Dum Dum Airfield and Jessop & Company near Calcutta. Several people were killed, and equipment was stolen. The militants moved towards Basirhat, attacking police stations and killing guards, but were eventually caught; Dasgupta and 39 others were arrested. The revolt led to the RCPI abandoning insurrectional tactics and joining parliamentary politics. In Assam, the RCPI continued armed uprisings from 1948 to 1952, advocating for peasant rights and Assam's independence from India. The Assam government cracked down on the RCPI, leading to an eventual loss of influence.

**p. 87. Atmaram Sarkar** | A figure from Bengali folklore; revered by magicians of the region. According to an essay published in the *Bangabasi* journal on 23 April 1892: 'Atmaram Sarkar is a proverbial personage, who used to confound all magicians by his own magic art, and was, therefore, a trouble to the whole race. The magicians at last laid a trap for him, and succeeded in putting an end to his existence. And so, since that time, no magician begins a performance without first striking the earth seven times with a broom in memory of Atmaram' (p. 416; quoted in: Marc Jason Gilbert, 'Mofussil Municipal Reform in Late Nineteenth Century Bengal: Nationalism and Development on Trial', *Journal of Third World Studies* 7(1) (Spring 1990): 84–115, here p. 98–99). An online source, the *South Asian Life & Times—SALT*, states that Atmaram was a magician, visionary and philanthropist who sought to enlighten people about the scientific basis of magic, debunking superstitions. This stance made him enemies among those exploiting people's religious beliefs, who spread rumours that he used dark arts and spirits for his magic. Villagers fell for these tales, and Atmaram's opponents seized the chance to tarnish his reputation. Ultimately, they murdered him at night, claiming his death was due to the wrath of spirits he allegedly conjured. The family of P. C. Sorcar, internationally famed Bengali magicians for several generations, have been known to claim descendance from Atmaram. It is only apt that Nabarun invokes this semi-mythical figure in *Beggar's Bedlam*, for Atmaram is intrinsically linked to the world of spirits that populate this novel: 'Even today, the legend of Atmaram and his spine-chilling fate lives on in the "magical" chants of the *madari*s (traditional street magicians of India)—'*Ja bhoot, tu ja. Atmaram ka matha kha!*' [Ghost, away you must flee, / Feast on Atmaram's head for me.]' (Priyanka and Partha Mukherjee, 'The Sorcars—Nine Generations of Magic!', *South Asian Life & Times—SALT* [Spring 2014], https://bit.ly/3AcTzV9, accessed on 2 August 2024).

**p. 91. the 108th Paramahansa, Sri Nigamananda Saraswati** | Paramahansa is an honorific title given to enlightened Hindu spiritual teachers; literally, 'supreme swan', symbolizing a sage who, like a swan comfortable on both land and water, is at ease in both the material and spiritual worlds. Nigamananda (1880–1935) was born Nalinikanta Chattopadhyay into a Bengali Brahmin family in Nadia District, West Bengal. Became a Hindu sannyasi, and achieved siddhi or perfection in four different spiritual disciplines—tantra, gyan, yoga and prema. Also authored five Bengali books based on these experiences.

**p. 92. Mohun Bagan couldn't have defeated** | Reference revered events in the history of Indian football or soccer. The Indian Football Association (IFA) was set up in 1893 in Calcutta, and the annual IFA Shield competition, which began in the same year, is one of the oldest football tournaments in the world. On 29 July 1911, Mohun Bagan Athletic Club, coached by Sailen Basu, became the first all-Indian side to win the IFA Shield by defeating the all-white East Yorkshire Regiment by a 2–1 margin. This was a historic moment for Indian football as well as the struggle for Independence, as the 'natives' beat the Englishmen at their own game.

**p. 92. humiliating defeat in Dhaka** | The Islington Corinthians, an English team known for touring globally, visited Dhaka on 21 November 1937. In a historic match, the Dacca Sporting Association XI, mainly comprising Dhaka University students, defeated the Corinthians 1–0, marking the latter's first-ever loss. This victory thrilled thousands of locals who celebrated the English team's defeat amid the rising tide of India's anti-colonial Independence movement.

**p. 92. call the state 'Bongo'** | In the late 1990s, the CPI(M)-led Left Front government in West Bengal sought to decolonize place names by proposing a change in the state's anglicized name to either 'Bongo' or 'Bangla,' reflecting its Bengali usage. Despite numerous efforts by subsequent governments, the state's name remains West Bengal. The capital city's name, always pronounced as Kolkata or Kôlikata in Bengali, officially remained Calcutta until 2001, when the state government successfully changed it to Kolkata to match the Bengali pronunciation.

**p. 93. Radhanath Sikdar** | (1813–1870). Bengali mathematician who joined the Great Trigonometrical Survey of India, a British colonial project that aimed to carry out a survey across the Indian subcontinent with scientific precision. In 1852, discovered that Kangchenjunga, which was considered the tallest in the world, was not really so. Compiling data about Mount Everest from six observations, eventually concluded that it was the tallest, at a height of 29,000 feet (8,839 metres). Officially announced this in March 1856, and this remained the height of Mount Everest till an Indian survey recalculated it to be 29,029 feet (8,848 metres) in 1955.

**p. 93. another Sikdar, Tapan** | Tapan Sikdar (1944–2014); leader of right-wing Hindu nationalist Bharatiya Janata Party (BJP) from Bengal. In 1998, won the parliamentary election from Dum Dum Lok Sabha constituency, thereby introducing the right-wing BJP as a force in West Bengal politics, so far dominated by left-wing parties such as the Indian National Congress and the various factions and allies of the Communist Party of India. The cult of God Hanuman has since been promoted by the BJP in West Bengal as part of its Hindutva agenda.

**p. 95. Ali Sardar Jafri** | (1913–2000). Urdu-language poet, critic and occasional film lyricist from Uttar Pradesh, India, known for his powerful verse; the citation of the Bharatiya Jnanpith award, which he received in 1997, states: 'Jafri represents those who are fighting against injustice and oppression in society'. 'The Blood Calls' is the translated title of his book *Lahu Pukarta Hain* (1965).

**p. 95. a blood-drenched Peshawar Express** | 'The Peshawar Express' is a story by Krishan Chander (1914–1977), which captures the brutality and chaos of the Partition of India in 1947. It is told from the point of view of the eponymous train ferrying refugees from Peshawar in Pakistani Punjab to Bombay in India. Passengers face constant danger and violence, with scenes of mass killings, forced conversions and kidnappings of Hindus, Sikhs and Muslims. The train symbolizes the horrors of communal violence and explores postcolonial themes of identity, otherness and race.

**p. 95. Bamboo Villa** | Erstwhile location of the Income Tax Department in Calcutta; presumably the tax itself or the (often unfair or arbitrary) demands made by the department are referred to as the 'recto killer'.

**p. 97. *Sonai Dighi*–type dialogues** | Composed by Brajendra Kumar Dey (1907–1976), *Sonai Dighi* (*c.*1970) is a 'Jatra pala'—a musical drama in the popular folk-theatre form of West Bengal. This kind of theatre is known for its extremely melodramatic dialogues, to which Nabarun refers.

**p. 98. a manure martyr like Nafar Kundu** | Nafar Chandra Kundu (*c.*1881–1907) performed an extraordinary act of courage in 1907. Walking down Chakraberia area in South Calcutta, he heard cries for help from an open manhole: two labourers were trapped inside. Ignoring the warnings of the crowd that had gathered, he entered the sewer and rescued both men but tragically lost his own life in the process; he was only 26. Though largely forgotten, a small memorial stands on Chakrabaria Road (South) to honour his bravery, now in a state of neglect, akin to other memorials to Bengalis that Nabarun describes in the novel.

**p. 100. the sahibs' cemetery** | Possibly South Park Street Cemetery, formerly known as the Great Christian Burial Ground, one of the earliest non-church cemeteries in the world, dating from 1767, housing numerous graves and monuments belonging to British soldiers, administrators and their families. Also the final resting place of several prominent personalities, including Henry Louis Vivian Derozio (1809–1831) and Sir William Jones (1746–1794).

**p. 101. Carvalho** | Portuguese captain Domingo Carvalho, who, in 1602, seized the salt-trading island of Sandwip along the south-eastern coast of present-day Bangladesh. Carvalho faced local rebellion and sought help from fellow Portuguese captain Emanuel de Matos, resulting in the island's division. The growing Portuguese influence alarmed the Arakanese king, who allied with local leader Kedar Ray to attack them in Chittagong. Although Carvalho's forces initially won, a second Arakanese assault in 1603 led to Carvalho's betrayal and beheading by former ally Raja Pratapaditya of Chandecan. See Deepashree Dutta, 'Portuguese in Bengal: A History Beyond Slave Trade', *Sahapedia* (9 August 2019); https://bityl.co/Qq6P (accessed on 2 July 2024).

**p. 101. Bhumen Roy** | (Dates unknown). Actor of stage and screen, whose film career has been documented from 1929 to 1942; Bengali and Hindi film credits include *Bishabriksha* (1934), *Taruni* (1934), *Khooni Kaun* (1936), *Swayambara* (1935) and *Pashan Devata* (1942). There is no immediately traceable record of him playing Carvalho on stage.

**p. 103. we wouldn't need to grovel and grasp for a Bengal Regiment** | During the First World War, the British Indian Army formed the 49th Bengalee Regiment in June 1917, composed primarily of Bengali soldiers from middle-class backgrounds. The regiment participated in the Mesopotamian campaign and helped quell a Kurdish rebellion, losing 63 soldiers before being disbanded in 1920. Notable members included poet Kazi Nazrul Islam, referenced elsewhere in this novel. Despite the revival of other regional regiments after India's Independence in 1947 (such as Punjab Regiment, Madras Regiment, Rajputana Rifles, etc.), the Bengal Regiment was not reinstated, a decision many Bengalis view as a deliberate slight, perpetuating the stereotype of Bengalis as weak, despite their significant contributions to India's Independence movement.

p. 105. **Harihar Seth** | (1878–1972). Eminent Bengali literary figure and historian born in Chandannagar, West Bengal, at that time a French colony. Contributed to several magazines and played a pivotal role in Chandannagar's social and educational development, including the establishment of the first women's high school, Krishna Bhamini Nari Shiksha Mandir. First president of independent Chandannagar after the 1949 plebiscite before the former colony merged with the Union of India in 1950.

p. 108. **happy hijras dancing** | In South Asia, the hijras—the indigenous male-to-female trans community—are traditionally believed to possess the power to bless families and bring joy. In subcontinental Hindu and Muslim traditions, hijras visit families during weddings or childbirth, performing dances and songs while offering blessings, and receiving money in return for their benedictions.

p. 118. **Jibanananda's short stories** | Reference to Jibanananda Das (1899–1954), the pre-eminent and hugely popular poet of mid-20th-century Bengal. Although celebrated for his poetry, Jibanananda published three dozen short stories, many of them set in the gritty Calcutta of the times. In the words of Allen Ginsburg, Jibanananda 'introduce[d] what for India would be "the modern spirit"—bitterness, self-doubt, sex, street diction, personal confession, frankness, Calcutta beggars . . . —into Bengali letters' ('A Few Bengali Poets', *City Lights Journal* 2 [1964]: 117).

p. 119. *Sholay* | A 1975 Hindi action-adventure film directed by Ramesh Sippy and written by Salim–Javed, which follows the heroic adventures of two criminals, Veeru and Jai, played by Dharmendra and Amitabh Bachchan, respectively. Regarded as one of the greatest and most influential Indian films ever made, *Sholay* is a 'Dacoit Western', blending the conventions of Indian bandit films with Spaghetti Western elements and influences from Samurai cinema.

**p. 121. Trailakyanath Mukhopadhyay** | (1847–1919). Indian public servant and prominent author in both English and Bengali. Curator of the Indian Museum in Calcutta and a pioneer of secular Bengali writing. His notable posthumous work, *Damaru-Charit* (1923), features humorous and satirical short stories set in colonial India, focusing on the life of the antihero Damarudhar, a dishonest man who ascends from a shop assistant to a landowner.

**p. 121. By the grace of Charnock** | Reference to Job Charnock (*c*.1630– 1692/93), an English administrator with the East India Company, often credited as the founder of Calcutta, a view that is not entirely uncontested—as is evident in the Raven's retort to the curator, a caricature of the blindly anglophile Bengali. In a 2003 judgement, the Calcutta High Court ruled that Charnock should not be considered the city's founder, as the area had inhabitants since at least the 1st century CE. Although Charnock did not establish the villages that formed colonial Calcutta, his determination to create an East India Company frontier on the eastern border of India significantly influenced the development of modern Calcutta. Often in conflict with Indian leaders and his Company superiors, Charnock faced accusations of mismanagement, theft, brutality towards Indian prisoners and—as the Raven points out—questionable morals. He is known to have lived with an Indian widow whom he had purportedly saved from her husband's funeral pyre—a claim that cannot be verified— and fathered several children with her, even though Charnock's mausoleum at St John's Church in Calcutta bears no mention of this wife, nor do the baptismal registers of his daughters in Madras (present-day Chennai).

**p. 123. Have you heard of Joseph Townsend** | There is mention of a Joseph, Joe or Josiah Townsend, sometimes 'Townshend', a friend of Job Charnock, in various early-20th-century texts, most notably in *Roving East and Roving West* (1921) in which English humourist E. V. Lucas (see 'Job and Joe', https://bit.ly/3SyVz0e, last accessed on 3 August 2024) quotes the poem 'Shoulder to Shoulder' that Nabarun reproduces on p. 124. Several historical accounts have claimed that this poem is to be found somewhere at Charnock's memorial in Calcutta, which, at least in 2024, is not the case. For many such debates, and for multiple opinions on Charnock and his influence, see P. Thankappan Nair (comp.), *Job Charnock: The Founder of Calcutta; In Facts and Fiction—An Anthology* (Calcutta: Calcutta Old Book Stall, 1977); full text available at: https://bit.ly/3Wz8As1 (last accessed on 3 August 2024).

**p. 126. Kolkata has a monument** | A reference to the 48-metre-high phallic column in the heart of Calcutta, originally called the Ochterlony Monument. Erected in 1828 to honour British Major-General David Ochterlony, it was rededicated in 1969 to the memory of the martyrs of the Indian Independence movement and renamed Shaheed Minar, even though the mononym 'monument' continues to be used in common parlance.

**p. 129. Operation Barga** | Land-reform initiative launched in 1978 in rural West Bengal by the newly elected Left Front government, aiming to record the names of sharecroppers (*bargadar*s) efficiently and bypass traditional settlement methods. Provided sharecroppers legal protection from eviction by landlords and ensured their rightful share of produce. Through parallel legislative moves in 1979–1980, the operation aimed to convert sharecroppers into landowners. Regarded as one of India's most successful land-reform programmes.

**p. 129. Sabai Bhoomi Gopal Ki** | Line from a philosophical couplet generally attributed to Vaishnava devotional poet Govindadasa (1535–1613): 'all the land belongs to Gopal, that is, God'. Later, Gandhian human-rights activist Vinoba Bhave (1895–1982) used it as a slogan for his Bhoodan (land-gifting) Movement, which attempted to persuade wealthy landowners to voluntarily give a percentage of their land to landless people.

**p. 130. In that procession march** | Nabarun names poets of Bengal from all ages, referring to lesser-known greats alongside celebrated names such as Michael Madhusudan Dutt, Rabindranath Tagore and Kazi Nazrul Islam.

**p. 130. Kanhapada** | (10th century CE). Also known as Kanhapa, Kanha or Krishnacharya; prominent poet of the *Charyapada*—a collection of mystical poems and songs of realization from the Vajrayana tradition of Buddhism, rooted in the tantric traditions of Eastern India. These works are the earliest known examples of Assamese, Bengali, Maithili, Bhojpuri and Odia literature.

**p. 130. Bhusukupada** | (8th century CE). Or Bhusuku Pa, also known as Shantideva; Indian philosopher, Buddhist monk, poet and scholar. Best known for authoring the *Bodhisattvacaryavatara*, an extensive poem that outlines the journey to enlightenment from the initial thought to full Buddhahood.

**p. 130. Hemchandra** | Likely reference to Hemchandra Bandyopadhyay (1838–1903), Bengali poet and lawyer at Calcutta High Court. A patriotic poet, his works reflected Hindu nationalism and advocated for women's rights and communal harmony. His masterpiece is the epic *Vratrasanghar* (1875–77, 2 volumes), inspired by the *Mahabharata*, exploring the triumph of justice over an unjust contemporary regime. Despite his literary success, he faced financial difficulties and died in poverty.

**p. 130. Bishnu De** | (1909–1982). Prominent Bengali poet, essayist, academic and art connoisseur, influential during the modernist and postmodernist eras. His seminal work, *Smriti Satta Bhabishyat* (1963), set a new standard in Bengali poetry.

**p. 130. Bijoylal Chattopadhyay** | (1899–1974). Multifaceted individual remembered as a poet, essayist, freedom fighter, editor, journalist, social reformer and village organizer from Nadia District, West Bengal. Influenced by Mahatma Gandhi, actively participated in the Non-Cooperation Movement in the 1920s, leading to several imprisonments. Wrote extensively on Gandhi, Tagore and Marxism. His most important work is *Shob-harader Gaan* (1929). After India's Independence, served as an MLA and continued his efforts in village development and communal harmony until his death.

**p. 131. A. N. M. Bazlur Rashid** | (1911–1986). Bangladeshi educationist and litterateur; author of more than 30 books, including the poetry collections *Maru-Surya*, *Shite-Basante*, *Rang O Rekha*, *Ek Jhank Pakhi* and *Mausumi Mon*. Awarded the Bangla Academy Award for Drama in 1967 and the Tamgha-e-Imtiaz from Pakistan in 1969.

**p. 131. Kalidas Roy** | (1889–1975). Bengali poet and teacher from the Tagore era; taught at several institutions, including Barisha High School and Mitra Institution in Calcutta. His poetry, influenced by Vaishnava thoughts, includes notable works like 'Chhatradhara' and 'Triratna'. Authored 19 books of verses, translated Sanskrit works and wrote critical reviews.

**p. 138. *Shiva Samhita . . . Gheranda Samhita*** | These two Sanskrit texts are among the three classical works on hatha yoga. *Shiva Samhita*, written by an unknown author from possibly the 17th century CE, comprises five chapters: the first two dwell on Hindu philosophy; the subsequent three cover yoga, the significance of a guru for a student, and various asanas, mudras and tantra practices. *Gheranda Samhita*, also dating from the 17th century, is one of the most encyclopaedic treatises on yoga. Organized into seven chapters with 351 shlokas or verses, it teaches 32 asanas and 25 mudras, among other things.

**p. 138. Vayaviyedharana mudra** | Verses 24–26 of *Gheranda Samhita* dwell on this 'concentration on air': 'With the practice of this mudra, a sadhaka [practitioner] achieves the power to travel in space [ . . . ] This dharana should never be disclosed to an undevoted and wicked person. By doing so, siddhi [knowledge] is destroyed.' See Niran-janananda Saraswati, *Gheranda Samhita*: *Commentary on the Yoga Teachings of Maharishi Gheranda Swami* (Munger, Bihar: Yoga Publication Trust, 1992), verses 24–26; full text available at: https://bit.ly/4dx8p7r (last accessed on 3 August 2024).

**p. 140. Go show your Ram to Advani** | Many Hindus believe that chanting the name of Lord Ram will ward off ghosts and spirits. The reference here is to Lal Krishna Advani (b. 1927), leader of the BJP, and the most prominent face of the Ram Janmabhoomi [The Birth-place of Rama] Movement in the 1980s–90s, centred on the claim that the Babri Mosque in Ayodhya, Uttar Pradesh, was built atop the birthplace of Lord Ram; hence the mosque must be demolished a Hindu temple built in its place. This highly contentious issue led to significant communal violence and protracted legal battles. Since the 1980s, the BJP, through Advani and other leaders, has projected Lord Ram as a unifying Hindu god.

**p. 145. Poush Mela** | Annual winter festival held in Santiniketan, Bolpur, celebrating the harvest season, one of the key components of which is the performance of Bengali folk music.

**p. 146. Kumud Ranjan Mullick** | (1883–1970). Notable Bengali writer and poet of the Tagore era, who mentored Kazi Nazrul Islam. His poetry, influenced by Vaishnavism, vividly depicted rural Bengal. Received several awards, including the Jagattarini Gold Medal, Padma Shri and Bankimchandra Subarna Padak.

**p. 146. Lal, Bal and Pal** | Lal Bal Pal—Lala Lajpat Rai (1865–1928), Bal Gangadhar Tilak (1856–1920) and Bipin Chandra Pal (1858–1932). Trio of assertive nationalists in early-20th-century British India. From 1906 to 1918, they championed the Swadeshi movement, advocating the boycott of imported goods and promoting Indian-made products. Their activism mobilized nationwide protests, strikes and boycotts against British rule. The movement declined after Tilak's arrest and the Pal's retirement. Lala Lajpat Rai was severely injured in a police lathi charge and died on 17 November 1928 from the injuries.

**p. 147. Ranadive era** | Possibly a reference to a communist, trade unionist and nationalist leader B. T. Ranadive (1904–1990). During the Indo-China War of 1962, Ranadive adopted a moderate stance, advocating for a peaceful resolution through negotiations. However, the ruling government at the time viewed his position as anti-national, leading to his imprisonment until 1966 alongside the widespread arrest and torture of communist sympathizers.

**p. 148. The beheading that Uttam Kumar . . . witnessed on that fateful, foggy morning** | Refers to the alleged killing of Saroj Dutta (1914–1971), a communist intellectual and poet active in the 1960s Naxalite Movement in West Bengal. The first West Bengal state secretary of the ultra-left-wing CPI(M–L) party; also editor-in-chief of the English daily *Amrita Bazar Patrika* in the 1940s. Arrested from the home of his friend Debiprasad Chattapadhyaya on the night of 4 August 1971. In the early hours of 5 August, Dutta was reportedly killed by Kolkata Police at the East Bengal–Aryan Club football ground in the Maidan area, not far from the Manohar Das 'tank' or lake mentioned by Nabarun. It is claimed that Bengali movie star

Uttam Kumar (1926–1980) witnessed the shooting during a morning walk, an incident that he recounted privately. In 1977, after the Left Front came to power, many Naxalite sympathizers petitioned Chief Minister Jyoti Basu for an investigation into Dutta's death; however, no investigation has ever been conducted. While Dutta's murder is widely acknowledged, there is no related report of a beheading nor of a skeleton being found in the Manohar Das lake. For more on extrajudicial killings in Calcutta during the Naxalite Movement, see *DNA*, 'Countering the Maoists' (12 July 2010): https://bit.ly/4dyI4G5 (last accessed on 4 August 2024).

**p. 153. Mahanambrata Brahmachari** | (1904–1999). Born Bankim Dasgupta in Barishal, present-day Bangladesh; Hindu monk and leader of Mahanam Sampradaya, a monastic organization. For his discourse on Goddess Kali, see Mahanambrata Brahmachari, 'An Essay on Ma Kali': https://bit.ly/3AdaaIv (last accessed on 4 August 2024).

**p. 153. dacoit Veerappan** | Koose Munusamy Veerappan (1952–2004), an Indian wildlife poacher, smuggler, domestic terrorist and bandit active for 36 years, known by his distinctive moustache. Was wanted for the deaths of approximately 184 people, including police officers and forest officials, for poaching around 500 elephants, smuggling ivory worth US$ 2.6 million and sandalwood worth US$ 22 million. Killed in a police encounter on 18 October 2004 near a village in Tamil Nadu.

**p. 162. Manohar Aich** | (1912–2016). Bengali bodybuilder, known as 'Pocket Hercules' for his 4-foot-11-inch height. The second Indian to win a Mr Universe title, securing victory in the 1952 NABBA Universe Championships. Celebrated for his influence on Indian physical culture, Aich credited his longevity to a simple diet and stayed active in physical training until his death at the age of 104.

**p. 163. Hamida Banu** | (*c.*1920–1986). India's first woman wrestler, known as the 'Amazon of Aligarh'. Debuting in 1937, dominated the wrestling scene for decades, challenging and defeating many Indian wrestlers and competing in Europe. Despite facing significant gender and religious stereotypes, she fought male opponents, garnering criticism and even physical assaults. On 2 May 1954, in Mumbai, Banu, standing at 5-foot-3 and weighing 230 pounds, defeated wrestler

Baba Pahelwan, a prospective suitor, in under two minutes. Later that year, also achieved a notable victory by defeating the Russian pro-wrestler Vera Chistilin, known as the 'Female Bear', in less than a minute. Banu won over 320 matches during her career, but following her high-profile wrestling matches in Europe, she vanished from the wrestling scene. Reports indicate that she suffered domestic violence from Salam Pahalwan, who allegedly broke her hands to prevent her from travelling again. To support herself, Banu turned to selling milk, renting out properties and selling homemade snacks.

p. 175. **Kokh Shastra** | *Ratirahasya* (translated as *Secrets of Love* or *Kokh/ Koka Shastra*), a medieval Indian sex manual written in Sanskrit by poet Kokkoka, also known as Koka Pandit, estimated to be from the 11th or 12th century CE. Unlike the ancient *Kama Sutra*, this text reflects the cultural norms of medieval Indian society. Comprising 15 chapters and 800 verses, it covers topics such as physical types, the relationship of sex to the lunar calendar, different kinds of genitalia, foreplay, sexual positions and stages of love, including weight loss and death. Classifies women into four psycho-physical types based on their appearance and physical features: Padmini (lotus woman), Chitrini (art woman), Shankini (conch woman) and Hastini (elephant woman).

p. 201. **Alamohan Das** | (1895–1969). Ppioneering industrialist; played a pivotal role in Bengal's economic development across pre- and post-Independence India. With a diverse portfolio encompassing jute, cotton, heavy machinery, pharmaceuticals and banking, he was a visionary entrepreneur. Established India Machinery Company, a cornerstone of India's nascent industrialization efforts; founded Dass Bank in 1939, which soon expanded to 60 branches across Bengal. However, following the Partition of India, the bank had to shut down as it lost most of its branches when East Bengal became part of Pakistan.

p. 211. **Herzen . . . Bakunin . . . Tkachev** | Leading figure in Russian thought, **Alexander Herzen** (1812–1870); credited with laying the groundwork for both socialist and agrarian populist movements. **Mikhail Bakunin** (1814–1876); foundational figure in anarchist thought; instrumental in shaping socialist and collectivist anarchist ideologies. **Pyotr Tkachev** (1844–1886); seminal Russian writer and revolutionary theorist whose radical ideas laid the groundwork for many of Vladimir Lenin's later principles. Often dubbed 'the First Bolshevik', his significant contributions to revolutionary thought are overshadowed by his relative obscurity in the historical narratives of the Soviet Union—and, by extension, among socialist enthusiasts of Bengal.

**p. 212. 'My name is Chin-chin-chu . . . my red headscarf'** | Two iconic Bollywood romantic songs—'Mera naam Chin-chin-chu' from *Howrah Bridge* (1958), written by Qamar Jalalabadi and performed by Geeta Dutt; and 'Hawa mein udta jaaye mera laal dupatta' from *Barsaat* (1949), written by Ramesh Shastri and performed by Lata Mangeshkar.

**p. 214. W. L. Jones** | Wilfrid Llewelyn Jones, *Ministering to Minds Diseased: A History of Psychiatric Treatment* (London: Elsevier, 1983); chronicles the evolution of psychiatric methodologies and treatments, and covers early physical treatments like hydrotherapy and blood-letting, medicinal treatments including psychopharmacology and antidepressants, and the rise of psychotherapy and behaviour therapy.

**p. 214. Sperry or Ornstein's work** | **Roger Walcott Sperry** (1913–1994); American neuropsychologist, neurobiologist, cognitive neuroscientist and Nobel Laureate. Severed the corpus callosum in cats and monkeys to investigate the functions of each brain hemisphere; discovered that the hemispheres operated independently—a condition he termed 'split-brain'—and allowed the animals to memorize twice as much information. **Robert E. Ornstein** (1942–2018); American psychologist, researcher and author. His book *The Right Mind: Making Sense of the Hemispheres* (New York: Harcourt Brace, 1997) deals with split-brain studies and other experiments or clinical evidence revealing the abilities of the right cerebral hemisphere.

**p. 232. Pala kings** | The Pala Empire, a dominant force in India between the 8th and 12th centuries CE, originated in Bengal. Named for its ruling dynasty, whose monarchs bore the title 'Pala' (protector), the empire extended its influence across much of the Indian subcontinent during its zenith.

**p. 232. Neither Hunter nor Majumdar have made any mention of them | William Wilson Hunter** (1840–1900); Scottish scholar and administrator. Member of the Indian Civil Service, he served in Bengal in the 1860s, and meticulously collected local lore and records. Seminal work *The Annals of Rural Bengal* (1868) significantly influenced the historical fiction of Bankim Chandra Chattopadhyay. **Ramesh Chandra Majumdar** (1888–1980); towering figure in Indian historiography; leading proponent of the nationalist school of history. Extensive research focused on the annals of India, author of works such as *Early History of Bengal* (1924) and *The History and Culture of the Indian People* (11 volumes, 1951–1977).

**p. 235. The God of the Road smiles and says, O Apu** | A reference to *Pather Panchali*, a popular Bengali novel by Bibhutibhushan Bandyopadhyay written in 1929, later adapted into a landmark film by Satyajit Ray in 1955; the protagonist's name is Apurba—Apu, in short.

**p. 236. historic coachmen strike of Calcutta** | Fuelled by nationalist sentiments, workers participated in numerous strikes in Calcutta during 1905–1906. Initially driven by demands for shorter working hours, labour rights, and the elimination of discriminatory wages, the strikes were significantly influenced by the broader struggle for Independence. Prominent freedom fighters, including Bal Gangadhar Tilak, who addressed the Printer's Union of Calcutta, supported these labour actions. In 1906, Eastern Railways workers in Calcutta protested wage disparities; Nabarun probably refers to this.

**p. 240. '*To little Ranu, from Bhanu-dada*'** | The prestigious Bengali literary journal *Desh* publishes a special autumn issue every year on the occasion of Durga Puja. Alongside novels, essays, short stories and poems, it often features hitherto unpublished correspondence between eminent personalities. One correspondent widely featured in *Desh* has been Rabindranath Tagore, who sometimes wrote under the pen name Bhanusingha—hence 'Bhanu-dada'. Although it is unclear who Ranu might be, Nabarun appears to be referencing the novel *Ranu o Bhanu* (1965) by Sunil Gangopadhyay, in which a fictionalized Tagore, grief-stricken after his daughter's death, finds solace in the company of a little girl named Ranu who had once written a letter to him. The novel is available in English as *Ranu and Bhanu: The Poet and His Muse* (Sheila Sengupta trans.) (Delhi: Supernova Publishers, 2012).

**p. 243. Santhal Rebellion** | Also known as the Santhal Hool, an uprising by the Santhal ethnic community in present-day Jharkhand and West Bengal against the East India Company and the exploitative feudal system. One of the first major uprisings by an indigenous community in Asia, it began on 30 June 1855, and led to the proclamation of martial law by the Company on 10 November 1855. The rebellion, which was led by brothers Sidhu, Kanhu, Chand, Bhairav, and their sisters Phoolo and Jhano, was brutally suppressed in January 1856 by the Company armies, leading to widespread killings. Karl Marx referred to this rebellion as India's first organized 'mass revolution' in his work *Notes on Indian History*.

**p. 246. Saigal, Robin Majumdar** | Kundan Lal or **K. L. Saigal** (1904–1947); legendary Indian singer and actor in Hindi films. Unlike later artists, sang his own songs on screen, pioneering a style later known as playback singing. **Robin Majumdar** (1919–1983); Bengali actor and singer most active in the 1940s and often called 'the Second Saigal' for his soulful voice. Starred in Bengali hits such as *Shapmukti* (1940), *Nandita* (1944) and *Kavi* (1949) and acted on stage for plays such as *Shei Timirey* (1952) and *Ulka* (1952). It is important to recognize that while Bombay or Mumbai became the centre of Hindi films in post-Independence India, Calcutta was once a major hub for national cinema. This context highlights Nabarun's reference to Saigal walking the streets of the city.

**p. 266. SUCI rally** | The Socialist Unity Centre of India (Communist) or SUCI is an anti-revisionist Marxist–Leninist communist party in India, known for its frequent protests against government policies. During the Left Front government's tenure in West Bengal (1977–2011), the SUCI's opposition to its policies often led to violent police crackdowns on their demonstrations.

**p. 273. Brest-Litovsk Treaty** | A peace treaty signed on 3 March 1918, between the new Bolshevik government of Soviet Russia and the Central Powers—Germany, Austria-Hungary, Bulgaria and the Ottoman Empire—that ended Russia's participation in the First

World War. The so-called Left Communists, led by Nikolai Bukharin and Karl Radek, were sure that each of the Central Power countries was on the verge of revolution. They wanted to continue the war with a newly raised revolutionary force while awaiting these upheavals.